BISON
BOOKS

D1528219

Other mysteries by Mignon G. Eberhart
available in Bison Books Editions

DEATH IN THE FOG

THE PATIENT IN ROOM 18

WHILE THE PATIENT SLEPT

M. G. EBERHART

FROM
THIS DARK STAIRWAY

Nurse Keate was walking down the long
corridor, when a whisper reached her out
of the darkness . . . "You must do it. He
will be murdered, I tell you. Murdered!"

INTRODUCTION TO THE BISON BOOKS EDITION

BY M. K. LORENS

University of Nebraska Press

Lincoln and London

© 1931 by Mignon G. Eberhart
Introduction © 1996 by the University of Nebraska Press
All rights reserved
Manufactured in the United States of America

☉ The paper in this book meets the minimum requirements of American
National Standard for Information Sciences—Permanence of Paper for
Printed Library Materials, ANSI Z39.48-1984.

First Bison Books printing: 1996
Most recent printing indicated by the last digit below:
10   9   8   7   6   5   4   3   2   1

Library of Congress Cataloging-in-Publication Data
Eberhart, Mignon Good, 1899–
From this dark stairway / M. G. Eberhart; introduction to the Bison books
edition by M. K. Lorens.
p.   cm.
ISBN 0-8032-6729-0 (pa)
I. Title.
PS3509.B453F76   1996
813'.52—dc20
96-1725   CIP

Originally published in 1931 by Doubleday, New York.

INTRODUCTION

M. K. Lorens

Mignon Good Eberhart, born in Lincoln, Nebraska, in 1899, entered her own thirties in the year of the great stock market crash that plunged the nation and the world headlong into the Great Depression. As the national economy stagnated after 1929, American writers—with the stubborn persistence of writers everywhere—seemed to flourish in the poorest of soils, and among Nebraska women writers there was a particular efflorescence. Willa Cather, their senior sister, had, of course, been a major literary figure since the publication of *O Pioneers!* in 1913. She had recently published *Death Comes for the Archbishop*, and was working on *Shadows on the Rock*, which would appear in 1935. That same year was to mark the emergence of Mari Sandoz, with the publication of *Old Jules*. Bess Streeter Aldrich would publish *A White Bird Flying* in 1931 and *Miss Bishop* in 1933.

But 1929 belonged to Mignon Eberhart, whose first Nurse Sarah Keate mystery novel, *The Patient in Room 18*, was published that year by Doubleday Doran. It was followed the next year by *While the Patient Slept*, which received the Scotland Yard Prize as best mystery. By 1931, the year in which she published *From This Dark Stairway*, Mrs. Eberhart had earned a solid reputation as a writer of well-crafted mystery novels in the "series" tradition which had become, in the twenties and early thirties, more or less the special province of women writers. The most famous of these, of course, were the indomitable Dorothy L. Sayers, whose Lord Peter Wimsey novel, *Five Red Herrings*, appeared that same year, and the ever prolific Agatha Christie, who had published *Murder at the Vicarage*, the first of her Miss Jane Marple novels, the previous year.

Male writers—E. A. Poe, Conan Doyle, and G. K. Chesterton, most obviously—may have created the subgenre that become a reliable standard of trade-book publishing, but by the 1930s the mystery category was already beginning to split itself into two distinct camps. Men, for the most part, wrote what mystery publishers still refer to as Hard-Boileds—the Dashiell Hammett–Sam Spade tradition, in which guns are always carried, noses are usually busted, and women are, at best, the motive for the crime or the reward for the victorious sleuth.

The classic detective novel in the Christie-Sayers tradition, to be referred to as the Cozy, came partially in response to the huge popularity of Hammett, and after him of Chandler, Ross Macdonald, and even Spillane. *Cozy* is a term that hints at a great deal more than it says, and the hints are arrogant and supercilious, if not out-and-out chauvinistic. I am not certain what genius of publishing or of book reviewing first coined it; but whoever he was—I assume it as a "he"—he deserves to remain anonymous.

Still, the word stuck, and is sticking yet among editors and publishers, and in the years following the publication of Mrs. Eberhart's first Nurse Sarah Keate novels, as her books and magazine stories found a wider and wider audience and were made into successful Hollywood films, the lines of demarcation between "women's mysteries" and "men's mysteries" became more and more rigid.

Dorothy L. Sayers had hoped to bring the novel of detection back into the mainstream of literary fiction, returning it to the days of Dickens, when a popular novel like *Bleak House* or *Our Mutual Friend*, or, indeed, *Great Expectations*, might have a mystery plot and still provide the complexities of character and theme and the amplitude and grace of style that define great fiction. But Miss Sayers was doomed to disappointment. It was the fate of her female followers to be consigned instead to a constantly narrowing cupboard within the larger room of mystery writing.

In time, the walls of this closet grew higher and were reinforced with concrete. If there was logic to it, it ran something like this.

Men write Hard-Boileds. Hard-Boileds deal with The Real World. If detective novels intend to be serious fiction, they had better be Hard-

Boiled. *The Maltese Falcon. The Big Sleep. The Third Man.* Conclusion: Men write Serious Fiction.

If women write at all, they may be assumed to write (a) romance novels, (b) children's books, (c) family reminiscences, or (d) Cozy mysteries. Though I myself have published five mystery novels that I wouldn't exactly call cozy, the mailman, bless his heart, still labors under the impression that I write children's books, and I forgive him, for I doubt that he is conscious of the size or the stale odor of the box he puts me in. Not until our own decade, with the "hard-boiled woman sleuth" books of Sara Paretsky, Sue Grafton, Sue Dunlap, and Linda Grant, have its boundaries been challenged—and there are still those of us who wonder if these books actually challenge the stereotype or merely shape themselves to fit the preexistent box. (Creating a woman who is harder-boiled than the male is, it seems to me, no great proof of independent thinking—no more, certainly, than the brilliant feminist idea of a few years back that women ought to wear jockey shorts. If you find it comfortable, then by all means do it. But no book ought to be written simply to prove women can break noses just as well as men.)

The great thing in writing, particularly the writing of popular fiction, which is as much bound by conventions as any Petrarchan sonnet or Horatian ode, is to be thoroughly aware of the prejudices for and against your chosen form, and then to use them, rather than to be used by them.

That is, I think, what Mignon Eberhart did in her long career as a mystery writer. It is why she was so successful, and why, after more than sixty years, a book like *From This Dark Stairway* still reads with such increasing interest, still seems a well-wrought and integrated book about people who exist on a realistic level and whose struggles with death and life mean more than they say.

Nurse Sarah Keate. A matter-of-fact name for a practical, unsentimental woman, who describes herself as "a middle-aged nurse, inclined to embonpoint and neuralgia." Not Sally Keating, as Hollywood named her in the movie adaptation. Plain, forthright Sarah Keate. Student nurses may turn queasy from a glimpse of the victim, whose bloodsoaked corpse is found in a darkened elevator; heiresses may affect hysterics; and vampish widows may flirt brazenly with the suspects in their husbands' deaths. But Nurse Keate marches straight to the operating room to see if the murder weapon, an amputating knife, is missing from the case. Oppressed by the strangling heat of a midwestern summer, certain she is being pursued and that her own life is in danger, Sarah is glad—as who would not be?—of the arrival of her policeman friend Lance O'Leary. But even his warnings do not deter her from her nurse's duty. On she marches, doing her job, making her lists of significant clues, keeping her notebooks. A thoroughly modern working woman to the end.

O'Leary—to the chagrin of Eberhart's feminist critics—waltzes in just at the end, after Sarah has collected all the important data, and naturally he knows at once who committed the crime. He saves her bacon at the final climax—for her refusal to pay court to death by letting it interfere with her duties leads her into many a cliffhanger—and though he gives her credit it is Lance who waltzes away as the hero of the hour, leaving Nurse Keate to return to her routine of chart-keeping, bed-changing, patient-soothing, and striking a delicate balance between obedience and surrender to that oiliest of chiefs-of-staff, Dr. Felix Kunce, better known as "Dr. Fulla Prunes."

Unenlightened, you may say. After all, any woman whose consciousness has been suitably raised would have had Nurse Keate saving O'Leary's bacon, or at the very least her own.

Mrs. Eberhart was, of course, writing in the early 1930s, we may cry in her defense, and she cannot be expected to reflect the enlightened values of our own time. But what defense could be more smug and patronizing? The working relationship between Keate and O'Leary seems to me, rather, a perfect emblem of the actual roles of men and women in the working world. Is it so uncommon for the woman to do the plodding work of amassing precise and telling detail and the male executive to use her work and reap most of its rewards?

But, come now. Is there anything *between* Sarah Keate and Lance O'Leary? Anything of romance? Certainly not the love-at-first-sight infatuation that occurs between her friend, Nancy, and one of the prime suspects in the case, no. But there is something. Something more interesting for remaining suppressed. O'Leary does not merely use Sarah as a workhorse or an unpaid secretary. He is solicitous of her, even tender. When she is attacked, there is "something like fury back of his luminous gray eyes." And she, though she says little, waits anxiously for his arrival. He makes only a brief appearance in the book, but so apparent is his feeling for this woman years older than himself that even the silly little student nurse, Ellen, is moved to exclaim "Gee! He likes you, Miss Keate."

"Well," replies Sarah, in her usual unflappable style, "I should hope so."

From This Dark Stairway is, like many of Mrs. Eberhart's novels, about people of overwhelming greed and passion caught in a moment of stasis, in which the world no longer turns as it ought to, in which values—except those of Nurse Sarah Keate—are momentarily in abeyance and masks are lowered.

There is almost always a structure—a big, isolated mansion in overgrown grounds, as in *Death in the Fog*, or in this case, the great, stifling hospital, silent and smothering, with the dark staircase leading down and down into its heart like a vortex. At the foot of the staircase, in the basement, lives the lowly orderly, asthmatic and desperate Jacob Teuber. At its head, on the top floor, is the empty operating room with its cases of gleaming and deadly knives.

And on the floors between, the nurses, a dozen different personalities, hiding their pasts and their sometimes-passionate presents behind the wilting starch of white caps and uniforms.

A great structure hollow at the heart, sheltering death.

Frightened people, small people, who want only to live.

And often, too, the rich invalid, the man or woman with money and little else. Cultivated, perhaps, and placated for his money. Seldom loved. The sense of slow death overtaken by sudden death. The sense of the inchoate greed that drives the world.

Across the street from Melady Memorial Hospital, St. Malachy's Church runs a shelter for lone men the Depression has driven onto the streets, the unemployed, the homeless. Inside the hospital, the rich invalid, Peter Melady, changes places unaccountably with a dead black man in the charity ward. In this oppressive world waiting for the renewing storm that will restore it, what is real and what is not? Who is the victim, and who the destroyer? Who is rich and who is poor?

To use the conventions of one's chosen form, and not be used by them.

Cozy mysteries like Mignon G. Eberhart's Nurse Keate novels are often accused of being merely amusements or puzzles. They are cute. They are "tasteful" and look decorative on end tables. They have no more to do with The Real World than do romance novels or books about how to serve a proper high tea. People die in Cozies, but nobody looks too closely at The Body. If there is blood, it is nice, clean, reasonable blood. The detective may suffer a few uneasy moments during the process of crime-solving, but in the final scene, his or her hands are clean and he or she sits in a comfortable parlor sipping tea and discussing the tidy and comforting outcome of the case.

Baldly stated, these are the stereotypes of the kind of book Mignon G. Eberhart began to write in 1929, and continued to write for the whole of a long career that earned her a Grand Master Award from Mystery Writers of America.

Quite honestly, I doubt very much if she spent so much as a minute worrying about whether she was Cozy or Hard-boiled, or even Mainstream.

As Sarah Keate would say, "I should certainly hope not."

FROM THIS DARK STAIRWAY

CHAPTER I

THE stairway stretched before me, the smooth rail shining darkly, the broad steps losing themselves in shadows and then emerging again at the top of the flight into the pale little area of green-shaded light about the chart desk. It is an old stairway, its steps shallow and very wide and covered so securely with some kind of rubber-like fabric that one's steps only make soft little thuds of sound upon it, and it begins at the first floor of the Melady Memorial Hospital in a splendor of carved walnut newel posts and leads solidly upward, turning abruptly but in a dignified fashion around landings, which are midway each flight of stairs, and around the intersecting corridors of each floor all the way to the fourth and last floor. Thus, climbing the old stairway gives one a sort of cross-section of the entire hospital; all along its turns one is offered vivid glimpses of the hushed but stirring life of the place—it is like putting a finger on the pulse of the seething, intensely engrossing entity which is our hospital world.

There is back of it a narrow and shabbier stairway leading from the first floor to the basement; and from the fourth floor a small flight of iron steps lead to a door on the roof. And alongside the wide stair well there runs from the first floor to the fourth a fairly new and modern elevator. This is an automatic affair with any number of buttons and stops and lights and things to push or pull in case of emergency, and it has a nerve-shattering way of giving a little lurch as it stops at the floor you have indicated and just before you open the grilled door inside the cage. I have never liked the thing and have a tendency, when using it, to keep my eyes glued to the rather large black button labeled "Emergency Stop" and to calculate somewhat nervously just what I should do, and how rapidly I could do it, if the silently creeping thing took a notion to stop between floors. It is narrow and long enough to accommodate stretcher trucks and it is very silent, being made especially for hospital use; so silent, in fact, that in the corridors we hear it only faintly and it indicates its presence at a floor by the red light in the cage shining through the opaque glass doors that lead from the elevator shaft into the various corridors. As I say, I have never liked it and frequently use the stairway in preference.

I did so then, letting one hand slip along the railing— a railing made smooth as the beads of any rosary by the pressure through the years of countless hands passing along its gleaming surface. The drama of the hospital caught at me then, I remember, as it always did at the thought of those hands—hands that were anxious or triumphant, jubilant with renewed promise or hopelessly weak with the need to touch some other hand which would no longer respond to any touch, be it ever so tender. Ah, the hands that had polished that railing, and the feet that had worn shallow hollows in the wide steps, and the hearts those steps had carried! There is a kind of coming face to face with essentials in a hospital, a casting away of vanities. Living and freedom from pain and peace, with perhaps what love life may give—these are the only things that are vital. Everything else is empty and futile and rather small and shabby beside these essentials. Anxiety and love and the need for peace surround one like palpable, breathing things on that old stairway that, for so many years, has led through the very heart of the Melady Memorial Hospital.

And there is also very perceptible in a hospital, particularly among the patients, a hurriedly acquired righteousness, a subduing of earthiness, a something which Lillian Ash referred to as a "when-the-devil-was-sick reform." She added further that it was humanity's poverty-stricken way of offering a bargain to God. In this, as in many things, I do not agree with Miss Ash. I hold rather that it is that instinctive reaching toward godliness which the reality of pain induces and that it is human and pitiable and lovable.

That hot night in early July I started up the stairway, letting one hand slide along the railing and holding with my other hand the small package I was bringing from Peter Melady's home. And the stairway led me straight into the strange and tragic affair which the newspapers so alliteratively and variously labeled Mad Mystery at Melady Memorial and Melady Murder Mystery and Murders at Melady Memorial. Well, it was mad and bad enough, in all conscience, and now that it is over I shall try to set down events as lucidly as may be. Though as to that there seemed to be nothing logical or lucid about the dreadful business.

It strikes me as curious that I should show no evidence of the rather horrible experience—though it does seem to me that the white streak in my abundant reddish hair which my white nurse's cap does not adequately conceal is a little wider, and the lines about my eyes, which are not exactly pretty perhaps but have remarkably keen vision, are a little sharper. Certainly I have lost a little in weight, but this is not a matter which troubles me.

To begin at the beginning I must go back a year or so

to the ill-advised day when I accepted the position of superintendent nurse of the east wing, third floor, of Melady Memorial Hospital. Not an easy task, for that wing is devoted to the care of the wealthier class of patients, many of whom are what Dr. Kunce calls whimsical and I call downright devilish. Especially during second watch, which is between midnight and dawn.

This is how it happened that that particular July day when Peter Melady—head of the Melady Drug Company, as perhaps you know, grandson of the founder of Melady Memorial Hospital, and himself chairman of the hospital board—came to the hospital as a patient of Dr. Harrigan's and demanded that I, Sarah Keate, give him nursing care, he was simply assigned to a room in my wing, as he would have been in any case. Of course, since he was Peter Melady discipline was stretched a little in his case, routine made a little elastic. Dr. Kunce gave orders, Nancy Page was sent to act as superintendent of the wing under my watchful eyes, and my time was made my own. Or, rather, Peter Melady's.

It was a curious fatality that brought Dione Melady, his daughter (married to her second cousin purely in order to perpetuate the Melady name and blood and fortune, so gossip said), to the hospital at the same time. Fatality and a severe case of sunburn.

It was the same fatality, assisted this time by a natural disinclination on her part to obey traffic laws, that brought Ina Harrigan to the room beside Peter Melady's, her right arm broken, one of her perfect teeth knocked out, and the long Packard roadster she'd just purchased into the garage for somewhat extensive repairs. She also had an unidentifiable bruise or two which were not exactly recent, but that is neither here nor there; Dr. Harrigan was known to be a man of violent temper, particularly when confronted with one of his young wife's escapades.

There we were then, that hot, still July night: Peter Melady and Dione Melady and Mrs. Harrigan all in the east wing, with Lillian Ash nursing the typhoid convalescent in the room opposite Ina Harrigan's, and Courtney Melady, who was Dione's cousin and husband and a gentleman of none too savory a reputation, wandering about, in and out of Dione's and Peter Melady's rooms, viewing the hospital, himself, and the world with cold, weary eyes. I had no idea, no premonition at all, of the drama that was about to begin. The actors were at their entrances, their lines on their lips, the stage was set, the drug-room key, the cork, the ugly amputating knife, the bit of white chewing gum were all at hand ready to play their own not unimportant rôles. And in the charity ward a Negro lay dying and I carried in my hand the Chinese snuff-bottle.

It had been a day of stifling and unseasonable humidity, the worst of a few days of extreme heat that had hung over the city, sending thermometers soaring, bringing victims of heat-stroke to the hospital, and fraying the nerves of the nurses. The first two days had been endurable but that day, Tuesday the seventh of July, was one of those days which seem to come once in a while and bring with them a sort of psychic unrest. There was uneasiness in the very air. A series of small accidents had occurred during the day, such as dropped thermometers and spilled medicines and leaky ice-bags; Nancy had had words with Miss Ash anent some missing sheets, Dr. Kunce had snapped at everyone all day in a most irritating fashion, and I, myself, had fought a headache since morning. Now, approaching nine o'clock in the evening, it was still hot, still breathless, and not a breeze stirred in the long corridors and high-ceilinged sick rooms.

The long climb up the stairway through the heat left me weary, and I stopped to rest a moment as I emerged at the third-floor corridor. It was very warm and very still. Toward the west stretched the long corridor of the children's ward and after that, gradually diminishing into darkness, the shadowy perspective of bare, gray white walls, dotted here and there by tiny red signal lights above blacker spaces that were doors, which was the charity ward. To the east stretched my own wing. At the chart desk, in a little recess directly opposite the stairway, sat Nancy Page. Her face looked weary but very young and pretty above her white uniform, and around her forehead and ears were dampish-looking little tendrils of hair which caught gold glints from the light above her head. She looked up, the pen still in her hand, and squinted her eyes a little in an effort to see beyond the circle of light cast by the green-shaded lamp. Nancy's eyes, by the way, have created much havoc in hospital circles, particularly among the internes.

"Oh, it's you," she said. "Dr. Harrigan left a message for you. He was in for a few moments while you were gone." As I approached her she eyed the little package in my hand curiously. "Did you get it?"

"The snuff-bottle? Yes. Although I had a difficult time convincing an elderly woman who calls herself Mr. Melady's housekeeper that I was not going to steal it."

"Here's a note Dr. Harrigan left for you. He told me he would be in again about midnight. What in the world does a Chinese snuff-bottle look like?"

I took the note and scanned it briefly; it was only a few words telling me he had left orders on the chart for the preparation of my patient for the coming operation, which was scheduled for the next morning, and that he would be in again about midnight, and was signed in the very small, neat handwriting which always seemed such an anomaly for a man of Dr. Harrigan's physical build and characteristics.

"It's odd he would trouble to leave a note," I said idly.

Nancy shrugged.

"It's because it is the great Peter Melady," she said. "Hurry up and show me the snuff-bottle, Sarah."

Seeing no harm in it I slipped the snuff-bottle out of the folds of tissue paper. I held the small blue thing in my hand a moment and then set it down on the glass surface of the chart desk.

"Why, how small it is!" said Nancy in an amazed way. And after a moment she added in a sort of whisper: "And how beautiful!"

Well, it was beautiful. It did not take expert eyes to see the beauty of the ancient thing, standing there on the desk. It was small enough to fit in the hand and very delicately made of some rich blue stone, lightly flecked with gold, which I learned later was lapis lazuli, carved very gracefully in the design of a pomegranate fruit and leaves. At least Peter Melady had said it was a pomegranate; it looked quite as much like an apple to me. The stopper was a round pink tourmaline, and attached to it was a slender ivory spoon which dipped down into the flat little bottle.

Yes, it was a beautiful thing. A bit of ancient China set down strangely on the bare, hygienic desk of an American hospital. I found myself thinking of hands again; what hands had carried that bit of jewelry, what ornamented fingernails had tapped at it? Manchu hands they would have been, for one had only to look at the thing to know that it had been made for princes, Manchu hands, long and slender and yellow and smooth, hands that, with the snuff-bottle, held secrets and cunning and wisdom.

"How beautiful!" whispered Nancy again. The tired look had left her face and she was leaning forward, her eyes shining. The pen dropped from her grasp and rolled on the desk, scattering a tiny trail of ink, as she stretched her slim fingers toward the snuff-bottle, touched it lightly and with a sort of reverence, and finally took the tourmaline stopper between her fingers and pulled it out.

"Look, Sarah," she said eagerly. "Look at the funny little ivory thing. It is exactly like a tiny, slender spoon. How did Peter Melady happen to have this?"

"He collects objects of art that appeal to him. It is merely a hobby with him," I explained with some authority, having been obliged to listen to an extended monologue on the subject by Peter Melady himself that very day. "And the intrinsic value of the thing has no meaning at all for him. His only criterion is his own taste. His collection of fans has been very highly complimented and he has the only collection of snuff-bottles outside the museums. If there is anything you want to know about Peter Melady's collections, just ask me. I am well informed."

Nancy also has a particularly engaging dimple. It is quite near the corner of her soft crimson mouth and has disturbed more than one masculine pulse. It showed briefly now.

"Hot weather always makes you snappish, Sarah." She pushed the snuff-bottle toward me and leaned with her elbow on the desk. "What a day it's been! I hope it cools off some during the night. There's not a breath of air stirring."

There was a sudden buzz and thump against the screen of the window back of her and she started a little nervously, glancing swiftly over her shoulder.

"Oh! It's another June bug. I wish they'd leave; it's past June. They are nearly driving me mad, thumping like that against the screen. I don't know what's the matter with me to-night."

"It's the heat," I said sympathetically.

"And the humidity. Yes, it really is the humidity," she repeated with a touch of irritation. "Everything I touch is damp and feels sticky."

There was a soft little click across the corridor and down a little; it was the little click a signal light gives as it is put on. We both looked in that direction.

"My patient," I said, and as Nancy took her pen again I picked up the blue Chinese snuff-bottle and approached Room 309.

Against the doctor's orders my patient had managed to prop himself up on some pillows and was smoking a long and vilely odoriferous black cigar, the smoke of which met me at the door.

"There you are," he said. "Did you bring the snuff-bottle?"

"Yes."

Peter Melady was a slight, shrewd-eyed man of fifty or more, his thin hair an indeterminate sandy gray, his mouth hard, and at the time he was very ill, indeed, although he refused to admit this and smoked his cigars and railed at the nurses and doctors and fought his daughter Dione and her husband with all the belligerence and obstinacy of his nature.

"Well, it took you long enough," he said in a disgruntled way. "Give it to me." As he reached for it he gave me a shrewd look. "Nice to have something pretty to look at in this bare hospital room," he added in an explanation that was neither flattering nor, as it developed, true. It was not entirely in order to have something pretty to look at that Peter Melady had sent me so urgently to his home for that Chinese snuff-bottle. I think I felt that, even then, though I said nothing; it is not for me to question the whims of my patients.

His spare hand with its blunt fingers and the fine sandy hair along the back shook a little as it reached for the snuff-bottle. When I emerged from pinning on my white cap in the bathroom he was still, apparently, gloating over the tiny blue bottle, turning and twisting it in his hands and screwing up his shrewd eyes so as to see through the cloud of smoke from the cigar which he held tightly between his teeth.

"Dr. Harrigan was in?" I said conversationally as I skillfully extracted a pillow from the heap under his head, thus lowering him to a position more nearly that advised by the doctor.

Peter Melady's sandy eyebrows lowered over his nose as I took the pillow but he did not protest.

"Yes," he said. "He's going to go ahead with the operation to-morrow morning all right. He thinks I'll get along well enough." He paused for a moment and then added in the most nonchalant way in the world: "I'll get along all right. But he's a damn fool all the same."

I lifted my eyebrows. While I cherished an opinion or two about Dr. Harrigan myself, still it did not become me to say so.

"A brilliant surgeon," I said, picking up my thermometer.

"Dissipated," grunted Peter Melady back of the cigar. His eyes did not leave the lovely bit of blue in his restless fingers. "Drinks too much. On the downhill grade."

"The best surgeon in B——." I shook the thermometer vigorously.

"Used to be the best surgeon in B——," amended Peter Melady. "Mark my words, Miss Keate, he won't last long. Look at the paunch on him. Look at the bags under his eyes. And he's not much older than I am. He thinks I'm in a bad way. Oh, don't shake your head, Miss Keate; I've got eyes. He thinks I'm in a bad way. But mark me, I'll last longer than Leo Harrigan."

"You can put entire confidence in Dr. Harrigan's skill," I said. "Will you let me take your temperature, please?"

"Well, ain't I putting confidence in his skill? You don't need to tell me he is the only doctor in the Middle West who can do anything for me. I know that." He slanted a sharp glance in my direction. "Do you think that otherwise I would put myself unreservedly into the hand of ——" He paused. He had been speaking in the lightly ironical way which was his habit, but he concluded in a suddenly hard and sincere voice: "—of my bitterest enemy?"

Well, of course, everybody in the hospital knew that Dr. Harrigan and Peter Melady, after being the closest of friends for years, had suddenly and unaccountably veered around to being the most determined of enemies. They could always be expected to take opposite sides of any matters of controversy, Peter Melady with money and authority on his side, Dr. Harrigan with the prestige of past success and the influence of his important patients on his side. And there is no doubt that, in spite of his faults, Dr. Harrigan was always a man to inspire loyalty, even now when he certainly was, as Peter Melady said, on the downhill grade and going at a pace faster than I think anyone outside the hospital realized.

"He'll pull me through if anyone can," said Peter Melady. "And I hate him. And he hates me." He finished on a note of such grim truth that I daresay I looked as I felt, more than a little shocked.

He shot another quick glance at me, smiled with one side of his hard mouth, and said in a more natural way:

"Come now, Miss Keate. You'll admit he's got no morals. Because he's the great Dr. Harrigan he gets by with things no other doctor would dare—or would want to dare. Doctors as a rule are a pretty decent lot. They couldn't get along if they were not. And Harrigan *was* decent. Until lately." He removed his cigar and shook the ashes airily over the side of the narrow, high bed.

"Dr. Harrigan still manages to cure his patients," I said dryly. "Open your mouth, please."

"Dr. Kunce is the coming man," began Peter Melady with every evidence of continuing the subject, but as he opened his mouth to insert the cigar again I slipped the thermometer adroitly under his tongue. He gave me a baffled look but held it there, and as I waited I thought of his last words. Dr. Kunce, the present head of the hospital, was certainly the coming man. I never knew by what gift of silky diplomacy he had managed to steer a straight course between Peter Melady's obstinacy and Dr. Harrigan's bluster but so he had done, greatly to his own benefit. However, it seemed to me that very lately Dr. Kunce had been underestimating Dr. Harrigan. Dr. Harrigan's influence was on the wane, that was true, but he was still powerful, still brilliant between the lapses we had so far managed to keep quiet, still unexcelled in the operating rooms. He had specialized in diseases of the nature of that from which Peter Melady was suffering, and when Peter Melady said that Dr. Harrigan was the only man in the Middle West who might cure him he spoke truly. So far, Dr. Harrigan had been obliged to postpone the necessary operation owing to the precarious state of Mr. Melady's heart reaction, but he had finally decided he could delay it no longer. I was pleased to find my patient in such optimistic spirits regarding the coming operation; that, as any nurse knows, is half the battle.

As I was taking the thermometer from my patient's mouth and managing at the same time to secure the forbidden cigar, the door into the corridor opened and Dione Melady stood on the threshold.

"For heaven's sake, Dad, why don't you have the door left open?" she asked in a complaining way. Her diaphanous pale mauve draperies trailed across the room and she sat down, wincing at the motion, in one of the wicker chairs near the window. The bandages on her back and chest made her look curiously bulky; she was actually of slight figure and build, and was of a kind of washed-out blondeness which had missed the wiry strength of feature and expression that was in her father's face. A young woman accustomed to having her own way, she was inclined to be pettish and was given to exaggerating her own troubles. If she had actually married her second cousin, Courtney Melady, in order to perpetuate the Melady name, so far she had not accomplished much in that direction. She had a curiously stubborn way of clinging to and making much of her dislikes, was inordinately interested in birth control— a subject of which the average nurse knows very little, although Dione was not easily convinced that this was true—and in the state of her own health. She really had got a very severe case of sunburn, due, I suspected, to sitting around on the beach in a bathing suit in which she fancied herself, but she made a commotion about it that was out of all proportion to the pain and discomfort it gave her.

Poor Dione! If I have lingered a little over her it is because her peculiarities of character had so much to do with what was to follow. I remember very well how she sat on the edge of the chair, her full, weak mouth pulled into petulant lines and her light, colorless eyebrows, along the line of which she had simply run a black pencil with no attempt at artistry at all, drawn upward.

"I can't stay on a bed with these horrible bandages, Miss Keate," she said in a thin, somewhat nasal voice. "So I came to see how Father was getting along. Since they are going to operate to-morrow after all, and a daughter's objection doesn't matter in the least, I hoped he was much better. But really I can't understand you, Father. Letting Dr. Harrigan operate——"

"Now, Dione, we've been over that time and time again."

"But it is so unreasonable, Father. I can't see why you do it!"

I cleared my throat.

"My patient must not be——" I began when Peter Melady silenced me.

"I've made up my mind," he said wearily. "You've nagged me for months about this. Now let's call it settled. Dr. Harrigan operates to-morrow morning and that's flat."

"I'll never consent."

"I don't need your consent."

"Now see here, Father, do listen to reason."

"Shut up!" said Peter Melady. It had the effect of an explosion. And he regarded his daughter with a kind of regretful fury as if he were wishing the days of spankings were not past.

"You are very rude," said Dione, "when I'm thinking only of your welfare. However," she added hurriedly as a sort of snarl came from her father, "I'll say no more about it. Will you leave us, please, Miss Keate?"

"You may stay for ten minutes," I said, "providing you do not worry or fatigue Mr. Melady."

At the door I met Court Melady. He was looking as spruce and powdered and unwrinkled as if the heat had not touched him, although at the edge of his thinning, gray-sprinkled hair was a little line of moisture. His cold, pouched gray eyes went past me to Dione and became if anything colder, but he smiled and asked me quite nicely if he might visit my patient.

"For ten minutes. Mr. Melady must not become fatigued." As I propped the door open so that my patient might catch any vagrant breath of air, I glanced back into the room.

"Oh, you sent for the Chinese snuff-bottle," Dione was saying, more liveliness in her voice than was customary, and Court Melady was leaning over the bed surveying the rich bit of blue in Peter Melady's hand with eyes that had momentarily lost their weariness and had become singularly intent.

It is strange that, as I looked at those three people, each so intent upon that bit of old China in Peter Melady's hand, I had no premonition of the terrible entanglement that was to concern each so nearly and in which each played such an important part. It is true that I felt unreasonably restless, but at the time I attributed my uneasiness to the sultry heat of the night.

And all the time things were reaching their preordained climax, although only one of the actors had, probably, any notion that it was to come so soon. Lillian Ash was caring for her patient, fretting on account of the heat and, likely, watching Ina Harrigan's door. Dr. Kunce was probably preening himself and looking enigmatic above his silky black beard at the dinner party which, as was brought out during the inquest, he attended early in the evening. Jacob Teuber was sleeping the hurried sleep of the hospital orderly who is apt to be called out at any or all hours of the night; Kenwood Ladd was sitting in Mrs. Harrigan's room smoking—I knew that because I caught a whiff of his cigarette smoke as I passed her door and, naturally, the frequent visits of that rising young architect to handsome, imperious Ina Harrigan would not go unnoticed in a hospital. And in the charity ward a Negro was taking a long time to die.

Too, Ellen Brody, a student nurse who, without knowing it, was the crux of the whole affair, was standing at the chart desk talking to Nancy as I approached.

That night began much the same as other nights except for the humid heat which seemed to grow heavier and more oppressive as the night advanced. Dione and her husband had left my patient's room without lingering past the time I had allowed them, and by eleven o'clock I had got my patient settled for the night and had myself tossed and turned on the nurse's cot in a corner of the room for a good hour before I concluded that there was no use trying to sleep. I rose, got into my crumpled uniform again, and slipped quietly from the darkness of my patient's room into the silence and dimness and emptiness of the long, darkened corridor.

No one was about and my skirts whispered against the shadowy walls as I walked quietly to the window behind the chart desk.

All around me the little bedtime murmur and bustle of the hospital had died away, lights were out in the sick rooms, and it was very still. From the children's ward which, as I have said, was on our own third floor and lay between the east wing and the charity ward at the extreme west end of the corridor, came the thin sound of a child's wail and from Euclid Avenue three blocks away I could hear the sound of a trolley car. Some June bugs, late that year, thudded and buzzed against the screen, tiny insects circled and circled about the chart-desk light until they fell exhausted on the glass surface of the desk. As I stood there trying in vain to get a cool breath of air, the child's wail hushed itself, the murmur of the trolley car became lost cityward where a faint radiance marked the presence of lights and people, three stories below me a few street lights made misty blobs of yellow in the soft, deep darkness, and the silence in the sleeping hospital became more profound as it got into its first slumber.

You can say what you please about winter with its accidents and spring with its babies, the summer months are by far the most difficult of the hospital regime. Especially when we are visited, as we usually are, though seldom so early in the summer, by protracted heat waves which, in our climate, leave us limp and exhausted and nervously fagged. I have often wondered how much the strain, the irritability, the excessive weariness induced by the weather had to do with the ugly business that was on its way. Man is not nearly so completely divorced from earthy influences as he thinks he is.

Not seeing that I was any cooler at the window, I moved over and sat down at the desk. It is, as I have said, in a little recess opposite the stairway, but is so arranged that any nurse sitting at the desk can see along the entire length of the east wing, thus noting the small red gleams of any signal lights above the sick-room doors. You have to turn your head a little to see along the westward-stretching corridor which, at that hour of the night, is rather too shadowy to suit my taste. A hospital is never cheerful, especially at night when the long, bare corridors, with deep shadows that are open doors, seem to stretch infinitely onward, and the tiny red signal lights here and there and the occasional faint green radiance of the shaded lights over the chart desks are indescribably eery. The stairway was a black well, wide steps leading upward and downward into shadow. And everywhere lay that stifling blanket of heat. It was actually a humid heat, as Nancy had said; everything I touched seemed damp and the old walls themselves were sweaty and moist.

I sat there for several moments, I suppose, leaning my head on my hand and keeping a listless eye on the corridor. Nancy Page and Ellen Brody, the two general-duty nurses in the wing at that time, were apparently busy in the sick rooms, and Lillian Ash, the only special-duty nurse in the wing, was not to be seen, although her patient's door was open and a green baize screen appeared to be across the doorway. Against the walls of the corridor were lined vases of flowers which had been set outside the various sick rooms for the night, and their fragrance mingled in a rather sickening way with the smell of antiseptics and ether and soup which lingers about a hospital.

Later I realized that it was exactly then that the last notes of the sultry, brooding overture died away, the waiting hush deepened, the curtain was rung up and the drama began. It began quietly with no hint of the turmoil and the horror it was about to disclose.

I suddenly became aware that someone was whispering. The whispers were singularly penetrative, as if uttered forcefully and vehemently. I was conscious that I had been hearing the sound for several moments.

CHAPTER II

I DO not know why those whispers at once affected me so disagreeably unless it was because, in the first place, my nerves were already a little unstrung and quicker to catch any hint of danger, and in the second place, contrary to what you might suppose, whispers in a hospital are not usual. There is nothing so exasperating to a nervous patient as whispering, and a nurse is taught to habituate herself to speaking in a low, clear voice.

As that vehement whispering continued I grew uneasy. The softly sibilant sounds wafted themselves through the quiet corridor in a peculiarly bewildering fashion and I could not at once decide whether they were coming from the stairway or from one of the sick rooms. Certainly the speakers could not be far from the chart desk. I rose, walked to the stairway and then along the south side of the corridor. At my patient's door I peered into the room. Mr. Melady was lying quiet, appearing to be asleep. The sound of whispering was more distinct there, however, and I crossed to the opposite door which was Dione Melady's. The door was open and a screen was across the threshold and two people back of the screen were whispering with such violence that I actually caught a phrase or two.

A few hours later I was to strive desperately to recall every nuance of inflection in those whispers, but there were only a few words that were really clear and distinct. One phrase was ". . . I will not do it . . ." This was followed by some quick words on the part of the other speaker which I could not understand, and then the first one said again, distinctly: "I can't. Don't ask me. It's out of the question." After this came a rush of whispers out of which I caught only a few words, but they were of a nature to make my flesh crawl. Someone on the other side of that screen said distinctly: "You must do it. He will be murdered, I tell you. Murdered."

And at that very instant Dr. Kunce spoke softly from the door of the elevator.

"Miss Keate."

Well, I daresay I was a bit confused, especially when Dr. Kunce's rather sharply aquiline nose came down over his silky black Vandyke and moustache. He does not have a pleasant smile. The smile itself is masked by the neatly trimmed beard and small moustache, and there is something about the contraction of his facial muscles that actually draws the tip of his nose downward. He is a handsome fellow of early middle age, which is anything you please in a man. He has a very pleasant way when he chooses, especially with feminine patients, is a little too stiffly mannered to get on well with the nursing staff, has liquid brown eyes with unbelievably long eyelashes, his dark hair is very silky as is his beard, his hands are delicate and well cared for, and he is always the very pink of sartorial perfection. His full name by the way is Felix Kunce, a nice enough name which, I am sorry to say, arouses undue levity among the student nurses who habitually refer to him as Dr. Fulla Prunes.

He is an excellent physician and surgeon, has remarkable composure and a rather nasty little gift of sarcasm. The recollection of this gift increased my confusion as I turned to see him standing a few paces from me, watching me with his nose down over his beard and looking, I must say, very handsome in his well-tailored dinner jacket with the black ribbon of the eyeglasses he affected for evening wear trailing across his gleaming shirt front— very handsome and very much out of place against the hygienic emptiness of the bare hospital walls.

The whispers ceased as if automatically when he spoke, and when he added a smooth request for me to accompany him to see the patient down in Room 301 I perforce followed him in that direction. I escaped as soon as possible, however, anxious to see who came from Dione Melady's room and to discover the meaning of those curious whispers.

But the corridor was still empty and there was not a sound to be heard. My patient had apparently not stirred; when I slipped quietly into his room I judged him to be sleeping soundly, for his breathing was very regular and quiet, he did not speak to me, and so far as I could see everything was quite normal.

The whispered words I had overheard continued to echo in my thoughts, but I did not accord them their true significance; people often employ highly exaggerated phrases. The thing that troubled me concerned the identity of the speakers; Dione Melady must have been one of them, but who had the other been? At eleven o'clock at night all visitors have gone and the inmates of a hospital are quite accurately disposed; there are no wanderers about the corridors and sick rooms. There are, of course, many times when the corridors are de- serted owing to the nurses being occupied in the various sick rooms, but the sick patients are always in bed at that hour. It was not Peter Melady who had been in his daughter's room, for he was sleeping; I did not think it was Ellen Brody, the student nurse. It might have been Nancy, of course, but I could think of no topic which would call for a whispered conversation of such feeling between her and one of her patients. I finally decided it must have been Ellen being urged to gratify some whim of Mrs. Melady's which was against hospital rules (as people will urge student nurses) and very properly refusing. It is true that this did not explain the matter very satisfactorily but there was no other common-sense explanation. When Nancy emerged from Room 302 down at the east end of the corridor, answered a signal light halfway along it, and finally came to sit near me at the chart desk whither I had drifted, I asked her if anyone besides the nurses had been in the wing during the last hour.

"Dr. Kunce just came in," she said in an uninterested way. "He is in 301 now." She made a notation on the chart, returned it to the rack, and leaned back against the white metal back of the chair in which she sat. She looked tired and dabbed at her forehead and lips with a wisp of a handkerchief. "Such a night! So hot!" She sighed.

"Hot as an oven," agreed Ellen Brody with somewhat startling fervor. She had a way of materializing without warning at one's elbow which was extraordinarily disconcerting. "Will you O. K. this chart for me, Miss Keate? I mean Miss Page. I keep forgetting you are superintendent now, Miss Page. Oh, and Miss Page, I can't find the drug-room key."

All three of us looked at the hook on the desk where it is customary to hang that key when it is not in use.

"Why, it isn't there," I said. "Are you sure it wasn't left accidentally in the door to the drug room?"

"Yes, ma'am. I just looked. It isn't there. I thought maybe Miss Page had it."

I glanced at Nancy. It struck me that she looked extremely white in the greenish light; white and tired, and

yet there was certainly anger in her eyes, which was entirely uncalled for, inasmuch as the various keys used by
the nurses are not infrequently mislaid. She was fumbling
in the pocket of her own uniform.

"Why, yes," she said suddenly. "I did have it. I must
have dropped it. Glance into 302, will you, Ellen? It
may have slipped from my pocket when I lowered the
head rest in there a moment ago. Or I may have dropped
it in——" Without finishing her sentence she was off
down the corridor; I did not join in the search and did
not even note where they searched. Nancy must have
found the key, however, and very shortly, for in a few
moments she appeared in the corridor again, met Ellen
and gave her the key, I suppose, for Ellen at once turned
toward the door to the narrow little drug room and vanished presently.

Instead of growing cooler it seemed to me that with
every moment the sultriness of the night increased. It
was difficult to breathe properly and every motion was
an effort.

It is singular how vividly I recall the smallest and
most trivial-seeming events of those brief hours before
midnight of July seventh. I do so, I believe, because each
was to acquire such grim significance in the grisly entanglement which was already involving us in its meshes.
I even remember Dr. Kunce's taking his leave and how
he rang for the elevator and stood there looking at
Nancy's bright hair, with his dark eyes rather narrow
between their silky eyelashes, until the blurred oblong of
red appeared behind the opaque glass door and he
opened that door and the grilled door inside the cage
slid smoothly back and in a moment the oblong of red
vanished downward. Shortly after that I went back to
the cot in my patient's room and did not see Dr. Harri-

gan when he arrived. I learned later, however, that he was in his wife's room when the faint shallow sound of the midnight supper bell, away down in the basement, tinkled sharply and a vague odor of coffee crept through the corridors.

Faint though it was, the fragrance was irresistible. I rose, again looked at my patient, and left the room.

And entering the corridor came face to face with Lillian Ash.

That in itself, of course, was no unusual thing. What was unusual was the look on Lillian Ash's face. It was a look of stark terror.

It was not alarm, or apprehension, or fright. It was terror.

Lillian Ash was a tall, blonde woman, well filled out but determinedly youthful with her carefully waved hair which seemed to have experienced a variety of bleaches and dyes, an elaborate complexion, and an easy smile. She looked rather like a Gibson girl grown buxom and a little hard, was not a particularly modern or efficient nurse, but a woman, one would have said, well able to take care of herself. Now, however, her face was a perfect mask of terror under its paint, and she was looking fixedly at a man who was just disappearing into Dione Melady's room. The man was Dr. Harrigan; one glance at those bulky shoulders and his tall figure and leonine head with its thick shock of vigorous, still defiantly black hair was enough to identify him, even if someone had not turned on the light in the sick room, which silhouetted his hawklike profile against the white walls beyond. And Ellen was standing there beside us in the corridor with her light blue eyes like dollars and her expression that of an inquisitive Irish terrier.

But when I brought my eyes back in some perplexity to

Lillian Ash the terror had gone from her face as completely as if it had never been. She yawned somewhat exaggeratedly, patted her mouth, adjusted her white cap and said:

"Going down to supper?"

I nodded and we started toward the stairway. I saw her give Ellen a sharp look which said as plainly as so many words: "Mind your own business," but otherwise she was quite natural and composed. I suggested waiting for Nancy to accompany us but she demurred, saying "For heaven's sake let's go on to the basement," for it might be cooler there. And under the light above the chart desk she looked remarkably fagged, the heavy pink powder on her face was all caked with moisture and her uniform limp and wrinkled with a little pinkish line of powder and perspiration around the neck line of the collar.

Nancy caught up with us as we rounded the second-floor landing. She said she had seen Dr. Harrigan when he arrived and he had told her, with the bluff good nature that made him so many friends, not to wait for him when the supper bell rang but to run along and get some supper; that he would be in the wing for some time likely but the student nurse could help him if necessary.

"Does he realize that the student nurse this month is Ellen Brody?" asked Lillian Ash with a little laugh.

"He saw her," said Nancy. "But really since she's been assigned to our wing I've begun to think she has more brains than we give her credit for. She's got quite marvelous powers of observation; she sees everything!"

"Oh, she sees things all right," said Lillian Ash somewhat sharply. "It's just common sense she lacks."

"Well, she does seem a little lacking in that direction," admitted Nancy.

"She can't do much harm in the fifteen or twenty minutes we take for supper," I said. "It's a good thing to give student nurses that little period of complete responsibility. Ellen is no worse than lots of them are. Heavens—it's worse down here than it is upstairs!"

How well I remember that meal—the long, white-plastered room with its narrow tables, the hot bright lights, the tiny bugs that had fallen on the cheap white cotton tablecloth, the pale tired faces of the night nurses with their disheveled hair pushed back from foreheads and ears and their white sleeves rolled up and their uniforms wrinkled. The June bugs kept thumping and buzzing against the black screens in a nerve-shattering way, Miss Jones came in a little late, murmuring wearily that a Negro in the charity ward had just died, and upstairs a grim and terrible drama was taking place.

Lillian Ash drank a cup of iced coffee in a rather thirsty fashion and left at once, saying something about her patient, but the rest of us lingered over the sandwiches.

"It's a horrible night," said Miss Jones presently. "A kind of creepy night." She paused and added with a little shudder, "I *hate* the charity ward!" She drank a little hot coffee, gripping the thick cup with fingers that shook a little and setting it down to stare thoughtfully at a tiny bug that was going in frenzied circles around and around on the white cloth.

"It's the kind of night when you feel as if something's following you all the time." She reached out, ended the bug's futile career with a blunt forefinger, and flipped it off the cloth. "Especially on the stairway."

"They ought to have lights at the landings," said Nancy Page soberly.

"Cost a few cents more. Dr. Kunce couldn't endure that," said Miss Jones.

"Suppose it does cost a little more," cried Nancy with an unexpected flare of temper. "Nurses have enough creepy things to do without having a black hole like that old stairway right under our noses every night. You feel that—*anything* might come crawling down those steps."

"From the operating room?" said Miss Jones flippantly, and then without any warning at all she shivered and quietly began to cry.

"It's just the heat," she sobbed warding off our sympathy and expostulations and dabbing at her eyes and cheeks with a napkin. "It's a perfectly h-hellish night. Give me some more coffee, will you?"

She was still sniffing when she walked upstairs between Nancy and me. We stopped at the first floor, I remember, to ring for the elevator, and had waited a moment or two for it, but it was apparently in use somewhere, so we took the stairway.

"Fine for reducing," said Nancy with a momentary dimple, which was rather an impudence on her part, Nancy having slim hips and no stomach, whereas there are times when I feel that I am practically all stomach. These are only at my lowest moments, however; while my figure is not exactly willowy, still I feel that it has dignity and authority.

"Damn this hospital," said Miss Jones as we reached the third floor, she having apparently launched upon a career of mild profanity. "A nurse's life"——She stopped suddenly, staring upward along the black steps leading to the fourth floor. We both followed her gaze but saw only empty stairs and shadowy landing. "—I thought something moved there on the landing. But there's noth-

ing. A nurse's life," she resumed, "is hell, if you ask me."
With which she started down the corridor westward.

Our own wing stretched emptily before us. Ellen was
busy in some room; it was quiet, peaceful, entirely normal.

So it was something of a shock to find that my patient
was not in his bed.

Was not in the room. Was not in the bathroom adjoin-
ing. Was not in the corridor. Was not in Dione Melady's
room.

About that time Ellen materialized at my side.

"301 has been keeping me busy," she said. "Your patient's gone upstairs Miss Keate."

"Upstairs!"

"Yes. Dr. Harrigan said they had to operate at once,
instead of waiting till morning. Dr. Harrigan himself
took Mr. Melady up on the truck. He said to tell you
there was not a moment to lose. He said he, himself,
would phone the office and arrange for it. And you're
to come to the operating rooms, Miss Keate."

"But—— Why, Ellen! Are you sure? I can't believe——" I turned to Nancy who had joined us. "I
never heard of such a thing. What on earth can have
happened!"

She shook her head although she looked rather frightened, muttered something incoherent about Mrs. Melady, and disappeared hurriedly into Dione's room.

The operating rooms are on the fourth floor directly
above us.

I hurried to the elevator and touched the button, pressing it again impatiently as, after waiting a hasty moment or two, the red-lighted cage did not glide into sight.
Then I turned quickly toward the stairway.

There was no one about that night on the fourth floor.

The operating rooms, X-ray rooms, laboratories, and delivery rooms are on that floor, and it happened that there were no babies arriving the night of July seventh and, with the exception of my patient, no emergency cases. Evidently the operating-room nurses and Dr. Kunce had not yet got awakened and dressed and to business, for only the dim night lights shone in the halls and the whole place appeared to be deserted. The ever-present smell of ether and, curiously, meat broth grew stronger and more nauseating as I approached the surgery.

The air was very heavy and hot and the glass door knob felt damp as if it were misted. The door was unlocked; Dr. Harrigan must have used his pass key. The bright white lights were glowing from the ceiling, lighting up the white walls and the glass cases of shining steel instruments along the walls and reflecting themselves in the shining black window panes.

But the tables were bare. And there was not a soul in the room.

Feeling more than a little bewildered, I glanced into dressing rooms and lavatories and even into the little waiting rooms, switching on lights as I went. Could I have reached the place before Dr. Harrigan and my patient arrived? But the door had been unlocked and the only keys belonged to Dr. Harrigan, Dr. Kunce, and Fannie Bianchi, the head surgical nurse. And the light had been turned on. And beside one of the tables stood a truck—which is not a truck at all, you understand, but is a high, narrow stretcher-like affair mounted on rubber-tired wheels. I glanced at the laundry mark on the corner of the sheet which was on the truck. It was marked in blue stitches "3E"; it was a truck, then, from my own east wing.

But where was Peter Melady? And where was Dr. Harrigan?

I hurried out of the surgery, again pressed the signal for the elevator, and when the cage did not appear hurried down to the third floor again by way of the old stairway, hastening my steps through its dark stretches of shadows which moved and wavered all about me. I remember that it was just then that I began to feel strangely apprehensive and that a curious excitement began to drum my pulses.

This was an unreasonable feeling; while Dr. Harrigan's abrupt decision and abrupter action were an unusual enough procedure, still ours is a world of safety, of quiet and peace and of rigid routine. The glimpses of human drama we get are confined to the sick rooms. Apprehension of danger in the usual sense of the word is quite out of place.

The third floor was deserted, although there were several unattended signal lights glowing eerily up and down its length and a sort of subdued commotion going on in Dione Melady's room.

I was at the telephone, intending to telephone to the office, when Ellen came flying out of 302, her cap over one ear, and her starched white apron rattling. I intercepted her.

"Ellen, are you sure Dr. Harrigan took Mr. Melady upstairs?"

"Why, of course, Miss Keate. I helped get him on the truck."

"You didn't go all the way to the operating room with him?"

"No, Miss Keate. By the time we had got him onto the truck and out of the room there were a lot of signal lights going and Dr. Harrigan said I'd better answer the lights and that he would take the patient upstairs himself."

"But why didn't he leave Mr. Melady here for me to bring upstairs?"

"Oh, Mr. Melady insisted on being with the doctor, Miss Keate. I think he was scared. And you know how stubborn he is. And Dr. Harrigan said he'd take him upstairs himself; he didn't seem to mind doing it at all." She cast an anxious glance over her shoulder and her skirts fairly quivered with impatience. "Please, Miss Keate, 302 is having a chill—and look at all those signals."

"Well, go on and answer them," I snapped.

Ellen's blue and white starchiness rattled hastily away and I turned toward the elevator; no use telephoning the office, since my patient and Dr. Harrigan had certainly gone upstairs. As I pressed the button for the elevator I heard the faint little click of truck wheels. A man in white duck and a truck on which lay a sheeted figure were emerging from the gloom of the west corridor. My patient? I hurried in that direction. The man was Jacob Teuber, one of the orderlies, a young, undernourished little man who suffers from asthma during the summer.

"Is that my patient? Mr. Melady?" I asked hastily without pausing to consider the irrationality of the inquiry; my patient, who had been taken to the operating room by Dr. Harrigan, would scarcely turn up coming from the charity ward in care of an orderly, on one of the tall gray ambulance-room trucks.

"No, Miss Keate," he said in a wheezing kind of voice. "It's a dead Negro from the charity ward."

"Well, you can't use the elevator. Something is wrong with it. I've rung and rung and it doesn't come."

"Something wrong? I wonder what's the matter. Maybe I can get it." Leaving the truck where it stood, he walked toward the elevator door back of me, while I stood there for a moment or two staring at the sheeted figure on the truck. I am not of a suspicious nature; still it occurred to me that it could do no harm to be sure the burden on the truck was actually what Teuber had said it was. True, the lines were longer than Peter Melady's would have been, and I have no more relish for seeing such things than anyone. But I finally leaned over and pulled out a corner of the sheet and lifted it.

Well, it was not Peter Melady. And I knew why Miss Jones had been hysterical at supper.

I let the sheet drop, tucked it in, glanced impatiently up and down the stairway, thinking that surely the operating-room nurses would be coming along soon, and turned again toward the elevator. Teuber was pulling at the door leading to the elevator shaft, and Lillian Ash, looking rather ill, was standing there watching him.

"No use pulling at the door," said Lillian Ash. "It won't open when the elevator isn't at this floor."

"No," said Teuber. "That's right. That's——" He broke off as if he'd run suddenly out of breath, and grabbed for a handkerchief, in which he tried to smother a wheezy attack of coughs.

"Sh—sh," warned Lillian Ash. "You'll wake the whole wing."

I ran hurriedly up the stairway again.

It was by this time nearly ten minutes since I had returned to the third floor from supper to find my patient gone. The thing was beginning to be a nightmare, and I felt more than ever as if I were in the grip of one of those endlessly futile dreams when I emerged upon the fourth floor and found things exactly as I had left them.

Lights burning, no one about, and the 3E truck standing emptily beside the operating table.

The feeling of excitement and apprehension closed more completely around me. My breath was coming quickly; my forehead, when I pushed back my cap, was wet.

So hot!

Such a strangeness in that still, fetid, ether-laden room, with its bright white lights.

I must call Dr. Kunce. I must telephone the office girl on the main floor. I must do something. I must stop this senseless going in circles.

As I passed the elevator shaft habit halted me and I rang and rang again. It was owing to the breathless stillness on the fourth floor that I heard the faint rumble of the approach of the elevator cage, followed by the unmistakable sound of the little lurch it gives as it stops at the floor indicated. No red light loomed into place, but I was sure the cage had arrived at the fourth floor.

I pulled at the door, which opened easily, and the night light from the corridor and open surgery door fell only dimly upon the elevator floor. Evidently the light in the cage had burned out. Thinking only of my oddly missing patient I stepped at once inside the cage, the doors closed, and I fumbled in the darkness for the third-floor button and pressed it. The elevator went noiselessly and slowly downward. The heat was worse in the closeness of the long, narrow cage; the air was heavy and warm and ill-ventilated.

Somehow things were all wrong—all out of place—unnatural. I was cold and hot at once and my hands prickled.

I got out at the third floor. The grilled door of the

cage and the glass door of the corridor both swung gently to behind me. The corridor was deserted. There was a light still in Dione Melady's room and the muffled sound of low voices. Teuber had gone with his truck. Lillian Ash had gone back to her patient. I started toward the telephone, determined to get some kind of action.

Something was wrong.

The girl at the switchboard in the office was asleep—dead—drowned—eloped. The hospital, save for the subdued murmur of sound in Dione's room and the thud of the June bugs, was as silent as the grave. There was not a sign of my patient or of Dr. Harrigan.

And something was wrong.

Something was very wrong about that bare clean corridor. Something was terribly out of place.

The telephone was holding my hands to the desk, but my chair was scraping backward and my knee bumped the desk edge.

Then I had torn myself from the desk and was bending over the floor.

It *was* blood!

CHAPTER III

Leading from the elevator to the chart desk ran an irregular and diminishing line of the prints of rubber heels. Dark and red and shining on the immaculateness of the scrubbed corridor floor.

My own heelprints stamped in blood!

I think the first thing I did was draw up one foot and look at the rubber heel on my oxford.

Then I was at the elevator, opening the doors. On the fourth floor the light had been dim, but here it shone directly into the cage. Just in front of the door where I had stood was bare. But what was that on the floor, shining darkly in an irregular lane? And what was that huddle just beyond, so near the door that I must have barely missed treading on that outflung hand?

I suppose I must have cried out, spoken; perhaps I screamed. At any rate Nancy and Ellen and Miss Ash were all at my side. Their faces were ghastly white; they were chattering, mumbling words, mouthing indistinct syllables. Then we were bending over, staring at that huddle.

It was Dr. Harrigan. No doubt about that. No doubt either that he was dead. And the handle of a Catlin amputating knife, its smoothly shining surface all smeared and smudgy as if a moist hand had gripped it, was protruding from his shirt front exactly over his heart.

We were frozen, bending over, half in and half out

of the elevator, none of us seeming to move or breathe. Then someone in frenzied mauve was thrusting her way among us, making incoherent sounds.

It was Dione Melady, pushing Ellen backward, leaning over to stare, and then toppling untidily against Lillian Ash's white skirts.

Well—somehow we dragged Dione into the corridor and got her onto her own bed. Someone was running with a flash of white skirts for spirits of ammonia, and I think we all lost our wits for just a moment. I can remember a sort of chaotic milling around, the clicking of signal lights by the patients who had been awakened by the noise, the feeling that we must do something, and the sickness of horror and shock. And I recall Nancy, as white as her cap, running from somewhere with the ammonia, Ellen, her face a sort of greenish yellow and her eyes nearly popping out of her head, simply standing in the middle of the corridor with her hands making funny flapping motions, myself at the telephone trying to keep my teeth from chattering, and Lillian Ash leaning over me, her breath coming in jerky little gasps from between her pale lips and her trembling hands pulling at the collar of her uniform as if it choked her.

Then I got the night girl in the office. Her voice woke to life under my words.

"Dr. Harrigan is dead. In the elevator. Here on the third floor. Call Dr. Kunce. Hurry."

I clicked up the receiver.

"Keep this from the patients. Tell them there was a trivial accident—anything you please. Answer the signal lights at once, Ellen. Stop flapping your hands like that. Shut your mouth and get to work. Pull yourself together, Miss Ash; will you help answer the signal lights, please?" I spoke involuntarily, actuated by my many years of putting my patients' welfare first. As a matter of fact I scarcely knew what I was saying. And in a sort of daze I returned to the elevator; I believe I had a sort of vague feeling that it couldn't be true; that we had made some ghastly mistake.

It was all too true, however.

And my patient? Where was he?

The next moment I was in his room; the bed was still vacant, no one in the room, no one in the bathroom. I was being very cool and very collected, making a systematic search, looking into the wastebasket, under my cot, behind the radiator. What was I looking for—a dead man in the elevator—a man with a knife in his heart—*what* was I looking for? It was something urgent. What was it? In the elevator—a man with a knife in his heart—my heel prints in blood . . .

A remnant of sense sent me to the bathroom, where I dashed cold water over my face and hands and things became clearer.

Then I was in the corridor again. Where was my patient?

Lillian Ash was standing at the door of the elevator bending over. She straightened up as I approached.

"It's terrible—terrible . . ." she whispered, the words sliding out in a slurred way. "Dr. Harrigan—he was so alive, always. So vital . . ." At least I think that was what she said.

There were feet now on the stairway, crowding faces, a subdued, seething turmoil.

There are a few things that stand out in my memory of those crowded moments. I remember Dr. Kunce's examination of the body, his sharp question as to our finding it, the incongruity of the evening clothes he still wore, the greenish highlights on his black pearl studs and his gleaming white shirt front, and the reluctant way in which he went to the telephone and told the office girl to notify the police.

"Do you mean—is it murder?" I whispered.

He nodded and said crisply:

"Couldn't be anything else, the way the knife is driven in. Anyway Dr. Harrigan isn't—wasn't a man to commit suicide.—Yes, the police at once. Tell them a man has been murdered here at Melady Memorial———" (I could hear the little shriek the office girl gave and Dr. Kunce's face darkened.) "And hurry. Then call Dr. Peattie and the other board and staff members. Ask them to come at once to the hospital. . . . Yes. Yes, that's right." He put down the telephone. "Yes, Miss Keate, it's murder. Does Mrs. Harrigan know?"

Ina Harrigan! I had forgotten she was in the hospital. I looked toward her door. It was still closed, as it had been all night in spite of the heat, and no signal light gleamed redly above it.

"She must be asleep," I said, and Dr. Kunce started toward her room, first turning sharply to the little disheveled group of white-faced nurses and internes which had already collected near the elevator. He said a low word which sent Miss Jones and one of the children's-ward nurses scuttling back to their respective duties and at which two internes went to stand at the open elevator door, a somewhat wild-haired and erratically clothed guard.

And at the same instant Nancy Page hurried to him, her eyes dark in her white face and her white cap slipped slantwise over her ruffled, shining hair, to ask him to look at Dione Melady. He made an impatient gesture but followed her.

I remember, too, the murmurous tremor and shudder

that arose in the waking hospital as the news flew like wildfire among the night nurses and the patients themselves seemed to sense the excitement and awoke and turned fretful and uneasy. Signal lights popped on continuously, the office girl telephoned up that the police and board members were on the way, and I came upon Ellen Brody in the linen closet, her face the color of a quince, being violently sick on a handful of towels.

I followed Dr. Kunce into Dione Melady's room, where Dione was going from one fainting fit into another, to tell him my patient had vanished. He looked up sharply at my first word, gave Nancy a few staccato orders, and beckoned me into the corridor.

"Now tell me, Miss Keate, exactly what you mean."

I did so, briefly and concisely. His teeth began to worry his lower lip; his fingers smoothed and smoothed his silky beard.

"Do you mean to tell me that Peter Melady has simply vanished?"

"That's exactly what I'm saying."

"Where is he?"

"If I knew do you think I'd be standing here trying to get it into your head that he's gone!"

I suppose we were both too agitated to consider professional etiquette. He began to swear under his breath and worry his beard. It struck me, curiously, that he appeared to be more concerned about Peter Melady's disappearance than about the murder of Dr. Harrigan.

And then before we could reach any conclusion at all, blue figures were tumbling up the stairs and overflowing the place and a tall man in a blue uniform was striding toward us.

"'I'm Sergeant Lamb from headquarters," he said briskly. "What's the trouble?"

"It's Dr. Harrigan," said Dr. Kunce. "He's in the elevator. He seems to have been—murdered. And Sergeant——"

Sergeant Lamb was bending into the elevator. We followed him. After one long, comprehensive look he turned toward us again.

"Yeah?"

Dr. Kunce cleared his throat; the faces all about us were excited and eager.

"Sergeant—one of the patients seems to be missing."

"Who?" Said Sergeant Lamb sharply. "Since when? What does he look like?"

Dr. Kunce drew a fine linen handkerchief from a pocket and touched his forehead and mouth somewhat nervously.

"Since midnight," he said. "And it's—Peter Melady."

"Peter Melady!" said Sergeant Lamb after a thoughtful stare. "Whew! Peter Melady! Search the hospital, men—sick rooms and all. H'm." Some of the policemen hurried off, Sergeant Lamb's mild blue eyes saw the telephone and he reached it, called a quick number composed mostly of O's and while he waited he said over his shoulder to Dr. Kunce: "Any idea who did this?"

"Not in the least," said Dr. Kunce, touching his lips again with the handkerchief. "Not in the least. It's completely inexplicable."

"H'm," said Sergeant Lamb again while he held a brief conversation with someone who answered to the title of "Chief."

And it was about that time that the board members began to arrive, shocked and protesting and one and all visiting the third floor, the laymen tiptoeing about and the doctors very grave and anxious, and fine old Dr. Peattie, who had given most of his life to Melady

Memorial, looking incredibly old and stricken as he heard the story and looked sadly at the burden the elevator held.

"This is Mr. Melady's nurse," said Dr. Kunce as Sergeant Lamb approached us again. "And it was she who found the body. I suppose you'd better tell him just what you told me, Miss Keate."

I did so. Much, it appeared, to Sergeant Lamb's interest, to say nothing of that of the board members. The various doctors began to look more and more anxious and exchanged guarded glances as I finished.

"And the point is, Sergeant Lamb—and gentlemen—" said Dr. Kunce—"the point is I was not told of this projected operation upon Mr. Melady—I mean the emergency operation which developed to-night. I knew, of course, of the operation scheduled to take place in the morning. And I'm inclined to believe——" He paused, took the telephone, asked a few rapid questions of the office girl, and turned again. "It's as I suspected. The girl in the office had heard nothing of any emergency operation. No one was notified of the change in Dr. Harrigan's plans."

"What do you mean by that?" inquired Sergeant Lamb, his long pale face and mild blue eyes looking perplexed. "Do you mean it is customary to tell you and notify the office whenever there is an operation? Red tape, huh?"

Dr. Kunce looked at him coldly.

"Not red tape at all," he said. "Do you think there is no system in a hospital! Doctors can't just pick up a patient and operate whenever they choose." His voice became less sharp and he added rather wearily: "I am what is called resident doctor of Melady Memorial; I am directly responsible for the hospital. And the girl in the office would know if Dr. Harrigan had telephoned to have the operating rooms ready and the operating staff on hand. Apparently he had not yet done so. These gentlemen are members of the governing board for the hospital; some of them are also staff doctors."

"I see," said Sergeant Lamb, looking brighter. Then he added, voicing and making definite a sort of unspoken implication which had been hanging in the very air, although, except for some meaning looks, no one had even hinted at it so far: "But it is Dr. Harrigan who was murdered. And Mr. Melady who has disappeared. If it was the other way around now—— Doors of the hospital locked at night?"

Both Dr. Kunce and I nodded emphatically.

"Windows? Fire-escape doors?"

"The windows have steel screens which are always kept bolted," said Dr. Kunce. "And the long windows" —he motioned toward the nearest which was at the east end of our wing "—leading to the fire-escapes are always bolted from the inside. It's owing to the danger of open drops in a hospital where patients are often delirious," he added in an explanatory way as Sergeant Lamb looked incredulous.

"We'll soon see if everything was locked to-night. And if so"—said Sergeant Lamb unexpectedly—"if so there's not much chance of an outsider getting into the hospital and killing Dr. Harrigan."

There was a sort of gasp among the board members, Dr. Peattie went gray white and sat down suddenly as if he had reached the end of his endurance, and Dr. Kunce dabbed at his mouth and forehead again.

"Well, there's always that possibility, isn't there?" said Dr. Kunce evasively, but Dr. Peattie held up his wrinkled old hand.

"No, no, Dr. Kunce. We can't evade it. We've always made the hospital as safe as bolts and bars will make it. And it has always been our policy to face problems openly and honestly. This is a blow. A blow. But we must face it in honor. No, Sergeant, much as I regret it I am obliged to tell you there is no such possibility. You are quite right."

There was a brief silence; a rather fat board member loosened his collar and wiped his perspiring red face. In the hot stillness a June bug thumped so loudly against the screen that everyone, I think, started a little and looked quickly that way.

"Perhaps someone came in during the day when the doors were open and hid," suggested the fat board member diffidently, with a nervous glance along the shadowy corridor and stairway and over his shoulder where the elevator cage still hung, its door a yawning black mouth. "I should think there might be any number of hiding places around here."

Dr. Peattie's face lightened for an instant; then he shook his head.

"No, it would scarcely be possible," he said. "All visitors are out of the hospital by half-past nine at night, and the nurses would immediately discover anyone who remained."

"Well, if anybody did get in," said Sergeant Lamb briskly, "he's likely here yet—providing we find that everything's locked or bolted as you say it is." He rose abruptly, stretched upward to his full gangly height and looking down on the shocked old face of Dr. Peattie. "We'll soon straighten this out, Dr. Peattie. Now I'll want to see you again, Miss—I understand it was you found the body. There's no time to be lost just now." He started toward the elevator cage again. Down the

corridor two policemen were trying the window leading to the fire escape.

"Suppose we convene in Dr. Kunce's office," suggested
Dr. Peattie, and with curiously furtive glances toward
the elevator and a muffled reference or two to painful
notoriety and hospital policy they straggled down the
stairway and out of sight. It struck me that there was
not much grief expressed for Dr. Harrigan's passing.
Well, I had not exactly liked Dr. Harrigan myself; still
I had worked at his side many, many times.

Dr. Kunce had remained and was talking over the
telephone to the office girl again. I caught his smooth,
low-voiced words: . . . "call each wing superintendent,
tell her an accident has occurred. The police have the
matter in charge and must be given any assistance . . .
keep it from the patients . . . the nurses must stay on
duty . . . no visits to the third floor . . . above all
things prevent a panic . . ."

Except for Dr. Kunce and myself and the policemen
here and there the east corridor was deserted, although
I could see far down along the west corridor sundry
heads peering out of doors and white uniforms and
kimonos in excited little groups here and there. Lillian
Ash had returned to her patient, Nancy was still with
Dione Melady, and Ellen was either busy or still sick,
which I neither knew nor cared. The only thing that concerned me just then was the whereabouts of my erstwhile patient. Where was Peter Melady? Could *he* have
murdered Dr. Harrigan?

It was possible, of course; he was seriously ill; still, he
could have walked if his heart had behaved and, while
very weak under the least exertion, one of Peter Melady's stubborn disposition might conceivably have summoned the physical strength to stab Dr. Harrigan. It

would have had to be without any warning at all, for Dr. Harrigan was much larger and stronger than Peter Melady. And Peter Melady was ill—very ill—with a heart we'd been coaxing along assiduously, trying to get it in shape for the necessary operation.

Dr. Kunce interrupted my shocked speculations.

"Mrs. Harrigan must be told of this," he said in his silky, carefully modulated voice. "Will you come with me, please, Miss Keate? She may take it badly."

Well, the little I had seen of Ina Harrigan had not led me to think that she was readily affected, but of course I followed him. She answered his low knock promptly and as we entered the room I found the electric light switch and pressed it, revealing the bare gray walls, the shining metal furniture, and the leather-backed chairs. Melady Memorial Hospital was furnished many years before the present color wave struck interior decorating and the effect is chaste and not without dignity but very barren and ugly.

I blinked a little under the brightness of the dome light in the ceiling; the room was hot and still, with the lingering odor of cigarette smoke mingling unpleasantly with some kind of heavy, exotic perfume.

Ina Harrigan was leaning languidly back against the pillows, the fine, flesh-colored lace of which, so far as I could see, her night gown consisted, looking indecently seductive and out of keeping with her bandaged right arm and the gray severity of the hospital room. Her black hair was becomingly tousled against the white pillow, her aquamarine eyes looked curiously alert between their velvety black lashes and not at all sleepy, and her mouth was a deep crimson line even at that time of night. She had a fine, dead white skin and never rouged, although, to quote Ellen, "what she does with a lipstick is

nobody's business." She was considered very handsome,
I believe, although her eyes were set a trifle too close
over the thin bridge of her nose to suit my taste, her
black eyebrows would have met had she permitted it,
and I did not like the lady's jaw line, which was rather
grim and hard and had more than a touch of cruelty.
For no reason at all I found myself envisioning her in
trailing velvets and furs and jeweled medieval head-
dresses, and as she looked half-smiling at Dr. Kunce
there flashed across my mind a picture from one of my
childhood history books. I could see it quite clearly, a
woman in a jeweled headdress who was labeled Lucrezia
Borgia, Duchess of Ferrara, fourteen hundred something, and while I did not recall just what the Borgia
person had done to get herself put into histories four
hundred years later I did recall the look in her face.
But I am not a fanciful person; the memory was gone
as quickly as it had come and Lucrezia—I mean Ina
Harrigan—had stopped smiling and her black eyebrows
were drawing closer together over her thin white nose.

"What's the matter?" she asked. Her voice was a
deep, velvety contralto which roughened under emotion.
It was rough just then. "Something is wrong. I can tell
by your faces. What is it? Has—my husband finally dis-
graced us?"

"Come, now, Mrs. Harrigan," said Dr. Kunce sooth-
ingly. Then under the look in her eyes abandoned his
attempt to break the shock. "Your husband is ill. Very
ill. He—in fact he is—dead."

Her expression did not alter in the least. Her aquamarine eyes remained coldly fixed on his face. Not a
nerve or a muscle in her face moved for a long moment.
Then as Dr. Kunce reached for the pulse in her left, un-

bandaged wrist her red mouth moved and moved again
and she said:

"What did you say?"

"Control yourself, Mrs. Harrigan," said Dr. Kunce in
what seemed to me rather unnecessary admonition. His
dark eyes were narrow and intent between those silky
long lashes. Womanish eyelashes they were.

"Control yourself, Mrs. Harrigan," he repeated. "Dr.
Harrigan died a short time ago."

Silence. Then: "What happened? Tell me the truth."

He told the truth, or as much of it as he knew, his
slender fingers on her pulse, his dark gaze holding her
cold, jewellike eyes. I must say she took it rather well.
Almost too well.

And it seemed to me that Dr. Kunce's much admired
bedside manner was a little more tender than the rela-
tion of doctor and patient quite warranted. At the same
time it was a sort of abstracted tenderness, as if he were
anxious to get a disagreeable duty done with in order
to see to more important issues. He went away as soon
as he decently could and left me to give her the sleeping
powder he'd ordered, take the list of relatives and
lawyers to be notified, and sit with her until she fell
asleep. She made him promise to tell her at once of any
developments, took the sleeping powder, and lay there
for some time staring into space, with a sort of tiger-
ish look about her jaw and not shedding a tear. In the
middle of a longish list of relatives the opiate took effect
and she dropped into a sound sleep. As I tiptoed softly
out of the room I found myself speculating on the uncertainties of the female temperament. Here was Ina Harrigan tight-mouthed and controlled, scarcely lifting her
voice, carefully restraining the shock she must have felt,
and across the corridor Dione Melady was going from

one faint into another merely because she'd looked at the body.

There was a stuffy, smoky odor in the corridor. I sniffed and coughed and Nancy Page emerged from Dione's room and saw me.

"Where on earth have you been, Sarah?" she said, and without waiting for reply continued: "The police doctor—they called him the medical examiner—has been here and the coroner and a lot of men with flashlight cameras. Can't you smell the powder? And then some strange ambulance men came and took the—the body from the elevator and—oh, Sarah, it's all so horrible." She shuddered. Her face was chalk white; she pushed her cap farther back on her head with a weary gesture. "And so hot!" She added with a gasp. "Lillian Ash says we will all be questioned. Is that right?"

"I suppose so," I said. "The patients seem to have quieted down."

"Yes. Sarah, when will they question us? What kind of things will they ask?"

"I don't know. Probably they will ask everything they can think of. And there will be an inquest."

Nancy shivered again. "Funny," she said under her breath. "It's so hot and yet I feel sort of chilly, too. Do you?"

I shook my head.

"A draft from somewhere," I said. "What on earth ails Dione Melady? Does she know her father has disappeared?"

Nancy did not reply at once. It was odd that I got the impression that she hesitated, for Nancy was, I had always felt, unusually direct.

"Well, you know she saw——" Her eyes widened a little and her soft young lips tightened and she put a hand to her throat as if to help get the words out: "She saw the body, you know."

And then without warning the full horror of the thing swept over me again and I felt myself once more in that hot, ill-ventilated elevator, shut in with a dead man— walking in his blood—— I must stop thinking of it. I must do something—something energetic. I would see what ailed Dione Melady.

"Have they found Peter Melady?" I asked Nancy.

She shook her head, her hand still at her throat, her dark troubled eyes looking somberly into mine.

"I'll see what I can do for Mrs. Melady," I said and pushed open the door to Dione's room and entered.

It was then only about three o'clock—somewhat to my surprise when I glanced at my watch, for the night had seemed endlessly long. There was still no breeze and the leather chair backs were sticky and damp to the touch and the room stifling in its heat. The two windows were flung up the entire length and the night sky was black and heavy. A light burned over the high, narrow white bed and there was a hot odor of camphor and smelling salts and rubbing alcohol. Dione Melady was lying on her face in a mêlée of tossed sheets, pale mauve nightgown, tumbled light hair, and bandages; ice-bags and several wet towels lay about, and as I approached the bed she flopped petulantly on her side.

"Court, why don't you *do* something!" she cried fretfully. "Heaven knows where it is by this time." Her words slurred a little but were yet sharp; she'd probably been given a mild opiate and was too bent on making trouble to relax and let it soothe her.

Someone had summoned Court Melady, and he rose then from the other side of the bed.

"Hush, Dione," he said wearily. His face looked much

older—fatigue, I suppose—and anxiety regarding his
father-in-law's disappearance; the lines showed sharply
under the light above the bed, the pouches under his eyes
were gray and puffy and he had lost the debonair manner which as a rule characterized him. His coat was hanging on the back of a chair and his shirt was open at the
throat, his bow tie pulled out of its loops and hanging
down on either side of his open collar. Still, somehow,
he did not look untidy. "Hush—here is Uncle Peter's
nurse. Perhaps she can tell us something."

Dione whirled, groaned as her bandaged shoulders
touched the pillows.

"You'd better try to sleep," I said. "When we find
your father he will be anxious to see you."

" 'When' you find him! She says 'when'! Did you hear
that, Court? I doubt if they are doing a thing to find
him. I knew it. I knew it all along. I knew no good would
come of having Dr. Harrigan operate. I'm glad
he's——"

"Dione!" said Court Melady sharply. "She isn't herself, Miss Keate."

She took a long breath and narrowed her weak lips
rather viciously along her teeth.

"Everybody knows Father despised Dr. Harrigan.
And so did you hate him. You know you did, Court."

"Dione, will you stop talking nonsense and try to
sleep?"

"You did! You hated him. You were jealous——"

"Don't flatter yourself," interrupted Court with a sort
of cold disinterest that was inexpressibly contemptuous.
Then he leaned suddenly over his wife and said something that was purposely indistinguishable to me, I think;
whatever the brief word was—or it may have been due

to the look in his cold eyes which was still extremely unpleasant when he straightened and faced me again—Dione stopped talking and a look very like fear came into her weak, flabbily pretty face.

"She is not herself, Miss Keate," he said again. "She is—er—very nervous always and somewhat subject to these attacks. Has been since childhood."

I believed him. Indeed, I could quite see Dione kicking and screaming and knocking her head against the floor—but not too hard—until she got what she wanted.

Her husband was wiping his face and neck with his handkerchief.

"Good Lord, it's hot in here. Is there a place to attach an electric fan? Yes, here's a wall socket. I'll have a fan sent right away, Dione. I'll bet it's a hundred in this room right now. And it's so terribly humid. Now, Miss Keate, sit down, won't you? You must be awfully tired. And tell us the whole thing exactly as it happened. Miss Page and Dr. Kunce told us what they knew but we want to hear your account."

Still subdued, Dione contented herself with nodding her head.

Not seeing that it could agitate Dione any more than she had already upset herself, I complied as briefly as I could.

"You didn't see Dr. Harrigan at all, then?" asked Court Melady when I had finished and Dione was uttering soft little moans, her face dug into the pillows and her whole attitude one of "Comfort me. I am the suffering one."

"No—that is, yes. I caught just a glimpse of him as he came in to see Mrs. Melady just at midnight."

Dione's moans stopped and her back, under the bandages, seemed to stiffen. Courtney Melady's eyes went to her in a curiously comprehensive look. After a moment he said:

"Well, I guess all we can do is wait. There seem to be these possibilities: either Uncle Peter left the hospital in some way and for some reason of which we know nothing, or he quarreled with Dr. Harrigan in a way that came to a physical struggle in which—er—Dr. Harrigan got the worst of it."

"Court!" shrieked Dione. "How dare you suggest that Fath——"

"Stop that!" I said sternly. "You'll wake everybody in the hospital."

She twisted around to give me a faintly surprised stare and then resumed her moaning.

"Or, of course," said Court slowly, "there's a third possibility. That is that Dr. Harrigan also killed Uncle Peter."

"With that knife wound in his heart?" I asked grimly, while Dione gave another little shriek and Court said to her furiously: "Will you quiet down, Dione!"

"No," he continued, addressing me again. "But he might have hurt Uncle Peter in such a way that——Oh, I know it doesn't fit," he broke off to say, as I daresay I looked my skepticism. "But nothing about the affair fits."

"No," I said. "Nothing seems to fit. But a doctor and his patient don't quarrel and struggle and—kill each other as you are suggesting. Anyone in his senses knows that. It is out of the question. Would Mr. Melady have trusted himself to Dr. Harrigan on the operating table if there were cause for such a desperate quarrel between them?"

"But apparently he didn't," remarked Court Melady.

"Well, apparently he didn't," I admitted. "But he

fully intended to do so to-morrow—this morning. And Ellen Brody says that Mr. Melady insisted upon staying with Dr. Harrigan—refused to be separated from the doctor. Wouldn't Mr. Melady have wanted to get in touch with someone else if he were at all apprehensive?"

At that Dione squirmed around to face her husband, and the two exchanged the first look of mutual understanding I had yet witnessed between them.

"Not necessarily, I think, Miss Keate," said Court Melady quietly. "Not, for example, if there were something which Peter Melady had left in his room which Dr. Harrigan—wanted."

"I don't understand you," I said after a moment.

Court Melady reached across to his coat pocket and fumbled for a cigarette, but he suddenly changed his mind and tossed it over on the table.

"Oh, tell her, Court," urged Dione. "Maybe she will know where he put it."

He gave her a cold look that held warning.

"It's—the Chinese snuff-bottle, Miss Keate. It has vanished along with Uncle Peter. Or I ought say, not perhaps along with Uncle Peter, but at the same time."

"The Chinese snuff-bottle?" I said incredulously. "You mean that little blue bottle I brought from his house for him last night?"

"Yes."

"And Dr. Harrigan wanted it?" I asked disbelievingly.

"We think so, yes."

"But—it is—why, that's absurd! Do you really believe that Dr. Harrigan—that Peter Melady——" I floundered. "Do you believe that a man would murder for a little blue bottle like that?"

Courtney Melady shrugged, went to a table near by, and poured himself a drink of the iced fruit juice that stood there.

"Oh, Court!" broke in Dione in a muffled way. "Not that glass. It's—been used."

He turned again to give her that coldly speculative look, only now it held a sort of knowledge. Or at least so it seemed to me, although he only said with a chilly smile: "My wife has the germ complex," and took a clean glass from the tray.

"And you think that Mr. Melady wanted to stay with Dr. Harrigan in order to be sure Dr. Harrigan did not steal the snuff-bottle? Is that what you mean?" I felt myself groping for a grain of logic in this strange mêlée of words, hints, half-meanings that resolved themselves into rather dreadful accusations.

"That is exactly what I meant," said Court Melady, finishing his drink. "That is exactly what I meant."

"Was the Chinese snuff-bottle so valuable as all that?" I asked, feeling somewhat disturbed as I recalled how blandly I had carried the thing in my hands along Euclid Avenue on my way back to the hospital, and how I had shown it to Nancy and how we had admired it. We—Nancy Page—she had liked it.

Another communicative look flashed between Court and his wife, then he shrugged again and said: "Not in itself, no. But there were several people who wanted it —rather badly. Among them Dr. Harrigan."

"Do you know where Father hid the snuff-bottle?" asked Dione eagerly, rising on one elbow. There was a sincere note of anxiety in her voice. The first I had heard.

"He had it in his hands when he went to sleep," I said slowly. "But I can't remember seeing it again. It was there when I turned out the light about ten, and although

I was in and out of the room and watching him almost continually until midnight I did not turn on the light again for fear of rousing your father, who seemed to be sleeping."

"By the way, Miss Keate, what did you think of Dr. Harrigan's decision to operate to-night?" asked Court Melady.

"I was surprised," I said cautiously. "The operation having been definitely fixed for morning, I did not see that there could be much reason for suddenly operating to-night. But Dr. Harrigan was the physician in charge."

"And you have no idea where he hid the snuff-bottle?" insisted Dione eagerly.

"Not in the least."

She looked at me doubtfully and then turned to her husband.

"Are you sure you searched the whole room, Court?"

"It is *not* in his room, Dione," he said wearily, with an effect of threadbare repetition.

"But we must find it. We must find it. Father was so stubborn in his notions. I told him that was a poor——"

"Hadn't you better try to rest, Dione?" said her husband, much as one might say: "Stop talking, you fool of a woman!" It occurred to me that Court Melady's words quite frequently said one thing and his voice another.

The door opened softly and a white cap, set at a rakish angle, peeped in. Below it was Ellen's face, still greenish-looking, and she said in a remarkably meek way:

"Dr. Kunce wants to see you, Miss Keate." Her eyes gave one scared look around the room, encountered Court Melady's cold gray gaze, and she all but slammed the door as she vanished.

"Better try to sleep," I said to Dione and left.

The corridor loomed again dimly bare, the westward length of it losing itself in shadows, the walls still gray and bare and the air sickening in its fetid breath. It was very dark outside, the stars disappearing while the black pall that comes before the dawn lay over a sleeping world. And along that corridor murder had walked.

Singular that on such a night one could feel hot and cold at the same time. My spine was chilly and shivery and my hands were sweating.

CHAPTER IV

DR. KUNCE and Sergeant Lamb were sitting under the green-shaded light above the chart desk. The doctor's sleek black dinner jacket and gleaming shirt front and the policeman's tight blue coat looked hot and unfriendly and very much out of place against the bare hospital walls. I glanced toward the elevator shaft as I passed it. The cage still hung there, but the red light shone again inside it; the door was propped open and an orderly—it was Teuber, for I heard his wheezy cough—was scrubbing the stained floor.

Scrubbing the floor! The shiver up the small of my back became more unpleasant. He might scrub that floor for the rest of his life and to me that hideous, meandering stain would still be there. Like Lady Macbeth's hand . . .

Dr. Kunce had noted my glance and spoke, interrupting my none too happy train of thought.

"The light in the elevator hadn't burned out, you see, Miss Keate," he said in his silky way that seemed to hold some secret meaning. "It was just turned out." And to the policeman: "You didn't think of that, did you?"

"Yes," said Sergeant Lamb. "I found that the bulb was only twisted in its socket until the current was broken. Will you answer a few questions, Miss Keate——" He stopped himself abruptly, peered intently at my hair, and said suddenly and with what I con-

57

sidered remarkably bad manners: "Well, there's no doubt about the color of *your* hair."

"Here, Miss Keate," said Dr. Kunce hurriedly, rising and coughing and offering me a chair all at the same time. "Won't you sit down?"

I sat down. I am bound to admit that from that moment on I felt a certain lack of friendliness for Sergeant Lamb. While I am no beauty and never was, still I have felt that my hair is rather nice, and I did not like Sergeant Lamb's tone concerning it. I doubted very much if he would prove to be a man of discernment.

"Have you found Mr. Melady?" I asked in a distant manner.

"No," said Sergeant Lamb. "No. He is certainly not in the hospital. We searched every square inch of the whole place, I think; no one is hiding in the building. I can say that definitely."

"Oh." I considered it slowly. "Then"—as Court Melady's third possibility came to mind—"then Dr. Harrigan couldn't have killed Mr. Melady in the struggle in which he, himself, was killed. The body would be some place near at hand. Or certainly in the hospital."

"Exactly," said Dr. Kunce. "Without admitting for an instant that Dr. Harrigan had any—er—ulterior motive in his sudden decision to operate at once upon Mr. Melady, still if he had had such a motive, and any harm had actually come to Peter Melady, we would have found his body. As to a struggle, however, I'm inclined to doubt the possibility of that. Dr. Harrigan died at once of that knife wound. And it seems to have been a singularly peaceful and quick death."

"Look here, Miss Keate," said Sergeant Lamb suddenly. With a mysterious air, like that of a magician drawing a rabbit out of a hat, he drew a paper-wrapped parcel from somewhere under his blue coat, unwrapped it carefully, his long, pale, damp-looking fingers very delicate in their touch, and showed me a knife.

I stared at the thing. The blade had not been cleaned but the bright steel handle shone under the light.

"What is this?" he said.

"But I told you——" began Dr. Kunce.

"I know what you told me," said Sergeant Lamb, his tone a throaty, nasal slur that grew to irritate me exceedingly. "But I'm asking her now. See? What is this, nurse?"

"It's—a knife," I said, moistening my lips, which felt hot and dry.

"Yeah, I know it's a knife, but what kind of knife is it?"

"It's an amputating knife. I believe that particular kind is called a Catlin."

"Catlin? What's that?"

"Just a name," murmured Dr. Kunce silkily.

Sergeant Lamb's light blue eyes showed a rather ugly white rim.

"I'm talking to this lady, now, Dr. Kunze," he said.

"My name is Kunce. Dr. Felix Kunce," offered Dr. Kunce silkily from behind his imperturbable Vandyke. Sergeant Lamb's pale, wide mouth tightened and I said wearily:

"It's just a name. That is, I mean the Catlin—the knife—Catlin is just a name for it."

Dr. Kunce's quickly lifted eyelashes drooped enigmatically and Sergeant Lamb's pale blue eyes shifted from one to the other of us in a manner that was half baffled and half threatening and wholly suspicious. He continued, however:

"Now then, Miss Keate. I want to ask you. Think of

that scene in the elevator when you found Dr. Harrigan dead. Think. This is the knife we found in his heart. Was it the one you saw?"

"I suppose so."

"Looks like that one?"

"Yes, of course. Only——" A quick recollection of that smudged and smeary steel handle protruding from his shirt front recurred to me and I said something incoherent and leaned forward. "Why, you've wiped the handle. See how it shines as if it had been polished. When I saw it there in the elevator it was all smeary—like a mirror when you put your fingers on it." I checked myself abruptly. I did not like the sound of my own words. I knew something of fingerprints and their way of turning out to be those of an innocent person.

Sergeant Lamb looked triumphant and did not restrain a quick and complacent glance toward Dr. Kunce, who sat like a very picture of silky secrecy and did not return Sergeant Lamb's meaning look.

"Fine," said Sergeant Lamb. "Now we are getting some place. I have my methods. Now, Miss Keate." He leaned forward. "Did you wipe the fingerprints off this knife?"

"Certainly not!" I snapped. "I didn't touch the thing."

"Come now, Miss Keate, in the shock and terror of the discovery you had made didn't you suspect that someone in the hospital was guilty of this terrible crime—some friend of yours, perhaps—and didn't you just lean over and wipe this knife——"

"I didn't touch it," I repeated crisply. "And I don't know who did unless it was you. Certainly it had marks on it that might have been fingerprints, but they weren't my fingerprints and as a matter of fact I was in no state

of mind to consider the matter at all. All I knew was
that Dr. Harrigan was there. Dead."

"Miss Keate is very tired," said Dr. Kunce in a
suavely sympathetic way that was somehow the reverse
of soothing. "She has had a terribly difficult night. She
really knows nothing of this affair, Sergeant. Might I
suggest that——"

"Oh, is that so?" said Sergeant Lamb. "Wasn't Mr.
Melady her patient? Wasn't she supposed to be taking
care of him? Didn't she use that elevator? Wasn't she
running around on the fourth floor about the time of the
murder?" He made a gesture with the knife he still held
gingerly. "Maybe now, it was *your* fingerprints you
wiped off that knife, Miss Keate."

I sprang indignantly to my feet. I am seldom at a loss
for words suitably to express my feelings, but I was at
that moment. Dr. Kunce rose, too.

"Come now, Sergeant Lamb. Miss Keate is beyond
suspicion. I think you'll do better to wait until she has
rested to question her. I assure you she will neither run
away nor conceal any knowledge she might have—er—
acquired."

Well, quite unreasonably I liked Dr. Kunce's defense
no better than Sergeant Lamb's accusation. But any
words becoming a lady could not have begun to do justice to the outrage done to my feelings.

"I don't know as anyone is beyond suspicion," said
Sergeant Lamb in a curiously threatening voice. His
thick, pale eyelids drooped a little as he surveyed Dr.
Kunce. "I have my methods. Sit down, Miss Keate, and
tell me the whole story again. Begin when the little nurse
in the blue and white uniform——"

"Ellen Brody," interjected Dr. Kunce softly, his liquid
dark eyes on the elevator door where the orderly was

picking up his scrub pail and brushes and starting for the stairway. The water in the pail was red; but then, it takes very little blood to discolor water.

"Say, now, who's doing this?" asked Sergeant Lamb. He did not expect an answer and looked rather put out when Dr. Kunce said at once in his silkiest voice:

"You are, I believe, Sergeant."

"—when she told you that Dr. Harrigan had taken your patient up to be operated on."

I did so, wearily. It seemed to me that I had told the story a hundred times. It had begun to take on set phrases. When I had finished Sergeant Lamb asked me a number of questions, seeming to try to catch me in some denial or inconsistency, but since I had told the affair as directly and briefly as was possible he did not succeed in doing so. He inquired at some length regarding the four times I had signaled for the elevator without success and especially regarding the fifth time, there on the fourth floor, when the darkened elevator cage had finally responded, bringing with it, unknown to me, its terrible burden. However, he looked more perplexed than I think he would have wished us to note, and appeared to be able to make nothing of it.

"Now let's see if I have it right," he said finally in a sort of résumé. "You came up from the basement and this student nurse told you Dr. Harrigan had taken your patient to the operating room. You went to the operating room but nobody was there. You came back down here by way of the stairway that time. Right?"

I nodded.

"You can't find him here and you go downstairs again. Still nobody is about and this time you take the elevator down—and the dead man is in it and you find him."

"Yes."

"How many times did you ring for the elevator when you say it didn't come. Four or five times?"

"Five times altogether. Once down at the first floor as we were coming upstairs from supper," I said slowly. "Once right here as I started to the operating room the first time. A third time as I started downstairs from the operating room. Then again here when I started on my second trip to the operating room. That was the time the orderly and Miss Ash were here in the corridor and he rang for it, too, and even pulled at the door, which wouldn't open. That's the fourth time. And then the fifth time, of course, was when I was on the fourth floor about to come down. That was the time the cage came to the floor and I heard it and opened the door and—and— got in and pressed the third-floor button and——" I found myself shivering so that I could scarcely talk intelligibly.

Sergeant Lamb turned to Dr. Kunce.

"Is there a desk like this and a light opposite the elevator shaft at any of the other floors?"

"At the second floor," said Dr. Kunce. "At the fourth the elevator shaft is just opposite the surgery and at the first floor the office door and telephone switchboard commands a view of the elevator."

"Then we ought to be able to find out where the elevator was all that time. It's likely the murder was done during that time. Now then, Miss Keate, do you have any idea where this knife came from?"

Refusing to meet Dr. Kunce's gaze, which I could feel upon me, I shook my head negatively. I did have an idea but I had no intention of sharing it. Things were a bad enough scandal as they were. I had no doubt the knife was from the instrument cases in the fourth-floor operating rooms and I rather suspected Dr. Kunce thought the same thing. And if it were true it would come out soon enough.

Sergeant Lamb was looking thoughtfully at the knife which he had left on the desk all this time, where it shone sinisterly from its nest of tissue paper. During the little silence Ellen materialized beside us, reaching for a chart. As she touched it her eyes fell on the knife; she made a sort of gulping sound as if she'd swallowed something she regretted, and made as swift a trip down the corridor and into the linen closet as I have ever seen. I gave a worried thought to the linen supply, straightened my cap, and wished I could get a full deep breath of fresh air. Dr. Kunce's forehead had a softly damp look, and drops were frankly standing out on Sergeant Lamb's face. Every so often one would detach itself from its fellows and roll in a little rivulet down his temple and pale cheek. When this happened he would pass the back of his hand over his face and then along his blue trousers.

Then the corner of my eye caught the red gleam from the elevator cage and my mind was wrenched back to the accumulating terror of the night.

"About Mr. Melady," Sergeant Lamb was saying slowly. "Had he any enemies?"

"I don't know, I'm sure. I suppose any man who has made as much money as Peter Melady has made has acquired a few enemies in the process."

"He is a rich man," speculated Sergeant Lamb. "But I mean did he have anything in particular that Dr. Harrigan might have wanted?"

I thought of what Court Melady had told me of the Chinese snuff-bottle and would likely have told of it, but Dr. Kunce spoke, softly and smoothly as usual, but I felt as if I had been interrupted.

"Not a thing, Sergeant," he said definitely. "Not a thing."

"He wasn't at any sort of business crisis?" went on Sergeant Lamb, as one who feels his way along delicate and treacherous ground. "At a place, I mean, where his absence or presence might mean something to somebody? We have had some cases of abduction, you know, for that reason. And to my mind it means quite a little to know whether Mr. Melady went away of his own will or not. If he went voluntarily he likely murdered Dr. Harrigan. But if he was taken forcibly away, that's another question. Who would benefit by his absence at just this time? Mr. Melady, now—did he have his fingers in several pies, so to speak?"

"No," said Dr. Kunce at once. "Mr. Melady is the head of the Melady Drug Company, as you and everybody in B—— knows. He is interested in nothing else. I can think of no one whom his absence would benefit. But it is impossible to believe that Mr. Melady would murder Dr. Harr——"

"There's Slæpan!" I said suddenly. "He was about to market it." I stopped. On the principle of the least said the soonest mended I have as a rule a wary tongue. Dr. Kunce's eyes leaped at me from between those long eyelashes and then became unfathomable again, and Sergeant Lamb all but pricked up his ears.

"What's Sly-pan?" he said at once.

Well, the mischief, if any, was done.

"Why, that's what Mr. Melady called a new anesthetic they have developed in the Melady laboratories."

"Funny name for it."

"Anglo-Saxon," said Dr. Kunce, watching the tiny bugs that fluttered against the screen of the window back of us. "Mr. Melady says that many drug formulæ have been given Greek names and he was going to give this one a pure English name. And he did. It means sleep. And speaking of sleep wouldn't we better try to get some rest, Sergeant? It will soon be morning and a very heavy and difficult day is ahead of us. I'm sure Miss Keate needs rest after such a severe nervous shock."

It was not like Dr. Kunce to be so considerate; I glanced at him rather suspiciously.

"You can go if you want to, Dr. Kunze," said Sergeant Lamb. "But I want to hear more about this Slæpan stuff."

"Kunce," observed Dr. Kunce in a disinterested way and leaned back in his chair again.

"You said it was an anesthetic. Ether or something like that?"

Dr. Kunce said nothing and I replied:

"In a way, yes. It completely anesthetizes the patient. But if it proves to be successful it will be much better than ether. It keeps the patient anesthetized for a much longer period of time, does not interfere with or check functional activities, and has no bad after effects."

He looked at me doubtfully.

"Keeps the patient under longer, h'm. Just how long?"

"Between two and three days," I explained briefly. "That way the first shock and pain of the incision has healed a little before the patient recovers consciousness."

Dr. Kunce was still looking at the window, which was beginning to be gray; curious that I felt the presence of his strong disapproval as definitely as if he had given it some physical evidence. It was almost as if he had taken my arm and pulled me away from Sergeant Lamb's alert ears—though all the time he simply sat there, quiet and unspeaking, his silken Vandyke catching a blue-bronze highlight like very heavy silk velvet.

"What do you mean by no bad after effects?" asked Sergeant Lamb interestedly.

"No nausea. No gas pains."

Sergeant Lamb became suddenly plain Lamb; he leaned forward confidentially.

"Say, not even any castor oil?"

"Well," I said cautiously, being always a conservative in such matters, "I wouldn't go so far as to say that."

"No; I suppose not," he said rather sadly. "I've had my appendix out," he went on with the air of a colleague. "Golly, I was a sick man. And I was scared. Funny but I kept thinking something was going to come crawling into my room from the corridor. Down low, you know, and I wouldn't see it coming on account of the bed being so high. I was scared. Must have had a hunch about this murder." He laughed and I felt another cold shiver start from the small of my back and creep upward. Well, he was not a man of social grace, certainly; I daresay he meant well.

"Indeed," said Dr. Kunce in a chilling way which hadn't any effect at all upon Sergeant Lamb. "If that is all now, Sergeant, suppose you let us go and——"

"Not by a long shot that ain't all," said that gentleman, coming quickly out of his reminiscent mood. "If this Slæpan stuff really does all that it is pretty important. Must mean a big thing."

"Why, yes, of course," said Dr. Kunce. "Any such formula, once proven to be successful, would revolutionize anesthetics. It would be a marvelous thing and it is sorely needed. A dozen big drug companies have been working and experimenting—with various different preparations —for years."

"And Mr. Melady got ahead of the others?"

"I wouldn't say that exactly," said Dr. Kunce. "Any

of the others may have developed as good or better a formula. But none is yet on the market. The whole affair, you see, is still in its experimental stage."

"Well, it looks to me," said Sergeant Lamb slowly, "as if the man who got this stuff on the market first would make an enormous profit."

Dr. Kunce shrugged.

"Possibly. The great thing would be the professional honor. I've always held," he went on suavely, "that the name of the man who first used it successfully should be given to the new anesthetic. Any number of chemists, doctors, druggists have been trying to find something that will be as practical as ether and have the enormous added advantage of doing away with the painful effects of ether. The man who accomplishes it first will be—remembered."

"Professionally," murmured Sergeant Lamb, his pale blue eyes looking shrewd. "But I think he'd want to own the formula, too. Most of us are mighty interested in the money a thing will make."

"Oh, doubtless," said Dr. Kunce frigidly.

"Could anybody who got hold of this stuff just pass it off as his own discovery and—get by with it?"

Dr. Kunce shrugged again.

"I presume so. Any number of people are working to find something of the kind; its discovery and use would be no surprise."

"This particular formula? Wouldn't everybody know it was discovered by the Melady Drug Company?"

"Not necessarily, unless they could prove it was stolen. And I doubt if they could claim it in any case, providing it was not patented—registered, you know."

"H'm," said Sergeant Lamb. "If anybody wanted to steal that now——" He did not finish his sentence at

once but sat looking at the desk top with a far-away look
in his pale blue eyes.

"So this new ether does all that," he said presently
with a contemplative air.

"What Mr. Melady called Slæpan is said to," said Dr.
Kunce noncommittally. "It is still, however, in the experimental stage."

"What does it look like?"

"Really I—can't say that I know much about it," said
Dr. Kunce, his liquid dark eyes meeting mine secretively.
He said it very smoothly, quite as if he himself had not
talked to me of Slæpan and what they hoped from it and
even showed me a small quantity of the stuff—it was a
liquid as yet though they expected to use it as a gas—
which had come direct from the Melady laboratories for
experimental purposes. There was some at that moment
in the third-floor drug room of the east wing, which had
been sent by Peter Melady, who at least had the courage
of his convictions and had suggested their using it for
him in the event he had to undergo an operation. Owing
to the state of his heart they had convinced him at last
that it would not be a true test.

Well, if Dr. Kunce thought the sergeant need not know
too much about Slæpan I was quite willing and did not
question Dr. Kunce's denial. He always put the hospital
and its welfare first; it was, I think, his sole pride and
affection; if he considered it discreet to say no more
about Slæpan I was willing to abide by his decision.

"If anybody got hold of some of the stuff couldn't he
have it analyzed?" asked Sergeant Lamb. "Then since
—or if—it isn't registered, he could make his own formula."

Dr. Kunce shook his head definitely.

"I don't think that would be possible, Sergeant. You

see, a thing like Slæpan would have to be very exact; in-gredients in a drug often blend so it is almost impossible to analyze them so accurately and exactly as to deduce the formula. Testing a drug for certain stated ingredients and analyzing it so exactly as to discover its formula are two different things. The first is comparatively simple. The second is practically impossible in a case like this."

"Maybe some of these other druggists and people who have been trying to discover the same drug knew that Mr. Melady had succeeded and wanted him out of the way. Maybe somebody was just on the verge of perfecting such a drug——"

"I think not," said Dr. Kunce coldly. "And anyway it is Dr. Harrigan's murder that you are investigating."

"But it's Peter Melady who's gone. And right after that murder. And this Slæpan would mean a lot to somebody. Who's that?"

We both turned at his sharp question to look down the east corridor. It was only Lillian Ash, however, her uniform wilted and clinging close to her opulent figure and her face, as she glanced at us, looking old and jaded. Her hair had come out of curl with the humid heat and was hanging in dejected-looking wisps over her ears. Well, it was a cruel hour of the night.

Sergeant Lamb leaned forward, peering in an interested way at her hair.

"Now what color would you call her hair?" he said as Lillian Ash disappeared into the diet kitchen. "Would that hair, now, be blonde?"

"It *would* be, yes," said Dr. Kunce softly, with a sort of feline relish.

"Blonde, huh?" murmured Sergeant Lamb thoughtfully. "And that little student nurse, what would you call her hair?"

"Miss Brody?" Dr. Kunce turned to me. "What color do you say, Miss Keate?"

"Brown," I said briefly, reaching for a chart pad in order to fan myself with it. The moving air felt warm and damp against my face. The still gray of early morning was crawling into the shadows of the place. But it was no cooler; I think that was the first dawn I have ever known—and I have seen many dawns—that gave no respite between the heat of the night and more intense heat of the day it was ushering into being.

"Brown," repeated Sergeant Lamb, still thoughtfully. "Not blonde, then."

"No," I snapped. "Not blonde."

It was just then that he reached into his tightly buttoned coat and took out the pillbox. It was a plain pillbox, very small, which he had probably picked up from the little heap of empty boxes someone had left in the wastebasket—probably it had been Nancy, for she had done some cleaning and rearranging in the east-wing drug room during the previous day. He opened the tiny box with an air of secrecy and held it toward me, inclining it so I could see what it contained. In it was a blonde hair, a single fine thread that lay in a light, soft curl and had a sort of bright glow so that it shone like gold where the highlights touched it.

"I found that," he said slowly. "—Can you see it, Dr. Kunze?—I found that caught around the handle of this amputating knife at exactly the spot where the blade entered Dr. Harrigan's heart."

Dr. Kunce seemed to stiffen as he bent his smooth dark head to look; you felt that there was a steel bar underneath all his softness and silkiness. And I felt myself grow suddenly a little sick. It was a blonde hair. And anybody knows that blonde women are not uncommon. But there seemed to me to be a sort of life about that hair—a golden shine to it. It looked like Nancy Page's hair, and I could not disguise that fact to myself, much as I should have liked to do so.

"And that isn't all I found," said Sergeant Lamb. He closed the pillbox carefully, taking an unconscionable time to fit the little lid accurately upon it and wedge it down. Then he laid the pillbox on the chart desk. Not far from it lay the soiled knife with its brightly polished handle. He fumbled again into his inside coat pocket.

I was looking at the pillbox. And my feeling that I may have, deep-rooted within me, the liveliest of criminal impulses, dates from that moment. And I must add that I displayed a facility in the business which is really shocking to recall; a facility which leads me to fear that I have submerged talents in that direction. It is the simplicity of the act which startles me; the ease with which I did it.

I stole the pillbox!

It was the simplest thing in the world. I remember thinking that I was not going to have Nancy's soft gold hair brought into the sordidness of a murder trial, and the next thing I knew I had dropped the chart pad on the floor, bent and secured it and one of the empty pillboxes out of the wastebasket at the same time, had leaned forward to replace the chart pad on the desk, and had used the pad as a screen during the split second it took to substitute the empty pillbox for the one that held the golden hair, had dropped the chart on the desk and the pillbox with the hair in it into the wastebasket—and was sitting back in my chair with as much composure as is possible in one who is obliged to hold her teeth tight together to keep her heart from leaping out.

Both men were intent on the thing Sergeant Lamb was unwrapping; so intent that neither had even glanced my way. Sergeant Lamb seemed to be experiencing some difficulty in getting it unwrapped, and Dr. Kunce was watching him with a set face whose stillness was belied by the gleam in his narrow dark eyes.

Gradually my heart retreated to a more normal place and I began, even, to feel a little glow of satisfaction. I have read the newspapers; I know something of all that rigmarole of science by which hairs are identified and finally convict their owners. At any rate Nancy would not be convicted by that hair.

Nancy convicted! Was it possible that I was sitting there in that infinitely familiar corridor figuring how one of our own small world could escape conviction for murder? It was not possible. None of it was possible. But it had happened.

"Why——" said Dr. Kunce suddenly and checked himself; his voice had lost its smoothness—it sounded outraged and protestant.

"Do you know anything about this?" asked Sergeant Lamb, all at once very sharp and insistent.

"No," said Dr. Kunce. "No." His voice was low again, but a little uneven. "Nothing except that it looks like a piece of white chewing gum. It's frightfully hot in here. Is there any iced water about the place, Miss Keate?"

"I'll fix some," I said. "It won't take a moment."

"Wait a minute, wait a minute," intervened Sergeant Lamb. "What about you, nurse? Do you know where this came from?"

It was indubitably a little lump of white chewing gum

which had certainly been chewed. So far as I could see it was only that and I said so with some asperity.

"Who chews gum around here?" asked Sergeant Lamb.

"No one," said Dr. Kunce. "Where did you find that? What has it got to do with the murder?"

"I expect to find out very soon," said Sergeant Lamb. "I don't know yet what it has got to do with the murder, but I found it stuck to the sleeve of the murdered man's shirt. Right near the cuff. Now then, you don't mean to say that nobody around here chews gum?" His incredulous inquiry robbed his words of none of their grim significance. A piece of chewing gum stuck to a murdered man's sleeve! Was there ever so trivial and foolish a bit of evidence! And evidence the man appeared to consider it.

"No one chews gum around here," repeated Dr. Kunce. "At least the nurses do not do so on duty. Their private vices are their own affairs."

If the appearance of the piece of gum had shaken him he had entirely recovered his suave composure.

"Maybe not," said Sergeant Lamb as one who says: "Have your own way but I know better." He added hopefully: "But some of the patients might like to chew gum."

I may have imagined an added secrecy in Dr. Kunce's veiled eyes, for he said easily enough:

"They might. Though I don't happen to know of any. Not in this wing, at any rate. Do you, Miss Keate?"

And as I shook my head Sergeant Lamb leaned closer to me, his face very moist and shiny.

"Did Dr. Harrigan chew gum?"

"No. Not that I know of."

"Did Peter Melady chew gum?"

"No."

"Do you chew gum?"

"No!" I snapped, suddenly and irrationally angry. "No. And if I did I don't see what that could have to do with Dr. Harrigan's being murdered. Unless you're implying that he was bitten to death."

Dr. Kunce rose decisively.

"Sergeant Lamb, it is nearly morning. I will have a very heavy day ahead of me—board meetings, reporters, police about the hospital, anxious patients and their relatives to reassure. The prosperity and name of a hospital rests to an enormous extent upon the safety and security which patients feel within its walls. Melady Memorial as an institution was not built in a moment and cannot be permitted to collapse in a moment. We must do everything in our power to avert very serious consequences of this—this terrible"—his silky voice tore a little just then but he went quickly on—"this terrible catastrophe. You must excuse me now; there are many things I must do—preparations I must make, staff doctors whose counsel I must seek. I shall hold myself at your service but I must leave you now."

Well, despite a tendency on Dr. Kunce's part toward oratorical effects (due, I suppose, to his far-away German ancestry), there is usually good common sense in what he has to say.

"But what about my patient?" I said hurriedly. "Where is Peter Melady?"

"God knows," said Dr. Kunce, and in the same breath:

"We'll soon have him," said Sergeant Lamb. "I'll have men scouring the town."

Scouring the town. Yes. But who would have looked for Peter Malady where, as we learned later, he actually was at that moment?

After a little more talk they left. I cannot begin to describe my feeling as I watched Sergeant Lamb take up the empty pillbox and put it carefully away in an inside pocket of that tightly buttoned blue coat. There was a panicky instant when I thought he was going to take off the lid, but he only pressed it tighter on the box. Then they were gone down the stairway, and the elevator cage still hung there beside me.

Dawn was gray and misty and it was difficult to breathe. The bell for five o'clock Mass was ringing from the chapel of St. Malachy's just back of the hospital. Three slow strokes, faint and melodious and grave through the heavy, heat-laden air, and then three more. I stopped counting and leaned over the wastebasket, finally crouching down on my knees. I was furiously opening and casting aside empty pillboxes which sent up various pharmaceutical odors when I found that Ellen was watching me curiously from across the chart desk. I did not offer to explain. Instead I said sharply:

"The next time you feel ill, stay out of the linen room; there's no need to deplete the towel supply so recklessly. Oh, and Ellen—just glance into the elevator, will you, and see if Teuber really got it clean."

I did not intend to make her feel ill again but she has a highly emotional stomach—a characteristic which, I fear, is going to make her nursing career a series of ups and downs. This time she included me, the red-lighted elevator, and the freshly scrubbed spots on the floor in one brief agonized glance and fled.

It was just then that I found the right pillbox.

I looked at the curled blonde hair for a long time. Only when the odor of coffee for breakfast came creeping through the still shadowy corridor and I took a long breath and realized that a rather dreadful day was beginning, I suddenly comprehended the weight I had laid upon my conscience. It was not, however, the fact that I had deliberately stolen the pillbox that troubled me, depraved though the admission sounds.

It was the fact that I remembered, and most untimely the memory was, that Nancy was not the only blonde-haired woman in the east wing. There was Lillian Ash who was blonde. And there was Dione Melady who was blonde. To my fevered fancy the world seemed suddenly full of blonde heads.

It was true, I argued to myself, that the three heads were, on their owner's bodies, easily distinguishable. Dione's hair looked faded and washed-out; Lillian Ash's had experienced a variety of bleaches and dyes and was at that moment a sort of bright ochre yellow, and Nancy's hair was bright and soft and vigorously gold. But it is not so easy to distinguish the exact shade of color in a single hair. The men of science of whom I have heard so much lately are doubtless able to do so, but I myself am not color blind. And at the moment the only thing I could have sworn about that hair was that it was not black.

Courtney Melady came quietly out of the door to Dione's room. I slipped the pillbox into my pocket. He advanced noiselessly along the corridor and paused beside me, his weary eyes looking out through the window to the hot, misty morning.

"Dawn," he said in a hushed voice. The night had not been kind to him. He looked his years and more; the pouches under his eyes were puffy and gray, the lines in his face and the look in his eyes were cold and hard and inexpressibly bleak. It was a look of disillusionment, of satiety. I was feeling rather kindly disposed toward him, the sort of sympathy one does feel for a man who has a nagging wife; but even at the moment I decided that in all likelihood the tales I had heard about Court Melady had their foundation in fact. No man of forty or thereabouts who has lived a reasonably hygienic and decent life ought look like that.

"It's going to be a dreadful day," he said after a moment or two. "It's hot already. I don't believe it cooled at all during the night. Mrs. Melady is asleep and I'm going out for some breakfast and a nap. I'll be at home if anyone wants me."

He turned absently toward the elevator and at the door drew sharply back and sheered over to the stairway. At the top he paused again and looked back at me.

"I'll order an electric fan for my wife," he said, and repeated: "It's going to be a dreadful day."

Presently I went into the room that had been my patient's and lay down again on the nurse's cot—whence I had risen so long ago to go downstairs for midnight supper.

I could not sleep for watching the door into the corridor.

Morning, real morning, finally came and with it breakfast and clusters of frightened nurses, white-faced and taut and whispering of the thing the night had held— and reporters and doctors and telephone calls and policemen everywhere and Kenwood Ladd.

And Kenwood Ladd. Coming to see Ina Harrigan with his eyes guarded and a great sheaf of salmon-colored gladioli under his arm.

CHAPTER V

I BELIEVE I have said very little about Kenwood Ladd. This is because, just there at the first, he was not at all a prominent figure. He was just one of Mrs. Harrigan's callers, a rather handsome young fellow of around thirty, an architect by profession who was planning a new house for Ina Harrigan and who came to see her about it rather more frequently than one would have thought the exigencies of house plans demanded. It was toward the end, after Lillian Ash's damaging testimony, that he became such an important factor in that strange and ugly drama.

He was, as I say, a handsome enough young man, fair with rather nice blue-gray eyes, a curiously tight look about his mouth, and a nice taste in tailors. He was not much younger than Ina Harrigan and had been riding with her, by the way, on the occasion of her ill-timed dispute regarding the right of way. He had escaped with only a cut on his cheek bone and a wrenched wrist, and I suppose he felt a sort of fellow-sufferer sympathy for Mrs. Harrigan. At any rate he came very often and kept her room supplied with somewhat unimaginative but lavish flowers and she seemed to like him to come. Certainly she spent enough time improving her appearance, forcing Ellen or the student nurse on day duty to hold a mirror for her and getting the sheets stained with lipsticks while she wielded her left arm skillfully and swore every time the mirror slipped. Ellen's vocabulary was becoming highly spotted, and once I caught her experimenting on her own innocuous young mouth with a lip paste so deeply crimson that it was nearly purple. The effect, before I made her scrub it off, was something scandalous.

Since then I have wondered how Kenwood Ladd must have felt that morning, his flowers under his arm, the morning paper with its headlines sticking out of his pocket, mounting that wide old stairway and knowing what he knew all the time. Knowing, too, what one of the nurses had seen. He did not know which nurse had stood there in the door; he had only caught, as came out later, the flicker of her white uniform. Certainly his mouth was tighter than usual, his eyes guarded; certainly he must have been frightened. And I can imagine him watching the four nurses who had been on night duty in the east wing of the third floor that night—the night of July seventh. Watching Lillian Ash, watching Ellen Brody, watching Nancy—watching even me, Sarah Keate. All the time wondering who it was and when she would tell. He knew the danger but not where it lay.

Morning then, with Kenwood Ladd and his flowers and newspapers, asking if he might see Mrs. Harrigan for a moment. Morning with Nancy and me off duty and trying to sleep in our rooms of the nurses' dormitory and failing and starting up at every sound. Morning with Ellen Brody terrifying the student nurses' dormitory with a recital of the events of the previous night and being sick again on her roommate's new silk kimona and getting fifty demerits from the training superintendent who knows nothing of adolescent psychology.

Lillian Ash was probably trying to rest in her patient's room, her weary eyes shut tight, her blonde hair straight and stringy from the heat and dampness, and her thoughts going in their desperate circle. And Miss Jones and Jacob Teuber were likely asleep, too; asleep and dreaming perhaps of a Negro who took a long time to die. And I know that Diona Melady was awake, for one of the day nurses in the east wing had an attack of hysterics and the head nurse for that wing threatened to resign before noon.

Yes, it was a bad day.

In the first place the sun did not come out once all day long, and yet it did not cloud up heavily and rain, which would have been a most welcome relief. Instead it remained gray and misty and hot. Terribly hot. Varnish grew sticky and smelled; drawers stuck, leather was damp and slick to the touch, the mirrors were faintly bleary, so that on looking into one you had an impulse to rub the film from your eyes. Uniforms were limp and wrinkled five minutes after they were donned, hair would not stay waved, noses were shiny and oily-looking. Patients were nervous and fretful, insisting on being in drafts with only sheets over them and then catching cold. Not, however, that there were what you could properly call moving currents of air, for there were not. It was dreadfully still, a sort of Turkish-bath stillness and steaminess, and the least exertion left you limp and exhausted.

And in the second place, while we who had been on duty during the night were supposed to sleep as long as we wished during the day, precious little sleep we got that day. It was to be expected, I suppose, but was none the less annoying, and not the least of our troubles were the demands of curious nurses, coming stealthily to our doors, knocking lightly but persistently and plying us with questions. This despite the *verboten* policy which

Dr. Kunce, with true German thoroughness, had under-taken.

"It is a question of morale," said Fannie Bianchi, who administers ether more skillfully than any nurse I have ever seen and is flippant about everything in the world but music and cats. "He figures the less we talk of it, the less we think of it. Prussian psychology. Silence and neither visitors to prowl our corridors nor newspapers to harrow our patients. As a consequence the patients are hounding us with questions, for of course they know something has happened, and I'm told that blue-black curses are coming in a steady stream from the men's ward due to the absence of the morning papers. They'll go quite mad if we don't get them the baseball scores this afternoon."

"But how do the patients know something has hap-pened?" I asked.

"It's in the air," she said and shivered and was all at once not flippant. "Do you suppose Dr. Harrigan really meant to operate on Mr. Melady?"

"I don't know. I suppose so. That's what he told Ellen."

"Then why didn't he arrange for the operating room?" she asked.

Well, I couldn't answer that, of course, and pres-ently she left, promising to bring me a newspaper which one of the special nurses had brought in and which was being passed surreptitiously around. Which accounted, I believe, for its draggled and limp state when it finally reached me.

The headlines were rather bad, but the account of the murder was correct and restrained. So restrained that I seemed to see. Dr. Kunce's blue pencil and the combined influence of a rather important board membership.

The hospital was treated with deference, ill health and despondency on the part of Dr. Harrigan was more than hinted at (with not a grain of truth and despite the fact that there was little question of its being suicide), Miss Sarah Keate, a night nurse, had found the body in the elevator; the missing fingerprints, the blonde hair, and the bit of white chewing gum were not mentioned, and the public was assured that the police had the matter well in hand. There was no mention, then, of Peter Melady's inexplicable disappearance. It was in the evening papers that that came out and already, then, the influence of the board had gone down before a news story; the papers were full of the affair, there were many pictures of the hospital and nurses, and the rather sinister implication of Peter Melady's disappearance at the time of, or immediately following, the murder of a man known to be his enemy was made the most of.

But that was in the evening. Many things were to happen before then.

I have often thought of the conflicting lines of evidence which so clogged and impeded our efforts to get at the truth. There was a mass of things, each having its own significance, and out of them all it was next to impossible to draw true conclusions. Yet, as we know now, the crime itself in the beginning was direct and simple and actuated by one of the simplest and most direct of motives. The curious arrangement of circumstances which made the crime inevitable was something no one could have foreseen. There was no scheming and plotting and very little planning. And there was no attempt at any time on the part of the murderer to cast suspicion upon anyone else.

Peter Melady could have given us the key, but no one knew where to find Peter Melady.

We also failed to reckon with one of the strongest of feminine'instincts; failed to reckon with it because we did not know that it had any bearing upon the case. And it was from the beginning, as I heard Sergeant Lamb remark somewhat ruefully, a case of *cherchez la femme.* Or as he put it knowingly: "Sharshay lay faym, eh, Dr. Kunze?"

"Kunce," said that gentleman softly.

Certainly bits of femninity kept cropping up. That blonde hair, for instance.

Feeling presently that it was no good lying on my back staring at the ceiling and seeing only the black depths of an elevator, I rose, put on a fresh uniform and cap after a tepid shower, and went down to an apathetic lunch of boiled cabbage, the odor of which lingered in a depressing way about the corridors all that day. Although I retained an impression of not having closed an eye I must have rested, for I did not feel sleepy at all, feeling instead strangely alert and wide awake. Up till then the horror and the rapid sequence of the events had drugged me into a sort of acquiescence. Now questions began to trouble me.

Where had the elevator been when I had rung for it? How had Peter Melady got out of the hospital? Why were Dione and Court Melady fully as much concerned about the Chinese snuff-bottle as they were about Peter Melady's disappearance? Had that knife actually come from the operating-room instruments? Had, then, Dr. Harrigan and his murderer presumably reached the fourth floor? *Where had the elevator been?*

I began to perceive that this question was of some importance. The cage had not been at the first floor, for I had rung for it there. It had not been at the third floor and it had not been at the fourth floor. That left only the second floor to be accounted for, unless—could it be stopped between floors? There was that button labeled "Emergency Stop"; what exactly did that mean?

I do not know what impulse led me to the fourth floor. Certainly it was in no effort to convince myself that the thing was real, for, admitting its strangeness, its horror, its ugliness which was so out of place within our peaceful, orderly hospital world, still and all the thing was entirely real to me. At any rate, immediately after lunch I toiled all the way upstairs—you could not have hired me to use the elevator—to the fourth floor. As I rounded the several landings of the stairway I caught, as always, a kind of cross-section of the hospital which included various glimpses of nurses, their white caps close together, scurrying internes and orderlies, an occasional blue-coated policeman which, in our world, is in itself an astounding thing, and there was a sort of restrained hub-bub going on in and around the main office, which is there at the west of the stairway on the first floor. However, in spite of the indications of the excitement with which the whole place seemed to seethe, it was nevertheless quiet and orderly in its outward aspects, and the routine of caring for the sick appeared to be going along with its usual despatch and exactness. My own wing looked scrubbed and quiet; a light or two burned down its length, and one of the day nurses whisked starchily out of a sick room and along the bare walls of the corridor. The halls and sick rooms were rather dark that day, owing to the weather, and every available light was burning and Dr. Kunce did not say a word about the expense. Even so the added light did not, somehow, lighten the somber emptiness and shadowy spaces.

The fourth floor had not, apparently, been in use that morning. It was quiet and bare and had that hot close atmosphere of unaired hospital rooms with the smells of ether and antiseptics and strong yellow soap and meat broth all blending together. The surgery was still, through someone's oversight, unlocked, as Dr. Harrigan had left it the night before. I remember that I fell to thinking again of the elevator; certainly at some time it had reached the fourth floor and discharged its load, for Dr. Harrigan would have had to unlock the door to the surgery and turn on the lights, and there was that 3E truck to prove further that he and his patient had actually reached the surgery. Why Dr. Harrigan had reëntered the elevator—what had happened to Peter Melady— were things I could not even surmise with any degree of certainty.

The 3E truck had been removed and the operating rooms were bare and clean and orderly and very quiet. Nothing was moved, nothing out of place; the instruments glittered back of the tight-fitting doors of glass.

Then I knew why I had come. The case of operating knives was directly below a case of scissors of all kinds of curves and blades; I looked carefully along the rows labeled "Surgical Bistouries" and found the vacancy at once, for the neatly arranged instruments had not even been pushed together to hide the gap. Of course, until there was a definite check of operating instruments one could not be sure, but it seemed to me fairly certain that the Catlin amputating knife had come from that very shelf. And, as was proved later in the day when a definite check was made of the instruments, I was quite right in my conclusion.

Then I looked carefully about the room. It was so still that, in spite of having switched on those bright, white ceiling lights, I began to feel a little uneasy. The clean white walls had witnessed a strange and terrible thing not very long ago; I felt closed in with terror and murder as if they were palpable things that had taken up their evil abode in that room.

Far down on the street below me I caught the faint sharp echo of an ambulance gong, and it restored me suddenly to everyday life. There was no use in lingering on that silent fourth floor.

It was as I turned off the light that I trod on something which shot from under my feet with a little bounce. It proved to be only a small cork apparently out of a medicine bottle; it had a penetrating and faintly familiar odor which I could not identify though I sniffed thoughtfully at it. I slipped it into the pocket of my uniform, touched my forehead and upper lip with my handkerchief, closed the doors, and went slowly down the wide, dark old stairway. The rail was slightly damp and sticky to the touch and very, very smooth under my fingers.

The office girl saw me as I reached the first floor.

"Oh, there you are," she said. "Dr. Kunce wants you in his office, please."

"Thank you," I replied. "Will you let Miss Bianchi know that the surgery is not locked?"

"Oh, boy, will I!" she said with a shiver. "All those knives and things up there!" She plugged in at the switchboard and eyed me avidly. "Isn't it terrible, Miss Keate? They say you found the body. How did he look?"

Well, she was like that. Unfortunately the door into Dr. Kunce's office opened before I could administer the lesson in manners she sorely needed. Dr. Kunce stood on the threshold.

"Oh, Miss Keate," he said. "Will you come in, please?"

Dr. Kunce's office is a rather handsomely furnished place of walnut bookshelves, softly glowing walnut desk,

deep rugs, and down-cushioned chairs which are uphol-
stered in a soft green stuff that I believe is called antique
velour and looks like nothing so much as velvet after the
cat has sharpened her claws on it. Even so it has a certain
opulence and beauty against which Ellen Brody's white
uniform and red eyes and huddled little figure looked
very dejected and out of place.

Sergeant Lamb was there, too, looking sternly at Ellen
and appearing to be none too happy himself.

"Here is a chair, Miss Keate," said Dr. Kunce, and a
brighter look flashed for an instant over Ellen's face and
was lost in dejection again.

"But you are supposed to see to it that every visitor is
out of the wing," said Dr. Kunce sharply as if continuing
the conversation which my arrival had interrupted.

"I know it," quavered Ellen. "It's just like I told you,
Dr. Kunce; Miss Page said it was nine-thirty and for me
to tell the caller in Mrs. Harrigan's room—that was
Mr. Ladd—and Mr. Court Melady in Mrs. Melady's
room, and the mother of 304 and the sister of 301 that
it was time for visitors to leave. That's all the visitors
we had that night in the east wing. And the visitors in
304 and 301 left right away, Dr. Kunce, and I saw them.
And Mr. Melady and this Mr. Ladd that was calling on
Mrs. Harrigan both said right away that they were just
going. But 301's light went on clear down at the end of
the corridor and he's sort of peevish and I hurried to
answer it and—and I didn't see them leave. And I know
Miss Page was busy at the same time because I saw her
in 302, right across the corridor from me. But we often
do that, Dr. Kunce; people always leave when it's time.
We've never had anybody trying to stay——"

"Never is a long time," said Dr. Kunce with silky

sharpness. "And student nurses do not question their superiors."

Two tears welled out of Ellen's eyes; they came easily as if many others had preceded them. She clutched a wet little wad of handkerchief tighter in her hand and sunk lower into the hot down cushions.

"I beg your pardon, Dr. Kunce, but I think——" I was beginning when he interrupted me. He is a fair-minded man, as a rule.

"Oh, I know what you are going to say, Miss Keate," he said impatiently. "And you are quite right. I know it's customary. If a visitor doesn't happen to leave when he's told to do so, one of the nurses always sees him. But in this case, you can see for yourself it puts us in a bad place. Sergeant Lamb and myself have been at some pains to check up on the entire hospital—patients, nurses, dormitories, wards, everything. And we thought we knew exactly who had been about the east wing or near the elevator during the hours from ten till the body was found. We found that every door and means of exit had been properly locked and that the night nurses of the east wing, third floor, myself, Dr. Harrigan, one of the orderlies with the body of a Negro, and the nurses in the east wing of the second floor are the only people whom we know to have been in that portion of the building. We say that portion of the building because we think there is no doubt but that Dr. Harrigan was killed in the elevator, hence his murderer must have entered the elevator. As you know, the east wing of the second floor is the isolation ward, and supper was sent up to the two nurses on duty there at present; they ate it at the chart desk, saw no one approach the elevator at any time during the hour between twelve and one o'clock, and provide a perfect alibi for each other. And the first floor is taken up entirely, at the east end, by the offices and the staff room. As I say the culpability of the patients themselves is not to be considered——"

"Mrs. Melady can walk," said Ellen unexpectedly, and cowered into the cushions as Dr. Kunce looked at her, but she added with swift breathlessness: "And so can Mrs. Harrigan."

"Is that right, Dr. Kunze?" asked Sergeant Lamb quickly.

"Kunce," said Dr. Kunce coldly. "Mrs. Harrigan's right arm is broken. And Mrs. Melady is scarcely of a physique to overpower and stab a man of Dr. Harrigan's build." He leveled a black look through those silky eyelashes at Ellen, who dabbed miserably at her eyes but even so maintained a ghost of her Irish-terrier expression.

"Do you mean to say, Dr. Kunce," I began in some anxiety, "that you and Sergeant Lamb have succeeded in narrowing the suspects to the people you have just mentioned?"

"That was what I was saying, yes," said Dr. Kunce precisely.

"But—but Dr. Kunce, do you realize that that limits it to—why, just to *us?* Just to those of us here in the hospital? Why—that's absurd!"

"You forget Peter Melady himself," remarked Sergeant Lamb.

"But Peter Melady was desperately ill. He couldn't have done it."

"What makes you so sure?" asked Sergeant Lamb rather eagerly.

"His state of health," I snapped. "And if you mean do I know anything about the murder, *I don't!*"

"If you will permit me to continue," said Dr. Kunce

coldly, adjusting the scarlet geranium which it was his custom to wear in the lapel of his light silk summer coat with as much care as if it were the only thing that engaged his attention—"if you will permit me to continue —I was saying, Miss Keate, that after some trouble and time we had narrowed the range of—er—suspects in this fashion until Miss Brody admitted just now that——"

"That this Court Melady might have been right here in the hospital all the time. And this Ladd fellow that's building a house for the Harrigans. For Mrs. Harrigan, I mean."

I looked at Ellen and Dr. Kunce looked in silky disapproval at Sergeant Lamb.

"So that's it," I said. "But you had told them both that it was time for visitors to leave?"

"Indeed, I did, Miss Keate," said Ellen earnestly.

"But didn't actually see them leave," said Sergeant Lamb.

"No," admitted Ellen in a small voice. "No."

"The office girl?" I suggested.

"Saw nothing of either of them," said Dr. Kunce. "Did you happen to see either of the men, Miss Keate, in the east wing that night? After nine-thirty?"

"No. But I don't recall being in Mrs. Harrigan's room before midnight. Or in Mrs. Melady's room."

"I was," piped Ellen. "I was in both rooms. But nobody was in Mrs. Melady's room except Mrs. Melady herself, of course. And I didn't see anybody in Mrs. Harrigan's room; she told me to go away and not bother her; that she didn't need any help."

"And all the doors had been properly locked," I said musingly.

"So it seems," said Dr. Kunce. "And so the police found them."

"But—no one having seen Mr. Melady and Ken-wood Ladd leave doesn't prove that either of them stayed right here in the hospital," I went on thoughtfully, although, being as interested in my own safety as anyone, I must say that the inclusion of two more names in that sinisterly short list of possible murderers gave me a more secure feeling.

"No," said Dr. Kunce in quiet agreement, and Sergeant Lamb cleared his throat noisily.

"No," he said. "But we'll see what they've got to say about it. You're sure about the rest of the place, are you, Dr. Kunze? It looks mighty big to me to be able to know just who was where between twelve and one—there's a whole hour to be accounted for. Are you sure you can rely on what the nurses have had to say?"

"My dear Sergeant Lamb," said Dr. Kunce somewhat testily, "I have assured you at least a hundred times this morning that routine and order is the very soul of a hospital. Nothing is left to chance; everything goes by clockwork, so to speak. We can absolutely depend upon the results of our morning's work. We have sifted the thing down to exactly the people I have mentioned": he began to check the names on his smooth, well-cared-for fingers—"There are the nurses, Miss Page, Miss Ash, Miss Brody, and Miss Keate. There is the orderly, Teuber. And there was myself. I've already told you that I went to the third floor near eleven o'clock to see a patient in Room 301, returned to my office, and sat here reading, not caring to go to bed while it was so warm. And I was here when Miss Keate called for help after she had found the body."

He stopped, poured himself some water from a glass on the table, and drank it very deliberately.

"Well, here's Court Melady and this Ladd fellow to

add to your list now," said Sergeant Lamb in a disgruntled way. "And you didn't mention Peter Melady."

"No," said Dr. Kunce. "I didn't mention Peter Melady." He said it very softly, without any expression
at all, and it was singular that I felt as if Peter Melady
had been definitely accused of the murder of Dr. Harrigan. And while I did not exactly like Dr. Kunce's sum-
ming up of the situation, still I had to admit that there
was no doubt he had, in his thorough way, checked every
person in the hospital for the period of time he mentioned. Which was no doubt tedious, but not so difficult,
owing to the fact that, while Melady Memorial Hospital
is fairly large as hospitals go, it is run, under Dr. Kunce's
jurisdiction, with a precision and exactness of routine
which leaves no loopholes. At the same time it occurred
to me that, in the very nature of the thing, it would be
quite impossible to discover the murderer by continually
narrowing a circle of those proved to have been about
the scene of the crime near the time when it was done,
as I am given to understand is a procedure sometimes
followed. It seemed to me rather that, if it were ever
solved, it would have to be by a tenacious following up
of any bits of evidence, of any scraps of this and that,
fingerprints and such like, which the newspapers refer to
as clues and which seem to have much significance in murder trials.

Although as to that there seemed to be nothing you
could properly call a clue in the murder case that concerned us and that thereby seemed so much more poignant and real than any mere newspaper murder. Unless
it was the blonde hair which at that time, still in the tiny
pillbox, was reposing in the lavender rubber depths of
my own hot-water bag, which happens to have an unusually large top. Or the bit of white chewing gum.

Ellen, forgotten for a moment, made an incautious movement and both men turned to her with a sort of pouncing air.

"Now, then," said Sergeant Lamb, "is there anything else you've forgotten to tell us about?"

"No, sir," said Ellen earnestly.

"Nothing else, Ellen?" said Dr. Kunce, his nose coming down over his Vandyke in an unpleasant fashion.

"No, sir. No, Dr. Kunce. It was just like I told you. Dr. Harrigan came at almost exactly eleven-thirty. At twelve o'clock Miss Page and Miss Keate and Miss Ash went down to supper, and right away after they'd gone Dr. Harrigan called me into Mr. Melady's room. It only took him a moment or two to explain that he was going to perform an emergency operation and I got the truck and helped get Mr. Melady onto it. Then Dr. Harrigan told me to answer the lights that were signaling by that time and that he would take the patient upstairs and arrange for the operating room. He went to the elevator and I saw him push the truck with Mr. Melady on it into the elevator and then he went in himself. And it was five minutes after twelve, almost exactly."

"Look here," said Sergeant Lamb doubtfully. "How do you happen to know exactly what time it was always? That don't look right to me. You want to tell us the truth about these things, young lady. Don't go fixing up a story."

Ellen bridled, encountered Dr. Kunce's velvety gaze and masked smile, and wilted again.

"I've got a new wrist watch," she said in a small voice. She held out her white-cuffed wrist. "See? It's the first one I ever had. It's got the second hand and all." Her voice gained a little in pride as she looked at the white-gold oval which sedulously aped its aristocratic platinum sisters in severity of design. She lost herself in admiration for a moment. "And I know what time it was when I saw Dr. Harrigan there in the corridor again, too," she said absently, gazing at the watch.

"*When you what?*"

Ellen dropped her wrist hurriedly.

"When I saw Dr. Harrigan again there in the corridor," she said hastily. "I—I guess I forgot that, too. I——"

"What do you mean?"

"Well, I guess Dr. Harrigan had come back to Mr. Melady's room for something he'd forgotten. Anyway, he was just coming out of Mr. Melady's room when I came out of the diet kitchen with beef tea for 301. I didn't pay much attention to Dr. Harrigan but hurried on down the corridor to 301 because he's sort of—peevish, you know. But just as I reached 301's door I looked down the hall toward the elevator again and Dr. Harrigan was just going into the elevator. And it was exactly eighteen minutes after twelve. I'm sorry I forgot, Dr. Prunes, but I guess it didn't matter much. He just went into the elevator and——"

"*What did you say?*" His voice was like a silk thread, cutting and fine. Ellen became incoherent.

"Just went into the elevator. He just went into the elevator and the door shut. That was all. Really that was all, Dr. Prunes. And at twelve-twenty, just two minutes later, Miss Keate came back and——"

"Dr. *what?*"

"Dr. Pr——" Ellen choked. A look of abject terror came into her face, she opened and shut her mouth helplessly, her eyes staring at Dr. Kunce as if mesmerized. "Dr. Prunes—Dr. Kunce—Dr. Prunes——" she babbled wretchedly.

"Then the last time you saw Dr. Harrigan alive was at eighteen minutes after twelve?" asked Sergeant Lamb, unwittingly restoring Ellen's reason. She tore her eyes from Dr. Kunce, said faintly "Yes," and ducked her head.

"You are sure it was Dr. Harrigan?"

"Yes."

"Couldn't have been anyone else?"

"No. I'm sure it was Dr. Harrigan."

"And you're pretty sure about the time?"

"I know about the time," said Ellen with more spirit. "I'm positive about it." She lifted her head for an instant, caught Dr. Kunce's eyes, and ducked it again.

"That proves then that at eighteen minutes after twelve Dr. Harrigan was still alive," said Sergeant Lamb with a touch of triumph. "We are beginning to get on a bit, Dr. Kunze. We are beginning to——"

"Kunce," said Dr. Kunce, turning his smoldering eyes upon Sergeant Lamb.

"Eh!" said Sergeant Lamb, startled. "What did you say? Oh, sure, Dr. Kunze, sure. I know your name. Is your watch right, Miss Brody? Are you sure it's right?"

Ellen nodded. She looked shrunken.

"Yes," she said feebly. "At least I set it with the clock in the office and it hasn't varied at all since."

"Have you got this, Dr. Kunze? At twelve-eighteen she saw Dr. Harrigan on the third floor again, coming out of Mr. Melady's room and going into the elevator. What time did you get back to the third floor and find your patient gone, Miss Keate?"

"Twelve-twenty," said Ellen, as if she could not stay her tongue.

"That right, Miss Keate?"

"I can't say exactly. It must have been about that."

"And you went right to the fourth floor and could find neither your patient nor Dr. Harrigan?"

"Neither," I said.

"How long did it take you to find your patient was gone from his room, inquire of Miss Brody, and get to the fourth floor?"

"About four or five minutes," I said. "No longer."

"And in that four or five minutes," pronounced Sergeant Lamb slowly, "Dr. Harrigan was murdered and his murderer, Peter Melady, escaped."

"Not necessarily," I said sharply. "I didn't discover the body for some time after that."

"Not very long after, Miss Keate. The office girl and Dr. Kunze say you called for help at exactly twelve thirty-two. Twelve minutes after Miss Brody saw Dr. Harrigan enter the elevator you, Miss Keate, find him there dead. Does that narrow our suspects, or doesn't it, Dr. Kunze?" he inquired, with an effect of rubbing his hands together, although he actually did no such thing.

"Possibly," agreed Dr. Kunce, stroking his beard; his eyes were still smoldering back of those long, womanish eyelashes. "Do you mind informing us, Miss Brody, whether you have 'forgotten' anything else or not?"

"No, Doctor. I mean yes, Doctor," said Ellen lucidly.

"Think now, sister," urged Sergeant Lamb. "Was there anything that struck you as being unusual? Anything at all out of the way during the hours just before midnight? Or even after the murder was discovered? Think."

"No," said Ellen, avoiding Dr. Kunce's gaze by the simple expedient of screwing her eyes shut. "No. Nothing at all." She stopped and then added in a casual way which, even to me, was exasperating and I scarcely dared imagine its effect upon Dr. Kunce. "Unless it would be

Miss Page getting so excited about Dr. Harrigan operating on Mr. Melady just then. That was right after I'd told Miss Keate what Dr. Harrigan told me to tell her and she had gone up to the operating room. Miss Page said," remarked Ellen in the most nonchalant way in the world, "that someone must stop it and Mrs. Melady said it would be murder, and Miss Page said it was too late to do anything, and Mrs. Melady said if she didn't stop it it would be murder and it would be her—Miss Page's —fault. They were awfully excited. I heard them talking through the screen across Mrs. Melady's door. I couldn't help hearing them," she added defensively, adding in a plaintive way: "Anybody could have heard it. Anybody. I didn't go to listen, but they were so excited! Especially Mrs. Melady. She sort of gets excited about things."

There was a brief silence. Sergeant Lamb was staring at Ellen with a speculative look in his pale blue eyes; the look of a man who has a new and interesting idea. And I think Dr. Kunce was interested, too, although his face is not easy to read. I myself had suddenly recalled the earlier whispered conversation I had heard just outside Dione Melady's door. What had they been saying— something about murder?

"Oh, yes," said Ellen unexpectedly. "And Miss Keate was on her knees to the wastebasket. That was queer. And I think Miss Ash was afraid of Dr. Harrigan."

CHAPTER VI

"WELL, now, what do you mean by that?" inquired Sergeant Lamb a bit fretfully, wrenched from one new and intriguing angle to look at another before he'd finished looking at the first. "Don't change around like that, young lady."

"Nonsense, Ellen," I said briskly, beginning to feel that the sooner I got Ellen out of the company of Sergeant Lamb, the better for everyone it might be. "Miss Ash did not know Dr. Harrigan at all. And I was only picking up something I had dropped." Which was true enough. But it seemed to my guilty conscience that there was a question in the eyes of the policeman; I wondered if he had discovered his loss, but did not see my way clear to eliciting that interesting item of news. I felt, however, uneasy and repeated: "Nonsense, Ellen. You are tired and hysterical. You ought have rest before night duty again."

That brought Ellen's eyes wide open again. She started forward, clutching at the arms of the chair and saying in a strangled way:

"Night duty, Miss Keate! Night duty. Do you mean—— Are we going to—— Oh, I won't go on night duty again! I won't go! I won't go!" She ended in a wail that almost choked her, for she caught Dr. Kunce's eye in the middle of it, and while I don't say there was murder in that dark gaze there was something very near it.

"Control yourself, Miss Brody," he said softly, reducing Ellen to a state of distraction of which I think he did not realize the danger. "This is an excellent time to learn that a nurse's first and foremost duty is the care of the sick and the observance of hospital routine. Certainly you will go on duty to-night." He stopped, merely I think to arrange a little speech in his mind, and I spoke quickly, knowing his liking for oratory and his deep affection for discipline.

"Might I suggest, Dr. Kunce——" I was beginning. "Miss Brody is very tired and needs—— Ellen! Ellen, don't do it here!"

Ellen gave me an agonized look.

"I'm going to be sick," she said in dull horror. "Right here. Oh, this beautiful rug——"

"You are not," said Dr. Kunce with swift firmness. He had that ability for meeting crises which a successful doctor must possess. Ellen was in the outer office, the door was closed again, and Dr. Kunce was settling himself in his chair, stroking his beard and looking with satisfaction at the still virgin rug before Sergeant Lamb had more than grasped the danger.

"Oh," he said, looking embarrassed, though I'm sure I don't know why. "Oh. Felt—er—dizzy, did she?"

Someone knocked softly at the door and opened it at Dr. Kunce's brief word.

"Mr. Courtney Melady to see you, Doctor," murmured the office girl.

"Ask Mr. Melady to come in at once."

Over Court Melady's gray-coated shoulder rose a slight commotion and disorder in the outer office, and I judged that Ellen was rather outdoing herself, poor child.

"Hello, Melady."

"How do you do, Mr. Melady."

Court Melady nodded to Dr. Kunce, gave Sergeant Lamb a straight, cold look from his lined eyes, said "How do you do, Sergeant?" and accepted a chair. He looked fully as weary as he had looked early that morning, although now, of course, he was perfectly groomed. He took out a very handsome linen handkerchief, brushed his forehead where his grayish, rather thin but carefully brushed hair was receding, and said:

"It's a warm day."

"Very," assented Dr. Kunce, his nose down over his beard.

"Well," said Court Melady. "What have you accomplished? Do you know where Uncle Peter—Mr. Melady —has gone?"

"No," said Sergeant Lamb briefly. He looked somewhat discomposed. "I'd never have said any man out of his grave could vanish as completely as Mr. Melady has vanished. Are you sure you can't think of any place he might be, Mr. Melady? You know him well, of course. Where do you think he would go in case he wanted to disappear for a time?"

"I can't imagine him disappearing at all of his own will," said Court Melady. "He is not of a retiring nature. If he went any place he'd go to his home. And he certainly is not there."

"Look here, now, Mr. Melady," said Sergeant Lamb in a sudden access of friendliness. "Suppose you tell us —er—confidentially—just how much you know about this. Peter Melady, being so fond of you, must have taken you into the secret. Now if you can just tell us what he was planning——"

"I don't know one thing about it," said Court Melady wearily, as if he had been asked that question a number of times already. "I've told you that. The whole thing's a complete mystery to me. And my uncle, I might add, was not very fond of me."

There was a brief silence. In the outer office subdued and numerous feet came and went and there was a sort of murmur of voices and busy telephones. It was very warm there in Dr. Kunce's office; the down cushions on my chair were almost unbearable. Sergeant Lamb was looking in a baffled way at Court Melady, and Dr. Kunce stroked and stroked his beard.

"Well, what about this new kind of ether he was about to put on the market?" asked Sergeant Lamb presently. "Do you know anything about it?"

"It is not ether," remarked Dr. Kunce softly and exactly.

"Not very much," said Court Melady. He reached absently into his pocket and found a cigarette case, took out a cigarette with fingers that were none too steady, and got the case halfway to his pocket again before he remembered to pass it and jerked it out again. Sergeant Lamb's fingers were already outstretched when Dr. Kunce refused on his own behalf, at which Sergeant Lamb gave a rather uneasy look about the room and withdrew his hand quickly without a cigarette.

"You don't mind if I smoke in here?" said Court Melady at once.

"Oh, not at all. Not at all," said Dr. Kunce, who happened to mind very much, cherishing as he does somewhat finical notions.

"You say you don't know much about this ether?" resumed Sergeant Lamb.

"Not ether," murmured Dr. Kunce behind his Vandyke, and Court Melady frowned and repeated:

"Not very much."

"Well, just what did you know?"

"About what everyone else seems to know. The stuff was worked out in the Melady laboratories but I've never had much to do with my uncle's business. I know only in a general way that Slæpan is expected to take the place of and be a vast improvement on ether. If it actually proves to be that it will be important, of course, and ought have enormous commercial possibilities. But as I understand it, Slæpan is still in the experimental stage. And I have known of several things of that sort that have not worked out very well in a practical way."

"At any rate the formula"—Dr. Kunce stopped to brush a speck of lint from his light silk sleeve "—the formula must be an interesting one."

Something flickered back of Court Melady's cold eyes and he said easily:

"As to that I can't tell you much, Dr. Kunce. You see, I've never even seen the formula. And being neither a pharmacist nor a chemist nor a"—there was a speck of lint now on Court Melady's sleeve and he took his time to brush it away—"nor a doctor, I shouldn't have known what the thing meant if I had seen it."

I have never known whether Dr. Kunce deliberately brought the matter of the formula to Sergeant Lamb's somewhat slow-moving attention or whether Sergeant Lamb had, himself, recalled its possible importance. At any rate, he said quickly:

"Where is this formula, Mr. Melady?"

"I'm sure I don't know," replied Court Melady after a rather tense moment of silence. He inspected the ashes on his cigarette, glanced about for an ash tray, lifted his eyebrows as he saw none, and repeated: "I'm sure I don't know."

"You don't know! But surely—wouldn't Peter Melady have put anything so important in a safe? In the bank? Or at his own office? Wouldn't he have had copies of such an important thing?"

"One would think so." Court Melady gently flicked the little blue end from his cigarette. The ashes drifted lightly to the rug and Dr. Kunce got up at once, reached with a sort of reluctant haste into a drawer, and brought out an ash tray which he set down at Court Melady's elbow. Court Melady murmured: "Thank you," and I had the odd impression of a battle fought in which Court Melady was victor. It was only a momentary impression and rather absurd in view of Dr. Kunce's unruffled composure and unfathomable eyes.

"However," resumed Court Melady, "anyone knowing my Uncle Peter would not have expected him to do the customary thing. I doubt very much if the formula is in any safe. And I know that there was no copy. Mr. Melady had entire confidence in his own—er—discretion."

"Do you know where the formula is, then?"

"No. If I did I should secure it and turn it over to my wife, who certainly, during Uncle Peter's—absence—has first claim upon it."

"Well, do you think it's possible, then, that Mr. Melady—er—hid the formula somewhere?" asked Sergeant Lamb slowly and fumblingly.

Court Melady shrugged.

"Sergeant Lamb, anything is possible with Peter Melady. He is a man of remarkable business ability; I admire and respect him highly. But I would never attempt to say what he might or might not do."

"Whimsical," achieved Sergeant Lamb adventurously. Court Melady darted a glance at him through the little veil of blue smoke. His weary eyes were narrowed to escape the smoke.

"Well," he said, "you might call it that. Obstinate is another word."

"What's your business, by the way, Mr. Melady?"

"I'm not in business," said Court Melady rather slowly. Dr. Kunce's fingers were quiet on his Vandyke for a second and then resumed their stroking.

"Not in business," repeated Sergeant Lamb. "Oh, you—er—live on your income?"

"In a way," said Court Melady, inspecting the end of his cigarette again. Then he added with an effect of candor: "My father was James Melady, Peter Melady's cousin. He left me sufficient money."

"Your wife is Peter Melady's daughter?"

"Certainly. You knew that."

"Does she—is she wealthy in her own right?"

"I think you are going rather far, Sergeant," said Court Melady coldly. "However, she has an allowance from her father and what I am able to supply."

"Never hard up, are you, Mr. Melady?" said Sergeant Lamb softly.

There was certainly anger in Court Melady's eyes but he only said with care:

"Everyone is at times, Sergeant. Even police officers out of a job."

"Do you mean that for a threat?" cried Sergeant Lamb, reddening.

"Not at all. Not at all. But I think you are straying from the point, which is—where is Peter Melady? That's your business, you know."

"My business is my own," said Sergeant Lamb. "Is your wife Peter Melady's sole heir?"

Very wary now were those experienced eyes of Court Melady's, and I knew that Dr. Kunce was watching him intently from under his long eyelashes. Well, I had heard rumours of Court Melady's unbridled fondness for card games at which, it had been whispered in B——, rather large sums of money were apt to change hands. Suppose Court Melady had needed money—suppose he had married his wife for her money—suppose . . .

It was a thought that was too unreasonable to pursue; I listened for Court Melady's reply.

"I think it likely," said Court Melady.

"Don't you know?"

"No. My uncle—and father-in-law—had not taken me into his confidence in that respect."

"And you know nothing at all of the whereabouts of this formula. This Sly-pan thing."

"Nothing," said Court Melady, and I'm sure I don't know why I felt so sure he was lying but I did.

"Look here, Dr. Kunze," said Sergeant Lamb, "maybe Peter Melady had that formula here in the hospital. Maybe that's why he disappeared. Maybe that's——"

"Do you mean Peter Melady disappeared because he brought the Slæpan formula to the hospital with him?" asked Dr. Kunce silkily. "I, myself, fail to see any connection of cause and effect."

"Well, I don't know as to that," said Sergeant Lamb. "But I'll bet this ether has got something to do with it. Wasn't the stuff registered—patented—whatever is done to protect such discoveries? What I mean is, could somebody just walk off with it and claim he invented it and get by with it?"

Neither of the gentlemen seemed inclined to answer the question. Court Melady smoked steadily and Dr. Kunce inspected the creamy wall straight ahead of him.

Finally Court Melady said, rather slowly and thought-fully:

"I can't tell you much about that. But I'm afraid just such a procedure is quite possible. You see, if it was not registered anyone who possessed the formula itself could claim it. There might be inquiry. There might be more than suspicion in professional circles. But after all how could it be proved that the—doctor, for instance, or chemist who might get hold of the formula and pass it off as his own had not discovered it? He could easily claim it for his own and could eventually, providing he had effrontery and influence enough, face down suspicion. And I feel sure it was not yet patented. Uncle Peter wouldn't have done so until he was sure it was successful; he had a sort of superstition about that. And this was by far his most important effort. Much more important than the various flu preventives and cough syrups and head-ache tablets that the Melady Drug Company puts out. But you are likely familiar with the Melady products?"

"Oh, sure," said Sergeant Lamb. "My kid takes Me-lady Malt Cod-liver Oil. Gained six ounces last week. Do you mean Peter Melady didn't want to register it until he knew it was successful? This ether stuff, I mean."

"That's my surmise. As I have said, he didn't take me into his confidence to any great extent."

"But couldn't the chemists who worked it out dupli-cate the formula if it was lost or stolen?"

Court Melady shrugged.

"I doubt it. What do you think, Dr. Kunce?"

"Probably not," said Dr. Kunce. "Things of that sort must be very exact, you know. They might do it eventu-ally—work the whole thing out over again—but it would take considerable time. Anyone who actually possessed the formula could have it registered and introduced as his own achievement before the Melady chemists could arrive at the identical formula. That's only my opinion, however. I am not a chemist, myself."

"Wasn't Peter Melady afraid somebody might try to steal it?"

"Life is one long, joyous battle to my Uncle Peter," said Court Melady, evasively. "Why all the inquiry about Slæpan? You haven't by any chance found it?" He ground his cigarette into the ash tray as he spoke and did not meet Sergeant Lamb's eyes, although it seemed to me that there was a certain eagerness in his voice.

"No," said Sergeant Lamb, "we haven't found it. We don't even know that it was stolen. I only thought there might be a reason there for Peter Melady's disappearance. It ain't right for a man to just vanish—without any reason we can discover."

"By the way, Mr. Melady," remarked Dr. Kunce smoothly, "when did you last see Peter Melady? You see," he added as if in apology, "since he was a patient here I am actively concerned in finding him."

Again Sergeant Lamb recalled himself.

"Yes, Mr. Melady. Just when did you last see Peter Melady?"

"About nine o'clock last night, I believe," said Court Melady easily.

"How did he seem then?"

"Quite as usual, I thought. The nurse, Miss Keate here, said he'd had a rather trying day owing to the extreme heat."

"Was he in good spirits?"

"Quite as usual," repeated Court Melady.

"Said nothing of anything worrying him?"

"Nothing at all."

"What kind of terms was he on with Dr. Harrigan?"

"You are asking me difficult questions, Sergeant Lamb," said Court Melady with a readiness that did not suggest any particular difficulty. "However, I believe that it is no secret that Dr. Harrigan and Peter Melady were not—on the best of terms."

"Do you know what the trouble was between them?"

"No," said Court Melady flatly and promptly. Very promptly.

"What time did you leave the hospital last night?" pursued Sergeant Lamb.

"About nine-thirty, I believe."

"See anyone on the way out?"

Court Melady shot a quick glance at Sergeant Lamb and then at Dr. Kunce, and replied rather carefully:

"I don't know that I recall anyone in particular. Why do you ask?"

"Did you go straight home?"

"No. No, I sat in Euclid Park for a while."

"About how long?"

"Really I can't say exactly. Why?"

"What time did you reach home?"

"It must have been around eleven o'clock or so. Still very warm."

"Did you see anyone when you reached home?"

"No. I let myself in with my own latchkey and went straight to my own room."

"None of the servants see you?"

"No," said Court Melady shortly. "What is the meaning of this inquiry?"

"Just that it would be lucky for you, Mr. Melady, if someone had seen you leaving or outside the hospital before the time when Dr. Harrigan was murdered and your father-in-law disappeared. Wife heiress to Peter Melady's estate—no alibi—confesses to being short of money—looks rather bad, doesn't it, Dr. Kunze?" Again there was the effect of rubbing his hands together.

"Oh, doubtless," said Dr. Kunce suavely. "Only—there's the rub again! It was not Peter Melady who was murdered. It was Dr. Harrigan."

"So that's what you're getting at," said Court Melady. He was not as coldly detached as he had been, but a man just accused openly of having had something to do with murder would not be exactly cool and detached, no matter whether he was guilty or not. "Well, you'll not go far in that direction. I was out of this hospital long before Dr. Harrigan was in it last night. Long before Dr. Harrigan was murdered. I know nothing about this murder. And for your own sake I'd advise a little more expedition in discovering the whereabouts of my uncle, Peter Melady. I don't think for a moment that he stabbed Dr. Harrigan and then escaped, and I doubt if you think so. Well, then—where is he? What's happened to him? Has he been—murdered, too?"

He paused and in the warm, silent room the question seemed to echo itself: Has he been murdered, too? Has he been murdered, too?

No one spoke and presently Court Melady shifted his position uneasily as if to break an unpleasant train of thought, lit another cigarette, and looked at Sergeant Lamb again.

"And you'd better get down to work and find out just what's going on before everybody's on your neck about it. Peter Melady is—rather an important figure in B——."

"Never you mind about that," said Sergeant Lamb bravely enough but not very happily. "It's my neck. And I'm going to have this thing settled in short order. Before this new lieutenant gets back."

"New lieutenant?" inquired Dr. Kunce quickly. "You mean this young fellow who was just recently appointed?"

"Yeah. Headquarters thinks he's great. The new administration got him the appointment; everybody knows that. They call him the gentleman police officer. Gentleman!" repeated Sergeant Lamb with regret. "That's what things are coming to. Yeah, he's lieutenant now of the Homicide Bureau. Or will be when he gets back Friday. He's been in Europe. That's the kind he is. The gentleman police officer! Him that was a private dick!" concluded Sergeant Lamb scornfully and yet with a kind of sadness. "And you know what that means!"

"One would say the gentleman is about to step into a pretty problem," said Court Melady.

Sergeant Lamb smiled.

"Yeah. Only I'm going to have this settled before he gets here. It's not such a problem. All these murders are simple—once you get the right slant on them."

"Oh, certainly," agreed Dr. Kunce, his nose coming down over his beard. "Once you get the right slant on them. This lieutenant must be young O'Leary. I recall reading something about the appointment not long ago."

"Yes," said Court, smiling. "It is one of the new administration's much heralded reforms. I met the young man at a dinner once. Last spring."

"So?" said Dr. Kunce. "Is he so remarkable?"

Court Melady shook his head, still smiling coldly.

"Perhaps, but he doesn't look it. A slight young fellow—rather ordinary. Drives a good car. Didn't have much to say. I don't imagine that any of our city's criminal class exactly shake in their shoes at the mention of his name."

"Is that Lance O'Leary?" I asked Sergeant Lamb with much interest.

"Yeah. Lance O'Leary. Know him?"

"He was a patient of mine once," I said shortly, not seeing it necessary to mention the fact that I happened to have known Mr. O'Leary rather well during a strenuous period of my life, of which I have told elsewhere; that, indeed, I had been able to give him some slight assistance once or twice.

Sergeant Lamb was eyeing me doubtfully.

"Well, see here, nurse," he said, not, I think, with intentional rudeness, "don't you go holding out on me just because he's a friend of yours."

"I assure you, Sergeant Lamb," I said at once and with some asperity, "I have no intention of 'holding out on you,' if by that you mean keeping secret information which might lead to discovering the murderer. In the first place I have nothing to hold out. And in the second place I do not make friends with my gentlemen patients."

Court Melady choked on some smoke just then and coughed rather vigorously, which somewhat marred the effect of my words, but even so Sergeant Lamb looked faintly apologetic.

"No, ma'am," he said. "You don't look like that kind of a . . ." I did not hear the rest of his sentence, as Dr. Kunce rose just then rather hurriedly and went to the door to ask if Mr. Ladd had come yet.

Apparently Kenwood Ladd was just entering the outer office and ready to see Dr. Kunce. Court Melady rose, too, somewhat anxious, I thought, to get away, and left after Sergeant Lamb mentioned that it might be well for him, Court Melady, to find someone who'd seen him after leaving the hospital the previous night. Sergeant

Lamb meant to be subtle, I suppose, but was just the reverse.

"Keep me informed, please, of any developments," said Court Melady as if he had not heard Sergeant Lamb's warning. "This failure to discover what has happened to Peter Melady is preposterous. My wife is beside herself with anxiety. Will you step up to see her during the day, Dr. Kunce? She is in an extremely nervous state. Hello, Ladd. Bad business here."

"Very bad," agreed Kenwood Ladd. "How do you do, Dr. Kunce?"

The office door closed behind Court Melady's debonair shoulders and the newcomer gave a rather sharp look around the room before he bowed distantly to me, said "Hello, Sergeant," in the general direction of Sergeant Lamb, and took the chair Dr. Kunce indicated. "You wanted to see me again?"

No one would have guessed that he was badly frightened. Life had not gone any too smoothly for Kenwood Ladd for the few months preceding the murder of Dr. Harrigan, and that ugly business must have been a sort of culminating blow. But his poise was perfect. Only once was it threatened.

"Well, yes," said Dr. Kunce softly. "We are obliged to make a somewhat detailed inquiry owing to last night's —tragedy. It's quite a task, you understand."

"It must be. An affair like that in a hospital with any number of people in and out all day long. I don't see how you can make much progress in such an inquiry."

"No?" said Sergeant Lamb. "Well, it's not such a job as it seems. We are narrowing it down. Narrowing it down."

"Ah," said Kenwood Ladd politely.

"You were a visitor in the east wing of the third floor last night?"

"Yes."

"You were calling on Mrs. Harrigan?"

"Yes."

"Friend of the Harrigans?"

"Why—yes."

"Know them well?"

"I shouldn't say that—no. I am building their new house out on Westwood Height. I'm an architect, you know. So I've seen something of them."

"Were you and Dr. Harrigan good friends?"

Kenwood Ladd's always tight mouth became a little tighter and his eyes narrowed a little under his level, sun-bleached eyebrows but remained steady.

"Not particularly. I know Mrs. Harrigan better, of course."

"Why 'of course'?" asked Sergeant Lamb.

"Did you ever try to build a house for a woman?" asked Kenwood Ladd a bit wearily, adding: "It's always the women who have the most to say about a house. The men let their wives do all the planning. It's one of the things," he went on in a disinterested way, "that adds brightness and joy to the architect's life. May I smoke, Dr. Kunce? Or isn't your office sufficiently removed from the rest of the hospital?"

"Sorry I don't have cigarettes. Oh. You have your own. There's an ash tray."

Dr. Kunce's words were gracious enough. But Kenwood Ladd gave him a look of surprise and replaced the cigarettes he had half drawn out.

"Do you mean you would rather deal with the women?" asked Sergeant Lamb, who apparently liked to be sure that two and two make four.

"Did I give you that impression?" said Kenwood Ladd.

"Well, what do you mean?"

"I mean," said Kenwood Ladd, looking bored, "that no one in his senses likes to fritter away the hours of his youth making innumerable blueprints for the same house. Or, rather, not the same house. It seldom is the same house when the ladies have got through changing their minds."

"Oh, you mean the women change their minds," said Sergeant Lamb brilliantly.

"Exactly, Sergeant," said Kenwood Ladd in an encouraging way. "And I change the blueprints. And I do it myself because the state of my—er—professional exchequer does not at the moment permit draftsmen. The business depression, you know. No building. Convenient alibi."

"Well, it's an alibi we're after right now," said Sergeant Lamb restively. "When did you leave the hospital last night?"

"Let me see . . . The young nurse in the blue and white striped dress came in about nine-thirty, I think, to tell me it was time for visitors to leave. I talked for a little after that. I'm afraid I can't say exactly."

"Where did you go when you left here?"

"For a walk," said Kenwood Ladd promptly.

"See anyone you knew?"

"Why—no. Not that I recall."

"Where do you live?"

"At the Westwood."

"That new apartment hotel?"

"Yes."

"Then somebody saw you come in?"

"I—believe not."

"You believe not? That's funny. Aren't there a bunch of boys and clerks around that place?"

"There's a night clerk. He happened to be in the inner office. Making out bills, I presume; he does that rather well."

"Nobody else about?"

"Not that I saw. It was a hot night, you know. The elevator boy was out somewhere. Getting a cold drink, likely. Anyway I don't recall seeing anyone."

"What floor do you live on?"

"Eleventh."

"Take the elevator up?"

"Why, of course."

"Know a lot about elevators, do you, Mr. Ladd?"

I think Kenwood Ladd had entered that office determined to keep his temper under all circumstances. He must have known that he could not avoid certain comment; his friendliness with Mrs. Harrigan could not have escaped notice. But it slipped a little here.

"Just what do you mean by that?" he asked sharply. His eyebrows were still level and inscrutable but his eyes were less guarded. Suddenly I liked him better.

"Just what I say. Do you know a lot about elevators?"

Kenwood Ladd took a deliberate moment or two in reaching for and selecting a cigarette and lighting it. He did it as if automatically and did not note Dr. Kunce's look of silky disapproval.

"Not any more than anyone, I presume," said Kenwood Ladd then, letting thin blue smoke surround his face. "If you mean, do I need an elevator boy to take me up to my own apartment, I certainly do not. The elevator boys at the Westwood are merely that many loose-change vacuums."

"You didn't happen to stop at a drug store anywhere? Soda fountain? Cigar store?"

It was just then that a rather curious look flashed into Kenwood Ladd's guarded face. Flashed into it and was gone, but I saw something like alarm back of those wary, purposefully steady blue-gray eyes.

"Why, no. I think not," he said quietly.

"It would be better for you, you know, if you had," said Sergeant Lamb.

"Explain that, please."

"I mean that no one saw you leave the hospital. And that the husband of the lady you were calling on was murdered at midnight."

I was a little astonished to note a faint but quite definite look of relief on Kenwood Ladd's face; it was nothing, however, that I can describe exactly. Just a barely perceptible loosening of the taut lines around his mouth, a quick, less carefully controlled gesture with which he lifted his cigarette. It struck me as singular that he appeared to be relieved at a statement which certainly carried with it the most unpleasant implications.

"Oh, of course," said Kenwood Ladd. "I rather expected that. Well, you can't get very far with it, Sergeant Lamb. I didn't murder Dr. Harrigan."

"Yeah?" said Sergeant Lamb. "Well, somebody did."

"I don't doubt it at all. And made a thorough job of it, from all reports."

His flippancy threatened the kindly feeling I was beginning to hold toward him. Afterward I knew it was a sort of defiance.

"Very thorough," said Dr. Kunce smoothly; he had been sitting like a graven image, his only motion those continually stroking fingers on his silky black beard and the movement of his veiled dark eyes. "All we want is an alibi, Ladd," he continued in a pleasant way. "Surely you can furnish that. You can see for yourself, it's merely a matter of form. They are obliged to inquire regarding everyone known to have been about the——"

"Scene of the crime?" finished Kenwood Ladd. "Well —I'll see what I can do."

"See here, now, don't you go fixing anything," said Sergeant Lamb, who had looked very doubtful at Dr. Kunce's idea of what constituted a mere matter of form and now became actively alarmed. "This is murder, you understand. Murder and abduction—well, murder, anyhow. We'll have no funny business. It's something more important than—getting into traffic jams."

Sergeant Lamb's brand of irony was rather strong. An odd little flush crept into Kenwood Ladd's face; it was attractive. You caught a glimpse of something nice and boyish under his modern mask of indifference. I think he knew of it and was just young enough to be annoyed thereby. He said sharply:

"I expected you'd try to hang something on me. Makes such excellent newspaper copy, doesn't it? The kind of stuff people like to read. Does it bring the efficiency of the police before a wider public?"

Dr. Kunce coughed softly and murmured: "Now, Ladd! Mere matter of form."

"That kind of talk doesn't get you any place, young fellow," said Sergeant Lamb severely. "And as far as that goes, *wasn't* you running around with another man's wife?"

"Oh, good God!" said Kenwood Ladd. "Not as you mean it, no," he added quietly.

CHAPTER VII

HE GOT up, strode to the window, and stood there for a moment, his hands jammed into his light tweed coat pockets. When he turned, the little flush was gone and his face was very white and rather desperately controlled.

"Well, how was it, then?" asked Sergeant Lamb, adding up his two's.

"Why—I've seen a lot of Mrs. Harrigan recently. I'd have no reason to deny it. I always see a lot of my clients. And probably I've been with Mrs. Harrigan more than I usually go about with a—client. I—well, I may as well tell you that building her house meant a lot to me."

"Financially, of course," interpolated Dr. Kunce smoothly.

Kenwood Ladd shot a quick look at the doctor's imperturbable face.

"Financially, of course. And professionally. But as it happens, I've been devilishly hard up lately."

"Well," said Sergeant Lamb slowly and somewhat skeptically, "do you know anything at all about this murder? Or about Peter Melady? Have you ever heard either Dr. Harrigan or his wife say anything that would lead you to think he was in danger? Had any enemies? Any enemies besides"—said Sergeant Lamb with a rhetorical pause—"besides Peter Melady?"

"Not a thing," replied Kenwood Ladd promptly.

"You and Dr. Harrigan were on good terms, you say?"

"Certainly."

"Miss Page to see you, Doctor," said the office girl from the doorway. She looked at Kenwood Ladd and patted her hair.

"Very well," said Dr. Kunce. "Do you wish to see Miss Page now, Sergeant? I don't think Mr. Ladd can help us any more just at present."

"I guess not," said Sergeant Lamb reluctantly. "But you stick around, young fellow. And see if you can't scrape up an alibi. But it's got to be a real one."

"Don't worry about me leaving town," said Kenwood Ladd somewhat grimly. "I haven't the money to get away. What's your concern in all this, Kunce? It's a new thing to see you in the character of a Sherlock."

Dr. Kunce stiffened.

"As resident doctor of Melady Memorial Hospital I am very deeply concerned," he said frigidly, and there was a little rustle and Nancy stood in the doorway.

Nancy is not beautiful. But somehow one has to remind one's self that she has not the classical requirements, so completely does she give the illusion of beauty. I don't know just where that illusion lies; whether it is in the softness of her bright hair and the way the light touches it to gold, or the grace of her slim body which is yet rather sturdy, or the smooth whiteness of her firm little chin below something rather special in the way of lips. Or it may be just the way she looks out of her eyes. Certainly she has always seemed to be the very essence of femininity; at least men seem to like to do things for her; to have an impulse to guard her from unreckoned dangers. And I remember once an interne wrote a poem to her which he called, not very originally, "Girl of My Dreams" and it began something like this: "The girl that all men dream of, 'Tis she, the girl I love" and went on like that for several pages. Someone found it and passed it gleefully around, with the result that the whole hospital was quoting the thing, much to Nancy's vexation and the interne's wounded embarrassment. But it's quite true that at the sight of Nancy there's usually a sort of recognizing look gets into a man's eyes; a look as if something inside him were saying: "There she is. Take a good look. You've been hoping to see her for a long time." It's respectful enough, but—well, men look at me respectfully, and it isn't at all the same look.

However, Kenwood Ladd appeared to be an exception to the general rule. He took one look at Nancy and seemed to have just remembered an important engagement elsewhere. That sounds abrupt but is exactly the impression he gave. He brushed past Nancy with the barest word of apology and closed the door smartly behind him and was gone.

"Oh," said Nancy rather breathlessly. Upon which Sergeant Lamb was at once moved to rise and say very gallantly:

"He's sort of upset, miss. Don't mind him."

"Indeed," said Nancy. "Did you wish to see me, Dr. Kunce?"

Dr. Kunce, as became a doctor, was another exception to Nancy's gift of being Nancy; so far as that goes he seemed to be entirely immune from any of the nurses' charms, which was as it should be. There is far less love-making in a hospital than the general public seems to think. It is difficult to grow sentimental over surgical dressings and temperature charts and digestive reactions. At the same time, it is true, there is something rather enticing about a nurse's severe white uniform and starchy little cap.

"Yes, Miss Page. We are making a detailed inquiry,

you know, and we want you to answer some questions. I
have asked Miss Keate to be present since she was so—
er—actively concerned in last night's affair. And—er—
Sergeant Lamb of the police."

"Oh," said Nancy again. "I—— How do you do?"

"Here's a chair, Miss Page."

Well, they asked her any number of questions, but
for the most part she simply corroborated, in so far as
she could, the story I had told them shortly after Dr.
Harrigan's body was found. Yes, she and Miss Keate
and Miss Ash had gone downstairs to midnight supper
at exactly twelve, she supposed, for that was when the
supper bell always rang. They had gone at once, upon
hearing the bell, leaving Ellen Brody alone in the wing
as was customary. Ellen was supposed to go downstairs
after the senior nurses had returned to get her supper,
but she didn't think she had last night.

"Why not?" asked Sergeant Lamb. "She had time,
didn't she, before Miss Keate found the body?"

"Ellen had had three bars of chocolate about eleven
o'clock," said Nancy briefly. "And anyway we were all—
well, very much concerned about the emergency operation which Dr. Harrigan was about to perform. None
of us understood it. I'm quite sure Ellen didn't go down
to supper at all."

"Go on," said Sergeant Lamb. "What next?"

Next, she thought, Miss Keate had gone up to the
fourth floor and she herself had hurried to Mrs. Melady.

"That's this Dione Melady?" said Sergeant Lamb.
"Why did you want to see her?"

Well, of course, I knew what Ellen had told and I
must say I felt a little anxious for Nancy's reply, particularly as I noted Sergeant Lamb's light blue eyes fas-

tened in a speculative fashion upon the soft little curls of bright hair under Nancy's cap.

"She is of a very nervous temperament," said Nancy without any hesitation at all. "I thought it likely she would be extremely alarmed about the operation."

"How would she know of it?" asked Sergeant Lamb.

Nancy did hesitate there. She looked white and tired and there were blue shadows under her eyes. But none of us looked fresh after such a night. She said:

"The family of a patient is always advised of any surgical work."

"You mean you told her?"

"Yes," said Nancy. I think only I felt that there was a sort of desperation in the admission. Her mouth set itself into soft straight lines, and there was something frightened back of the very determination with which she met Sergeant Lamb's pale gaze.

"You told her? In the middle of the night when you knew she was apt to get all upset about it?" asked Sergeant Lamb. "That don't look right to me."

"Miss Page was quite right in the matter," said Dr. Kunce at once. "Epecially in view of the highly irregular circumstances."

Sergeant Lamb leaned forward; I believe he thought to take Nancy by surprise.

"Miss Page, why did you say that someone must stop it and why did Mrs. Melady reply to you that it would be murder and that it was your fault?"

Well, I had to admit that I did not like the effect his sharp question had upon Nancy. Not even Sergeant Lamb, who knew her not at all, could have failed to see the apprehension that leaped into her eyes, and Dr. Kunce swept his long lashes upward to give her one swift, keen look.

"I don't"—said Nancy in a breathless way—"understand you."

"Oh, come now, Miss Page. Someone overheard your conversation with Mrs. Melady. Why did you say someone must stop the operation? What did you mean?"

"Why—why just what I said."

"Why did you say that?"

"Because Mrs. Melady became extremely nervous about it. She had objected to the operation all along, you know. She felt it was unsafe and she made it clear that she expected me to stop the thing. That's why she said it would be my fault if it were permitted to take place. A nurse usually agrees with a highly nervous patient and besides"—Nancy had become more composed—"besides, I really thought it ought to be stopped. I was sure Dr. Kunce would not approve." She stopped and added without any effect of overemphasis: "I felt he ought know of the entire circumstances at once."

"Quite right," said Dr. Kunce, his nose coming down over his beard approvingly.

"Still," said Sergeant Lamb, "it's funny Mrs. Melady said it would be murder. That's exactly what it was, you know. Now why should she have said murder?"

"But it was not Peter Melady who was murdered," murmured Dr. Kunce softly.

"Maybe so; maybe not," said Sergeant Lamb morosely. "I don't know yet as to that. But I do know Mrs. Melady said 'murder' and I want to know why." His pale blue eyes focused themselves with much suspicion upon Nancy, who lowered her eyes and said nothing. When Nancy lowers her eyes so her lashes make a soft dark line against her young cheek one has an almost irresistible impulse to defend her. I said at once and quite without my own volition:

"Mrs. Melady is apt to say almost anything, Sergeant Lamb."

And Dr. Kunce said:

"Yes, Sergeant Lamb. I shouldn't give anything Mrs. Melady said much weight. She is of a hysterical temperament. Apt to say ridiculously exaggerated things."

"H'm," said Sergeant Lamb, who was nobody's fool. "Still it's funny she said it would be murder and it was murder."

"But it was her father she feared for," I said impatiently. "She was afraid all along that the operation would be too much for his strength. And it was Dr. Harrigan who was murdered. I don't see that there is much connection between her hysterical objections to her father's undergoing an operation and the fact that Dr. Harrigan was found murdered. And to my mind Peter Melady's unexplained disappearance is of as much importance as Dr. Harrigan's murder. In all my experience I have never had a patient simply disappear. A man in his condition of health and in his night clothes can't have gone far. In fact, after all you've said about the hospital being locked up, I don't see how he can have got out of the hospital at all."

It appeared to be a troublesome point.

"We are leaving no stone unturned," said Sergeant Lamb, looking glumly down his pale nose. He had, I was to find, a large supply of stock phrases. Dr. Kunce gave me the look of a man who fears he's going to be nagged.

"We are doing everything possible to find him, Miss Keate," he assured me in a harassed way. "I agree with you entirely. It is an unprecedented situation so far as my experience goes. But——" he shrugged. "You see, I am helpless. All we can do is put the matter in the hands of the police. And for your information," he added firmly, "the hospital *was* locked. Every possible means of entrance and exit was locked as is our custom. We have made sure of that. And Peter Melady is *not* in the hospital. I, myself, have searched."

"Certainly, Dr. Kunce," I said at once. I am afraid of no man, but I know my duty as a nurse.

"Peter Melady," said Sergeant Lamb, his pale eyes reverting to the dampish-looking little curls about Nancy's face—"Peter Melady will be found if he's above the ground. What color is your hair, Miss Page?"

"What color—— Why—why, it's brown." Nancy looked somewhat startled and repeated: "Brown, I think. Light brown."

"You wouldn't call it yellow, now?" said Sergeant Lamb thoughtfully.

He reached inside his coat. I sat very still while he drew out a pillbox and slowly opened it, talking: "Your hair looks sort of yellow in this light. I guess it's blonde, anyway, isn't it, now, Miss——" He stopped abruptly. In fact, he choked. It was with considerable interest that I watched his pale eyes stare incredulously into the interior of the little box, his long, pale forefinger explore it diligently and his face become a bright geranium color. There was a small residue of some kind of white powder in the pillbox and it seemed to infuriate him. He blew violently into the box, sneezed, coughed, and whirled upon Dr. Kunce.

"You took that hair!"

Of course, Dr. Kunce said at once and very emphatically that he had not taken any hair and did not know what Sergeant Lamb meant by such an outrageous statement. Sergeant Lamb felt no reluctance at all in explaining exactly what he meant, and matters were becoming quite lively when the office girl knocked to say that the reporters were there again.

A reporter has a most interesting effect upon persons about to be interviewed. Dr. Kunce and Sergeant Lamb instantly and simultaneously became bland, calm, and harmonious. The guilty pillbox disappeared and Dr. Kunce rose, smoothing his Vandyke and glancing into the mirror beside the door, and dismissing Nancy and me in the pleasantest of fashion. The reporters—there were three of them, all youngish—stood aside for us to pass. I have always attributed the fact that we were haunted with reporters from then on as much to Nancy's appearance at just that moment as to anything else. I am probably wrong about this, for the events at Melady Memorial certainly were of a nature to fill the news columns of B——'s papers for some time to come; still, I recall very distinctly the fact that not one of them stirred until Dr. Kunce said rather sharply: "Well—will you come in, gentlemen?"—and Nancy disappeared into the corridor.

At any rate, Sergeant Lamb had not thought of me at all in connection with the vanished gold hair. I glanced at Nancy's hair as we climbed the stairs (it was a weary climb but no one seemed to wish to use the elevator), and wished I could be sure that the hair I had come by was not hers.

Curious that she said nothing to me of Sergeant Lamb's inquiry. Curious that she did not offer to talk of the tragedy of the previous night. But perhaps she was thinking the same thing of my own silence.

"Hot," she said as we reached the second floor. "These uniforms are terrible in such weather. I'm sure you've got a corset on, Sarah; I should think you would perish. I've got practically nothing under my uniform and still I'm no cooler. If they didn't put so much starch in these dresses . . ." Her voice trailed away into nothing and presently resumed: "I'm going to get some sleep. I couldn't rest this morning. See you at six. Dr. Kunce says for us to share night duty for a time—with Ellen, of course. And there'll be Lillian Ash in the wing, too. Sarah, do you dread night duty?"

"Why, yes," I admitted. "Who wouldn't! But nothing will happen. It will be all right. Lightning doesn't strike twice in the same place. It will be all right."

She looked at me sombrely for a moment.

"I hope so, I'm sure," she said and drew her hand sharply away from a chance contact with the stair rail. "Such a terrible day," she said somewhat breathlessly. "Everything you touch is sort of—sticky. Like blood."

"Why, Nancy!"

"I didn't mean to say that," she said in a sort of whisper. "It's—I'm tired. Silly. It's so hot."

With that she whirled away down the corridor toward the nurses' dormitory in the south L and I followed. And it wasn't until I had reached my own room and looked in the wardrobe and under the bed and locked the door that I overcame the feeling of extreme discomfort up the small of my back.

I saw neither Sergeant Lamb nor Dr. Kunce again until evening. I spent the intervening hours sitting in my room, the door securely locked and the lavender hot-water bag, a pillbox with a blonde hair in it, and a small cork on my lap. But I was not in a state of mind even to attempt to draw any conclusions. I could only go over and over the events of the previous night in a weary, incredulous circle. And I dreaded the coming hours of night duty in that silent, hot, night-lighted wing.

I believe it was then, too, that I first became conscious

of that feeling of being in danger, of being continually watched and reckoned with, which was not to leave me during the whole of the dreadful affair. Which was, indeed, to become more and more definite. I scoffed at it at first: I was letting my nerves run away with me; I was overwrought; I had had a shock; the heat and the fatigue were making me fanciful. Thus I was to argue sensibly with myself. But that singular feeling of being under surveillance persisted. If I walked alone down a dimly lit corridor, I felt that there were footsteps following me. My skin would crawl and my neck muscles twitch, but when I would finally turn to look, there was never anything there. Except once or twice when I imagined that I saw something vanish around the corner of the stairs or into a room; in each case it was likely only a nurse going about her legitimate business.

When I went down that dark old stairway it was usually with a panicky certainty that something was back of me, following me, step by step. And in the narrow, poorly lit, and often deserted hall of the nurses' dormitory my fears became more definite and terrifying. And it began that afternoon when, as I sat there on the bed, staring absently at a spot opposite me which happened to be the glass door knob leading to the corridor, the door knob began to turn. It turned softly and slowly, but I'm sure it turned. There'd been no preliminary footsteps and no one called to me. When I finally got to the door and unlocked and opened it there was no one there. No one in sight anywhere.

Naturally I found myself dreading night duty, but any amount of dread could not stay its arrival.

The day nurses were frankly glad to be relieved, and we found the wing quiet and orderly. It seemed almost impossible that the routine of the hospital could go along so smoothly on the very spot, almost, where so few hours ago a man had been murdered. But, of course, it did. We have a habit of discipline; the routine of baths and diet trays and clean linens and dusting and bed-making and charts and doctors' calls carries itself along. But it would be too much to say that things were quite as usual, for they were not. The seething undercurrent of excitement and terror had become more urgent with the coming of the night. The old walls themselves brooded with the secret they held. Nurses and patients alike were nervous and uneasy, and some of the nurses were openly afraid at the prospect of the long, hot hours of night along those shadowy corridors and darkened sick rooms. The night air was heavy and humid and the summer darkness fell like a black, secretive mist, creeping along open spaces and into corners and laden with heat.

The head nurse for the day relinquished her keys to me with a sigh.

"Dr. Kunce said you were to resume duty as superintendent, with Miss Page assisting you for the time being," she said, and as I nodded, continued: "I suppose he meant until your patient turns up again. Well, if you ask me, he won't be back. Not if he can help it. Everybody thinks he killed Dr. Harrigan. Maybe it was in self-defense." She glanced down the corridor and shivered, although there was a little ridge of perspiration along her forehead and her uniform was limp and damp. "I don't envy you night duty," she said. "It's been bad enough during the daytime, but you couldn't pay me enough to coax me to stay here at night. With the elevator right there."

"If you think Peter Melady killed Dr. Harrigan," I said waspishly, "then there's nothing to be afraid of, for Peter Melady has vanished as completely as if the earth had opened and swallowed him. Are you afraid of ghosts!"

I had spoken in derision and was not prepared for her reply.

"Yes," she said, "I am. And I wouldn't go into Peter Melady's room to-night for anything in the world. I'm psychic," she concluded simply.

"Psychic fiddlesticks!" I said, "You're scared."

She gave me a look of cold rebuke and changed the subject.

"Mrs. Melady has been in a tantrum most of the day, as you can see by her chart. Here are the orders. I think you'll find everything is all right, but it's been a bad day. Upset, you know. Police searching Mr. Melady's room and talking to Mrs. Harrigan and Mrs. Melady and even Miss Ash. I suppose they questioned you, too. And they said not to clean Peter Melady's room. As if I would if I could get out of it!" She pushed her cap back. "Mrs. Harrigan has smoked exactly three packages of cigarettes. Well, I'm going, thank heaven." At the stairway she paused, looked over her shoulder at me, hesitated, and finally returned.

"I wouldn't take any chances about anything to-night, if I were you, Miss Keate," she said forgivingly. "Evil has been let loose here. Hatred and strife. Murder. They exist as separate and individual forces, you know. They hang over the place where they've been active. Murder begets murder." There was a simplicity of conviction in her manner that was exceedingly unpleasant. She straightened her cap again. "In all probability, however, if murder had been directed toward you it would have reached you last night. Of course, these forces get tangled up sometimes—are misdirected. But mind what I say, *murder is walking in this corridor right now!*"

With which dubious reassurance and a sort of sibylline look over her white shoulder she left me, her white cap bobbing downward and out of sight.

I turned to find Ellen at my elbow. Her eyes were nearly popping out of their sockets.

"Oh, my gracious me, Miss Keate! Did you hear what she said! It isn't true, is it? Murder can't just go walking around all by itself, can it?"

I opened my lips with the intention of telling Ellen not to be a fool. Instead I heard myself saying soberly:

'I don't know, I'm sure." And was only brought to my senses by Ellen's turning a faint yellow-green and clutching at my arm and demanding that the police search the wing again.

"Nonsense, Ellen. All they've done all day is search the hospital. Stop gibbering. 301's light is on; you'd better see what he wants."

There was after all something sporting about Ellen. She gave me a rather wild look but rolled up her cuffs grimly and sped down the corridor in the direction of the small red light. Privately I reflected that any number of policemen could not get their clutches on the impalpable thing that actually did seem to brood over that wing. The door to the elevator shaft was black and the door to Peter Melady's room was black and the June bugs attracted by the light were beginning to bang at the screen back of me and there was not a breath of air to be had.

Well, there would not be much work to be done that night, with Nancy and me and Ellen all on duty and Lillian Ash taking care of the only patient we then had who required very particular care. I remember thinking that as I sat down to glance over the charts. I was never more mistaken in my life.

I had not any more than got into the intricacies of Dione Melady's chart, which gave every evidence of it having been a large day in Dione's life, when Mrs. Harrigan's light went on with a vicious little click.

Her door was open with the green baize screen adjusted so she could see into the corridor. The night light was on over her bed, her black hair pushed back from her white face, her nightgown extremely diaphanous, and a magazine lay face downward on the sheet.

"Good heavens, it's hot in here," she said irritably, her heavy black eyebrows drawn together. She looked her age and more that night; there were fine lines around her eyes and a sort of sunken look under her cheek bones. "Haven't you a cooler room? I suppose they are all alike to-night. But I want something cool to drink. And someone to fan me."

"I can get you an electric fan," I suggested.

"I don't want an electric fan. They annoy me. Send that student nurse in to fan me."

"Miss Brody is busy, Mrs. Harrigan. Wouldn't you like a special nurse for a few days?"

She gave me a black look.

"I don't want a special nurse either—listening and watching and snooping into my own affairs. I'll tell you exactly what I want and when I want it."

I didn't doubt that. But it did not become me to say so; one of the trials of being a nurse is that you must so often soothe when you feel like smacking.

"It's hot everywhere," I said. "I'll send you in something cool to drink."

"Send me some ginger ale," she said. "And you needn't say there isn't any because my husband"—she did falter there, but only for a second, and she repeated the word coolly and with a certain defiance—"my husband had some sent in for me and there's a lot left. Unless your nurses have been drinking it."

At the door she called me back.

"These sheets are like a Turkish bath." She moved restlessly on the pillows. The motion brought her face into bright relief and the fine, sharp lines about her eyes were more clearly perceptible. I could never understand the aquamarine depths in Ina Harrigan's eyes. Instead of appearing shallow as light-colored eyes so often do, they were strangely limpid and knowing and secretive and yet perfectly expressionless in their clear green-blue. They actually had the color and the unfathomable look of the sea. She affected aquamarines in jewels, I remember, and a little heap of jewelry, long earrings, a heavy bracelet or two, and several rings that I suppose she had stripped off on account of the heat lay incongruously on the white porcelain top of the bedside table and sent out pale green-blue flashes. Certainly she was decorative but I myself prefer something a little less exotic and more healthy-looking. Though as to health I doubt if Ina Harrigan had ever had a day's illness in her life; her broken arm was sheer accident, of course, and bad temper. She groped with the unbandaged hand for a cigarette out of a nearly depleted package of Chesterfields that lay near the little heap of glittering jewels, asked me to hold a match for her, which I did with as poor a grace as I could contrive, and said:

"Blow out that match! You are singeing my nose. Have those police gone?"

"I believe so."

"What a day they have given me!" She took a quick puff or two, narrowed her eyes, flecked a shred of tobacco from her deeply crimson mouth, and added casually but with a sharp glance at me: "Are there no visitors to-night?"

So that was what she wanted.

"No, Mrs. Harrigan. No one except Mr. Courtney Melady. Dr. Kunce has permitted no visiting to-day."

Which was true. There were hordes of morbidly minded people who appeared to have picked up a newspaper, read about the murder, and immediately bethought themselves of some acquaintance whom they could visit who was then a patient in Melady Memorial Hospital. One of the minor annoyances of those days was the way in which we were beseiged with visitors wandering in and telephone calls.

"So Dr. Kunze says no visitors," remarked Ina Harrigan. "Well, if anyone calls to see me this evening, I insist upon seeing him. Dr. Kunze can go to the devil with his orders and you can tell him I said so."

"With pleasure, Mrs. Harrigan," I said blandly and left. I met Ellen in the corridor and sent her to the refrigerator in the diet kitchen for Mrs. Harrigan's ginger ale.

It was just then that Dr. Kunce and Sergeant Lamb rounded the corner of the stairway and approached me. They had both cast aside their coats but looked no cooler.

"How is Mrs. Melady?" asked Dr. Kunce at once.

"About the same, I believe."

"About the same," repeated Sergeant Lamb dubiously. "Well, we'd better try to talk to her anyway. We haven't got anything out of her yet. Eh, Dr. Kunze? But I can't say I hope for much. Not if she gets to carrying on like she did this morning. Say, isn't there some way you can quiet her down a little?"

"There is not," said Dr. Kunce wearily. "Will you

come with us, Miss Keate? Mrs. Melady needs quite a little attention, you know. How is everything going?" He walked to the chart desk, glanced rapidly through the charts, frowned over Dione Melady's, nodded over the others, and asked rather abruptly if Mrs. Harrigan had given me any message for him.

I resisted an evil impulse to give her message literally and said merely that she wanted to see any caller who might come that evening.

"Oh, certainly," said Dr. Kunce. "Under the circumstances we must make an exception of Mrs. Harrigan. Her lawyer may be calling. He's making the—er—arrangements for her. Try to make things go as smoothly as possible in that quarter, Miss Keate. It's an extremely unfortunate situation."

I went down to 301 to tell Nancy to let any caller for Mrs. Harrigan come up, and then followed Dr. Kunce and Sergeant Lamb into Dione Melady's room. I was just in time to hear her spirited denials of knowing anything at all about her father's disappearance and her equally spirited demands to be let alone. Dr. Kunce, his silky composure somewhat ruffled, was about to withdraw when she suddenly sat up in bed.

"Where is the Chinese snuff-bottle?" she cried. "Find that, if you must find something. Did you search his room?"

"We searched Mr. Melady's room, of course," said Dr. Kunce. "What do you mean? What bottle? And what has it to do with your father's disappearance?"

"The Chinese snuff-bottle," she flashed angrily. "The blue lapis bottle. The formula for Slæpan was in it!"

And as no one spoke for a moment she added rather sulkily:

"Court didn't want you to know; he said if it was

known that it was gone everyone would start looking for it and perhaps somebody would find and steal it. But I think the police ought to know so they can look for it. It's very valuable, you know."

"The ether's at the bottom of it! Just as I said," cried Sergeant Lamb. "Do you think somebody stole the formula?"

"How should I know?" said Dione, still sulky, and flatly refused to say any more.

I believe that in view of her disclosure they again and very thoroughly searched Peter Melady's room. At any rate they lingered in his room for some time; it was exactly ten o'clock when they finally emerged, for I happened to be in the corridor and saw them go down the stairs. There was a look about Sergeant Lamb's back which led me to think he had not been successful in discovering any particular clue. But it was clear to me, of course, that the Slæpan formula's having been hidden in the missing snuff-bottle gave a new and highly significant view to the whole affair. To my own knowledge there were a number of people who might conceivably wish to get possession of that formula. But even so there were not many—not in fact, one—whom I could imagine doing murder for it.

After Nancy had asked Mr. Ladd to leave—he had, it developed, arrived during our brief interview with Dione, his arms full of flowers and magazines. And I remember how promptly he left at her request and how white and grim his face looked under the chart-desk light as he started down the stairway—after, as I say, he had gone, and Dr. Kunce and Sergeant Lamb had gone and we had got our patients toothbrushed and bathed and rubbed with alcohol and settled for the night, things were very quiet. We had been a little late that night, and the rest of the hospital had already sunk into its heavy slumbrous silence. Ellen and Nancy and I came and went, doing quietly what was to be done, our skirts whispering along the shadowy corridor and our rubber heels making soft little pads of sound along the rubber floor runner. Our patients were a little restless and uneasy, but I think that was owing to the heat.

Eleven o'clock came and passed and then twelve with the faint sound of the midnight supper bell. We took turns, I remember, going down to supper; Miss Ash and Nancy went while I stayed with Ellen, and upon their return Miss Ash remained in the corridor with Nancy until Ellen and I got back on duty again. Lillian Ash looked extremely haggard; her face was flabby, her heavy powder a pinkish paste, and her hair, she complained, would not stay in curl.

"Another day of this heat will kill me," she said. "Didn't that young Ladd come to call on Mrs. Harrigan to-night?"

"Yes."

"Not waiting long, is she?" remarked Lillian Ash. "Nor grieving much. I wonder—did the police find out anything to-day?"

"I don't know," I said. "If they had, I'd not be apt to know it."

She gave me a thoughtful look.

"There's not much goes on around here that you miss," she said with none too flattering an implication, and disappeared into her patient's room.

One o'clock came and two and it was yet hot. The trolley over on Euclid Avenue had stopped running long ago, and it was very quiet. 302 had awakened and turned restless, and Nancy was in his room at the far end of the corridor wrapping him in sheets rung out in tepid water, with the door closed to prevent drafts. And Ellen, too, had vanished into some sick room, where she was probably fanning an uneasy patient.

A woman must have employment for her hands; otherwise she is apt to think. As I sat there at the chart desk, watching the corridor from force of habit, my thoughts naturally turned to the ugly affair of the previous night. Or rather they did not turn that way, for it already fully occupied my mind; even when I was busiest it seemed that only one part of me was intent upon what I was doing. The other, the inner me, was going in rather erratic and certainly terrifying circles. Indeed, it would have been impossible not to be continually aware of—well, of that dark elevator door, of the long shadowy reaches of bare corridor with black spaces for open sickroom doors. Of its emptiness. Of my patient who had vanished so mysteriously, so inexplicably. Of Dr. Harrigan's dead face. Of the knife. Of those bloody heel prints. Of the silence in the hospital.

It was so strangely still. A stillness that held a sort of violence.

Again that feeling of being watched came upon me, so that I looked all about me, searching the shadows of the blank doorways, the dimness of the long corridor, the black corners, the dark secretive well of the old stairway. I saw nothing and shrugged away that sixth sense which was trying to warn me. Strange how we civilized people fight our instincts: call them nerves and such like.

Impatiently I rose, went to the diet kitchen, and opened a bottle of ginger ale. I don't think it was one of Ina Harigan's. The drink was ice cold and very bubbly and stung my throat. I was no cooler but I felt more normal. As if I'd conquered a danger.

And just as I took a long, freer breath a large June

bug which had managed to find its way into the hospital and up to the lighted diet kitchen thudded with a nerve-shattering bang against the top of the refrigerator, righted itself before I could hit at it with the bottle opener, and *drove straight for my hair!*

It clawed and twisted with its horrible brown legs and buzzed in a very frenzy, and I suppose I was in a sort of frenzy, too, for I remember fighting to get it out, pulling at my cap and hair, gasping for breath.

Then I knew that someone was screaming. Someone in the east wing was screaming. It was a high-pitched scream which stopped all at once as if it had been choked off.

I suppose I dropped my frantic hands so that the June bug released itself somehow, I don't know. But I was in the corridor. And Lillian Ash was pointing and crying shrilly:

"In Peter Melady's room! In Peter Melady's room!"

I was conscious of Ellen and Nancy and Lillian Ash crowding after me as I snapped on the light and hurried into the room and stopped.

Dione Melady was lying in a huddle of mauve chiffon on the floor exactly at our feet. Her face was purple, her tongue hanging out, her eyes bulging horribly. But she was gasping raucously and still alive.

CHAPTER VIII

THE police came at once and searched the place and found precisely no one and nothing out of the way except that the screen to the window which in our east wing opens onto the fire escape was open. And since I myself knew that no one had escaped that way, since I would certainly have encountered him in the corridor as I hurried from the diet kitchen, and since Ellen and Nancy and Lillian Ash each denied having unlocked it, it appeared to have no particular significance. I was inclined to call it accident.

No one had seen any intruder; no one appeared to know anything of the business, and as we had only Dione's tale to go on and it was hysterical and almost unintelligible, it is perhaps not so surprising that the police made no progress. I believe they did attempt a search for the Chinese snuff-bottle, but looking for that tiny blue thing in the hospital, where there might be a thousand places to hide it if one so wished, was rather like looking for a needle in a haystack.

It was, I remember, the work of only a few moments to get Dione onto her own bed and get air into her lungs and apply restoratives. I sent Ellen to telephone for Dr. Kunce, but he was asleep, the office girl said; at least she was obliged to ring the telephone in his small suite of rooms several times before he replied. I suppose, too, he stopped to get into some clothing and call the police, and all in all we had completely restored Dione to her senses by the time he arrived on the third floor. Her tongue was already so swollen she could scarcely talk, and there were cruel marks on her throat where those strangling fingers had gripped it. I looked carefully at the bruises and thought: "Two hands did that. It took two hands. It was not, then, Ina Harrigan."

"She'll be all right," said Dr. Kunce. "It's mostly nervous shock we'll have to guard against."

Somewhat to my disapproval he ordered me to give her a mild hypodermic of morphine and sat there, his stethoscope dangling from his hands, and watched me give it. Dione groaned as I thrust the needle into her arm, and almost immediately the morphine made her momentarily talkative, as it does so many people, and we could not make her stop, although the words were blurred and almost indistinguishable.

"I found the snuff-bottle," she said at once. "It was under the mattress on Father's bed."

"But it couldn't have been," said Dr. Kunce, losing his silky composure for a second or two. "It couldn't have been. We looked there just to-night."

"It was," insisted Dione, gasping. Her story was faltering, but we were able to piece it together and it was substantially this:

She had felt positive that the Chinese snuff-bottle was still hidden in her father's room. He had laughed and had shown her and Court how cleverly he had rolled the thin paper on which the formula was carefully written and slipped it into the snuff-bottle so that the paper lay tightly against the oval hollow of the small bottle. And when they both objected, saying that if that was the only copy he had, as it was, it ought go in a vault or in his own office safe, he had assured them—angrily, I gathered —that he knew what he was doing. That it was safer in his possession. From Peter Melady's manner of speaking, she, Dione, felt sure he had determined upon some hiding place within the room, and she felt positive that he would not have permitted himself to be taken out of that room by Dr. Harrigan before he had hidden the snuff-bottle.

"He knew Dr. Harrigan hated him. And would have given anything to possess the Slæpan formula," said Dione mumblingly and beginning to speak with the peculiarly cheerful deliberation of one who is just getting under the influence of morphine.

Anyway, she had gone to his room, certain the police had overlooked the snuff-bottle. And they had. She had found it almost at once. And just as she got it into her hands someone must have reached inside the door and snapped off the electric-light switch. She just knew that there was someone in the doorway and that the light went out. And then someone had——

At this point we were obliged to hold her hands and tell her she was quite safe, that everything was all right, that she'd only had a fright.

And through it she insisted wildly but with increasing drowsiness that she did not know who her assailant was. That she had just caught the motion of someone in the doorway. Just as she drifted off to sleep she said a peculiar thing:

"And such a queer smell. Smell. Right beside me. Right—under—my—nose—right—under . . ." And that was all.

It was, quite naturally, after the brutal and murderous assault upon Dione Melady that panic actually entered Melady Memorial Hospital. It was more than panic. It was stark terror. And I say it was a natural development because it proved to us that the murderer of Dr.

Harrigan was still about and had managed to get in and out of a locked and bolted hospital. Either that, or, which was worse, it was someone of our own small hospital world, someone free to come and go at his will. I say it proved to us that Dr. Harrigan's murderer was still about; that is not quite correct for, of course, we could not be sure that whoever it was who came so near to killing Dione Melady was also the person who murdered Dr. Harrigan, but that was the natural conclusion. It was certainly more likely that there was only one person who had access to the hospital and was wandering about with murderous intentions than that there were two. And I don't know which was the more terrifying thing to believe; that is, whether it was someone of our own hospital world, or whether there was an unknown way in and out of the hospital which made the murderer free to come and go. (It is true that, the night Dione came so near death, he might have entered by the fire escape and that unbolted screen, but I knew he had not escaped that way. And he certainly had escaped.) Some of the nurses thought one way, some the other. There were times when I was inclined to both opinions and that simultaneously. The newspapers took the stand of a homicidal maniac for an issue before reverting to Peter Melady, thus occasioning much excitement in the city.

But in the hospital there was sheer terror.

It was after that, too, that I began to take a more active hand in the matter. I felt that Sergeant Lamb was willing but slow; had there been no danger—— But there was. The murderous assault upon Dione proved that there was definite and active danger in the old hospital which was the more menacing because its source was unknown. I longed for Lance O'Leary's arrival, but that was still three days away, and much can happen in three days. And nights. I can't say that I accomplished much; still I added my bit to that strangely accumulating dénouement.

I say there was terror in the hospital and that is exactly the truth of it. An old hospital such as Melady Memorial is full of shadowy turns and passages and corners and narrow storerooms, and I can't begin to express the feeling of uncertainly and apprehension that gripped us as we went about our work, entering the various rooms, passing along those endless corridors and up and down the wide old stairway, going to the basement for our meals and the dormitory for our hours of rest, and feeling that at any moment one of us might be the next victim. The nurses fell into the habit of doing as much work as possible in pairs, and I think none of us opened and entered an unoccupied room alone if we could avoid it.

It was worse for the night nurses, although the day nurses had to bear most of the brunt of the inevitable commotion and inquiries. But the night nurses had the long hot nights of darkness and fear; and those stark dreary hours between three and five o'clock in the morning when vitality is at the lowest, when the game doesn't seem worth the struggle, when weary souls ebb with the night.

And Dr. Kunce could not, as he wished, double the number of nurses on duty, owing to so many graduate nurses of the city being out of town on vacations. Moreover those left on the register suddenly developed urgent reasons for not taking any work just then. Indeed, it was as much as we could do to keep our present staff from becoming seriously depleted; Dr. Kunce was obliged to take firm measures, and there was a prompt and quite correct rumor to the effect that any nurse who found it necessary to leave at that time would never enter Melady Memorial in a professional capacity again. I daresay the only reason the hordes of anxious relatives who kept the telephones busy permitted the members of their families to remain as patients was that Melady Memorial Hospital is really the only hospital of importance and prestige in B——.

It was after four o'clock in the morning before we managed to get things quiet again. We nurses had been obliged to search the sick rooms ourselves, which was no pleasant task, but, of course, we could not have policemen blundering about in the sick rooms again, frightening and annoying our patients. Especially in the plutocratic east wing.

And some of our patients had heard Dione's scream and the resultant commotion, and we had to draw largely upon our inventive powers to soothe them. But with dawn things were normal again, except for various policemen who were still in the east wing and the occasional appearance of Sergeant Lamb's pale, weary, harassed-looking face.

It was in that hour that I began the notes which, Mr. O'Leary has been good enough to say, were such a help later on. I don't know as to that. I do know that they were the result of much thought, of much arguing with myself anent this or that possibility, of much putting down something which might be evidence and then striking it off as further thought proved it to be no evidence at all —and of many tedious lines of reasoning which, in the end, left me as baffled as when I had begun. Finally, however, I did arrive at a sort of chart, written on the back of a blank temperature chart taken from a pad on the chart desk.

On it I made a list of those people who, chiefly because

of their presence in the east wing near or at the time of the murder, might conceivably include the murderer of Dr. Harrigan. I did not even attempt to solve the minor mystery of the very recent assault upon Dione. Under each name I placed every item that, on going over and over the events of the last two days and nights, I was able to recall which might have some bearing on the case. I am not ordinarily of a suspicious turn of mind and I was aghast on reading my notes to find the curious bits which I had dug from my memory and whose connection with the murder was pure surmise on my part.

I give my notes almost as I made them; erratic, not particularly logical, unintelligible to anyone who did not know the whole story of the affair as I knew it. After some thought I began with Lillian Ash and I believe it was under her name that I finally accumulated the most thought-provoking items. For Lillian Ash was in the east wing. Lillian Ash had left supper earlier than the other nurses and thus might have had greater opportunity to secure that amputating knife and kill Dr. Harrigan.

But he was seen alive at 12:18, only two minutes before I myself returned to the third floor, and I had seen nothing which would tend to incriminate Lillian Ash.

Why had she looked so frightened when I came upon her there in the corridor just before we had gone together to supper? She had been looking at Dr. Harrigan; evidently they had met in the hall. Her interest in the Harrigans had always been rather keen, as I recalled it; but I could not recall her having nursed for Dr. Harrigan. Was it possible she had known them at some previous time? I put down, "Possible connection with Harrigans," and went on.

The next item was "Gold hair," with a question mark

after it. While I feared that hair was Nancy's, feared it
so strongly that I dared not turn it over to the police to
be analyzed, still it could have belonged to Lillian Ash,
so far as I knew.

She was in the corridor when Teuber had tried to open
the elevator door and had looked terribly ill and shaken;
quite as if she'd just had a blow or some kind of shock.
And she had tried to keep him from pulling at the elevator door. *Had it, then, been at the third floor all the
time?* It might have hung there, since the light was
turned off, without any of us knowing it. (Here again
developed one of those tedious long lines of surmise regarding that puzzling affair of the elevator, which took
me exactly nowhere.)

Lillian Ash was left alone in the corridor while Teuber
wheeled his truck away down the west corridor toward
the freight elevator (which I assumed at that time, but
assumed correctly because there is only the freight elevator besides the main elevator). True, she could not
have had more than two, or at the most three, minutes
alone. Still it was possible that she could have stabbed
him during those moments, provided, of course, that Dr.
Harrigan had had no warning of her intention.

And there, again, was a stumbling block. I could not
imagine Dr. Harrigan simply standing still and permitting himself to be killed. People don't do that. But, of
course, it had been dark in the elevator if the doors were
closed; he might not have seen the knife, since someone
—the murderer, in all likelihood—had turned off the
red light in the elevator.

Well, then, provided that she had managed the opportunity, she might possibly have killed him during those
few moments, or even during my first trip to the operating room, when I was absent from the third floor for a

longer time. But Ellen and Nancy had both been very near the elevator; Nancy, indeed, had been in Dione Melady's room with the door open, and had thus been in a position to note anyone entering or emerging from the elevator. And she had, apparently, seen nothing out of the way.

It was about then that I began to perceive that, while any murder is bad enough, a murder in an elevator is peculiarly troublesome. If we could have fixed definitely the floor at which the murder occurred we might have come closer to the truth. As it was, we knew well enough just where Dr. Harrigan was killed, but we could not discover where the elevator had been and that, according to my notion, was of considerable significance. As it was, it was extremely difficult to know just whom to include in that list of suspects I was attempting to make.

Since I had begun with Lillian Ash, I continued with the other nurses, Nancy and Ellen. Under Ellen's name I could only write: "Opportunity as to time and securing knife, presence in wing at time of assault upon Dione Melady; no motive." I could think of nothing more and felt, indeed, that there was some absurdity in thinking of round-eyed Ellen Brody in such a connection. Under Nancy's name I placed the same items, for while she had returned from supper with me, she was, of course, in and about the corridor during ten of those important twelve minutes. And there was that annoying gold hair which I feared had belonged to Nancy, and also, after some very sober thought, I added: "Interest in snuff-bottle, and anxiety as to resultant police inquiry." I added the last item dubiously, and must say at once that I did not actually suspect Nancy of murder; I included her in my list of suspects only because she was present, and honesty compelled me to add those items.

Then there were Dione Melady and Ina Harrigan.
Against both of them I could place "Opportunity."

True, her having been so nearly murdered herself
would appear to exclude Dione; still, she might certainly
have wanted to dispose of Dr. Harrigan if she felt that
it would be murder to permit him to operate on her
father. Could she have felt so deeply about the matter
as to commit murder herself to prevent the operation?
She did not, truly, appear to be a woman capable of such
an extremity of filial devotion; she was, however, of an
irrational and ill-balanced temperament. She was anxious
about the snuff-bottle but that was no more than natural
when one considered the extreme value of the formula
she knew it concealed. There were also—here, too, my
memory woke to life—those whispers coming from behind the screen in Dione's room. Those strangely vehement whispers which had actually ushered in the ugly and
terrible drama. I recalled perfectly the few words I had
heard. Someone had said: "I can't. Don't ask me," and
someone else had said: "You must do it. He will be
murdered, I tell you. Murdered." And it was not apt
to be pure coincidence that within a few hours a man
was murdered. In light of what had actually occurred the
whispers took on a sinister meaning; who had possessed
that prescience? One of the speakers must have been
Dione.

There was, too, that later conversation between Dione
and Nancy which took place during my frenzied search
for my patient, and which Nancy had explained as
smoothly to Dr. Kunce and Sergeant Lamb. I put aside
my distinct impression that Nancy had been a bit more
adroit than her simple explanation demanded, as well as
the indubitable fright in her eyes when she was questioned. If Dr. Kunce and Sergeant Lamb were satisfied,

why not I? But the earlier conversation, those vehement whispers earlier in the night, troubled me more than a little.

After some rather anxious thought I jotted simply: "Presence in wing, whispers, emotional temperament, and objection to operation"—and returned to Ina Harrigan. As the items on the chart multiplied themselves I began to feel that either I was of a singularly suspicious turn of mind or there were deep-lying ramifications of the grim problem that faced us which would not be easy to discover and bare.

I judged Ina Harrigan to have the psychological capacity for cold and deliberate murder. That is a rather dreadful thing to say but is quite true. However, I did not enter my opinion of her mental make-up on my growing notes. However much we may think we know of psychology there are twists and turns in anyone's mind which are simply inexplicable. No one runs continually true to form. To everyone come exceptions. Especially if the emotions are involved. I may be old-fashioned in this respect; still I have viewed life for a number of years and not, I think, blindly. And my opinion is, to put it briefly and colloquially: you never can tell.

So I did not make a note of Ina Harrigan's emotional capacities; I did say that she was known to quarrel with Dr. Harrigan. Of Kenwood Ladd's frequent visits I said nothing beyond the bare fact; I had no reason at all to suppose that Ina Harrigan might wish to dispose of one husband in order to get another.

Which brought me to Kenwood Ladd's possible presence in the hospital at the time of the murder. And after Kenwood Ladd I also wrote, "Court Melady, Teuber, Dr. Kunce, and Peter Melady," and sat back looking at the array of names. There were also the nurses who had immediate access to the elevator on the second floor, but I was inclined to believe that Dr. Kunce's checking of the whereabouts of the nurses had been thorough and accurate. So I felt that I had included everyone who might be at all connected with the affair by reason of, primarily, his or her possible presence. And after the assault upon Dione that very night, it did seem that the business was concentrating itself in a rather grisly fashion about my own east wing.

After each of those names I wrote: "Presence in wing at some time during night." After Kenwood Ladd and Court Melady I wrote simply: "No proof that he left hospital before midnight"; after Jacob Teuber's name I wrote: "Presence on third floor during *twelve minutes.*" I did not need to say what particular twelve minutes. And it was just then that it occurred to me that, so far as I knew, he was the only man in the east wing corridor during that important twelve-minute period. And somehow I much preferred to believe that a man's hand had driven that knife into Dr. Harrigan's heart. Too, Jacob Teuber knew where the instruments were kept, and he knew every detail of routine in the hospital. He lived in the hospital and as easily as anyone might have managed to get through the halls unobserved and to the east wing and could have so nearly strangled Dione. And even then I felt that Dione's assailant and the murderer of Dr. Harrigan were identical.

True, I could not imagine thin, young Jacob Teuber setting out upon a career of violence. Especially during the summer months when he was almost exclusively occupied with his asthma. I say "his asthma" because he habitually referred to the affliction as "my" asthma as if it were a particular brand of the disease. When it was at its worst there was even a quality of pride in his wheezy voice. But as I have said, you never can tell, so down went Jacob Teuber's name along with the rest, and I resolved to discover just how long he had been in the charity ward, and what motive he might have had for stabbing Dr. Harrigan.

But there was the difficulty of discovering a motive in every case. Especially in regard to Dr. Kunce, who certainly was in and about the hospital and might conceivably have slipped past the office girl without being seen and got to the elevator and thence to the fourth floor and the amputating knife and—his victim. It was possible, of course, but not at all likely. The night office girl has unusually sharp eyes and a keen curiosity about other people's affairs. And I could not believe that Dr. Kunce, resident head of Melady Memorial Hospital, would do murder. Jacob Teuber, for all his asthma and youth and inoffensiveness, was much the more likely suspect of the two.

I suppose it was thinking of Jacob Teuber and his ready attempt to get the elevator for me that recalled Lillian Ash to my mind.

Lillian Ash and—— I must have made some sudden motion or even spoken, for the two policemen who were still about both turned and looked suspiciously at me. I coughed vigorously and folded up my chart and put it carefully into the capacious pocket of my uniform.

I was suddenly as positive as I could ever be of anything that Lillian Ash had wiped the fingerprints from the handle of the Catlin amputating knife. I had caught her in the elevator directly after we found the body, bending over Dr. Harrigan's dead face. She was the only person I could recall even approaching the elevator alone from the time we found the body until the police arrived. And she had looked terribly shaken and horrified.

I was, as I say, quite positive that she had polished those smears which had certainly been fingerprints and palm prints from that shining, mirror-like handle. Why she had done so was something I did not know. If they were her own fingerprints—— But that would have to be proved.

CHAPTER IX

IT WAS with a distinct feeling of having gone farther than I intended that I decided not to go into the matter of Peter Melady's mysterious disappearance just at the moment. Not in my notes; it was, of course, impossible to keep my thoughts from dwelling upon it at some length.

Besides it was high time to be getting our patients washed and toothbrushed and ready for breakfast before the trays came up.

It was with relief that I handed the keys over to the head nurse for the day. She had heard, probably, of the affair of the night and must have slept very little, for she looked extremely white and tired. She did not refer in words to her warning of the previous night—which, on all counts, was fortunate. I was in no mood to hear, "I told you so," even from a psychic.

Breakfast was a rather hideous meal, with no one eating much and all of the nurses whispering a great deal and looking over their shoulders and nearly jumping out of their skins if a dish rattled in the kitchen. Following it I went at once to my room, disregarding any inquisitive inquiries along the way and, contrary to my expectations, fell at once into a sound sleep. Even a nurse, who is accustomed to somewhat erratic periods of rest and not too many of them at times, does grow exhausted.

I remember thinking sleepily as I dozed off that, murder or no murder, I had to have sleep. I was not so brave, however, as not to lock my door; I believe I even pushed the dressing table before it. If anyone silently approached my door and twisted the door knob he would find himself disappointed.

The inquest took place that afternoon. As I emerged from my own room about one o'clock or so and was going downstairs I met Dr. Kunce coming out of the men's surgical ward with an interne at each elbow. He stopped me and motioned the internes to one side.

"That screen for the window in the east wing which leads to the fire escape," he said, "was locked when Miss Page looked at it, as is her custom when she goes on duty. And no one in the east wing will admit unlocking it. And no one will admit hiding that snuff-bottle, either. But it was not there under the mattress when Sergeant Lamb and I searched the room earlier in the evening. Someone in the east wing must have placed it there at some time during the night. Are you sure, Miss Keate, that you, in and about the corridor all night, saw no one who might have hidden the snuff-bottle? Or unlocked the window?"

"I saw no one," I said slowly and carefully. "No one who did not have a perfect right to be there in the east wing."

"That's what I thought you'd say," he remarked somewhat cryptically, his nose coming down over his beard. Without another word he went on, his escort following him, and I did not see him again until the beginning of the inquest.

It was held in the long staff room on the first floor and took on a distinctly formal air from the massive mahogany and slippery black leather with which the room is furnished. It was still very hot and sticky and all the windows were raised to their full height, but the room yet had an unaired atmosphere of leather and stale cigar smoke and meat broth, and under it all the faint but ever-present odor of ether. All the board members were present, and all the staff doctors, and any number of policemen in their hot blue uniforms. There were some reporters, of course, with extremely quick eyes, and a sprinkling of outsiders. Ina Harrigan was there in a remarkably fetching sea-green negligee which exactly matched her eyes and a wheel chair for which there was no earthly need, it being her arm that was broken, not her leg. She looked, however, very handsome and very frail and very touching and I could almost see tears in the eyes of the jury. Her lawyer stood on one side of her; one of the day nurses on the other.

Dione Melady was not there, but Court Melady sat in the back of the room with Kenwood Ladd. It was curious that, while the two men did not resemble each other in the least, there was on that occasion exactly the same expression in each face. It was, I decided, an expression of wariness, a guarded look. It was as definite in Kenwood Ladd's handsome face and carefully aloof eyes and tight lips as it was in Courtney Melady's older, world-weary countenance.

There were a number of nurses, too, our white uniforms looking no doubt much cooler than they felt, and a few internes.

Well, it proved to be a long-drawn-out affair which yet appeared to move with considerable expedition. I listened intently to every word, but there were actually only a few things, when I came to sift down all that had been said afterward, which were news to me. The first came along at the outset of the inquest, after the time and manner of Dr. Harrigan's death had been detailed in such a way that even Ina Harrigan lifted a wisp of chiffon handkerchief to her face and I think all of us felt rather ill—as I say, the first item of news came during the testimony of a very studious-looking gentleman with enormous, smoke-tinted eyeglasses, who told what he had to tell dryly and rapidly. It was as he got to the end of his testimony that he informed his listeners that the prints on the door knobs of the elevator doors, surgery doors, instrument-case latch, and elevator buttons belonged to one of the nurses—upon which I endeavored to look inconspicuous; there was a sort of rustle and many glances cast toward the corner of the room which was more plentifully dotted with white uniforms—and that the electric-light bulb in the elevator showed distinctly, and superimposed upon other prints, *the fingerprints of Dr. Harrigan himself!*

Dr. Harrigan's own fingerprints! Then Dr. Harrigan had himself turned out that small red light, leaving himself in darkness.

It seemed to me that this point must be of considerable significance, but I could not for the life of me determine how or what. The coroner, to whom, of course, it was not news, did not pursue the matter. I was a little disappointed, although I realized that his real object was to prove that murder was done; the real inquiry was to follow.

Another moment of interest to me came during the office girl's testimony, which I give, not because it brought up any particular and startling bit of evidence, but simply because it gave me a clearer picture of things on the main—that is, the first—floor during the night of July seventh.

I omit the preliminaries. Her name was Marie Hill and she was a very pretty child in a pert way and seemed to relish her position, paying much attention to the arrangement of her skirts and seeing no one but the reporters.

"Your duties, then, are to manage the switchboard, make a record of telephone calls, and give information to visitors and act generally as an office girl?" said the coroner finally.

"Yes, sir."

"Do you remember the night of July seventh?"

"Oh, yes, sir."

"Is your desk in such a position that you can see the entrance door of the hospital?"

"Yes, sir."

"Can you also see the elevator?"

"Yes, sir."

"You would see anyone entering or emerging from the elevator?"

"Oh, yes, sir. Always. I can't miss it when I'm at the switchboard."

"Your working hours are what?"

"Nine to six, sir. And it's too long. Everybody's hours are long here at Melady Memorial."

"Never mind that. You are at the switchboard all that time?"

She said "Yes" to that, too; rather fervently, with a side glance at Dr. Kunce, as if she regretted her rash little remark about long hours. Which, by the way, was true enough; Melady Memorial is not modern in that respect.

"What doctors came to the hospital the night of July seventh after nine o'clock?"

"Only Dr. Harrigan, sir. And, of course, Dr. Kunce."

"What time did Dr. Harrigan arrive?"

"At eleven-thirty."

"How did you happen to note the exact time?"

She hesitated and said: "I've nothing much to do at night, you know, just sitting there watching for emergency calls all night. I sort of—watch things that go on in the hospital. It gets pretty lonesome—that big empty corridor. So I—well, I usually know what's going on. I remember thinking it was late for Dr. Harrigan to be calling and wondering if one of his patients was bad. But none of the nurses had telephoned for him."

"Did you see Dr. Harrigan again?"

"No, sir."

"Did he speak to you when he came?"

"No, sir. He acted like he was in a hurry. I thought it was funny because usually Dr. Harrigan—well, you know—talked to us all."

"Did you see him again?"

"No, sir."

"Did he call you and ask to be connected with any-one in the hospital? Dr. Kunce, or Miss Bianchi?"

"No, sir. He didn't call me at all. The first I knew was when Miss Keate called——"

"Did anyone enter the elevator after nine o'clock?"

"Yes, sir. Dr. Kunce. He came in from a dinner party all dressed up and he left his hat in the outer office and went straight to the elevator. I didn't notice the time exactly, but it was about half an hour or so before Dr. Harrigan arrived."

"Did you see Dr. Kunce again?"

"Oh, of course. He came back down by the elevator and asked me about a call or two and then went to his own rooms."

"And after that who used the elevator?"

"Nobody but Teuber, going upstairs to get a—one of the patients who had died."

"Did anyone approach the elevator?"

"No—oh, yes, there was, too. Miss Page and Miss Keate and Miss Jones, when they came upstairs after midnight supper, stopped at the door and rang, but the elevator didn't come, so they went on upstairs."

"You are sure that was all?"

"Yes, sir."

"Can you see the stairway also from your desk?"

"The last few steps of it. There at the bottom where the big newel post is."

"So you know just about who goes up and down stairs?"

"Oh, yes, sir. At night."

"Tell us who used the stairway between nine o'clock and the time the murder was discovered."

"I don't believe I can remember all the visitors that left. Not to name them, anyway. But all the visitors are out of the hospital by nine-thirty. And after that there was only—why, there wasn't anybody at all until time for supper at midnight. Then, of course, the nurses came down on their way to the supper room. And when they'd finished supper they came back upstairs and the student nurses went down. But it was about that time the murder was discovered—or a little later. I know I was just finishing the sandwich one of the girls brought me. And there wasn't any operations came in that night, or any emergencies or any confinements. There was that one death. A Negro in the charity ward. Miss Jones, the head nurse there, telephoned down to me before she went to supper to send an orderly up to take him down to the ambulance room and for me to notify the undertakers. He didn't have a family to notify. I did and Mr. Teuber answered and came up as soon as he was dressed and went up for him. The dead Negro, I mean."

"What time was that?"

"Miss Jones telephoned just at twelve and the orderly went past the office and upstairs—that is, by the elevator, you know, on account of the ambulance room truck he took up with him—in about five minutes or so."

"When did he return?"

"Oh, I didn't see him. He had to come back by the freight elevator, I suppose."

"What makes you think that?"

"Why, it's the only other elevator. And anyway Miss Blane——" She stopped and cast a guilty glance at Dr. Kunce. But Dr. Kunce might have known he couldn't keep a hospital full of nurses from talking of the murder. "I happened to be talking about it to Miss Blane and she said she saw him. I was wondering how he got the truck with the Negro on it down to the ambulance room, after I heard about Dr. Harr—about the murder in the elevator. And she said he used the freight elevator there in her wing in the southwest L. They never use the freight elevator at night because it makes such a lot of noise."

Sergeant Lamb leaned over and whispered something in Dr. Kunce's ear, who beckoned to an interne and said something in a low voice and sat back again, suave and composed, while the interne slipped quietly out the door.

"Do you know Mr. Courtney Melady?" the coroner was asking.

"Oh, yes, sir," said Marie Hill promptly.

"Is he here?"

"Oh, yes, sir." Her eyes went so straight to Court Melady that it had the effect of a pointing finger. Everyone looked that way but found Court Melady's face cold and inscrutable and entirely unperturbed, although Kenwood Ladd, next to him, looked extremely uncomfortable.

"Did you see Mr. Melady leave the hospital the night of July seventh?"

"No, sir."

"Could he have left without your seeing him?"

"He might have," she said at once, "if he had gone promptly when all the other visitors were leaving. I'm busier at the switchboard then than later. He could easily have gone without my seeing him."

"Do you know Mr. Kenwood Ladd by sight?"

"Yes, sir," she said eagerly, looking at Kenwood Ladd at once with a fervency of interest which he did not return. As others followed her look he stared stonily before him, probably made no less furious by his unpleasant prominence than by the flush which crept boyishly into his face.

It was at that moment I believe that the door opened and Miss Jones, Jacob Teuber, and Miss Blane, the head night nurse in the south L of the third floor—that wing which adjoins the west wing at its end—sidled into the room, herded by the interne.

"Did you see Mr. Ladd leave the hospital?"

"No, sir," she said decidedly.

"Are you sure? You weren't sure about Mr. Melady."

"Oh, yes, I'm sure," said the office girl wistfully. "I'd have seen Mr. Ladd."

A little whisper of laughter was frowned down by the coroner and Kenwood Ladd's face became a deeper scarlet, though not a line of it altered.

"You are positive, then, that Mr. Ladd did not pass the office? Not even at the time when you say you are busy and that someone might have passed without your seeing him?"

"I did not say some visitors might have passed without my seeing them," she replied spiritedly. "I said Mr. Melady might have passed and I might not have noticed him. But I know Mr. Ladd didn't."

"How can you be so sure in that case?"

"Because I remember thinking it was funny I hadn't seen him and that he must have not come to the hospital that night. You see I—we—well, you know. We are all sort of interested in him. Coming so often and all."

Dr. Kunce, sitting not far from me, did not move, but if I had been the unlucky witness I would have taken to my heels on encountering the look in his soft dark eyes. I think, in fact, she longed to do nothing else and was only restrained by her awe of the police, for she half rose, cast a frightened look at the coroner and Sergeant Lamb, and sat down again, her eyes going anxiously back to Dr. Kunce. She forgot the reporters for the first time. And although I am no more suspicious than most women, it was just then that I began to wonder if Dr. Kunce's wish to spare his beautiful patient any annoyance was entirely actuated by his feeling of responsibility as head of the hospital in which her husband and Dr. Kunce's colleague had been murdered and in which she herself was a patient.

"Coming so often?" said the coroner.

"Well—to see Mrs. Harrigan, you know."

Upon which Mrs. Harrigan's lawyer bent over her hastily, and the nurse fanned vigorously with a folded newspaper, and Mrs. Harrigan held the delicate handkerchief to her eyes again, and Dr. Kunce bent forward and whispered to Sergeant Lamb who, in turn, held a whispered conversation with the coroner. The reporters looked on with a sort of weary interest, and Kenwood Ladd stared straight before him, appearing quite oblivious of the looks cast in his direction, though his eyes were not very pleasant. The unlucky office girl made matters worse by saying with unexpected defiance:

"Dr. Kunce says we mustn't talk about the patients

and visitors, but I'd like to know how anybody can help it when a man calls as often as him and with flowers and all——"

"Did you see Mr. Ladd at all that night?" interrupted the coroner.

"No, sir. Not once."

"Would you have seen anyone leave the hospital after you had news of the murder?"

"Oh, my sakes alive, yes," she said, again forgetting the reporters.

And after a few questions relating to the time when I had called her, which she said was exactly twelve thirty-two, and what I had said, she was dismissed.

Miss Jones then was questioned briefly as to what time she had sent for an orderly.

"The patient died at twelve," she said in a scared voice, "and I called for an orderly right away. Then I went down to supper. Miss Leming, the nurse in the ward, said Teuber got there in just five or ten minutes and had to wait until I got back from supper to get the forms, the order to the undertakers and all that. Dr. Kunce had looked at the patient earlier in the night when we knew he couldn't live, so the death certificate was all right. It took me some time after I got back from supper to get things ready, and when Teuber finally left the charity ward it was just before twelve-thirty. I remember because it took such a long time and we were busy that night."

"Just before twelve-thirty? How long before?"

"Oh, not more than two or three minutes. I was in the door and saw him going down the corridor, where he met Miss Keate there near the elevator. She seemed to stop him and say something and look at the truck with the—the body on it and I went back to work."

Teuber himself, looking very much distressed and wheezing more than a little, told the same story, thus providing an excellent alibi for Miss Jones had she needed one. He added that Miss Keate had gone on up-stairs again as he turned and took the truck back along the corridor to the freight elevator in the south wing.

"I had to do it," he said with an apologetic look toward Dr. Kunce. "It made a lot of racket, but it was the only way to get the body down, and I knew the under-takers would be wanting it right away. Miss Ash was there in the east wing when I left it, sir," he said anx-iously. "She saw me. I didn't do anything. Miss Blane was in the south wing and she asked me why I was taking the freight elevator when it was against the rules. She said I'd wake all her patients. And I told her the regular elevator was stuck somewhere and I'd have to get the body downstairs."

"How long after receiving the call to the charity ward did you reach the third floor?"

"Why, I—I had to dress, you know. And then go to the ambulance room to get a truck. It must have been between five and ten minutes."

"You used the main elevator to go up to the third floor?"

"Yes, sir."

"You saw nothing unusual?"

"No, sir." A fit of coughing interrupted him; pres-ently he wiped his glistening face and went on: "Nothing at all, sir. When I reached the third floor I pushed my truck out and went on along the corridor. I didn't see anyone until I reached the charity ward."

"Was no one in the east-wing corridor?"

"No, sir. Not a soul."

"When you rang for the elevator there at the first

floor, how long was the cage in coming to that floor? I mean, from what floor would you say it came?"

"Well,"—the young orderly looked perplexed but anxious to please—"that's hard to say. But I believe it came from the fourth floor. At least it was too long a wait for it to have come from the second floor. I'm sure of that. But I couldn't be just positive as to whether it came from the third or fourth floor."

"You are sure it was after twelve-five that you rang for the elevator? It wasn't before that?"

"No, sir. I mean yes, sir. I mean it couldn't have been before that, considering my having to dress and all. But I can't say for sure."

"And the elevator was empty at that time?"

"Yes, sir."

"And you did not approach the elevator again till about twelve-thirty, when you came back with the truck on which lay this—er—body, and at that time you met Miss Keate?"

"No, sir. Yes, sir."

Miss Blane on being questioned corroborated his tale in so far as she could.

"Did anyone besides the orderly use the freight elevator during the night of July seventh?" Asked the coroner finally.

"No, sir," she said positively. "I'd have known it, for it makes such a racket. Sounds like an earthquake."

"There was nothing unusual or out of the way occurring in your part of the hospital that night?"

"Nothing at all. It was a quiet night—that is, until the police got there."

Lillian Ash when called also corroborated Teuber's testimony, although she did not do so very gracefully,

looking indeed very reluctant and rather ill and not appearing to relish her share in the inquiry.

". . . And the elevator seemed to be stuck somewhere, so he took his truck back along the west corridor
toward the freight elevator and Miss Keate went back
upstairs to the operating rooms and I went back to my
patient. It was just a moment after that that I heard
Miss Keate call out and I hurried out into the corridor
and she was standing there at the elevator door."

She shuddered violently just as she said "elevator
door," and a kind of sympathetic shiver went over the
audience.

"Was your patient awake?" asked the coroner.

"No. He had a good night—until all the commotion.
He slept most of the fore part of the night."

"H'm," remarked the coroner weightily. He might as
well have said: "Then he can't furnish you an alibi," for
I think that was in everyone's mind. The reporters one
and all were suddenly alert and Lillian Ash's large hands
twisted a little in her lap and a slow dull red crept under
the layers of powder on her face.

Well, he continued to question her at some length regarding the night of the murder, and I remember the
harassed look on her face as if she'd not slept for nights,
but she said very clearly that she knew nothing that might
have a connection with the murder, and to all his questions told practically the same tale that Ellen and Nancy
and I had told Sergeant Lamb regarding the finding of
the body and the events previous to that discovery. She
was presently permitted to take her seat again among
the other nurses, and Ellen, Nancy, and I were called
next one after the other and were disposed of very
quickly. I suppose Sergeant Lamb felt he already knew
everything we might have had to tell the coroner. The

jury was much interested and, indeed, so was the small audience interested in my own testimony. The coroner asked very particularly about my two fruitless trips to the fourth floor in search of my patient and Dr. Harrigan.

It was rather singular how Peter Melady's name kept coming into the inquiry. It was, of course, unavoidable, and every time anyone alluded to him there was a very tangible and definite quickening of interest on the part of the audience. The inquiry concerned primarily Dr. Harrigan's death, but Peter Melady's disappearance was so much a part and parcel of that death that it could not be entirely disentangled. The obvious assumption was, naturally, that Peter Melady had stabbed Dr. Harrigan and fled. Self-defense was more than hinted several times, and the well-known enmity between the two men was brought into the inquiry. During Court Melady's brief testimony he was asked quite exactly about this.

"I only know they were not on good terms," he said coldly. "I know nothing of the reasons for their quarrel."

And when pressed he said flatly that he knew nothing of his father-in-law's business.

He kept his temper admirably, even when the coroner asked him somewhat pointedly if he, himself, had been friendly with Dr. Harrigan and if there was not some way in which he could prove just where he had been during the hour in question.

"No one saw you leave the hospital, you see," added the coroner more deferentially, as if he had remembered that, after all, this was Court Melady who would eventually inherit the Melady money and influence. "And we are trying to check up on all the visitors in the east portion of the hospital that night."

He might as well have said what he meant: the visitors who, by any stretch of the imagination, could have had an interest in doing away with Dr. Harrigan. Court Melady's blank, cold gaze became blanker and colder, and he said in a detached way that he had no alibi at all for that night, if that was what the coroner meant.

"Not at all," said the coroner politely. "Not at all. Thank you, Mr. Melady. Er—oh, just a moment more, Mr. Melady."

As Sergeant Lamb pushed a note onto his desk and Court Melady waited impassively, the coroner glanced at the note, looked disapprovingly at Sergeant Lamb, but said:

"One more thing, Mr. Melady. Do you mind telling us just where you were between one and three o'clock last night?"

Court Melady's cold face did not alter in the least degree, although he must have known that the coroner was inquiring in a not particularly adroit way as to the murderous assault upon Dione Melady. That was another affair which, to my mind, was indissolubly connected with the murder. It was not, however, openly mentioned.

"Why, not at all," said Court Melady in an extremely cold and unpleasant way. "I happen to have an unshakable alibi for last night, Coroner. I got into a card game at my club after leaving the hospital about half-past nine. It lasted until Dr. Kunce telephoned to my house around three o'clock, was told to call the club, and did so and talked to me. He told me of what had just occurred, of what had been done, and that my wife was asleep and advised me not to come to the hospital until morning, as I could do nothing. I went back and—er—finished the game and spent the rest of the night at the club. Any of the gentlemen with whom I was playing can give you a complete corroboration of this. I'll be glad to give their names to Sergeant Lamb. Does that answer your question fully enough?"

"Oh, quite, Mr. Melady. Quite," said the coroner, managing to convey apology to Court Melady and disapproval for Sergeant Lamb's insistence in the same breath.

So, I thought to myself, sitting back against my chair again, that was all Court Melady had to say. While there was no proof, of course, that Dione's assailant and the murderer were the same person, still I felt convinced that this was true. So if Court Melady was able to provide a true alibi for the latter affair it went a long way, in my opinion, toward establishing his innocence of the murder. Not that I had particularly suspected Court Melady; I had included him in my sinister list merely because of his possible presence in the hospital that night and because he had known Dr. Harrigan and was so closely connected with Peter Melady.

There followed a long and tedious questioning of Dr. Kunce and various nurses relating to the people in and out of the hospital that night and particularly during the time between twelve and one. I did not relish this part of the inquest—not that I exactly relished any of it— for at its close I was more than ever convinced that the murderer must be among those few persons whose names appeared on the list I had made. Which was not only frightening but rather absurd in that there was not one whom I really could suspect of doing a murder. But in what was to all practical purposes a hermetically sealed hospital, with patients in their beds and under the eagle-eyed care of nurses, who are, in turn, continually under one another's observation, and with details of routine so exact and so definite that practically every moment is accountable, there is not much opportunity for people wandering about the corridors and up and down elevators. Dr. Kunce appeared to take a silky satisfaction in this public evidence of his own admirable administration. And as I say, I began to feel more and more certain that the purely physical matters of time and space and opportunity limited the affair rather rigidly to the brief list I had made. Which was in itself a grisly thought. And at the same time there was not one person on it whom I could conceive of committing so ugly and violent a crime. But I suppose murder remains an inconceivable thing to most of us.

I believe I did not mention the detailed testimony which went to prove that Dr. Harrigan had been murdered and had not committed suicide. The position of the knife (which had been taken apparently from the case in the operating room, as Dr. Kunce had reluctantly testified), the position of the body, the point at which the knife entered the heart, various all too clear photographs—all this was made much of in terms that were so highly scientific and businesslike that they were to many of us just so much talk. Much time was given this point, also, though I think the fact that it was murder was clear from the beginning. No one, seeing what I had seen, would have had any doubt of it.

And I have not mentioned Ina Harrigan's testimony, which was brief and conducted with considerable sympathy and heavy-footed delicacy on the part of the coroner. She knew nothing, it appeared, of any enemy who might murder her husband or of any reason for that murder; the shock and grief had made her ill; she had last seen Dr. Harrigan between eleven-thirty and twelve on the night of July seventh when he stopped in her room to talk to her and bid her good-night, and he had been in good spirits and certainly had had no premonition of his death. Her wheel chair, negligee, trained nurse, and bandaged arm combined to give an entirely erroneous impression of frailty, and somehow she managed to convey the feeling that she and Dr. Harrigan had been extremely loving and devoted, which was, as I knew, an almost equally erroneous impression. She was thanked and dismissed in an apologetic manner.

Nevertheless heads turned with unabated interest when, some time later, Kenwood Ladd was asked to testify.

He did so most ungraciously and I give what he had to say merely because it was of interest to me owing to my own perplexity regarding him. I was in two minds as to Kenwood Ladd from the beginning.

"You were a visitor to the third floor of the Melady hospital the evening of July seventh?"

"Yes."

"Upon whom were you calling?"

"Mrs. Harrigan."

"You are drawing up plans for a new house for her?"

"Yes."

"When did you leave?"

"I can't say exactly," said Kenwood Ladd. "It was after the little student nurse came to the door and told me it was time for visitors to leave. Certainly before Dr. Harrigan was killed."

The coroner, having made quite a point of the exact time at which Dr. Harrigan was last seen alive, said at once:

"Oh, certainly, Mr. Ladd. No doubt you talked with someone on your way home or upon arriving there? Someone who can corroborate your statement?"

No, he hadn't, he said, quite as directly as he had admitted this damaging fact to Sergeant Lamb previously. He had taken a a long walk in the park he said, it being so very warm, and he did not remember seeing anyone when he arrived at his hotel.

And upon being questioned as to his whereabouts on the night of July eighth he said briefly that he'd been having an attack of indigestion and had had a doctor.

"I'd got hold of some bad liquor," he said bluntly and a bit defiantly. A confession which did him no good; B—— takes its liquor surreptitiously and seriously and considers any public allusion to its drinking in very bad taste.

As in the case of Court Melady there was nothing which directly connected him with the murder and presently the coroner dismissed them. There was certainly no reason to hint that presumably grief-stricken Ina Harrigan had had a young lover in the person of Kenwood Ladd who might have become so emotionally entangled as to murder her husband. There was no definite bit of evidence on which to base such an implication. But people being what they are, there was distinct speculation in the curious eyes that went from Kenwood Ladd to Mrs. Harrigan and back again. The trouble was, I suppose, that he was so exactly the engagingly aloof type of youthful masculinity with whom a woman might easily imagine herself in love. There was even that little flush creeping into his face now and then to prove he was not so entirely aloof and inaccessible as he appeared. Even I, long past the years of indiscretion, felt that, while he might readily be Ina Harrigan's lover, he could not possibly have murdered her husband. Which only goes to prove that a middle-aged nurse, inclined to embonpoint and neuralgia, has her moments of romantic fancy.

He sat down beside Court Melady again and I could

only see his crisply blond hair and the straight inscrutable line of his eyebrows and his narrowed blue-gray eyes. *And his blond hair.* Was it possible that the gold hair upstairs in my lavender hot-water bottle was from his head?

I had been so sure it was a woman's hair, as it was rather long, but while it certainly curled there was as certainly a look about Kenwood Ladd's hair of vigorously controlled waviness. I could imagine him wielding brushes determinedly in an effort to make his hair lie flat and in place. The longer I looked the more certain I became that the gold hair in the pill-box might as easily have belonged to Kenwood Ladd as to either Nancy or Lillian Ash. Or Dione Melady. Again the world seemed exclusively populated with blondes and I turned my attention wearily back to the inquest.

It was not long after that, following a long-drawn-out train of routine inquiry which, to my mind, did not accomplish much, that the jury made its decision. We waited for that a long time, during which the room became suffocatingly hot, and when an orderly brought a pitcherful of iced water to the coroner's table and a glass out of which the coroner drank thirstily and with evident satisfaction, everyone in the room eyed him enviously and the rustle of uneasiness and impatience increased. Even Dr. Kunce looked disturbed and worried his beard and adjusted the red geranium in his buttonhole. At some time or other Dr. Kunce had lived in the South and he still, in the heat of the summer, affected the light silk suits so popular in New Orleans and other Southern cities. He looked very handsome in them, especially with the scarlet geranium which he so often wore, and I caught several reporters looking interestedly at the suit and no less interestedly at the geranium.

I learned later that the delay on the part of the jury was due to one of them insisting on a decision that Dr. Harrigan had come to his death at the hands of Peter Melady. He said and maintained, and with justice, that there was something fishy about Peter Melady's disappearance. Heat and hunger, for it was near dinnertime, finally broke his resistance and the verdict, when it came, was only what had been expected. There could have been nothing else. It was that Dr. Harrigan had come to his death at the hands of "a person or persons unknown," which to me is a phrase which has always a sort of irony.

We straggled out of the room.

A little group composed of Dr. Kunce, the coroner, Sergeant Lamb, and Mrs. Harrigan's lawyer and some of the staff doctors—Dr. Peattie, who looked very ill and worn with fatigue and anxiety, among them—was completely surrounded by reporters. Court Melady and Kenwood Ladd stopped to bend over the drinking fountain in the corridor and then walked toward the main entrance together. The dinner bell rang as I reached the stairway; on the way to the basement Lillian Ash caught up with me.

"Terribly hot," she said, panting. "I hope the student nurse who was with my patient this afternoon during my hours off has got along all right."

"How is your patient?" I asked.

"So, so," said Miss Ash. "The hot weather is bad for him. Keeps me busy. I'm not getting much rest. And it will be a good ten days before he is out of the woods, so to speak."

"By the way," I said in as casual a voice as I could assume, "did you ever nurse for Dr. Harrigan?"

She gave me a quick look and I thought she was going to stop there on the stairway, but she did not.

"No," she said. "Did you?"

"Oh, many times," I replied. "You didn't know him, then?"

She shrugged.

"As one knows of the various doctors. I haven't been here long, of course. I don't know any of the staff doctors well."

"Where was your home?" I asked idly. "I don't remember having heard you say."

She gave me a quick look and said nothing for a perceptible second or two. I felt that she was groping for a name. Then she said, with just a suggestion of triumph in her voice:

"Hollywood."

"Ah." A place of shifting population; it would be difficult to trace one woman. Then I caught myself up shortly. After all, I had no reason to believe she had actually committed murder. "This is a horrible affair, isn't it?"

She shuddered, put one fleshy hand up to push back a dry strand of blonde hair which had fallen over her eyes, and then passed the hand wearily across her flabby-looking face. The heavy powder she used was smeary with moisture, and the lines from her nose to her mouth looked deep just for the moment as we passed under the light at the foot of the basement stairs and entered the hot, steamy dining room.

"Horrible, yes!" she said. There was a little catch in her voice, and a moment later I noticed that her hand on the glass of tea was shaking and trembling and she was staring at the white, cotton tablecloth as—well, much as Lady Macbeth might have looked at her hand. Upon which flight of fancy I adjured myself not to be a fool.

And realized that my own hands were none too steady.

CHAPTER X

WHEN I reached the east wing to go on duty that night I found Nancy already there, talking to the day nurses, who looked hot and tired and were very glad to be relieved. After they had gone and Ellen was removing dinner trays, Nancy and I chatted for some time—of the heat, of the June bugs that began to bat against the screens as twilight fell and the lights in the corridors attracted them, of 301 who'd been troublesome about his diet—of anything and everything but that which was uppermost in our thoughts. And every time we let our eyes wander that way, there was the black door leading to the elevator shaft just across the few feet of corridor from us.

I did, however, overcome my reluctance and asked her in so many words just how long she'd been in Dione Melady's room during the time after our return to the third floor after supper and my own discovery of Dr. Harrigan's body, the night of July seventh.

"Every moment of it," she said at once. "Mrs. Melady was hysterical."

Every moment of it; that went far toward eliminating Nancy and Dione from my brief little list.

"And you saw no one entering or leaving the elevator during that time? You were almost opposite it."

"Not quite opposite, Sarah. And anyhow I was obliged to close the door finally as Mrs. Melady became excited and began to talk loudly. I was afraid she'd wake patients in near-by rooms. So I heard or saw nothing." She paused, looking at me somberly. "Do you know, Sarah, whether they are going to make any arrests?"

"Why, I suppose they will eventually," I began, and just then Kenwood Ladd arrived, stepping out of the gloom of the stairway. It was odd how we all managed to use the stairway that week despite the heat and the long climb. No one cared to step inside the elevator. Even the rubber-tired dumb-waiters, laden with heated meal trays for the sick patients, were sent up by the freight elevator and then wheeled along the lengthy stretch of bare corridors to the east wing.

Nancy, I remember, rose to accompany young Ladd to Mrs. Harrigan's room. She had just got into another fresh uniform which had not become limp yet and which looked very crisp and white and cool, her blonde hair caught bright little gleams from under her starched, piquant white cap, and she looked extraordinarly young and lovely in spite of the faint blue lines of fatigue and worry under her eyes.

"May I see Mrs. Harrigan?" asked Kenwood Ladd. I think that for just a moment he forgot what one of us knew, for as he stood there looking down at Nancy the tight line of his mouth relaxed a little, the hunted look left his face, and his eyes were all at once quite bright and alert and not at all aloof.

Then Nancy murmured something and he said: "Thank you," and followed her toward Mrs. Harrigan's room.

When Nancy came back she stood looking at the glass top of the chart desk for some time before she said:

"He's terribly attractive, isn't he?"

"Who?" I looked up from 301's vagaries as noted on his chart. "Oh, that young Mr. Ladd? I suppose so."

And after at least five minutes of meditation she added:

"I don't believe he's interested in Mrs. Harrigan at all."

"You think she's the aggressor?" I asked, smiling.

Somewhat to my surprise Nancy flared up at once.

"You needn't laugh," she said sharply. "That's exactly what I think. She's—like that."

She stopped herself abruptly and after a moment added in a sort of whisper, with her eyes wide and staring rather fixedly at the desk top:

"It's a horrible mess all around."

"What do you mean?"

"You know what I mean." She lifted her small shoulders in a shrug, pushed a soft little wisp of hair back off her forehead, and reached into her pocket for a powder compact. Nancy was one of those nurses who carry a vanity case as regularly as a thermometer, for which I thought the more of her. "Well, I can't do anything about it," she said. "I'm going down to coax 301 to eat his lettuce. He says he's already eaten so much that his nose is beginning to wiggle and his ears grow long and pink and he'll eventually be made into somebody's fur coat." Her smile did not reach the dark troubled depths of her eyes, but her firm little chin was set.

Kenwood Ladd did not stay long that night. I happened to be in the corridor when he left. I noted that on his way to the stairway he looked rather searchingly up and down the length of corridors and then in a disappointed way at me.

It was not until we had got our patients comfortably settled for the first quiet hours of the night that I began to think over the matters the inquest had brought up. There were several things that seemed to me to be rather curious. For one thing the Chinese snuff-bottle and the formula for Slæpan had not been mentioned. But after some consideration I found myself agreeing with the policy of silence; certainly if they were obliged to discover the criminal by means of such clues it was better not to put the criminal on his guard. I suppose, too, that that was why there had been no mention of the bit of white chewing gum. I knew why the gold hair had not been mentioned. I had no doubt that Sergeant Lamb looked upon every blonde-haired person connected with the hospital with aggravated suspicion, but he scarcely dared admit that the real bit of evidence had been stolen from him.

On sifting down the mass of alibis and evidence which the afternoon had brought forth I found there was only one item which was entirely new to me and which might have an important effect upon the development of the case. I refer to the fact that Dr. Harrigan's own fingerprints were found upon the electric-light bulb in the elevator cage, thus appearing to prove that he, himself, had turned out the light by simply twisting the bulb until the current of electricity was disconnected. There was something entirely contradictory about it—as there was, indeed, about so many aspects of the case. I had assumed that the murderer must have turned out the light in order to attack Dr. Harrigan.

I glanced down the corridor. At its east end, before a window and just in front of the fire escape, of course, a broad policeman was tilted back at a perilous angle on one of the small white metal chairs, and while neither the pose nor the gentleman was handsome I am bound to say that I have seldom seen anything more agreeable to look at. Not far from me along the westward corridor sat another policeman, and I had no doubt that Dr. Kunce had seen to it that there were others placed at strategic points about the silent, long corridors of the sleeping hospital.

Ellen and Nancy were both, apparently, busy. I looked at the various charts, noted carefully the orders for the night, saw that no signal lights were glowing unattended, and drew from my pocket the chart on which I had made my notes and which I had been at some pains to transfer from one pocket to another on changing uniforms.

I smoothed out the wrinkles in the sheet of paper and leaned over it.

So far as I could see there were few changes to make. True, Miss Jones had an ironclad alibi, but I had not considered her as being a likely suspect. Ellen, Lillian Ash—nothing at all to change or modify. After Jacob Teuber's name I was obliged to cross out the word "Opportunity"; while he was certainly in and about the elevator when bringing up his truck between five and ten minutes after twelve—which made it either immediately before or immediately after Dr. Harrigan's using it to convey Peter Melady to the fourth-floor operating room —he was as certainly in the charity ward during the time from ten minutes after twelve, at the latest, until I myself had seen him emerge with his burden. And Dr. Harrigan had been seen alive at eighteen minutes after twelve and had been murdered during that interval. However, I left the orderly's name on my chart, for it seemed possible to me that he might unwittingly know something of the crime; I made a mental resolution to question him, myself.

It was just here, I remember, that I began to do what I had told myself was impossible to do—that is, to eliminate certain names from that list. I was convinced in my own mind that neither Nancy nor Ellen could be guilty of murder; innocuous little Ellen was an absurdity in that connection, and while Nancy might have the will and the determination to carry through such a ghastly project, still there was nothing in her healthy, hard-working, gay young life to offer a motive, much less an inclination. In the long gray hours of second watch one gets to know one's fellow nurses rather well; if there is anything of cowardice, any neuroses, any lack of moral stamina it comes out during those weary hours before the dawn when the ordinary defenses are down. And I knew Nancy to possess courage and common sense and humor and tenderness—an ideal combination and one which, automatically, it seemed to me, eliminated Nancy's name. It was true that there were certain things I should have liked explained, but nevertheless I drew a mark through "Nancy Page," and felt I had done well.

Dione Melady was another name which I felt in justice I must eliminate; not only did she and Nancy offer an alibi for each other for most of those twelve minutes which had proved to be so important, but there was the added item that she could not have so nearly strangled herself. And I felt convinced, intuitively perhaps but I thought correctly, that her assailant and the murderer were one and the same person.

I did not, however, rule out Court Melady and Kenwood Ladd, although each had an alibi for the night on which the snuff-bottle was taken from Dione, which was, of course, though it seemed some time ago, actually only the previous night, the night of July eighth. It was perhaps inconsistent to retain both names as suspects, but alibis have broken down on inquiry many times, and I was not convinced that both of them had been out of the hospital on the night of the murder. True, the presence of either was extremely unlikely, but until we had more

exact knowledge regarding each I proposed to consider
them suspects. Besides, eliminating both those names
would have left my sinister little list so ominously short
and limited.

There remained Ina Harrigan, Dr. Kunce, and Lillian
Ash. I had no definite knowledge either for or against
Dr. Kunce; I did not think it very reasonable to suppose
that he had stolen up to the fourth floor (how, in the
face of the office girl's testimony, I couldn't even surmise), taken the amputating knife, killed a prominent
surgeon who was in many respects his rival, spirited
away an equally prominent patient, and then turned
around to conduct a vigorous and searching inquiry. His
behavior all along had been that of an innocent, if much
perturbed, man. Since he might have been able to do all
this, I left his name on my chart. He could, too, have got
to the east wing unobserved on the previous night and
stolen the Chinese snuff-bottle from Dione. He knew,
whispered something inside me, what the snuff-bottle
contained. However, I did not think it at all likely,
though to be just I had to admit its possibility.

Ina Harrigan's arm being broken did not eliminate her
so far as I could see. She could not have strangled Dione
Melady, but she could have killed Dr. Harrigan. I remember experimenting with my left hand, going through
the presumable motions of thrusting that knife into Dr.
Harrigan's heart. In fact I became so absorbed in stabbing into the air above the chart desk and figuring
whether or not she could have done it with her left hand
and deciding that she could, that I forgot the two policemen and was only reminded of their presence when the
one near me cautiously brought his chair forward until
its front legs touched the floor and began as cautiously
to rise. And the policeman down at the east end of the

corridor had already got to his feet and was poised in a sort of "pointing" attitude with one foot actually lifted and his jaw thrust forward when I looked that way. Both of them were staring at me.

I lifted my left hand, stabbed it violently into the air again, let it reach the chart rack that time, and snatched out a chart, over which I bent. Out of the corners of my eyes I saw the two policemen settle slowly back into their chairs. It was some time, however, before they tilted relaxedly against the wall again, and as I went about my duties all the night I was conscious of their combined and steady regard which indubitably held an element of suspicion.

Ellen flashed out of a sick room presently, asked me some question, and flashed back again. It was growing late, although the trolley cars still thumped along over on Euclid Avenue. The air was still sickening in its hot breath, the flowers in the vases along the walls looked wilted and made grotesque little arabesques of shadows, there were various little bangs and buzzings from the screen back of me, and the chart on which I had made my notes was half covered already with infinitesimal insects who had worn out their little lives circling madly around the light. I brushed them away, replaced the chart, and bent again to my erratically scribbled notes.

Ina Harrigan then might certainly have killed Dr. Harrigan and, such are the intricacies of matrimony, might conceivably have had a motive. She also had had opportunity, though going into the corridor, entering the elevator, and stabbing Dr. Harrigan at a time when there were various people coming and going in the corridors would have taken an amount of daring which was almost incomprehensible. It would have taken the courage of desperation. There were also ways and means to be considered: the problem of securing the knife, of getting into the elevator and out again, of doing it all unobserved. Could she have possibly done it during the short two minutes between the time Ellen had seen Dr. Harrigan enter the elevator and our own arrival on the third floor? I considered this for some time, but was finally obliged to give it up and go on to Lillian Ash.

And here was a name which I must definitely suspect. There was only one reason that I could see for her wiping the fingerprints from the handle of the Catlin amputating knife, which I was morally certain she had done. Moreover, what was that she had said at the inquest? She had said that Jacob Teuber had turned after his failure to discover the whereabouts of the elevator cage and had taken the truck with its grisly burden back along the west corridor past the charity ward again and that she had returned to her patient's room. *But her patient had been asleep.* She might have been in that corridor for possibly—well, it couldn't have been more than three of those important twelve minutes. Time was an important feature of the tanglement in which we found ourselves, and I wished that we could figure more exactly such things as, for instance, the time of my two visits to the operating room; however, I have a good memory and usually an accurate one, and I felt sure that at the most not more than three minutes could have elapsed during my absence from the third floor on the occasion of my second and final trip to the operating room.

Now then, if the elevator had been at the third floor —but there I stuck, for the elevator had not been at the third floor. True the cage might have hung there without our knowledge owing to its being darkened, but there again I stuck, for I remembered Teuber pulling at the door into the shaft which, had the elevator been at that floor, would have opened readily. After some thought I determined to ask the young orderly just how vigorously he had pulled at that door. And there was the emergency stop to consider; if it had held that dark elevator cage at our floor for some time it made our problem simpler. Or did it?

I sighed wearily, rubbed my hands over my tired eyes, looked down the corridor in time to see Nancy enter 302's room with a glass of orange juice, reflected that it was so far an unusually quiet night considering the heat, and went back to the last name on my list. I stared at it for a long time.

Peter Melady.

Just how was Peter Melady involved in the murder? And above all things where was he?

It did not seem within reason that a man should enter an elevator—and vanish from the sight of man.

The most exhaustive search, according to Sergeant Lamb, had failed to discover even a trace of him. His home, his business offices, his clubs, the homes of his friends, every hospital or hotel he might have entered had been thoroughly canvassed; taxi drivers, railway-station officials and porters, even newsboys and early milk-truck drivers had been sought out and questioned but to no avail. Too, the papers had been crowded with the news of the Melady Memorial Murder and of Peter Melady's inexplicable disappearance until there could not be an inhabitant of the city who had not heard of the affair. It was true that, owing to a stubborn notion on the part of Peter Melady, who was inclined to have notions, he had never posed for a picture, and although the reporters scoured the town for a photograph of him there was none to publish. But at the same time he was well known in the city.

Complicating the matter further was his very serious physical disability. While there was a decided and natural tendency to thrust the blame for the murder on his shoulders—and I had to admit that it was the only reasonable explanation for his otherwise inexplicable disappearance—I yet maintained my belief that it would have been physically impossible for him to kill Dr. Harrigan.

It did seem curious to me that Dr. Harrigan should have decided to operate just when he did, instead of waiting until morning, and I began to wonder if Dr. Harrigan had really intended to operate just then. Certainly we had discovered no evidence that that was his intention beyond his announcement to Ellen and his taking Peter Melady *out of his own room*. Was that a pretext which would permit Dr. Harrigan to return, search the room and—*find the Slæpan!* Court Melady's hints recurred to me. Nothing could have been easier than for Dr. Harrigan to return to the fourth floor and when I found him there explain that he had changed his mind about the projected operation and would wait until morning after all, upon which he might have ordered me to take the patient back to his room. And I, naturally, could not have questioned him. Such goings-on would have been entirely outside my experience as a nurse. Still it was a possibility.

301's light went on just then and I hurried to answer it. He kept me for some time, and then 303, who had insisted on going to sleep with the electric fan turned full on him, had a chill. A moment of panic caught me as I reached the door of the dark, narrow linen closet, but I glanced down toward the nearer policeman, took a deep breath, and snapped on the light. There was nothing there, of course; only neat white rows of sheets and pillow cases and towels and blankets all neatly folded.

It was just as I was emerging from the linen closet with a blanket over each arm and some metal hot-water bottles poised upon them that my subconscious—if that's what it is—clicked suddenly.

Why, of course! That might easily have been just what Dr. Harrigan did. Had not Ellen said very distinctly that Dr. Harrigan appeared to have "forgotten" something, for he returned to the wing and was entering the elevator again, his errand probably achieved, at exactly eighteen minutes after twelve? And knowing Peter Melady as well as Dr. Harrigan had known him, he—Dr. Harrigan, that is—had likely judged that the Slæpan formula would not be far from its stubborn and notional owner. Peter Melady could not possibly have taken it with him to the operating room; he must have concealed it somewhere in his own room. Had Dr. Harrigan found it? Had he had it in his possession when he entered the elevator that last time? Had someone followed him? Was that the reason for the murder?

Peter Melady might have guessed his intention—and perhaps he had suspected him all along, for had he not been reluctant to let the doctor out of his sight even for a moment? Had he not insisted on accompanying him? If Peter Melady had been left alone in the operating room while Dr. Harrigan returned to search his room, he might have risen, snatched the knife, which is a deadly-looking affair, and followed Dr. Harrigan, determined to protect his own property. He might have been waiting for Dr. Harrigan in the elevator when Dr. Harrigan entered it.

That would explain the presence of the empty truck. But it would not explain why Dr. Harrigan's, and not Peter Melady's, fingerprints were on the electric-light bulb. And I still did not think Peter Melady's strength equal to such demands. Moreover, there again was the problem of Peter Melady's escape from the hospital.

It was as I reached that snag that my patient began to comment with much fluency and versatility through his chattering teeth, and I found I had turned the fan full on him again under the impression that it was an electric heater. Not, I believe, an extraordinary thing to do, for they have some similarity. But I had some difficulty in soothing the patient.

When he was finally relaxed and beginning to complain about the warmth of the blanket I left him and walked to the east end of the corridor. The policeman was still sitting there, directly in front of the window which leads out onto the fire escape.

"I want to be sure the screen is bolted," I said, and he rose grudgingly and moved to one side, eyeing me with distrust. The screen was bolted then, of course. Who in the east wing could have taken the bolt off during the previous night? And why? I knew that the police had thus far been unable to discover the intruder of the night of July eighth.

I stopped at the door of Dione Melady's room, saw that she was sleeping quietly, the bandages on her throat looking hot and bulky, noted that the other patients were quiet and comfortable, glanced again through the orders for the night to be sure none had been overlooked, and sat down once more at the chart desk.

That night, the second night after the murder, stands out in my memory for several reasons. One is the fact that I came tardily to perceive that Peter Melady must be found before any progress might be made toward the solution of the ugly affair. Another was the calm and quiet that existed in the wing and continued even past the little midnight stir of pulses and temperatures to be taken and fans and cool drinks to be brought and draw sheets to be pulled straight and weary backs massaged. I say it was quiet and calm; it was, however, neither peaceful nor tranquil; the guarding policemen, the black door to the elevator shaft, the deep shadows of the stairway, the yawning black doors into sick rooms, Peter Melady's silent empty room all precluded the peace and the security which tranquillity demands. But it was quiet. There was no disturbance of any kind, if we are to except Dione's waking along about three o'clock and insisting that there was a visitor in her room. Upon my turning on the light in order to prove to her that there was no visitor about, she said she hadn't meant that kind of visitor. And when I asked what on earth she did mean then she said:

"A visitor. From the other world. It walked across the room and rustled that newspaper. It was Father, I'm sure. Reading the newspaper."

Upon which Ellen, who had followed me, turned a faint green and vanished into the bathroom, and I told Dione somewhat tartly that she'd been dreaming and anyway there weren't such things.

"And if there were," I said, "it couldn't read a newspaper in the dark."

"Why not?" said Dione—which stumped me.

"Plenty of reasons," I snapped, not being able to think of any. "Come now, I'll fix your pillows and you try to get to sleep again."

"He's dead," she said thoughtfully. "I believe he's dead after all. And he's trying to tell me something. What is it, Father?"

She spoke in a natural and matter-of-fact way, quite as

if someone were standing in the corner of the room just back of the screen. I must admit that my spine crinkled at her tone, but I said crisply:

"Don't let me interrupt you, then," and left.

And found my hands cold and my heart thumping when I reached the bare, dark stretches of gray corridor. After all, where *was* Peter Melady?

It was shortly after that that I found the scribbled note from Dr. Harrigan. Those strangely scrawled words which apparently meant so little and which were to trouble me with their very triviality; their triviality and that curious matter of the handwriting.

I had taken Peter Melady's chart down from the rack and was studying it, finding my opinion of his physical condition confirmed at every entry, when I came upon this:

"Miss Keate, come at once to fourth floor." It was signed, as was usual with Dr. Harrigan, merely "L. Harrigan, M. D."

I read and reread the brief message and then sat there looking at the thing. Quite evidently it had been written during that last mysterious hour of Dr. Harrigan's life. In the excitement following my return from supper that night I had not thought to look at my patient's chart. But instinctively a nurse associates the duty of watching a patient's chart only with the patient qua patient: and this patient of mine had indubitably disappeared. I suppose that is why I had subconsciously dismissed all thought of the chart from my mind.

There were two things unusual about the little note. One was that it was not written in the usual space for orders and it was, of course, not customary for a doctor to leave such a cursory message for a nurse to follow her patient and the surgeon to the operating room; but then nothing about that projected operation was customary. And the second was the matter of the handwriting. Dr. Harrigan's usual handwriting was very small and neat and meticulous in its spaces and its *t*'s and *i*'s. And while I felt positive that Dr. Harrigan had himself written the note—for there were certain characteristics that were unmistakable—still there was the most peculiar looseness about the writing, something quite clear to the eye and yet rather intangible. The loops did not meet with his usual exactness, the *t*'s were crossed but not with the precise neatness that was his habit. There was somehow a lack of coördination about it; an uncertainty. Yet it was his handwriting.

I puzzled over the thing for some time, considered and rejected the possibility that he might have been drunk, and finally tore off that much of the chart and put it away in my pocket to be stored with the growing collection in the lavender hot-water bottle. I could make nothing of it, but the thing perplexed me more than a little.

It was during the slow, hot, dragging hours of that night, too, that I began to note certain questions on my chart blank; they ran like this and I felt that, if I could discover the answers to even a few of them I would have at least made a beginning toward a solution of the problem:

Where is Peter Melady?

Why did Dr. Harrigan enter Dione Melady's room directly after his meeting with Lillian Ash? (He was not her physician and the social relationship between the two families was not such as to permit a merely friendly call at that hour of the night.)

What, if anything, does Lillian Ash know of the Harrigans?

Could the elevator have been at the third floor all the time?

If Dione Melady found the Chinese snuff-bottle the night of July eighth, who had placed it in Peter Melady's room? It was not there when the room was searched a few hours earlier. And who took the bolt off the screen to the fire-escape window and why?

Where is the snuff-bottle now?

Ask Ellen if Dr. Harrigan was drunk when she last talked to him.

Was Nancy's desire to stop the operation due to anything more than a natural apprehension as to its irregularity?

There were many more questions I could have noted, of course, but just then Ellen came to make some entries on 304's chart and I asked her at once if Dr. Harrigan appeared to have been drinking when she last saw him.

"Oh, no, Miss Keate," she said promptly. "He wasn't drunk. I remember him saying how hot it was. And I offered to get him some ice water, but he said he'd just had some ice water in Mrs. Melady's room. He wasn't drunk."

"In Mrs. Melady's room?"

"Yes. She asked me to tell him she wanted to see him. Wanted to know how she thought her father would get along. I told him and he went in to see her, after he came out of his wife's room. He wasn't there long, Miss Keate, because it was not long after you'd gone downstairs that he called me into Mr. Melady's room to tell me he'd decided to operate at once and to get the truck."

"Why didn't you tell me that sooner?" I said in some exasperation. Perhaps all my questions had as simple and innocent answers! "Is there anything else you haven't mentioned?"

"No, Miss Keate. No, ma'am. Nothing," she assured me earnestly. "You didn't say anything about that. And it was nothing strange."

Her white cap bobbed away. The two policemen were still heroically seated on those hard little chairs and must have been numb from the waist down. Occasionally one or the other would get up, stroll down the corridor, peering into every shadowy door and corner, exchange a word or two with the other, and disappear perhaps for a short time down the west corridor or the stairway, always returning shortly to his own chair.

That was the night, then, of July ninth; breathlessly hot, guarded by policemen, and very quiet.

Dawn came, still hot and giving promise of another stifling, airless day.

The head nurse for the day came reluctantly and wearily to the east wing. As she took the keys she said:

"Peter Melady is dead."

"What! Has he been found!"

"Oh, he hasn't been found that I know of," she said carelessly as if that were a minor matter. "But he's dead. Did 301 take his oatmeal gruel? He's been awfully stubborn about it lately."

"What do you mean? Why do you say Peter Melady is dead?"

She gave me a weary and slightly bored look.

"Why, he was here in the hospital last night. In spirit, I mean." She paused and informed me again: "I'm psychic."

"See here, have you been talking this way to Mrs. Melady?"

"Well—a little. She asked me a few things. She's extremely telepathic, you know. Not psychic," she explained with the air of one drawing a fine distinction. "But extremely telepathic. If she would cultivate her thought——"

"Cultivate nothing," I said bitterly. "She can't think."

And I left the east wing for the day, feeling more thoroughly disgruntled with the world in general and the hospital in particular than I can ever remember feeling. But I must admit that never, never since that day have I felt comfortable or easy in the presence of that woman. And twice on the stairway I jerked suddenly about, positive that someone was following me. There was no one.

After breakfast I went at once to my room. I did not see a newspaper and did not know it was to be a day of almost frenzied activity on the part of the police, owing to the popular indignation as to the security of Melady Memorial, which happens to be one of the objects of civic pride in B——. It was that morning, I learned later, that Court Melady and Kenwood Ladd and even Dr. Kunce were grilled unmercifully at police headquarters and Sergeant Lamb finally came out to the hospital, accompanied by members of his staff, and reduced various nurses and hospital attendants almost to hysteria. That was the day, too, that the district attorney took a hand in the matter himself and came to B—— on the morning train, arriving red-faced, perspiring, and righteously indignant. It was a cloudy day of sweltering heat.

I slept till noon.

As I was dressing my eyes fell on the newspaper for the day following Dr. Harrigan's murder; I had folded it and left it on my bedside table. Pinning on my cap, I found myself reading over and over a single paragraph which was in small type and wedged in between the weather reports and Local Items. It read:

"Early this morning the body of a Negro was found in the basement of St. Małachy's Cathedral. Since last winter when the unemployment situation became acute a room in St. Malachy's basement has been left open to accommodate vagrants, and it is assumed that the Negro, a man of about forty, was trying to find help when he died. There were no means of identification found. The body is at the city morgue waiting indentification."

In five minutes I was at the telephone booth nearest my room, hunting feverishly for the telephone number of the undertakers who take care of our charity cases and are paid by the county. I found and called it.

"This is Miss Keate at Melady Memorial," I began steadily, after a voice had answered. "Our records are not quite complete as to the case you had the night of July seventh. It was a Negro, wasn't it? A man?"

"Just a moment, please," he said. "I'll look it up."

It was dreadfully hot in the little booth. I could not get my breath properly. Then his voice came through the receiver again.

"No, Miss Keate. That was a white man we had from the hospital the night of July seventh."

CHAPTER XI

I DO not recall getting downstairs and into Dr. Kunce's office but there I was, flourishing my newspaper. Sergeant Lamb was there and several policemen and, of course, Dr. Kunce. They were incredulous, excited, plying me with questions, with Dr. Kunce hurriedly telephoning to the undertakers and telling the office girl to have his car brought round to the door and Sergeant Lamb saying there was a police car outside and trying to get into his coat and asking me if I was sure it had been a Negro who died in the charity ward.

"I saw him, I tell you. I saw him. Here, you are trying to get your arm into the wrong sleeve."

He accepted my help without, I think, knowing it.

"If that's Peter Melady and he's been murdered and buried these three days it'll be hell," he said. "Casey, get out there and get the Chief on the phone. Where the devil's my cap! We'll have to get a permit to open the grave before we can identify him. Burns, get the police car started and at the door. We'll be out right away. What in hell are you all standing around like a bunch of——" Just then and most fortunately for the morals of everybody concerned Dr. Kunce clicked up the telephone and turned around, interrupting Sergeant Lamb's flow of language.

"It was a white man, all right. Buried him early the next morning. He was small and sandy-haired and around fifty years old. There's not much chance of it not being Peter Melady."

"Well, you'll soon have a chance to see," said Sergeant Lamb grimly. "How did he die? Murdered?"

"The undertaker said he'd judge from natural causes —heart disease. He said they had sent him the wrong certification from the hospital but he was gone on his vacation, just got back yesterday, and the night man was new to the business. His assistants fixed up the thing and buried the body." Dr. Kunce leaned his dark head on his hands and groaned. "Careless, but you can see how it happened. There was their case, a charity case with no family and dead from natural causes. They had no reason to think anything was wrong. He thought it merely a matter of confused records. The main thing was the body and there it was."

"Well, come on, Dr. Kunze, if you want to identify him. I'll see you later, Miss Keate."

"Kunce," said Dr. Kunce softly and followed.

The news was over the hospital like wildfire. I suppose the office girl started it from her post of vantage and the excited nurses fanned it furiously along. The truth was bad enough, but already the wildest added rumors were floating about, and it was only the promptest and most decisive action on the part of the steadier nurses which prevented a panic. As it was, one of the student nurses was caught walking out a back door with her traveling bag in her hand. Miss Jones collapsed into a faint that was so prolonged and complete that it looked like death itself and finally, when she learned she would have to go to identify the body of the Negro, it took all the nurses in the dormitory to get her into street clothes. And the day head nurse in my own east wing had a violent attack of hysterics, aserting wildly between spasms that she'd seen the ghost of the dead Negro walking out the elevator door. Considering the terms of familiarity she appeared to maintain with ghosts, I thought it highly inconsistent of her to be so affected that she had to be released from duty and given a sedative. I administered the sedative and gave her a very particular Triple Bromide, one which smells like all the vilest smells of the world rolled into one and multiplied. The odor alone has been known to bring recalcitrant patients to their senses. She hinted that I leave the small glass on her bedside table, but of course I saw the nauseous dose safely down her throat before I left.

And when I returned to the east wing to reassure the girls still on duty and to get someone to help out for the rest of the afternoon I looked at that elevator door with some misgiving.

After all how *had* that dead Negro got out of the hospital? Across the driveway? Into the basement room of St. Malachy's?

Around four o'clock, Dr. Kunce telephoned some message to the office girl, in the course of which it developed that the man who had been buried Tuesday was truly Peter Melady. They had got Court Melady's permission to perform an autopsy, after which, Dr. Kunce said, he would return to the hospital.

I was still in the east wing when this last item reached us. By that time, doubtless at Sergeant Lamb's orders in the face of this new disaster, a number of policemen were about the hospital, permitting no one to leave and peering suspiciously at the nurses, although I never knew just what they expected to accomplish at that late date.

No one had dared tell Dione Melady, but I think she guessed something was wrong, for she turned very irritable and inquisitive and her light snapped on fifty times, I'm sure. It was burning, I remember, when Dr. Kunce finally returned, accompanied by Court Melady and Ser-

geant Lamb, and went at once to her room. She took it
rather badly, I believe, in spite of the nonchalance with
which she had mentioned such a possibility during my
watch of the previous night. I did not wait, however; I
felt in no frame of mind to soothe and comfort Dione
Melady. They told her simply that he had died of heart
disease (as, it developed, the autopsy showed), and
glossed over the gruesome circumstances of his disappearance as best they might.

It was not long after that that I was summoned to
Dr. Kunce's office. Sergeant Lamb was there, of course,
and there were a scattering of policemen, Dr. Kunce, and
a red-faced gentleman, coatless, with his shirt damp about
the shoulders and back, who sat in front of the fan, completely usurping it, and smoked a very thick cigar, which
must have annoyed Dr. Kunce excessively. He proved to
be the district attorney and said very little beyond occasional grunts; he had, however, an extremely expressive
and versatile grunt. Miss Jones was there, too, in her hat
and a summer street dress of shantung; she looked dreadfully ill and white and was answering their inquiries
shakily.

Dr. Kunce motioned me to a chair and I subsided
quietly.

Yes, Miss Jones was saying, she and Teuber had
placed the body of the Negro, then properly tagged, on
the truck and Teuber had taken it away and that's all
she knew about it. She repeated at some length the story
she had told at the inquest and asked rather faintly if she
might have a glass of water.

"And I know it was a Negro. And I don't know how
his tag got on the body of Peter Melady," she said with
a shudder as Dr. Kunce gave her the water.

"Where is this Teuber?" asked Sergeant Lamb.

"Outside," said one of the policemen.

"Well, bring him in."

"May I suggest that you let Miss Jones go?" said Dr. Kunce softly. "She has had a trying week on account of the heat and all and must go on duty to-night."

"Oh, sure," said Sergeant Lamb. "But see that you don't try to leave, miss."

"Is that the nurse who telephoned the undertakers?" asked the district attorney suddenly, indicating me with a jerk of the cigar.

"Yes," said Sergeant Lamb unpleasantly.

"H'm," remarked the district attorney. This was a very subtle grunt which seemed to compliment me and insult Sergeant Lamb in the same breath; I say this because I felt a distinct sense of elation and Sergeant Lamb, shaken no doubt by the recent development and perhaps sensitive, turned a furious pink and asked one of the policemen why in hell he didn't open the windows. The windows were already open.

"A warm day," murmured Dr. Kunce in a placating way. He looked as haggard and worn as any of us there in Melady Memorial, but his light suit was immaculate though wrinkled, his red geranium only a little wilted, his silky dark beard smooth and unruffled, and his dark eyes secretive back of those long eyelashes. It was in the coffee-colored pockets about his eyes, in his yellowish pallor, in his slender fingers stroking and stroking his beard that the strain he was under evidenced itself.

Just then Jacob Teuber was ushered into the room by a fat policeman beside whom the orderly looked more shrunken and ill-fed than usual. He was wheezing, too, so agitatedly that they had to wait for him to get over the attack, which added to Sergeant Lamb's impatience.

"Here," said Dr. Kunce, "take a drink of water."

But Teuber motioned away the water, wiped his streaming eyes and his face with a handkerchief, pulled down his white sleeves, and said:

"It's all right, now."

"Now then, Teuber," began Sergeant Lamb, "let's have the truth about this. Just why did you give the undertaker Peter Melady's body instead of the dead nigger?"

Well, I suppose his question would have frightened anyone; there was certainly a very gray look about Teuber's thin face.

"I know what you're talking about, of course," stammered the orderly nervously. "It's all over the hospital and I—I've been trying to think and I—I don't see how it could have happened." He turned appealingly to Dr. Kunce. "Really, Dr. Kunce, I did everything all right. Miss Jones and I, we loaded him onto the truck and I took him along to the elevator and met Miss Keate —oh, it's just as I've told you all along. After I couldn't get the elevator I turned right around and took him down by the freight elevator and right straight to the ambulance room ready for the men from the undertakers, and they came and put it into the ambulance and"—he lifted his thin shoulders—"and there you are. That's all I know."

"See here, Teuber, you're lying," said Sergeant Lamb. "You're lying. Come out now with the truth."

"That's the truth, sir," cried Teuber. "I'll swear it was the Negro."

"Are you trying to make us believe that the undertakers' men took that Negro's body out of the hospital —actually got it into their ambulance—and on the way to their establishment somebody substituted Peter Melady's body? Listen to me, Teuber. There were two men on the undertakers' ambulance that night——"

He paused and Teuber, his bony, moist-looking hand beginning to twist in front of his white duck jacket, nodded soundlessly.

"—and both these men swear that they did not stop on any pretext between the ambulance door of this hospital and their own establishment. Now what have you to say to that?"

"I—I don't know," faltered Jacob Teuber, his weak eyes going here and there about the room and finally coming to rest upon the rug at his feet. He looked, I must say, the very picture of guilt. Suddenly he flared up defensively. "I took the body of that Negro straight down to the ambulance room. And the undertakers came and got it. And nobody can make me say I didn't!"

"All we want is the truth," said Sergeant Lamb more kindly. "Come now, confess that you changed bodies and tell us why you did it."

"I've already told you all I know about it."

Dr. Kunce, who had moved a bit restlessly a time or two, leaned forward.

"You see how it is, Teuber. You are the only man who *could* have changed bodies. Why you did it, God knows, but you must have done it."

But Teuber, though increased fear leaped into his eyes at the sound of Dr. Kunce's silky voice, shook his head stubbornly.

The district attorney gave a preliminary grunt, at which Teuber flinched, and said:

"If I understand it right, your business was to take this dead Negro on this stretcher affair down to a room in the basement and hand it over to the undertakers' men when they arrived with their ambulance. Right?"

"Yes."

"How long was it before they arrived?"

"I can't say exactly. They'd been notified right away and I suppose it was ten minutes or so after I got the body down to the ambulance room. But I didn't have my watch; I can't be certain."

"When did you hear about the murder?"

"Just after the ambulance left with the body. I started back to my own room there in the west wing of the basement floor, and already the other orderlies had heard about it and upstairs the nurses and all were running around telling each other. Nobody knew what had happened except that Dr. Harrigan was dead and that Dr. Kunce had told the office girl to call the police. So, of course, we thought he must have been murdered."

"You are sure you locked the door—the outside door, that is—of the ambulance room after the men from the undertakers' had gone?"

"Oh, yes."

"And you saw nobody else in the basement? Anywhere —corridors, ambulance room—whatever rooms there are down there?"

"Not a soul," said Teuber dejectedly, as if he wished with all his heart he had seen someone. Which I have no doubt he did wish.

"Heard nothing unusual?"

"Not a thing."

"Nobody slipped out the door while it was open? You might have had your back turned."

"No. I'm sure of that."

"You started a search—guarded the doors and all— immediately upon your arrival?" asked the district attorney, addressing Sergeant Lamb.

"Certainly. At once. We were at the hospital within

—seven minutes at the most following the call. Perhaps five minutes."

"You called for Dr. Kunce at twelve thirty-two?" asked the district attorney, whirling around toward me.

"So the office girl says."

"Well, did you?"

"I believe so," I said haughtily. "You will understand that I didn't look at my watch."

"And you"—turning to Dr. Kunce—"how soon did you get upstairs and telephone the police?"

"It took me probably three minutes or so to reach the third floor after the office girl got me on the telephone and gave me Miss Keate's message. Then I made a brief examination of the body and told the office girl to call the police and board members."

"The time of the call from the hospital was noted on the police blotter as being twelve-forty, if that's what you are after," said Sergeant Lamb in a gloomy way though with much respect.

"In the meantime you were downstairs in the—er—ambulance room, handing over that Negro to the undertakers' men?"

"I suppose so," said Jacob Teuber uncertainly, as if he were not sure just where that admission might lead him.

"And Sergeant, you and your squad couldn't have got here until about twelve forty-five. That sounds like quick enough work but"—the district attorney leaned back, took a quick puff from his cigar, and continued: "—but it's too bad it wasn't just a little quicker. The undertakers' ambulance had plenty of time to get away. Also Dr. Harrigan's murderer. Apparently it was not Peter Melady. In fact," he went on in a more leisurely way, "I don't see that you are accomplishing anything. We found

Peter Melady and the autopsy proved he died from natural causes. We'll probably find out eventually just why those bodies were swapped. But I don't see that we are any closer to finding out who killed Dr. Harrigan. Or why." He turned suddenly to Teuber again and snapped in a crisp and sharp voice as if to take the orderly off his guard: "How long did you leave that body alone in the ambulance room?"

"I—you—no, no!" denied Jacob Teuber wildly. "I didn't. I didn't. I didn't leave it alone." He began to choke and wheeze again very violently. The attack was not feigned—I knew that. But I was suddenly quite sure he was not telling the truth.

"See here, young man," I said abruptly, ignoring the startled looks from the district attorney and others, "you are not telling the truth. And unless you're as dumb as a post you'll see that you'd be far better off if you *had* happened to leave that dead Negro alone in the morgue or the corridor for a few moments. I'd advise you to tell the truth. Dr Kunce won't discharge you for that. And you can take my word you'll be much better off."

But he stuck to his story with the strange hysterical obstinacy which one often sees in physically weak or somewhat stupid people. And presently from very weariness they were obliged to let him go with a warning not to leave the hospital.

"Not that it would be much use to try to get away," added Sergeant Lamb, continuing a bit more affably as he turned to me: "We'd like to ask you a few questions, Miss Keate."

And it was not until a good half hour had passed that I realized why they were questioning me so closely, going over and over again the brief story I had already told so many times. The reason, when it occurred to me, was not a nice one. For who had been known to be wandering about between the third and fourth floors, ringing for the elevator and looking for Dr. Harrigan, but I—Sarah Keate? And who had found the body? And who had been Peter Melady's special nurse—thereby, and for a reason that seemed quite clear to Sergeant Lamb but not to me, having had an interest in sending his dead body along to the undertakers instead of the body of the Negro?

"But you did approach the truck where this nigger lay and look at him?" insisted Sergeant Lamb at one point.

"I did," I said acidly. "And not being in the habit of lugging dead bodies about I did not slip Peter Melady's body under the sheet and walk downstairs with the other body." And found myself shivering.

"Come, Sergeant Lamb," said Dr. Kunce softly. "Really I must protest. Aren't you going too far?"

The district attorney grunted, whether in agreement or not, I could not determine, and Sergeant Lamb said plaintively:

"Well, wouldn't this Slæpan stuff do her as much good as anybody?"

The district attorney stirred restlessly.

"When did you say this new lieutenant—this O'Leary fellow—would be in town?"

"Day after to-morrow," said Sergeant Lamb.

"Why doesn't he stay in town? What's he gadding about for?"

"He's just received his appointment," said Sergeant Lamb briefly. Then a slightly happier look crossed his harassed face. "I thought maybe I could have this thing all settled and the murderer awaiting indictment by the time he got here. I don't know as I will," he confessed honestly. "But I'm not going to be sorry to hand it over to this young fellow they say is so good. We'll find out what he'll do about it."

"Well," said the district attorney somewhat sharply, "I think it's high time somebody did something."

"What would you suggest?" asked the Sergeant in a bland and very respectful way. Upon which the district attorney's wide face assumed a soft purple tint and Dr. Kunce said:

"The trouble is, it is so contradictory. If we assume the motive to have been the theft of the snuff-bottle with the Slæpan formula in it, the obvious thing to do would be to locate the possessor of the snuff-bottle. And, of course, the range of suspects is likely limited to those who knew Peter Melady's idiosyncrasies and who might have guessed—or even known—that the formula was in the snuff-bottle. But as for you suggesting that Miss Keate had anything to do with the murder, you are just wasting time. You may not feel like taking my word for it, but there it is."

Again I disliked, and quite irrationally, Dr. Kunce's championship.

"That's as may be," said Sergeant Lamb, giving me a dark look. "But I'll grant you it's contradictory enough. If that Slæpan formula is at the bottom of it—and it certainly is the only motive we can get a hint of—and even granting that Dr. Harrigan had managed to get the thing away from Peter Melady, that doesn't explain this business of getting Peter Melady's body out of the hospital and buried. If Peter Melady killed Dr. Harrigan and then himself died from heart disease, *who* got his body into the undertakers' ambulance? And *why?* That's the big question. Why? Or were Peter Melady and Dr. Harrigan both put out of the way by a third person? That's the ground we've got to take."

"No," said Dr. Kunce decidedly. "I agree with the findings of the autopsy. Peter Melady was not murdered. He died a natural death."

"Maybe," said Sergeant Lamb. "But I think he was murdered. Maybe he was threatened and died of fear and excitement. Maybe the murderer struggled with him and that brought on his heart attack. But I think it was actual murder, for otherwise there would have been no attempt to conceal his body."

"And," I said crisply, "if I had had any guilty knowledge of this wicked crime do you think I would have discovered and told you where to find the body of Peter Melady?"

Sergeant Lamb favored me with another doubtful look.

"You can't tell about women," he said dourly. "Come now, Miss Keate, isn't there anything you know that might help us?"

There was the whereabouts of the gold hair, of course. But there was nothing else of which I definitely knew. I felt positive that Lillian Ash had wiped the fingerprints off that knife, but I could not have sworn it. As far as that goes, there were a number of things I surmised and a number of things which greatly interested me, but very few which were definite evidence. However, I felt it was only fair to tell Sergeant Lamb everything I had in mind. Everything, of course, except about the gold hair which was not in my mind, so to speak, but in the lavender hot-water bottle. I knew that when Lance O'Leary arrived and found me an active figure in the business, he would question me extensively and listen very patiently and attentively to everything I had to say. And I don't mind saying that, while I did not expect Lance O'Leary to produce the criminal as a magician produces rabbits, still

I did expect him to make a little more progress in that direction than Sergeant Lamb had made. Having known Lance O'Leary rather well for a number of years I could scarcely help being somewhat biased in his favor. So, for that very reason, I felt I must force myself to do the fair thing; I must oblige Sergeant Lamb to listen to the whole story of surmise and suppositions and lines of inquiry which I had built up. He might draw his own conclusions or he might draw no conclusions, but that obviously was my duty.

So far I had told him only the briefest of facts in the briefest of ways. Now I would give him my impressions, yes, even my suspicions of Lillian Ash, distasteful though it was for me to do so. I was reaching into my pocket for my notes in order to present my story in a systematic fashion when Sergeant Lamb said:

"Don't be all day about it, nurse. If you've got anything to say, get it out. And I want facts, mind you. Facts. Not any of your opinions."

Well.

I was not angry, I think, so much as wounded. I rose at once. I did not even look at Sergeant Lamb.

"Is that all?" I asked Dr. Kunce. "I should like to get upstairs as soon as possible. The hospital is very much agitated about all this."

"Wait a minute. Wait a minute," said Sergeant Lamb, aware possibly that he had offended but not in what manner.

It was at that second that the door was flung violently open and Lillian Ash stood there in the opening.

She just stood there, very quiet and still except for her quick breathing, after that violent introduction. The room became very still, too; a throbbing, sultry, heat-laden stillness, while we stared at the woman on the threshold. Her hair was straight and stringy under her white cap; her uniform was wrinkled and none too fresh. Her fleshy face had grown flabby in the last three days, the muscles sagging so that she looked older, and her eyes had deep leaden marks under them. Every vestige of her usual manner of bright and determined youthfulness had left her and she looked—I searched for the right word and found it—she looked beaten.

Everyone in that close, overfurnished little room must have known at once that she was about to say something of the extremest importance. But it was at least a minute before anyone spoke. A long sixty seconds, seething with the turbulence of things yet unsaid. I remember the district attorney's dropped pink jaw and his absent-minded clutch for his cigar.

Then Lillian Ash moistened her full, dry lips.

"I've come," she said in a strangled way, "to tell you something."

Her voice broke the stillness. Dr. Kunce sprang upward, motioned her to a chair, and closed the office door.

"Shan't I go?" I offered with some reluctance.

"Let her stay," said the district attorney, giving me a rather penetrating look and waving his cigar in my direction. "Now, then—what's all this?"

"I've come to tell you something," said Lillian Ash again. "I——" She choked, put her hand to her throat, and finally said: "It was Kenwood Ladd. I couldn't tell you before. It—it's such a terrible thing——" Her voice broke and she sat staring into space with a wide, blank look as if she were actually seeing the ugly sight which her words brought to us, and she went on in a sharp whisper: *"It's a terrible thing to accuse a man of murder. To send him to death."*

And then closed her eyes and leaned against the chair

as if the very breath had gone out of her body with her whisper.

Well, it is a dreadful thing to make a statement which, when proved, is going to send another human being, living and loving life as much as yourself, on that long ignominious road which ends so hideously and so shamefully. True, it had not seemed to me that Lillian Ash was the imaginative, sensitive type of person whom that duty would affect so profoundly; still, as Sergeant Lamb had remarked, you never can tell about a woman.

"Kenwood Ladd!" cried Sergeant Lamb. "Ladd! Just as I thought——" He checked himself abruptly and went on with more pomposity: "Come, now, Miss Ash, don't make any rash statements. It's a serious thing, you know, to send a fellow to the hot—the electric chair." He amended the brutal phrase hurriedly, which convinced me that, after all, he meant well.

"It was Kenwood Ladd," said Lillian Ash again. Then she took a long breath, sat up, and said rapidly: "He did not leave the hospital the night of July seventh until after twelve o'clock. I don't know when he left, but it was not before twelve. He stayed in Mrs. Harrigan's room. I was nursing a patient right across the hall from Mrs. Harrigan's room and I saw. He simply closed the door so no one would see him and stayed. Once Ellen Brody went to the door and opened it but went away right away at something Mrs. Harrigan said and, I suppose, didn't see him. Finally about eleven-thirty Dr. Harrigan came and opened the door and went in. I"—she did hesitate there, but for only a moment—"I—well, I took a pitcher of ice water as if I'd understood Mrs. Harrigan had asked for water and went to the door and opened it. Mr. Ladd was facing me, and Mrs. Harrigan was sitting in a chair, and Dr. Harrigan was standing

with his back to me. And the two men were quarreling in low, terrible voices. It was worse because they were
afraid of being overheard. And as I opened the door,
Dr. Harrigan was swearing and said: 'And I find you
here with my wife again,' and Kenwood Ladd said"—
her voice had been getting lower and lower and was
husky and strained and painful to hear—"and Kenwood
Ladd said: 'I could kill you for saying that, if you
weren't an old man.' Then Mr. Ladd seemed to see that
there was someone at the door—only the night light over
the bed was turned on and the door was in shadow, so
I suppose he only saw my white uniform. And I set the
pitcher on the table by the door and was back in my patient's room before Mr. Ladd reached the door of 307
and opened it again and I saw him look up and down the
corridor. But he didn't see me, of course. And he closed
the door again. Just as the supper bell rang Dr. Harrigan came out of the room. I went on down to supper. I
wasn't hungry and came upstairs right away again, but
my patient wanted the door to the room closed and then
drifted off to sleep, and I was afraid to open the door
again until he was in a sound sleep and I would not be
apt to wake him. So I don't know exactly when Kenwood
Ladd left the hospital. But what I've told you is the
truth. And I can swear to it."

The amazing thing about it was that it did appear
to be the truth, at least so far as it went; to my notion
there was considerable proof lacking that the young
architect had actually killed Dr. Harrigan. But it was
true that he was in the hospital at very close to the time
the murder actually occurred. He admitted that at once
and not half an hour after Lillian Ash's entrance into
Dr. Kunce's office. They had sent for him immediately
and he had come without protest. He looked rather gray

and very tight-mouthed; I think he had been fully alive to the danger of his position from the beginning.

"Oh, I've been expecting it," he told Sergeant Lamb. "I knew some nurse was there in the doorway. Anyway"—he said somewhat enigmatically, his eyes on Lillian Ash—"I'm glad it was you and not——" He left that sentence unfinished and went on: "It's been hell wondering when it would come out. I'd have told at once but Ina—Mrs. Harrigan wouldn't have it. Well, there it is. I was here until midnight, yes. And I quarreled with Dr. Harrigan. And I said I could kill him for what he said. That's true enough. But I didn't kill Dr. Harrigan."

"How did you escape?" asked Sergeant Lamb.

That curious little flush crept into Kenwood Ladd's face, but he replied in the most nonchalant way in the world:

"It was not escape. I left by—by way of the roof."

"The roof!"

"The roof and then down the fire escape."

"But the door to the roof was locked. All the doors were locked."

"The door leading from the little iron stairway onto the roof has a night latch, I suppose," said Kenwood Ladd. "I've wondered how you came to insist that all the doors were locked. I suppose the police tried it from the outside."

"Well, I'll be damned," said Sergeant Lamb; he shot a look of fury toward the police then in the room, and the district attorney fixed his eyes on Sergeant Lamb and said: "H'm," in an eloquent fashion which did not appear to soothe Sergeant Lamb.

"Any other of these 'locked doors' have night latches on?" asked the district attorney.

"No," said Dr. Kunce.

"H'm. So that's the way of it. And I suppose when you got into the hospital and choked Mrs. Melady and stole this bottle thing, you got out that door again."

"I was not here that night," said Kenwood Ladd steadily. "I've got an alibi for that night. But I am admitting I was here the night Dr. Harrigan was murdered."

Well, if he was guilty he deserved short shrift. If innocent, it was a difficult enough position; I could readily understand that Ina Harrigan might have been bored and restless, might have urged him to stay, laughing at hospital rules and customs as she would; they might have talked on and on without realizing that, for a hospital, it was growing late. Then Dr. Harrigan, always a man of violence, had arrived and, possibly because he felt like quarreling, had plunged into the most brutal accusations which were, so far as that present moment was concerned, patently absurd.

"What time did you say you left the hospital?"

"I didn't say. And—and that's the trouble. I don't know. It was a few minutes after Dr. Harrigan left the room. Mrs. Harrigan said to wait until the nurses had gone to supper and the corridor was deserted and told me about the little stairway to the roof. Naturally she didn't want the office girl or any of the nurses to see me. And I waited."

"But it was after twelve?"

"Yes. Very shortly after twelve. I've been telling you the truth all along, though: I really don't know exactly what time it was."

"Do you know what time Dr. Harrigan was killed?"

"I heard at the inquest, yes. Sometime between twelve-eighteen and twelve thirty-two, wasn't it?"

"And you admit you were here at that time?"

"I admit nothing of the kind. I tell you I left just a short time after twelve."

"But you can't say when," said Sergeant Lamb in a derisive voice which was not necessary in order to point out the weakness of Kenwood Ladd's position.

"No. I can't," said Kenwood Ladd. "But I didn't kill Dr. Harrigan and you can't prove that I did."

"Don't be so sure about that, young fellow. Are you familiar with the plan of the hospital?"

"Not precisely. I know the general plan, I suppose— that is, the entrance and the third floor. And Mrs. Harrigan told me about the flight of steps leading from the fourth floor to the roof."

"I don't doubt that you know the third floor. The east wing in particular," said Sergeant Lamb, and the young architect flushed again. But he disposed some cigarette ashes in the tray with a steady hand, kept on smoking steadily, which he had done ever since entering the room, and returned Sergeant Lamb's look with narrowed, careful eyes.

"You know where the operating rooms are?"

"I do now, yes. After hearing the inquest. I don't believe I knew then."

"You knew where the instruments were kept?"

"No."

Sergeant Lamb smiled.

CHAPTER XII

IT WAS just then that a stenographer arrived from police headquarters, with his tablet and pencil in hand. He first took Lillian Ash's story, and after that I presume the inquiry took on a more official character. I do not know, for Miss Ash and I were permitted to leave.

At the door I lingered to speak in a low voice to Dr. Kunce.

"You found the body of the Negro?"

"Oh, at once. It's the same. Miss Jones identified him. He was dressed, by the way, in the clothes in which he was brought here. The tag had been removed from him, of course, and there was nothing to identify him. But we are sure it's the same body. So there's no need for the nurses to fear it is still about the hospital somewhere."

"How did it get there—into the basement room of St. Malachy's?"

Dr. Kunce shrugged.

"How should I know?"

Once in my own room I got out the pillbox again and decided presently that I should have no peace of mind until that hair was analyzed and its ownership determined. And there was the scrap of paper, too, with Dr. Harrigan's message to me; that curious message, not quite coherent and written so loosely, so unlike Dr. Harrigan's usual handwriting. And I wished with all my heart that Lance O'Leary would arrive; even the delay or another day seemed far too long. The situation had grown incredibly bad and ugly. Even I, who am, as a rule, the most prosaic and unimaginative of women, felt very clearly and definitely the danger in the silent old hospital—the threat in its shadows and its thick walls and its high-ceilinged corridors and sick rooms.

And all the time, in the heat, that inquiry was going on down in Dr. Kunce's office; eager, avidly determined questions, guarded replies, going on and on during the desperately hot hours of the afternoon. I can imagine that interview from the little I saw of it; the sweltering heat, the sweat running down the men's faces, the yellow tablet of the stenographer and his flying pencil, the subdued undertone of the electric fan, the smell of the district attorney's cigar, smoldering and going out and having to be relit, the breathless atmosphere in the over-furnished, crowded room, and Kenwood Ladd's young, desperately guarded face. There must have been something of torture in that face, too; he'd known his danger all along. And even if he escaped, if they failed to trap him into some damaging admission, if they could not, at the last, prove him guilty, there would still be that sensational story to toss to the newspapers. Of the two people concerned, it was curious that I felt that Kenwood Ladd would suffer most thereby. I think I am not blaming the woman in the case unduly; it really seemed to me that there was a sort of shell of extreme selfishness and hardness about Ina Harrigan which would make her impervious to such a wound.

With Lance O'Leary's longed-for arrival in mind I got out my scribbled notes, took some fresh paper, and made a sort of résumé of the affair. It took a long time, and when I had finished I was exactly where I started. The ominously short list was precisely the same, except that there was an added and important item below the name of Kenwood Ladd.

There was Courtney Melady, against whom I had no evidence that I could see—except the possibility of his presence in the hospital the night of the murder, and I considered this highly improbable (though as to that, I had considered Kenwood Ladd's presence just as improbable until faced with Lillian Ash's staggering evidence). Then there were Dr. Kunce, Teuber, Ina Harrigan, and Lillian Ash.

Of them all there was definite evidence only against Lillian Ash and Kenwood Ladd. Yet I was morally certain that one of these six names was that of Dr. Harrigan's murderer.

Outside the shadows were lengthening. Another night was on its way. From my window I could see a strip of languid lawn, and the hot asphalt which looked swollen and elastic with heat. Numerous cars were passing, their occupants craning their necks to stare at Melady Memorial. The sun had not been out all day but the clouds were no heavier; they seemed to hover lightly but densely over the world like a gray blanket, holding the moisture and heat close to the earth. The extreme humidity made things appear weary and exhausted; even the thin leaves of the Chinese elms that bordered the street hung heavily like slow little drops of green syrup. Nothing moved except the automobiles, and they went as slowly as they dared in order to permit their morbidly minded passengers to get a good look at the place.

I stared thoughtfully at the scarlet cannas in the middle of the strip of lawn, thought how curiously tropical an air had come upon us with the humid heat, and turned back to my notes again.

Peter Melady I did not consider as a suspect, although,

not knowing just when and how he had died, one could not know what he had or had not done before death overtook him. The autopsy showed that Peter Melady had died a natural death. At the same time deliberately calculated shock or over-excitement might have been arranged so as to bring on his death, in which case he would have been murdered as surely as Dr. Harrigan was murdered with that knife.

In the case of the Negro there was no doubt. He had been dead when I looked at him. So he couldn't have dragged himself, poor thing, out of the hospital and across to St. Malachy's. Or got himself into clothes!

I sat up excitedly at that. Someone had even got that body into clothes, purposely taking off anything that might connect the dead Negro with Melady Memorial hospital and putting on its own clothes which, as is customary in such cases, Miss Jones had likely made into a little roll and sent down with the truck.

St. Malachy's is, of course, just around the corner, facing the street on the opposite side of the square; the basement room where the Negro's body was found has an entrance which is not far from the back drive of the hospital and the door at which the ambulance usually stops.

On an impulse I rose, straightened my cap, and went to the basement. It was not without some trepidation that I hurried along those narrow basement halls but I saw nothing to alarm me. The door to the ambulance room was open as is customary; it is only the door to the mortuary itself, where the large ice boxes are placed, which is kept locked—largely, I've been told, to prevent ambitious young surgeons from making informal and illegal post-mortems of baffling cases. I nosed around in the ambulance room for some time, finding nothing of interest and incurring some highly gratified attention on the part of a burly policeman who entered the room as I was examining the outside door which was locked.

"Trying to get out, are you?" he said most rudely.

In the hall I encountered Teuber and stopped him.

"When you took that Negro down from the charity ward did Miss Jones put the bundle of his clothes on the truck also?"

"Yes, Miss Keate."

"See if the bundle is in the supply room, will you?"

I had no right to make the request, of course, but he was amiable and went at once to the small supply room where a dead patient's belongings are left so that, if they are not eventually claimed, they can be cleaned and used for charity. He returned quickly, shaking his head.

"No, Miss Keate. It isn't there."

"Are you sure you put it there?"

"Oh, yes. On my way to my room for——" he stopped, and a look of consternation spread over his face, and a paroxysm of wheezing racked his thin body. I waited until it had subsided and then said sternly:

"Then you left the body of that Negro in the ambulance room alone, no one with it, while you went to your room for something?"

He nodded miserably.

"How long were you gone?"

"I don't know exactly, Miss Keate. But it wasn't long. My asthma was bad that night and I went to get an inhaler. Please don't tell Dr. Kunce. He'll fire me sure. And my asthma is so bad this is the only kind of job I can hold."

"Why, you idiot! Don't you see that you are apt to be arrested for murder yourself? Or for something any-way," I went on, feeling somewhat confused as to the exact nature of his offense. "You were in charge of the body, at any rate, from the time it left the charity ward until the undertakers came for it. Who else but you is responsible for changing the bodies? You'll be much better off telling the truth about it. Dr. Kunce won't discharge you for the negligence of leaving the body alone for that length of time. At least I don't think he will. And even that would be better than to be arrested for murder."

Well, I could see that I had frightened him, but he still insisted that I keep his dereliction from duty a secret.

"Where was the key to the outside door while you were gone from the ambulance room?" I asked finally.

At which, if possible, he looked more terrified and said:

"In the lock of the door, Miss Keate. I'd unlocked it so the men from the undertakers' could get in if they happened to arrive while I was gone. Dr. Kunce will kill me if he hears about that."

"Well, I shouldn't blame him! The door, then, was unlocked for—how long? Ten minutes?"

"Maybe."

"You realize, of course, that you've upset all Dr. Kunce's careful investigations and statements as to the hospital being locked?"

He nodded wretchedly, wiped his nose, and gave a rather pathetic wheeze, upon which the policeman came to the door of the ambulance room, regarded us both suspiciously and a bit hopefully, and then lounged against the door casing, straining his ears, no doubt, to hear what we said.

"I don't see how we can avoid telling, Jacob," I said more kindly. "It is so very important. You see some-

one had plenty of time and chance to change bodies——"
I stopped abruptly, frowning at the thought that still
we had to explain how on earth Peter Melady's body had
been got down to the ambulance room with the main
elevator not running, and after a moment continued:
"—and escape if he wanted to, after taking that Negro's
body into the basement of St. Malachy's. No, I can't keep
it a secret. But I'll speak to Dr. Kunce about you, myself. That's the best I can do."

He assented to that listlessly and miserably, as if he'd
already been discharged, and answered my other questions in an apathetic manner.

No, there'd been no one about in the basement. At
least he had seen or heard nothing out of the way. He
got back to the ambulance room just a moment or two
before the undertakers' men arrived. The body was just
as he had left it, he thought, covered with a sheet, there
on the truck. No, none of them had looked at it; why
should they? The men had just loaded it into the ambulance and left and he'd locked the door after them.

"Didn't you notice the difference in weight?" I asked
impatiently.

"No, the undertakers' men lifted it."

"Oh, by the way, you remember when you were starting downstairs with this Negro and I had been ringing
for the elevator and I met you?"

"Of course, Miss Keate."

"Well, didn't you try to open the elevator door?"

"Why yes. But I couldn't get it open."

"You wouldn't say, then, that the elevator cage was
already at the third floor? With the emergency stop on
to hold it there?"

He shook his head doubtfully.

"The door would have opened in that case, Miss

Keate." He paused and then went on informatively: "If the emergency stop had been on it would have held the cage all right, so no amount of ringing could have brought it to another floor. But I could have easy opened the door if the cage had been there at the third floor. You see, the electric power and a——"

"I quite see, thank you," I said loftily, not liking his pedagogical air. "I'll do the best I can for you with Dr. Kunce."

I left him and made my way upstairs again. Dr. Kunce was in the outer office giving some orders to a nurse from the OB ward, and when he had finished I told him what Teuber had admitted to me. In the face of the orderly's extreme apprehension it was curious that Dr. Kunce should have almost welcomed the news. It was not at all what I had expected, for he is as cranky a man as I have ever seen on points of hospital routine and management. He looked almost pleased. He questioned me with a smooth silkiness that was very near to eagerness, and to my astonishment appeared to have swung completely around to the belief that some intruder had stolen into the hospital, killed Dr. Harrigan, and escaped. I suppose it was either that, to him, or a belief in Kenwood Ladd's guilt and thus Ina Harrigan's becoming involved in the affair. I have never known just why I felt so sure that he cherished a secret tenderness for Ina Harrigan, but there the notion was, full-fledged and vigorous, in my mind.

"He escaped," went on Dr. Kunce with smooth satisfaction, "by the opened door of the ambulance room."

"And stumbling upon Peter Melady's body, he carried it with him down to the ambulance room, placed it on the truck, and took the body of the Negro with him in his mad flight," I said.

His silky lashes drew closer together.

"I think that will be all, thank you, Miss Keate," he said, dismissing me as coolly as if I'd been an impertinent little student nurse.

Several nurses were gathered in a little knot, near enough to the office to be easily accessible to the office girl, in case her alert ears caught any bits of news, and far enough away to make a hasty retreat in case Dr. Kunce appeared. They looked avidly at me as I drew near, but I daresay I did not seem in any too sociable a mind, for no one questioned me.

Nancy was waiting for me in my room, turning the pages of a *Nurses' Record* and looking very weary and tired.

"They've still got Kenwood Ladd down there in the office," she said. "I think it's a shame and a disgrace."

"What? Making an inquiry into murder?"

"Torturing him!" she cried with a little rush of feeling which she quickly stifled. "I mean," she went on in a quieter way, "making anybody suffer so this terribly hot day. Trying to trap him, wear him down until he confesses to something he—didn't do."

"But—maybe he did. Maybe he murdered Dr. Harrigan."

"He didn't!" she cried. "He didn't!" And turned to stare out of the window—blindly, I think, for her voice had shaken.

"He might have," I said quietly. "How can you tell that he didn't?"

She whirled at that.

"By looking at him," she said. "By looking at him. Why he—he couldn't do that!"

"I'm afraid he could," I said, troubled. I did not like the way she had spoken. She was too vivid, too dark-eyed, too shaken; in an age when much is made of trivialities but one's most cataclysmic feelings are carefully covered, the feeling must be very cataclysmic indeed to emerge. And here was Nancy, cheeks flaming, mouth red and none too steady, tears brimming hotly—defiant, tremulous, tender all at once, and in such a state about a man at whom she'd only looked a few times. But I suppose that's the way things are; you go along in a casual and contented way and then one day there's a word or a look or maybe just nothing at all and your heart is wrenched out of your body and twisted.

Well, well—"men have died and worms have eaten them but not for——" I caught myself up shortly, fearing I had spoken aloud. In view of the circumstances, it occurred to me that that particular thought was not well chosen.

Moreover, Nancy was of a nature to take things hard; she savored experiences too vividly, too fully to escape them unscathed; if she even had a cold she had it more violently and more wretchedly than anyone else in the dormitory. And furthermore, I couldn't remember Nancy having fallen in love before (*jumping* in love would be a more appropriate word, I thought somewhat waspishly to myself)—not even with the sinfully handsome young interne who'd finished his interneship in May and left us, thereby permitting the temperature of the entire nursing staff to drop a degree or so. With one exception, which was Nancy. And another which I trust I need not indicate.

"I'm afraid he could," I said again, thoughtfully. "Nancy, my dear, is there anything troubling you? Forgive my asking, but you've looked so pale and anxious for the last few days."

Well, heaven knew I wasn't inquiring about her feeling toward Kenwood Ladd; that was clear enough. But her face went faintly pink and then white and she said:

"Why, no, Sarah. Nothing, that is, except—just the state of affairs here in the hospital. I suppose I've got nerves like anyone else. And—it's pretty awful, you know. I passed an empty room this morning and saw something white in it and screamed. And it was nothing but a sheet hanging over a chair. That's the way I am, and I'm not the only one."

Which was all quite true. But I felt dissatisfied; her voice was not natural; her eyes avoided mine. And I felt still less satisfied when I found, after Nancy had gone, that my notes had apparently gone with her. At least I could not find them on the table where I'd left them, or anywhere about the room. Of course, someone else might have entered the room while I was in the basement and taken the notes and gone before Nancy arrived, but I doubted it. Yet Nancy was as a rule overpunctilious about such things as laundry lists and postcards and telegrams.

I told myself that she had probably been doing some calculating herself (as everyone in the hospital no doubt was doing), saw my notes, the purpose of which was so obvious, saw perhaps Kenwood Ladd's name, and took the notes from a perfectly natural curiosity. Love affects people so very queerly. I clung stubbornly to that well-known fact, but in my heart I wished Nancy had told me what she knew. I feared that there was something she was concealing, through loyalty perhaps, or a mistaken conception of her duty, but nevertheless concealing.

My fear confirmed itself at dinner, when Nancy appeared looking more troubled than ever, resembling, indeed, a very lost and worried little ghost with soft gold hair and a nurse's uniform. She watched me covertly and said not a word. It was a sorry meal, altogether, chiefly of cold roast beef and a jellied salad which the heat had reduced to baffling incoherence. It was terribly stuffy down in the basement room and not cheerful, and our heads jerked as if on a single wire when someone dropped a pan in the kitchen. And Fannie Bianchi, who is a maddeningly deliberate eater, left her custard dessert untouched rather than remain alone in the room when the rest of us were leaving. Not that the custard was anything to regret; there is nothing more insidiously calculated to shake one's faith in humanity than a quickly cooked custard pudding.

As we rounded the turn on the first floor I glanced down toward the office. There was a subdued hubbub of nurses and staff doctors and police, but I saw nothing of Kenwood Ladd.

But when we reached the third floor Ellen came flying to meet me, her Irish-terrier look in full control and her cap over one ear.

"Dr. Kunce and Sergeant Lamb and a man with a yellow tablet are in Mrs. Harrigan's room," she said eagerly. "And Dr. Kunce said for you to come and bring some aromatic ammonia, Miss Keate. I could have brought it myself," she added in some disappointment, "but he said you. Do you know what I think? I think Dr. Prunes is sweet on Mrs. Harrigan."

"Why?" said Nancy.

"Oh, just the way he looks at her, and lets her have her own way."

"That will do, Ellen," I said sternly, after waiting to see if she was going to add any interesting item. "Such comment is not respectful."

If there was ever a woman who did not need aromatic ammonia that woman was Ina Harrigan. I saw that the instant I opened the door to her room and stepped inside. I daresay Dr. Kunce with his feeling for propriety preferred a nurse to be present during the interview and may have felt he could trust my discretion.

I remained during the entire half-hour or so, standing as unobtrusively as possible in the background and all ears. I was interested to note that of the four Ina Harrigan herself was by far the most composed. Even the stenographer looked hot and ill at ease and had a tendency to chew his pencil during the slight pauses.

It was just dusk, I remember, a breathlessly hot summer twilight, and there was only one light, the one above the bed, in the bare, high-ceilinged room.

"And so you insisted on this young Ladd staying on after the visitors were told to leave?" Sergeant Lamb was saying as I entered the room.

"I did nothing of the kind," said Ina Harrigan coolly, her low voice as smooth as velvet. "I permitted him to remain. It was rather absurd, you know, being sent away like a child at such a ridiculously early hour."

"But Mrs. Harrigan, didn't any of the nurses on duty come to your room to get you ready for the night?" asked Dr. Kunce, ever alert to any infringement upon his rules.

"Oh, yes," said Ina Harrigan. "The little student nurse came. I had turned out the light and when she opened the door I told her to go away and not bother me. Mr. Ladd was sitting over by the window and she did not see him. It isn't as if I were helpless, you know. I can get around quite nicely. For instance," she went on in an irritating way, "I can brush my own teeth quite well."

"Handy with your left arm, are you?" inquired Sergeant Lamb with interest.

Her aquamarine eyes glittered.

"Not any more than anyone else, I should imagine. What do you mean by that?"

"I mean," said Sergeant Lamb, making four, "that somebody certainly killed Dr. Harrigan."

She lay there, relaxed against the white pillows, her black hair smooth now and sleek, the lace of her nightgown soft and delicate against the smooth white shoulder of her unbandaged left arm, her straight black eyebrows drawn together over the thin bridge of her nose. Her mouth was such a deep crimson that it was almost purple, and there was that feline look about her jaw I had noticed before. In fact there was a suggestion of smoothness and sleekness and graceful and cruel strength about the lady which was distinctly feline. There was a sort of pantherish look in her strange light eyes, a graceful rippling of muscles when she moved.

"I thought you'd get around to me presently," she said with an effect of indolence, though her eyes had that waiting look. "Are you charging me with my husband's murder? Because, if so, I shan't say a word until I see my lawyer."

"Well—now," said Sergeant Lamb. "No, I'm not charging you with Dr. Harrigan's murder. But I want to know what you've got to say about this. We've got young Ladd under guard, one of our best men trailing him, but we don't want to arrest him till we're a little more certain of the lay of the land."

And then it began again, question and answer, question and answer, with Sergeant Lamb waxing rather angry and wiping his glistening forehead with his hand and Ina Harrigan cool, controlled, evasive until pinned down to "Yes" or "No" by Sergeant Lamb, and even then somehow untouched and victorious. Toward the last she became insolent.

"Yes, my husband quarreled with Mr. Ladd. He quarreled with everyone. If you're going to accuse everyone who ever quarreled with Leo of murdering him, you'll have too many suspects for your jail."

"What time was it when Kenwood Ladd left this room?"

She smiled.

"Poor Ken! How he hated that fire-escape business." She took a cigarette from the package on the bedside table, waited while Dr. Kunce, his face masked and enigmatic, held a light for her, and then looked at Sergeant Lamb again.

"What time, did you say? Why, I don't know exactly, but it must have been before—let's see, when did that student nurse last see my husband alive? Twelve-eighteen, wasn't it? Well, Mr. Ladd left before that." Her eyes were sea-green and mocking, her crimson lips amused.

"See here," said Sergeant Lamb, "I'll trouble you to remember that this is a serious business."

"My dear man," said Ina Harrigan, "how quaint! *You* telling *me* it is serious." She expelled a trail of blue smoke quite expertly from her thin white nostrils and added: "I am the widow."

Upon which I was interested to note a rather odd look of reflection in Dr. Kunce's dark gaze; after all, pantheresses, or whatever lady panthers are called, are not exactly creatures of the hearthstone.

"Yes," resumed Ina Harrigan coolly. "He left before twelve-eighteen. I daresay if put to it I could swear that."

"My dear Mrs. Harrigan," said Dr. Kunce, his nose

coming down over his beard, "we are sure that you are anxious to bring the murderer of your husband to justice." He turned in an explanatory way to Sergeant Lamb. "Mrs. Harrigan is in an overwrought condition. She is really very anxious to help us."

"Oh, yeah?" said Sergeant Lamb, wiping the sweat from his forehead and eyeing Ina Harrigan with skeptical blue eyes.

"Oh, by all means," said Ina Harrigan in a flat voice which was not even intended to be convincing.

"But you did hear Kenwood Ladd threaten to kill Dr. Harrigan?" persisted Sergeant Lamb.

That did touch her; she took a long moment to adjust the bandage on her right shoulder to an easier position, holding the cigarette between her lips in the meantime, until the smoke made a little blue haze around her face. Then she said calmly enough:

"I could have killed him myself. And you can make anything you want to make of that. Dr. Harrigan was a man of violent temper and a violent tongue. He was in the habit of making the most brutal accusations."

"With no foundation at all, I suppose," said Sergeant Lamb, who was, as I have said, nobody's fool.

"None at all," she said smoothly, then appeared belatedly to catch his meaning. "None at all," she repeated sharply, the latent ferocity one felt in her stirring and peering for an instant out of her sea-coloured eyes. "None at all, and I'll thank you to remember that, my good man."

It was about then, I think, that I found myself watching for the gap that showed now and then as she spoke, the gap along the upper right side of her perfect teeth that was there owing to the motor accident which had brought her to the hospital. The bruise about her lips had healed at once, but owing to the circumstances she had not yet been to a dentist and had the gap bridged. It was curious that, as often as I had talked to her I had not noticed the gap before then, although if I had stopped to think I'd have known it must be there.

Something—some memory—some connection was drumming at me, striving to become definite.

"See here, Mrs. Harrigan, what do you know of your husband's quarrel with Peter Melady?" asked Sergeant Lamb.

"I know everything about it," said Ina Harrigan coolly.

"Everything?" said Sergeant Lamb. "Well, then, what caused it?"

And at that instant the little nudge of consciousness made itself coherent. Under pretense of getting a pitcher of water from the bathroom I walked to that room, turned on the light, and went to the little shelf for toothbrushes and tubes of this and that and toilet articles. There, stuck carelessly behind a great bottle of green bath salts, I found what I sought: several unopened packages of chewing gum. White, of course. And in the wastebasket below the shelf were two small lumps that had been chewed; little lumps exactly like the one Sergeant Lamb had found there stuck to the murdered man's sleeve.

It was so clear that I could not understand how I had missed it so far. Vain, anxious, and careful about her appearance, Ina Harrigan had been carefully shaping little bits of white chewing gum and wedging them into the vacant space along the right side of her mouth. A little spasm of mirth caught me as I reflected on the difficulties of the thing, the gum slipping and having to be continually replaced with her tongue, or sticking to

her cigarette or troubling her when she talked and forgot the thing. She had probably only placed it there when
she expected to be seen, and that evening she'd been
taken by surprise. I scooped the bits of gum into a piece
of paper and returned to the sick room.

"I know everything about their quarrel, and I don't
mind telling you in the least," Ina Harrigan was saying.

CHAPTER XIII

"It was all," she continued, "over Dione Melady."

She paused, glanced at Dr. Kunce and then at Sergeant Lamb, stuffed the pillow more comfortably under her sleek head, and went on with the most aplomb in the world:

"It happened about five years ago, three years after Leo had married me. I knew it all along but it didn't matter. Although I could never see what he thought was attractive about Dione; she was always a muddled, wishy-washy kind of person. Cold as a little fish. I can't think what Leo expected to come of it. I don't know just how far it went; far enough I presume. Anyway Melady *père* discovered it, there was a terrible scene, and Peter forbade the house to Leo and married Dione off to her second cousin." She paused again and then added reflectively: "Personally I thought Leo was well out of it. He'd have tired of Dione—a morbid-minded girl without an ounce of honest passion about her. But that's the reason for the quarrel between Peter Melady and my husband. There's been a lot of talk about it, but no one knew the truth. Except perhaps Court Melady."

Sergeant Lamb cleared his throat; he had looked faintly embarrassed during the more candid bits of Ina Harrigan's tale, but was now himself again.

"What's your own opinion about this murder, Mrs. Harrigan? Do you think that quarrel may be back of it?"

"I couldn't say. But in that case they'd have had to kill each other, wouldn't they? Both of them died."

"How did Dione Melady take all this? Was she—er —resentful?"

"At being interrupted in her illicit love affair with my husband, you mean?"

"Er—yes," said Sergeant Lamb. I daresay he was not accustomed to freedom of speech in a woman of what he would consider a respectable class. I think Ina Harrigan's cigarettes, her crimson mouth, her lace nightgown, her lack of grief for her dead husband, and her candor all had a sort of cumulative effect upon him so that, from then on, I am convinced that he considered her an abandoned woman. For my own part I was inclined to think that Ina Harrigan had kept a cool and discreet head through any adventures she might have had. Not that I was interested in Ina Harrigan's virtue. Or lack of it. It was only that, with Nancy in my mind and the way she looked when she defended young Ladd, I did hope the young architect had not involved himself too deeply with his handsome client.

"I don't know," she said, yawning a little. "I don't know, I'm sure. Leo was furious. Felt a fool for getting caught, I suppose."

It was just then, I believe, that Dr. Kunce brought up the subject of the missing formula, about which Sergeant Lamb questioned the lady at some length, eliciting from her exactly no information at all save a bare admission that she knew of the thing and that Leo had known of it.

"Perhaps Leo did intend to steal the thing," she agreed imperturbably. "He'd have liked to get it away from Peter Melady of all people. But how should I know what he did! I know I didn't want the thing. Nor did Kenwood Ladd."

And that was all Sergeant Lamb succeeded in getting out of Ina Harrigan. I think, however, she was frightened under her cool mask of nonchalance. Evade Sergeant Lamb's inquiries though she had, she must have known that she could not evade forever; that there was a time coming when she would be forced to reply directly and with an appearance of the truth. She was too intelligent and too worldly wise not to know that things looked black for Kenwood Ladd and thus for herself.

"She won't be so slick with her go-to-hell air pretty soon," said Sergeant Lamb, wiping his forehead as we emerged into the corridor.

Opposite us was the door to Lillian Ash's patient's room; the door was open, with a screen across it, and above the screen I caught a glimpse of a white cap moving silently out of sight into the blackness of the twilit room beyond.

It was to escape Lillian Ash's prying ears that I drew Sergeant Lamb and Dr. Kunce into the room that had been Peter Melady's. The stenographer hovered on the threshold while I snapped on the light and showed them the bits of white gum and explained their use.

"Well, I'll be damned!" said Sergeant Lamb slowly, his pale blue eyes nearly popping out of his head. "Well, I'll be damned!"

"Yes, I thought you would be," I said cheerfully.

Dr. Kunce was stroking his Vandyke."

"This doesn't prove anything," he said, and somehow I was convinced that he had known about the gum all the time, although I was never to know definitely for, of course, I dared not ask. "It might have got stuck to Dr. Harrigan's shirt in the most innocent of ways. He may have leaned over to——"

"To kiss her and she bit him instead," finished Sergeant Lamb. "Or maybe she got mad and threw it at him. No, no, Dr. Kunze. This is the first bit of definite evidence I've had, and you're not going to talk me out of it."

"But if she were guilty would she have left other gum about so it could be so easily seen?"

"She didn't know where she lost it. Probably in the excitement of the moment it dropped without her knowing it. Dropped there in the elevator when she leaned over to view the dastardly work of her paramour."

Well, I dated back to the era of Mary J. Holmes myself; still, I felt it was not necessary to employ her vocabulary. I felt it the more strongly because I was really shocked at the ghastly vision his lurid phrase conjured up. I could almost see Ina Harrigan leaning over that huddle in the elevator, her sleek black hair disheveled, her crimson mouth hungry and cruel, her aquamarine eyes avidly curious, her sea-green chiffons pulled back with one white hand so as not to dip in that spreading lane of blood. There would have been a sort of Clytemnestra-like look on her face and she would have been panting a little, perhaps, her mouth opening, and the chewing gum—— No! That effectually destroyed the picture. For the life of me I could not imagine Ina Harrigan hanging her mouth open in such a way that a bit of chewing gum would fall out. Ellen, now, might easily do so, but not Ina Harrigan.

"Paramour fiddlesticks!" I said acidly. "If you arrest young Ladd on the strength of his presence and his quarrel with Dr. Harrigan and this silly bit of chewing gum, you are making a sad mistake. Anyway the chewing gum indicates that Mrs. Harrigan is guilty rather than young Ladd."

"Well, maybe she helped him. Or maybe she gave him some gum," said Sergeant Lamb owlishly. And when I smiled briefly and Dr. Kunce looked affronted, Sergeant Lamb said, "Well, I don't see why not."

"You can take my word for it, she didn't," said Dr. Kunce shortly.

"Maybe. But see here, Dr. Kunze, did it ever occur to you that you expect me to take your word about a lot of things?" The shrewd look I was learning to respect had come into Sergeant Lamb's pale blue eyes. "A lot of things. Maybe that's why I'm not getting any place."

"Just what do you mean by that?" Dr. Kunce's silky voice had a smooth edge of anger. "Have I not devoted my time to this problem for the last three days? Have I not permitted you to pursue your investigations? Have I not given you every possible assistance?"

"Oh, sure, Doc," said Sergeant Lamb, still with that shrewd look in his eyes. "I ain't complaining any. But I do think——"

"A gentleman to see you, Dr. Kunce," said Ellen, materializing in the doorway.

The gentleman was beside her and proved to be Ina Harrigan's lawyer, one Thomas Wepling by name, a short, slender gentleman of something over fifty, gray-haired, and very neat and precise in his gray suit in spite of the heat. He wore eyeglasses with wide rims and a black ribbon which looked deceitfully severe and, at the moment, an exceedingly distressed expression. For the effect he was to produce he might as well have carried a bomb in one of his neat pockets.

"Dr. Kunce," he began at once, "I must see Mrs. Harrigan. Dr. Harrigan's funeral is to-morrow, you know, and a number of relatives have arrived in the city, and at her wish and theirs I opened the will, although it is not customary to do so.before the funeral. But Dr. Harrigan had put away a substantial fortune, you know, and I—er—presume there was some anxiety. And I must see Mrs. Harrigan at once."

"Was there something unusual about the will?" asked Sergeant Lamb after a brief silence.

Mr. Wepling passed a lavender handkerchief which smelled of violet sachet over his gray head and said:

"Most unusual. Most unusual."

"Might one ask—er—is this apt to be a shock to Mrs. Harrigan?" inquired Dr. Kunce, silkily concealing his curiosity.

"Well," said the lawyer cautiously, "she won't like it."

There was an expression on his face very like that of a patient who says: "If I've got to swallow that bad medicine, let's get it over with." He added: "May I see her at once?"

As Dr. Kunce turned to lead the way to Mrs. Harrigan's room again, Mr. Wepling touched his arm nervously and said:

"Hadn't the nurse better come, too? It may affect Mrs. Harrigan very seriously, since she is ill."

Dr. Kunce nodded briefly in my direction and I followed. Dione Melady's door was open and the light on above the bed. She was propped up against the pillows with the fan turned full on her, stirring her light hair and the newspaper she was reading. The bandage was off her throat, but the black and purple bruises showed distinctly. Court Melady was there, too, sitting in one of the wicker chairs before the window. Away down the hall I saw Nancy's white uniform flash into a sick-room door; Ellen was stooping absorbedly over a chart, a policeman lounged before the window at the east end of the long corridor, and Lillian Ash's white cap showed for an instant above the screen of the door of her patient's room as we entered Ina Harrigan's room again.

If she was pleased to see us again she successfully controlled the emotion. She said, in fact:

"Well. What now?" in no very pleasant voice.

"My dear Mrs. Harrigan," began the lawyer nervously, "a very unpleasant duty devolves upon me. Most unpleasant. Yes. That is, most unpleasant."

"Well, what is it?" Her full low voice was rough now, and there was a distinct look of anxiety in her aquamarine eyes, which had narrowed quickly between those straight, thick black eyelashes. Her white nose looked thinner; her cheek bones sharper. "What is it? Have you opened the will?"

"Well, that is to say, yes. Yes. I opened and read the will. That's—er—that's why I'm here." He began fumbling in his inside pocket and drew out the bomb, which was folded very tidily in a long manila envelope, around which were slipped a number of rubber bands quite as if the lawyer had placed them there in what was to be a futile effort to restrain its explosive qualities. Holding the envelope in his hand he took off his eye glasses and began to polish them with his handkerchief. There was an undeniable feeling of tension in the air. Ina Harrigan was sitting bolt upright in bed, exposing a quantity of lace nightgown which the stenographer, who had trailed along with us, was regarding with considerable interest. Sergeant Lamb, his face damp and hot-looking, and Dr. Kunce, stroking his beard, had their eyes glued upon the envelope.

"Oh, hurry up," said Ina Harrigan at last, as Mr. Wepling blew his breath for the fourth time upon one of the lenses of his eyeglasses without achieving the desired result. "You don't have to read it to me. Tell me what it is. What is the matter? Didn't my husband have anything to leave me? Had he thrown it all away?"

"Why, no," said Mr. Wepling. "He had a sizable estate. Yes, a sizable estate. Considerable property in bonds. Quite a nice fortune. Yes, quite a nice fortune."

"Well, then, what's the matter with you?" said Ina Harrigan, looking relieved. "If he had plenty of money there's nothing to worry about. I was afraid he'd lost everything he had."

"He'd plenty of money," said Mr. Wepling, looking acutely distressed. "Plenty. But you see—— Well, the trouble is—— Well, he did not leave it to you."

After one incredulous gasp Ina Harrigan sprang out of bed.

The stenographer gave a sort of squawk and, his nicer instincts prevailing, fled to the corridor. Sergeant Lamb became a bright pink, and I seized a green-blue chiffon affair that lay over the foot of the bed and flung it around Ina Harrigan, who was advancing with a kind of pantherish tread upon the lawyer. She clutched the negligee about her in an absent-minded fashion and Mr. Wepling retreated a step or two.

"Wait, my dear Mrs. Harrigan! Wait! Let me tell you! Wait!"

She halted. Her negligee trailed on the floor behind her and quivered and shook a little, and looked, in fact, rather like a lashing tail.

I think Lawyer Wepling did not relish his position. He looked highly uneasy, glanced anxiously toward the door whither lay escape, his clean tidy hands worked nervously on the envelope and as she said "Well?" harshly, he gulped and began to speak very rapidly, first absolving himself of blame.

"I knew nothing of all this. Believe me, Mrs. Harrigan, I knew nothing of it. I had suggested to Dr. Harrigan several times that he have his will properly drawn up and he'd always given me to understand that it would be done. He never mentioned this will and I did not know of it at all until I came upon it among his papers directly after the murder. I did not open it until to-day. It was made a long time ago. A number of years ago, in fact."

"Who——"

"The will leaves all his property to—to his first wife."

There was a silence. Ina Harrigan did not move. The lawyer began again, agitatedly:

"It was made some years ago. Before his divorce from his first wife. But so far as I can discover, there exists no other will. Of course, we can see that you get a share, but by far the bulk of the estate will go to his first wife—if she is still alive."

"Oh, she's alive," said Ina Harrigan. She had lapsed suddenly into a frowning, brooding silence. She walked slowly back to the bed and sat down on its high edge, staring at the floor. She was not a woman to waste time raging, infuriated though I knew her to be; it was at once with her a question of expedience what to do next. I could almost see her revolving this or that plan in her mind.

"You are sure there is no other will?"

"I'm sorry, Mrs. Harrigan," said the lawyer, with a thin little laugh which must have been induced by nervousness. "I'm positive there is no other. We have gone into his safe-deposit box, his safe at home, and at his offices—have made the most extensive search."

"It's nothing to laugh about," she said sulkily, giving him a black look. Her left hand fumbled for a cigarette, she lit it automatically, evidencing a nice skill in using her left hand, and began to smoke, still frowning at the floor through the soft veil of smoke.

"You are going to break that will," she said.

"But—it's perfectly valid in every respect. I can get you your share according to the laws of the state, but that's all I can do. There's no irregularity at all about the will."

"Well, it's your business to find one," she said without troubling to look at him. Her voice was very low and rough, like a throaty purr.

"A—er—might I ask—you say his first wife is alive. Do you know where she is?" inquired Mr. Wepling diffidently, eyeing his client with some uncertainty. As well he might.

"I said she was alive. I'd likely have known it if she had died. He would probably have heard of it and told me. I know nothing about her, except that he treated her abominably. He'd never have dared treat me like that. But I wasn't afraid of rages. She was. She couldn't manage him as I did."

"She must be notified," said Mr. Wepling worriedly. "Her name is——"

"Lillian," interrupted Ina Harrigan. "Lillian Something-or-other."

"That's right. Here it is. Lillian Ash Harrigan——"

I suppose one of us exclaimed. I'm sure Sergeant Lamb stepped suddenly forward. Ina Harrigan leaped to her feet again and stood there with narrowed eyes that glittered coldly like aquamarines. And Lawyer Wepling's eyeglasses fell to the length of the ribbon and his precise mouth hung open a little.

"Lillian Ash——" said Ina Harrigan in a harsh whisper.

I was the first to speak intelligibly.

"She's right across the corridor, Mr. Wepling."

Sergeant Lamb whirled his gangly body about and was out of the door and into the corridor like a hound to the scent.

"Evidently you don't read the newspapers, Mr. Wepling," explained Dr. Kunce softly. "There's a Lillian Ash here in the hospital. One of the nurses. She gave some evidence at the inquest. It may not be the same Lillian Ash. We'll soon see."

"She killed him," said Ina Harrigan in an extremely vicious and unpleasant way. "She killed him. She knew about that will. She wanted that money." She did not look handsome, standing there, raging, her painted lips drawn back a little from her teeth, her white nose thin and cruel, her jewel-like eyes actually catching and reflecting the light in the most uncanny way.

"It may not be the same Lillian Ash at all," repeated Dr. Kunce in a soothing way, although I caught again that reflective look in his gaze as he watched Ina Harrigan; I daresay Dr. Kunce's drops of German blood produced in him a leaning toward domesticity, and taking Ina Harrigan to wife would be about as peaceful as taking a lithe and healthy young panther to one's arms.

"How long has she been here?" asked Mrs. Harrigan suddenly.

"About three months."

"What's she doing here? Did Leo get her a position?"

"No. She's nursing. She is, of course, a registered nurse. But Dr. Harrigan had nothing to do with her being here. She presented her credentials, got her name on the register, and has been nursing private patients—usually here at Melady Memorial, I believe."

"He knew she was here, though. He was likely making love to her again."

"No, no, Mrs. Harrigan. I doubt very much if he more than saw her about the corridors. And I can't recall that she ever nursed for him."

"That is right, Dr. Kunce," I offered. "I think she tried to avoid him. In fact——" I checked myself abruptly. No need to make a case against the poor woman, and anyway Sergeant Lamb had heard what Ellen had said. A most damaging witness now, was that bland remark of Ellen's: "I think Lillian Ash is afraid of Dr. Harrigan." If she were really Dr. Harrigan's divorced wife, returning to B—— and making her living as a nurse in the very hospital to which he brought most of his cases, no wonder she was afraid. Especially if she had to depend upon her own earnings, as I was certain she did. Dr. Harrigan was always a man of violent and unreasoning rages, and I think few things would have more completely enraged him than to discover his former wife nursing and living right under his nose. The comment, the curiosity, the gossip would have been most irksome to him. But it seemed likely to me that poor Lillian Ash had been merely anxious to escape his attention and earn her bread and butter. And of course it might not be the same Lillian Ash.

But it was.

She admitted it at once. Afterward I decided that she had been taken by surprise and, her nerves frayed and ragged with the strain of the last few days, had not even tried to convince Sergeant Lamb she was not Dr. Harrigan's long-divorced wife. Or perhaps she realized that she would have to come forward and declare herself sometime if she wanted the estate that was due her and which she must have needed so sorely, and that denial now would make matters enormously difficult later on. But whatever her motive or lack of motive she did admit that she was his first wife.

"He was a devil," she said, with the most amazing simplicity—a simplicity which was poignantly honest. And then she repeated the words I had heard her speak there at the elevator door so shortly after the murder. "But he was so alive. So vital," and looked helplessly from Sergeant Lamb to the lawyer and then about Ina Harrigan's room.

"So you killed him," said Ina Harrigan.

I was caught by the strange little scene before my eyes. The two wives staring at each other, each so typical of her day and generation. Lillian Ash had probably been the exact type of prettiness that her day demanded—hair curled and pompadoured, high-bosomed, round-hipped, corseted within an inch of her life. And Ina Harrigan was of her own day—sleek, uncorseted to what must have been an exciting degree, deliberately emotional where Lillian would have been sentimental, lightly ironical where Lillian would have been secretly skeptical, both of them highly sexed, both of them selfish and rather hard, and both of them touched by Dr. Harrigan's forceful, imperious personality; a personality which had been bluffly good-humored and lovable at one moment, and brutally passionate at the next. I mean, a raging passion of anger; I knew nothing of Dr. Harrigan's more tender moments, and cared to know nothing of them, although I did know that, right up to the last, he always had an eye for what he'd have called, "a handsome figure of a woman." I've heard him say that more than once.

"I did not kill him," Lillian Ash was saying. She said

it weakly, flabbily, without an ounce of the brazen, determinedly bright and youthful manner which was customary with her. Later I knew what had left her so haggard, so flabby, what had given her that beaten, old look, but at the moment it only increased my secret suspicions of Lillian Ash. "I kept out of his way. He didn't even know I was in the hospital. Until——" She faltered. "—Until the night of his death. We met for the first time in fifteen years that night. But I didn't kill him."

It was just then, and something to my vexation, that Ellen appeared at my elbow with the breathlessly whispered message to the effect that 301 had got out of bed and was walking about the corridors in his night clothes trying to find a cooler place to sleep, and she and Nancy couldn't do a thing with him. So I was obliged to leave.

Once I came on the scene 301 returned to his own room without demur beyond a plaintive murmur that the corridor was cooler. But when I'd got him into bed he looked up at me and said.

"I want a policeman."

"You—*what!*"

"I want to see a policeman. I want to see——"
He reached carefully under his pillow and pulled out a newspaper. "Never mind how I got this paper," he interpolated sternly. "I knew something was going on here. And I want to see this policeman. This Sergeant Lamb. I've got"—he continued, leaning back and giving me a sort of triumphant look—"I've got something to tell him. I know something. Something important."

And it was important.

After vainly trying to get him to tell me and waiting impatiently until Sergeant Lamb and the others came out of Mrs. Harrigan's room, and finally getting Sergeant Lamb into Room 301, with Dr. Kunce and the stenographer following, we found it was important. Very important.

For he had seen Kenwood Ladd leaving the elevator door at exactly twenty minutes after twelve.

"It clinches my case," cried Sergeant Lamb excitedly. "It's done, Dr. Kunze. We've got our man. I'll make the arrest at once."

It was this way, according to the witness:

"It was hot that night," he said. "And I thought the corridor might be cooler. So I watched my chance to get out there while the nurses were gone to supper. But every time I looked it seemed like somebody was in the corridor; I saw Dr. Harrigan take the truck with his patient on it to the elevator, just like Miss Brody told, and then Miss Brody was bobbing around a lot, so I went back to bed. But it was awful. Finally I got up again and went to the door and peeked out. And I saw this Kenwood Ladd there at the elevator door, his hand on it! And as I looked he hurried over to the stairway and went upstairs. And just then Miss Keate and Miss Page and another nurse came into the corridor from the stairway that goes down. So I—er—decided to go back to bed. And if you hadn't tried to keep the murder a secret from the patients I'd have told you long ago."

"How do you know it was Kenwood Ladd?"

"Here's his picture in the paper."

"That was quite a distance to see, and the halls were not light," said Dr. Kunce.

"He came right under the light from the chart desk," said 301. "And anyway, I'm far-sighted." Which, as a matter of fact, was true.

"Where did you get that newspaper?" asked Dr. Kunce, jealous of his reign.

"I hope you don't think I'd tell," said 301 impishly. "I hope to get more the same way."

They finally left, talking furiously in hushed voices all the way down the corridor and out of sight down the stairs. Even the matter of the chewing gum and the startling development as to Lillian Ash's identity had been lost in this new evidence.

Hoping that 301 would stay in his bed like a Christian, I walked slowly along the hot, still corridor, noted there was not a signal light burning and that the door to Ida Harirgan's room was closed and that Court Melady still sat in Dione's room, and then retraced my steps to the diet kitchen. I noted that the light was on and the door partly ajar, so I pushed the door further open. In common with the other nurses I had no desire to enter even a lighted room without a kind of reconnoitering peek beyond the door. I was not, however, prepared for what I saw.

Kenwood Ladd, himself, was standing in front of the gas stove. He was holding a girl tight in his arms. He was kissing the girl and the girl was Nancy. I rather imagine it was the first time they had kissed and they stood there pressed against each other, mouth to mouth and knee to knee and body to body, quite as if they were welded into one. Neither spoke, neither stirred, neither appeared to breathe; to all intents and purposes they were lost to the world.

Being a fool of an old maid I withdrew as silently as I had approached and went away still thirsty and with a kind of full feeling about my throat. Then I smiled faintly at the thought of Sergeant Lamb going furiously forth to arrest Kenwood Ladd, and Kenwood Ladd, having apparently escaped his police guard, turning up right there in the east wing. In the diet kitchen which Sergeant Lamb had just passed by. Kissing Nancy. Nancy. And Kenwood Ladd—— I sobered then. Kenwood Ladd and the staggering evidence which had accumulated against him. Police in only a few moments would be looking for him, hounding him, dragging him to jail. And perhaps—justly.

Mechanically I set about preparing my patients for the night. I did not see Kenwood Ladd when he left, but he couldn't have been long with Nancy in the diet kitchen, for in just a few moments I saw her going about her work.

I thought our patients would never get their various whims suited that night, but the wing finally did become quiet and slumbrous. It was after the last wakeful patient had drifted off to sleep—not a signal light burned and Ellen was sitting at the chart desk doing exactly nothing —that I recalled my lost notes.

Those notes. If Nancy had actually taken them, it was a good time to make sure.

The policeman seated at the stairway eyed me darkly as I sped past but made no move to stop me. I remember that in the dark hall of the nurses' dormitory the feeling of being watched and even followed swept over me with such force, such definite menace that I nearly turned back. I think I should have turned back had not Nancy's room been nearer than the stairway. And I actually broke into a quick light run, my skirts rustling and hissing between the dark walls. Once in Nancy's room I locked the door. In less than five minutes I had found my notes, which had been slipped under the blotter on her desk. I might say now that I never asked her why she took them; I did not need to ask.

I found also the blue Chinese snuff-bottle.

CHAPTER XIV

IT WAS under the rug before her writing table. I suppose it was lucky that I stepped on it and bent to look. Not an hour later some policemen from headquarters who'd been attempting to search the hospital reached the nurses' dormitory, and in the morning when I came off duty I found my room had been ransacked. I think there had been the intention of searching the whole hospital; a monumental task and to my notion a foolish one if they were looking for either the tiny Chinese snuff-bottle or the slip of paper on which the Slæpan formula was written and which must have been very small and easily concealed. But perhaps I'm wrong in saying it would have been foolish to search for the Chinese snuff-bottle, for they'd certainly have found it in Nancy's room. The policemen, by the way, did not apparently more than glance at the lavender hot-water bag which was hanging openly and frankly above the shoe cupboard in my room; at any rate my small cache was still there the morning after the search.

I remember that after my first painfully shocked moment of recognition, when I touched the smooth surface of the Chinese snuff-bottle, and then pulled it out from under the rug and stared at its delicate rich blue and the little gold flecks against the blue and the smooth pink tourmaline stopper, I pulled out that stopper and the tiny ivory spoon attached to it and squinted in a vain endeavor to see into the bottle and discover the formula. I could see nothing, of course, so I took a long pin from

Nancy's dressing table and experimented, finally convincing myself that there was nothing, no paper of any de-
scription, in the bottle. She'd taken the formula out, then,
and there was no telling where she'd hidden it. I looked
about the room, I remember, but without much spirit,
for I was profoundly shaken by my discovery and wished
with all my heart I had not gone near Nancy's room. I
could scarcely escape the conclusion that she was somehow implicated in the ugly business of murder and theft.

True, I at once began to reason out extenuating circumstances. She had been involved innocently; she had
been deceived or overpersuaded by—well, by whom?
Kenwood Ladd?

A sound of some sort outside the door caught my ear.
I approached the door and bent to listen. There was no
sound of movement, but I was sure I could hear something breathing, breathing heavily, as if it had been running, just outside the panel of wood.

I'll not deny that I was suddenly and unreasonably
terrified. The sleeping hospital, the darkened dormitory
rooms, the isolation—if I screamed would anyone hear
me? How near was someone sleeping? Whose rooms lay
near? My own, Miss Blane's room across the hall, Miss
Jones's room next door—all the nurses on night duty.

I was still bending, trying to distinguish the sound of
that heavy breathing from the thudding in my ears and
the desperate pounding of my heart, when all at once it
was gone—if, indeed, it had ever existed,—and I heard
someone coming along the hall, starched skirts rustling,
and the low murmur of voices. My fingers were trembling
but I managed to find and turn the key in the door and
open it. Miss Jones was at the door of her own room
with Miss Leming standing beside her. The front of
Miss Jones's uniform was a bright scarlet and she said

she'd dropped the jar of mercurochrome and had to change uniforms; Miss Leming had come with her because she, Miss Jones, was afraid of the darkened corridors. Both of them were rather nervous, although, to my inquiry, they said they had seen no one. I waited while Miss Jones buttoned herself hurriedly into a fresh uniform and returned with them to the third floor, viewing the lounging policeman with a relief that was not unmixed with exasperation. Why couldn't he have been about when and where he was needed! But I did not tell him of my experience; I could not be sure how much of it was real and how much due to my overstrained nerves.

I had taken the snuff-bottle, of course, thrusting it into the bosom of my uniform, where it felt warm and hard and sinister against my skin. And this was the only time when I deliberately and with malice aforethought, so to speak, treated Sergeant Lamb unfairly. I resolved at once not to tell him of the snuff-bottle and where I had found it. I do not defend myself; still, I think I have as firm and high a sense of duty as the average woman, and I simply could not involve Nancy in the ugly affair. I did intend, however, to tell Lance O'Leary of it when he arrived; I felt that he would be cautious and just.

And I must add that by the time I had got back to the east wing I had evolved an explanation by which Nancy was merely the tool of Kenwood Ladd; I did not attempt to explain to myself just how.

With that in my mind the brief little conversation I had with Nancy along about twelve o'clock was something of a trial. She joined me at the chart desk, where I sat pretending to study a chart and actually going over and over in a rather frantic mental circle my ominously limited list of suspects.

"Sarah," she said at my elbow, and as I looked up

quickly she added: "Why, Sarah! What is the matter? Why do you look at me so strangely?"

Nancy guilty of murder! Nancy conniving at theft! Looking at her, I knew it was nonsense.

But still there was the snuff-bottle. What had she done with the formula? I decided then and there that if Kenwood Ladd had drawn her into the business he deserved his punishment, and I vowed grimly to myself to see that he received it.

Aloud I said:

"You startled me. I didn't hear you coming," and settled my cap, which had slipped to one side at my sudden motion.

"Isn't it awful!" she said, emphatically enough, but still with an air of detachment. "Everybody jumps if you so much as sneeze. But cheer up, Sarah. Things aren't so bad."

I caught myself on the verge of appropriating Sergeant Lamb's: "Oh, yeah?" and said instead:

"Indeed."

"Not so bad," she said softly, hunting for a chart. "Where is 301? Oh, here he is. Do you know that man was out perambulating the corridor in his night clothes? Yes, he was."

"Don't I know!" I said rather bitterly. "I had to get him back to bed."

"I started after him but stopped for a moment in the ——" she checked herself, blushed vividly, and said— "the diet kitchen."

"Indeed," I said again with much fluency.

"Yes." She kept on hunting through the charts, then let her hands relax and slipped down into the chair beside me with a little rustle of her white skirt and said surprisingly:

"Sarah, he's the dearest man God ever made. And I love him. And he loves me." Upon which she closed her eyes as if to shut the glory in, folded her hands under her chin, and smiled as if nothing else existed but the enchanting memory back of her white eyelids.

"Oh, Sarah," she said softly, "you don't know what's happened to me."

Didn't I!

A phrase of Ellen's rose with irresistible force to my lips.

"Don't kid yourself," I heard myself saying, as much to my own shocked surprise as to Nancy's. Her eyelids flew open, her hands dropped, and I rose abruptly and walked away. Knowing what I knew, and, worse, suspecting what I suspected, it was more than I could endure to sit there and listen to her.

I carried on my duties almost automatically that night, my mind circling distractedly from one thing to another: the Chinese snuff-bottle, the mystery of Peter Melady's death, the grisly substitution of the bodies, my own discovery regarding the bit of white chewing gum, the appalling weight of evidence against Kenwood Ladd, my own suspicions of Lillian Ash, and this new knowledge that she'd been Dr. Harrigan's wife. Poor Lillian Ash, trying so desperately to appear young, avoiding Dr. Harrigan, remembering with terror past cruelties and humiliations—remembering and trying to forget—trying so determinedly to cover her lack of modern nursing methods only in order to insure herself a living. It seemed keenly ironical that, all along, she'd been amply provided for in Dr. Harrigan's will. Perhaps she had known it, after all—perhaps she'd known it and wearied, during those hot nights of the struggle and—murdered him.

Lillian Ash, Kenwood Ladd—Dr. Kunce, Teuber, Ina

Harrigan, Court Melady—wearily I went over and over
that short list of names, until they actually took on a sort
of rhythm, like a chant. Yet I rejected each name indi-
vidually.

And so the night passed—hot, slow, exhausting, with
the policemen in the corridor and Nancy going about in
a sort of beatific daze, though I noted that she took no
chances with the dark stair well or the various shadowy
corners, despite her somnambulant aspect. Ellen, blue
eyes wide, scared for her life of every flickering shadow
but game. Ina Harrigan—bitter, probably; certainly re-
vengeful—lying on the pillows in Room 307, planning
and planning. Dione sleeping, I suppose; or lying awake,
making up her mind to defy her husband and tell the
story which was to be her contribution to the entanglement, and fearing every step that went past her door,
and touching the bruises on her throat.

Lillian Ash couldn't have slept much behind that green
baize screen; she went to supper, I remember, pallid and
worn and said not a word, and I can imagine her, during
the slow, hot hours of second watch, turning and twisting on her narrow cot, and hoping and fearing. And wondering if her last desperate effort had failed after all.

And there was I going about my work while my
thoughts spun in that maelstrom of uncertainties and
anxieties and fears and all the time a primitive feeling of
danger—danger to me, Sarah Keate—was pulling at me,
urging me to take care, to avoid that shadow, to turn on
this light, to be sure there was nothing in the gloom behind the refrigerator, nothing back of the shower curtain
in this bathroom, nothing in the shadow back of the bed
in that sick room—to watch, to take care.

Morning finally came, reluctant in its hot gray mist. A
dull little pain was beginning to throb along my left tem-

ple, and there was a sort of twitching inside my elbows that I always get when it's going to storm.

The day nurses straggled on duty, weary with the hot night and looking as if they had not slept. Nancy walked downstairs with me. She was singing, I remember, in a light soprano which was barely above a whisper, it was so soft, and was yet very clear and tender. I even recall the words: " 'Deep in my heart, dear, I have a dream of you, Fashioned of starlight, Perfumed of roses and dew . . .' " It was exactly there that Miss Blane caught up with us.

She'd smuggled in a newspaper and, with a quick glance to be sure Dr. Kunce was not in sight, she showed it to us. The little song froze on Nancy's lips and I remember how her mouth retained the shape of its faint smile but was suddenly distorted and ashen and pitiful as she stared over Miss Blane's white shoulder. For the headlines were splashed in great letters across the entire sheet.

Kenwood Ladd had been arrested for the murder of Dr. Leo Harrigan. He was being held at the Euclid Avenue police station to go before the grand jury at its convening. It was expected that there would be a true bill, as the evidence against him was convincing.

The article went on to compliment the police and the district attorney upon their astute and rapid action in tracing the criminal. It mentioned somewhere that the new lieutenant of the Homicide Bureau was fortunate in arriving home to find his first case finished for him and done well. That particular newspaper was against the incoming administration.

When I met Dr. Kunce in the corridor an hour later I asked what he thought of the matter..

"It's bad for young Ladd," he said, and upon my inquiry it developed that there was an added point or two against him of which I had not known, although what I already knew was conclusive enough. His alibi for the night of the murderous assault upon Dione Melady, said Dr. Kunce, had broken; the doctor he had called to his apartment said he had not been called until nearly four o'clock in the morning, thus giving Kenwood Ladd plenty of time to escape from the hospital after so nearly strangling Dione Melady, go home, and call the doctor. That was bad, for unconsciously I had put considerable faith in that alibi. But it also developed that one of the patients in the men's ward on the first floor, the windows of which face the alley back of the hospital, had seen something. He had been sleepless on account of the heat and along about twelve-thirty—he guessed the time owing to having heard the supper bell sometime previous— he had heard a subdued sound of steps in the alley and a sort of scuffling sound. He had raised himself on his elbow and peered out the window. It was too dark in the shadows of the alley to see anything clearly, but he had been able to distinguish two men, one of them apparently so drunk that he had to be almost carried along by his companion. They'd staggered around the corner of the church, the one almost dragging the other, and just for a second the street light fell dimly on them and the man supporting the, presumably, drunken man had been wearing a light suit. But that's all he had seen. And of course, it was easy enough to prove that Kenwood Ladd had been wearing a light summer tweed the night of the murder.

"None of it is exactly conclusive," said Dr. Kunce wearily, "except the evidence 301 gave us last night. Young Ladd says, regarding that, that he came from— er—Mrs. Harrigan's room, turned toward the elevator, intending from force of habit to take it, heard you and Miss Page and Miss Jones on the stairway, and rather than wait for the elevator and be seen, hurried over to the stairway and ran up to the fourth floor. Sounds fishy, of course. But it may be true. You see, he was frightfully hard up; might have wanted the Slæpan formula. Although he refuses, so far, to admit it, and they have not been able to find either the snuff-bottle or the formula among his things."

"But why should he have substituted Peter Melady's body for the Negro's body?"

Dr. Kunce shrugged.

"We don't know. He refuses, so far, to confess, although Sergeant Lamb expects a confession before the day is over. Sergeant Lamb thinks that was to cast suspicion upon Peter Melady."

"I see," I said slowly. "On the theory that everyone knew of the enmity between Dr. Harrigan and Peter Melady, and if Peter Melady simply vanished, the natural thing to believe would be that he was the murderer. The Negro's body, of course, could not be so easily identifiable as Peter Melady's, had it been left in the church. Dr. Kunce—I feel sure Peter Melady was murdered."

"How, Miss Keate? The autopsy showed nothing out of the way. His heart simply stopped beating."

"Extreme agitation could have caused it," I said crisply. "Anyone wanting him out of the way had only to excite him beyond his strength."

"Nonsense, Miss Keate. You are letting your imagination run away with you. One murder is enough. I must ask you, for the good of the hospital, not to repeat what you've just said. You have no foundation for saying it, have you?"

"Common sense," I said with asperity and turned away.

The day then beginning was destined to be an important one. In the first place it was as hot as any of its predecessors and very still. The thermometer in the main hall had actually touched 101 by noon, which was very near to being a record in our part of the country, and the barometer beside it had started falling in an ominous fashion. It was a gloomy day, with smothering, light gray clouds, and breathlessly still as if waiting. I don't think a leaf stirred.

The newspapers which managed to get themselves smuggled into the hospital made much of Kenwood Ladd's arrest, permitting the citizenry to breathe more easily—providing, of course, they managed to get any breath at all, for the air had a sort of density and heaviness which actually made you gasp under the least exertion. Nancy, looking now like the palest of sad little wraiths, with blue hollows under her eyes and all her new delight sunk into tragedy, disappeared directly after breakfast.

I, myself, tried to sleep and did manage to drop into an uneasy slumber, dream-haunted and restless. I awoke with a conviction that someone had just been rattling a key in the lock of my door. No one replied when I called out, but I imagined I heard a furtive footstep or two in the hall. It was all nerves, I told myself, but decided it was no good trying to sleep when it was so hot. So hot and humid and dreadfully still.

Finally I dressed, pulling on each garment wearily and feeling not at all refreshed from a tepid shower, and wishing women needn't wear so many clothes. I slipped the blue snuff-bottle into the bosom of my uniform again.

There was, even then, I recall, a feeling of something waiting, something impending, and I remember going over to the little calendar on my desk and figuring that Lance O'Leary could not possibly arrive until the following day, and with this the sensation of helplessness which I was experiencing increased. I know exactly, now, how chickens feel when they scamper so madly to cover at sight of any shadow that passes over them. There's just the flying shadow; they can't see the thing that makes it; it may not be a hawk at all. But their instinct sends them scuttling, feathers flying, for shelter. It's precisely the way I felt. It's an unreasoning feeling, something you can't control. I knew that Peter Melady was dead, and, that very morning, was being buried again. I knew that Kenwood Ladd was safely under arrest. Either of them might have murdered Dr. Harrigan—must have, in fact. I knew that the dead Negro was actually dead and buried and could not possibly go prowling about the corridors. But I still felt like pulling my white skirt over my head and crawling under the bed, exactly as a hen ruffles her feathers and crawls under a hedge.

Along about noon I went downstairs. I met Fannie Bianchi on the way. Her uniform was soiled and she looked tired and not at all flippant and pulled me out of the way of the little group of nurses on the stair landing. She looked cautiously around her and whispered.

"We had two operations this morning. Dr. Kunce operated. And listen to this, Sarah. We had finished counting sponges and all for the last one, and Dr. Kunce was sewing up the wound and I was just standing there at the head of the patient with the ether cone, and I got to sort of looking around, and the instrument cases are right opposite me there, you know, and I got wondering if everything was there. And"—she looked quickly over her shoulder again and leaned nearer me—"and after the patient had been taken away and they were cleaning up I got the check list. And Sarah, there's another knife gone. One of the longish curved bistouries; you know, with the sharp edge on the inside of the curve. And what I want to know is where's the thing gone to?"

The little group of nurses were disappearing around the corner of the stairs, murmuring as they went. Away down the first-floor corridor something on a lunch tray jangled. A sickening smell of ether clung to Miss Bianchi's uniform. Above us and below us loomed the shadows of the stairway. So hot. So still.

Then she said, still in a whisper:

"Had I better tell Dr. Kunce?"

I nodded. Forced myself to speak past the stiffness in my throat. Now I knew exactly what I feared.

"Tell him. Yes. At once. And the nurses should be warned."

"They'll be terrified," said Fannie Bianchi. "It's pretty bad already. Still—I think they ought know."

"The police—they ought search for the knife."

She nodded but said somberly:

"You know as well as I that there's too many hiding places in this old barn of a place. They'd never find it. Don't tell me the murderer is dead and buried—or locked up in jail. He's right here in this hospital. Or has access to it," she added with more spirit. "I don't mind saying I'm scared for my life."

I was still in the corridor near the main office when she emerged from a brief interview with Dr. Kunce. She was scarlet-cheeked and her dark eyes were blazing angrily.

"He says I don't know what I'm talking about!" she said hotly. "Said I hadn't checked right. I'm going to tell every nurse I can reach. They ought know somebody's about this place with that awful knife." She paused thoughtfully for a moment and then added:

"You know how sharp Dr. Kunce makes us keep everything."

I knew, of course.

She kept her word about warning the nurses, with the result that two of them took to their beds with sick headaches before lunch and the rest huddled in scared little groups with signal lights burning unattended and the patients fretful and justifiably furious at the neglect.

Dr. Harrigan had been buried that morning, with hordes of relations turning up and wanting to see Mrs. Harrigan and being refused. Mrs. Harrigan, assisted by one of the day nurses, had got herself up in the deepest of mourning, attended the funeral in the company of Mr. Wepling, and had returned to the hospital, swearing at her widow's veil, which was made of heavy black chiffon and touched the floor and must have been terribly warm, jerking off her black crêpes and smoking furiously and demanding ginger ale. The day nurse got it for her, and there was some speculation as to why she'd returned to the hospital when she might as well have gone to her own home and had a trained nurse come in daily to dress her arm—or rather change the soiled bandages; the arm itself was in a cast. I think she was shrewd enough to place herself so far as possible in a position which might extract sympathy from the relations, upon whom she'd certainly have to depend for help if she expected to contest Dr. Harrigan's will.

Peter Melady also was buried that morning, but at a later hour. It was a strange irony that their cemetery lots had been bought at the same time, years ago, and adjoined. I can imagine the two mounds so near each other, left alone at last with the newly turned clay and the mounds of flowers wilting under the dreadful heat.

And all the time the barometer was dropping.

Dione and Court Melady had, of course, attended the latter funeral. Dione's sunburn was much better by that time, although Dr. Kunce had advised her to stay in the hospital until it was quite healed and until she was over the nervous shock. She had insisted on the soothing oil being rubbed off and her shoulders and back powdered when she dressed to go to the funeral, and when she returned she was in tears of pain, demanding fresh tubes of Unguentine and yanking off her hot white chiffon so hurriedly that it tore across the back. Whereupon she seized a pair of scissors from the dressing tray and demolished the gown then and there instead of giving it to the young student nurse who could have mended and worn it quite nicely. A student nurse's salary does not provide an over-abundance of gowns.

It was while she was enjoying her little tantrum that Dione sent for me. I never knew why she preferred to tell me rather than go directly to the police, unless it was because she hoped that Court would not so readily discover that she had been the informant. Not that it was damaging to Court; I think he'd objected to her telling it merely from a man's preference to let another man's business alone. And he may have thought, as I did, that it was rather absurd to drag Dr. Kunce into the affair.

For it was about Dr. Kunce. She rambled more than a little in her high, complaining voice, while her eyes went here and there below those penciled eyebrows, one of which had smeared downward across her temple. The gist of the thing was this: Dr. Kunce had known all about Slæpan. He had been determined that it should be associated with his name. For months he had been trying to convince Peter Melady that Slæpan ought to have a definite stamp of medical and surgical approval, and who better qualified to give it that stamp than himself? He had become, I gathered, quite disagreeable about it in his smooth, insistent way.

"He acted as if he'd actually had a share in discovering it," said Dione, watching me. "Just because he and Father had talked of it so much. He said it was a big thing. The biggest thing since the discovery of the uses of radium. He said it was of incalculable value. I don't say, you understand," she interpolated, "that I think he murdered anybody. But I do think this formula ought be found. Why, it's *mine!* And Dr. Kunce certainly wanted it; maybe he's got it.—Look here, Miss Keate, what's this tale that's going around the hospital about a knife missing from the operating rooms? Is there a knife gone?"

I never lie; still I have professional discretion.

"No." I said. "Certainly not."

I could see that she didn't believe me. And when I left her it gave me a little chill to hear her lock the door behind me. Close and lock the door on such a day, when her only hope for physical ease lay in taking advantage of any vagrant current of air that might sift through the long corridors!

And I remember descending the dark, quiet old stairway, slipping my hand along the smooth rail and catching my breath when a board somewhere above me squeaked. When I turned there was nothing to be seen.

Once in the main hall I paused. I was in two minds as to the information Dione had just given me. As information it amounted to very little. Any doctor—even good old Dr. Peattie, who had set such a fine and proud code of ethics for the younger doctors of B—— to follow—

would certainly have been intensely interested in such a thing as Slæpan purported to be.

But, in view of the existing circumstances, I think I should have told Sergeant Lamb of the matter, or at least sent him to Dione, had he been about, but so far as I knew he had not been near the hospital all day. There were, then, no policemen about the place; I suppose Sergeant Lamb had thought it somewhat inconsistent to guard the hospital from a murderer whom they'd locked up in jail.

I loitered over to the barometer. It was still falling; it would storm before night. There was already a hint of threat in the hot, still air; a feeling of fullness and of menace, a hushed, pregnant waiting. The storm when it came would be bad.

Someone in the little nurses' parlor near me was playing the piano; it was Nancy, for I knew her precise, delicate touch on the keys. She was playing very softly so as not to disturb any patient, but the notes were clear and distinct. It was the second movement, I believe, of the sixth Chaikovsky symphony, the *Pathétique,* and it blended too perfectly with the feel of things.

I moved to the window and stood there looking out on the quiet lawn. The window was open and the air hot and dense. Not a leaf stirred, not a bird sang except a robin out of sight somewhere, that was singing its curious little rain song—three low notes in a soft minor which was clear and light against the interwoven tapestry of the music. The clouds were heavier with the presage of storm. There was a singularly clear light that made the colors of things stand out with unnatural distinctness; the green lawn was accented with yellow, the sky looked slate gray above the purple-green of the treetops, the cannas were a deep crimson that picked itself out sharply from the green foliage. The whole thing combined to induce in me one of those extremely poignant moments when everything about you is new and unfamiliar and yet enormously significant and as much a part of you as your own hand.

The music back of me broke off and did not resume.

Around me the old hospital was silent, shadowy, very still. It was waiting, too. Waiting. Was someone there— with that curved knife—also waiting? And for whom?

"Sarah. Sarah Keate."

It was a quiet voice; rather grave. I whirled.

Lance O'Leary was standing there in the gloomy corridor. He was smiling; his hands were out toward me.

Well, I won't deny I was glad to see him. I do deny, however, that I was so glad that I wept, as he meanly taxed me with later on. And there was no necessity at all for his putting one arm around my shoulders and patting my back with the other; I was not choking. I will admit that I clutched his coat lapels with both hands; I did it deliberately, having a distinct impression that if I let go he might vanish and I should be left again in that silent hospital.

After a moment or so, he drew me into the office and on into Dr. Kunce's office. It was empty, he told me, Dr. Kunce being with one of the patients he'd operated on that morning. The office girl looked at us curiously, and Lance O'Leary shut the door carefully and got me into a chair. Then he straightened up, smoothed his ruffled lapels, and smiled.

He was browner than usual and a little heavier; his prolonged holiday had been good for him. His light brown hair was very smooth, his gray eyes very clear, his slight figure lithe and extremely well tailored.

"I see," I said, running my eyes over his gray suit and

fastening on something quite handsome in the way of ties
—"I see that you've been buying trunkloads of clothes."

"Sarah," he said soberly, "English tailors have the
world beat. You ought to see the clothes I've brought
back."

"I don't doubt it. You're as vain as any peacock. Well,
it's high time you got back—Lieutenant."

He smiled again at that. Lance O'Leary has always
had a nice smile. It lights up his whole face in the most
engaging way and is one of the reasons, I suppose, why
I've a sort of partiality for that young man.

"Just wait till we clean up the city," he said, and then
became really grave. "Sergeant Lamb cabled; the cable
caught me on the boat. I took a plane from New York as
soon as I landed. That's how I'm a day ahead of the time
they expected me. But apparently there was no need for
such haste. I understand the thing is settled; at least so
they tell me at headquarters. The criminal jailed and
awaiting indictment." His clear gray eyes were watching
me closely.

I shook my head.

"I don't believe Kenwood Ladd killed Dr. Harrigan,"
I said slowly. "And I think the—the killer is here. Now.
In the hospital. Waiting for somebody else. And whoever it is has got a knife. And I think—well, I think I am
the one he's waiting for."

He did look shocked at that.

"Why, Sarah!" he cried, staring at me. Then his
mouth tightened and he said more briskly: "Let's have
the whole story. It doesn't matter how long it takes.
Don't omit a thing. Tell me everything."

I did so. It took a long time. The look of intense con-
centration, of remoteness from the world, which I knew

so well, came into his face at my first words; his eyes were very clear and shining and alert.

And I shall never forget what he said when I'd finished. He said:

"Well done, Sarah," and added casually: "Of course, you know who killed Dr. Harrigan."

"No! Do you know?"

"Why, naturally. You've told me. How can you help knowing? The name is here, one of your own list of suspects." He paused, looking at my scribbled notes, and then said, thoughtfully:

"Curious, isn't it? If that Negro hadn't died there would have been no murder."

CHAPTER XV

SINCE I had told Lance O'Leary the story of the affair much as I have told it here, although much more hurriedly, still the telling took some time. It grew darker in the small, overfurnished office. Once Lance O'Leary rose, went to the door, and told the office girl to see that we were not disturbed; I don't know whether it was his handsome new clothes that impressed her or his way of speaking, but no one, not even Dr. Kunce, came near. Another time I observed him fumbling absent-mindedly into his pocket, whence he extracted a small and very shabby stub of a pencil which he turned and twisted in his fingers during the whole of the remaining tale. He did not interrupt me once, although when I gave him the Chinese snuff-bottle he examined it eagerly, looking with keen interest at its gorgeous blue and gold and its smooth pink top before he slipped it into a pocket. And when I had finished and leaned back against the down cushions of the chair and rubbed my aching eyes, he made the casual remark which I have quoted to the effect that I had told him who murdered Dr. Harrigan.

"I couldn't have told you," I said wearily. "I don't know, myself."

"Oh, yes, you do. If you'll only think a moment. But never mind. I know. And it's not going to be a simple matter to get the murderer arrested and convicted. And you see——" He left the sentence hanging in the air while his clear gray eyes, grave now and very thoughtful, watched through the window the bright green of the tree-tops against the black sky. "I wonder how long this storm is going to hold off," he murmured irrelevantly. "Terribly hot, isn't it!"

I nodded lifelessly. He looked cool and immaculate and unwrinkled, but I don't doubt he felt as warm and sticky as anyone.

"You see, Sarah," he resumed soberly, still with that clear and yet unfathomable gaze lost in the greens outside the window. "My business is always serious enough; anything is serious that has a human life as the wager. Thank God, I don't often have murder cases. But this time it is particularly complicated in view of the political situation here. This much bragged of reform has got to justify itself. This very new appointment of mine has likely been the subject of much adverse comment. And justly adverse if I can't—come across, so to speak. Produce the goods. Now I'm idealistic enough to think that gentlemen in politics is the cure for—well, there's no need to go into my theories on that subject. The point is I've got to go warily. I can't antagonize members of the staff. I couldn't make a fool of Sergeant Lamb if I tried, and I don't intend to try. I do think that with all the public clamor for an arrest they may have been stampeded into making one. At the same time the evidence against Kenwood Ladd is pretty bad. But what I'm trying to get at is this: I've got to be damn sure I'm right. I've got to have motive, everything, ready to prove before I go ahead."

He stopped, lost himself for a moment in thought, and then said, turning to me:

"You haven't asked me who killed Mr. Harrigan and Mr. Melady."

Mr. Melady!—he agreed with me, then.

"No," I said aloud.

"What's the matter? Don't you want to know?"

"I—why, certainly."

"Sarah," he said in a sort of scolding way, "I believe you're afraid to know."

"I'm not afraid. I just feel tired, I think. It's the heat. And you said—you said it was one of my list of suspects. It's such a short list. Our own hospital world. And I ——" I shivered and braced myself. "But I'd better know, of course. Who did it? And don't say it was Nancy. Because I'd never, never believe you."

He looked away from me quickly.

"No, Sarah, you'd better not know. I didn't realize how deeply you felt about all this. You couldn't possibly know the truth and act in a natural way. And I've still got to prove it, you know. But you must promise me to be very careful. I must tell you that you've been in very grave danger all along. The risks you have taken have been terrible. It frightens me to think of it." There was a feeling in his last words that brought me out of the chair.

"See here," I said, "I'm going straight upstairs and put on my hat and leave this hospital and never come back."

"That's exactly what I'd advise you to do," he said quite soberly. "But I don't think you'll follow my advice. I can't quite see you leaving at such a time. But for heaven's sake, Sarah, listen to me. Keep yourself in some-one's company all the time; stay with two or three of the nurses, Miss Page or this Ellen girl. Don't walk down a corridor alone or enter a room alone or use the elevator. Don't let any pretext take you alone to any part of the hospital. You see it's no use trying to discover the hiding place of that knife right now. And I've got to get some proof as to motive before I can make an arrest; now that

I know where to look for it, it may be simple. But in the meantime remember what I've told you. I was never more serious in my life."

I was sitting down again; not voluntarily.

"Do you mean I am really in danger?" I said huskily.

"In very grave danger. You see, you are the only living person who knows and will testify of that thing which may convict the murderer. Yours will be the convicting testimony. You with your own eyes saw and heard that which will bring the murderer to justice. But don't look like that. I'll protect you. I just want you to—coöperate with me."

"I'd like a drink of water."

He brought it for me and I drank it and sat up and pushed my cap back.

"Feel better? Understand me, Sarah, I'm not going to let anybody get hold of you. I'll see that you're as safe as human power can make you, if you'll just help me a little. You see, I don't like the idea of that knife being at large in the hospital.

"Although," he went on in a reassuring way, "since Kenwood Ladd has actually been arrested and put in prison for the murders, it is very likely the murderer will feel more secure. I think we can pretty well count on that. Now, Sarah, I've got to send a few messages; get the police to look up some things for me. I'm going to use the telephone and I don't want that little office girl to listen while I talk. Will you engage her in conversation while I put my calls through? And then wait for me, for I want you to go upstairs with me."

It was more difficult to keep the office girl engaged in conversation than one might think. She put his calls through with expedition and showed such keen interest in seeing that he got his numbers that it was only by bringing up the matter of the mysteriously missing knife that I attracted her complete attention.

"Isn't it terrible!" she said. "And me sitting here all day long at the switchboard! If I was on night duty I'd just pass out. I'll bet the night girl is good and scared."

Lance O'Leary put in several calls and held rather extended conversations. At the last one the girl turned to me.

"That was police headquarters," she said.

It was at that instant that Dr. Kunce came in, smooth and suave in his light silk suit. He was, however, in an uncertain temper; you could see that at a glance. I did not doubt the nurses had had a difficult day. The office girl stopped talking abruptly and reached for her memorandum pad, which he scrutinized sharply.

"Ah, Dr. Kunce," said O'Leary, opening the door of the inner office. "I took you at your word when you offered to assist me and have appropriated your office this afternoon."

"Quite right, Mr. O'Leary. Quite right. Anything at all that I can do—although I really feel the case is settled. But I suppose there is a matter of tying up the ends —so?"

"Tying up the ends," assented O'Leary gravely. "We still have to convict, you know. Looks like a storm, doesn't it?"

Both men turned toward the window, and I followed their glance out to that still green lawn and the bright crimson cannas and on to the quiet leaves of the Chinese elms.

"Sky's black already," said Dr. Kunce. "It can't hold off much longer. I wish it would storm and get it over with." There was a little surge of feeling in his words which he quickly suppressed, and added: "Makes the sick patients nervous, you know. Restless. Everybody's nerves are on edge, anyway."

"I should imagine they would be," said O'Leary quietly. "Now, Miss Keate, will you show me the east wing——"

I was conscious of Dr. Kunce's sharp glance which was like—well, it was like a sharp, shining needle sewing a silk thread. That sounds fantastic, but it is exactly what occurred to me and I am about as fanciful as an oyster.

The corridor was deserted. The eery light from the storm-waiting world outside made the shadows deeper, the lights pale and weary-looking. The broad steps of the stairway went upward through the still shadows, and the smooth rail caught green highlights from some light. I turned that way, but O'Leary continued past the stairway.

"We're going by way of the elevator," he said.

I followed him, of course. The red cage was there at the first floor so we did not have to wait for it. O'Leary pulled back the grilled inner door and I stepped into the narrow, hot elevator. The little red light was shining now just above my head, and the corners were empty and clean.

O'Leary pressed the third-floor button, and as the thing began its uncannily silent ascent he looked in a speculative way at the light.

"So Dr. Harrigan turned that out himself," he murmured. "H'm. You say Dione Melady did not approve of the projected operation?"

"Most decidedly not."

"And when you found the note to you in Dr. Harrigan's handwriting your first thought was that he'd been drinking?"

"Yes. But, as I told you, he had had nothing but some ice water in Mrs. Melady's room."

He nodded.

"Here we are. What a strange little lurch! Makes you feel the cage has made up its mind to drop with you in it. But here's the third floor. Just a moment, Sarah. About this Slæpan—you say it puts a fellow out for three days?"

"It's supposed to, yes."

"Didn't you say you had some here? In the drug room for this wing? May I see it?"

"Why, certainly. I'll get the key."

The head nurse relinquished the key promptly, although, I think, with misgiving, and Lance O'Leary and I let ourselves into the narrow, small drug room with its carefully labeled bottles and drawers and trays.

"Dr. Kunce left some here, rather than in the main drug room, because there wouldn't be so many people in and out who might be curious about it. It's in this drawer. It's a liquid at present, though I believe they intend to manufacture it in another form."

"Because of its—bad taste?"

"No. I understand it has no particular taste. Just for the conven—— Well—I can't seem to find——"

"Couldn't anyone take some of this Slæpan, have it analyzed, and thus make his own formula?"

"No," I said absently, searching the drawer. "I believe the ingredients blend in such a way that the exact proportions are difficult to determine and, of course, in this case the formula must be very exact. Ah, here it is. But—why, look! The bottle's empty!"

"I thought it would be," said O'Leary composedly. "You see it was stolen before the murder. The stuff was almost colorless, wasn't it?"

"Almost. A sort of light honey color. Something like the camphorated oil in that bottle."

"Soluble with water, I suppose."

"I don't know. You might ask Mrs. Melady; she would know. Or Dr. Kunce."

"Your Dr. Kunce appears to be an honest man," murmured O'Leary. "He hasn't used the stuff for experiment, has he?"

"No, I'm sure he hasn't."

"Well," said O'Leary, "let's go into Mrs. Melady's room and ask her why she returned the bottle."

"Mrs. Melady!"

"Why, certainly. It's as plain as the nose on your face. She was afraid to have Dr. Harrigan operate on her father. Peter Melady decided to have Dr. Harrigan operate and a date—the coming morning—was set. Mrs. Melady, being as stubborn as her father, would not give up, and decided she must stop the operation. She probably asked one of the nurses to help her; yes, that's exactly it, and you heard them whispering about it. Probably the nurse refused—it was likely this Miss Page—and Mrs. Melady managed to get the stuff anyhow. Then all she'd got to do was get Dr. Harrigan to her room, which was simple enough. She had poured the Slæpan into some ice water and while he was in her room she either asked if he didn't want a cold drink or he saw the ice water and asked for it himself. Nothing more natural on such a night. He drank it and—just how soon would it take effect?"

"Within twenty or thirty minutes."

"Good, that explains much. But wait a minute; could she have given him so much that that would have killed him?"

"No. I know something of Slæpan, of course. One of

its points was its safety. It would take a long time for
him to recover, but there was not enough in that small
bottle to kill anybody."

"Then we have it. Dr. Harrigan had got Melady upstairs and had himself come down to the east wing of this
floor again. Likely to search for and secure the Slæpan
formula. Knowing Peter Melady so intimately as he had
known him, he must have guessed that he would have
brought the formula with him, rather than let it out of
his own hands. When he came upon the snuff-bottle hidden in the room he must have found the formula in it at
once. We can't be certain about that yet, but it seems
reasonable. If he once got that formula patented as his
own, all the lawsuits Peter Melady could institute could
not take it from him, and who was to say that he, himself, had not worked it out as an ether substitute? By that
time the dose he'd unwittingly swallowed was beginning
to take effect. His muscles were not coördinating properly and we have that slovenly written message to you.
I think you are quite right in your surmise that he did
not intend actually to operate on Peter Melady until
morning and that, in that event, it would have been in all
probability a successful operation. Then I suppose he began to feel sleepy and—well, we can't be sure of this; I
doubt if we shall ever know. But it seems very likely that
he simply collapsed there in the elevator. His last conscious thought must have been to reach up and turn out
the light, hoping he would not be disturbed. And thus he
was an easy mark for an assassin."

"I think," I said slowly, "that you are going too fast.
Much too fast."

"Nonsense, Sarah," he said impatiently. "Don't you
see! It explains that stumbling block. How could a man
of Dr. Harrigan's physical strength have been stabbed

so quietly and neatly without even a struggle? That wasn't right—wasn't logical. He might have been shot, except for the noise. But sticking a knife into a man's heart is not so simple as it is made out to be. The assailant has got to approach his victim, and there's almost bound to be a struggle of some kind. The victim is almost sure to recognize the danger and try to escape it."

"I think you're jumping at conclusions," I said. "But if you want to see Mrs. Melady she's right down the corridor."

He did and would, and I accompanied him.

And something to my astonishment Dione Melady acknowledged the theft of the Slæpan without any visible contrition. She admitted giving it to Dr. Harrigan in exactly the manner outlined by Lance O'Leary.

"I suppose Nancy Page has told," she said. "Well, I did it. I didn't care how I managed so long as I stopped the operation. But I certainly was scared when I saw Leo Harrigan there in the elevator—dead. And I made Nancy promise not to tell about the Slæpan. His death hadn't anything to do with the Slæpan I gave him."

"You had asked Miss Page to help you carry out your plan?"

"Yes. But she refused. Even when I told her that Father would be murdered if that operation took place next morning. So I took the key to the drug room; slipped it out of her pocket while she was bending over to straighten the sheets. But she missed it and came and made me give it up, so I had to watch my chance and slip into the corridor and get the key off the hook above the chart desk. Heavens, what a time I had sneaking along the corridor and getting into the drug room and getting the Slæpan. I took the small pitcher from my room along with me and just poured the Slæpan into it then and there. Then I poured ice water into it when I got back to my room. But I was pretty smart about it. I even returned the key so Nancy wouldn't know. Miss Ash was standing right there in the corridor at the door of Mrs. Harrigan's room and didn't know I passed back of her, going and coming."

There was actually a note of pride in her voice, like a spoiled child boasting of its naughtiness.

"The corridor must have been pretty well traveled that night," said O'Leary dryly. "So you just replaced the empty bottle in the drawer?"

"Of course. 'Way back where it might not be seen right away. Do you think I wanted anyone to find it in my room?"

"You say you were frightened when you discovered Dr. Harrigan had been killed?"

"Oh, yes. Scared to death. And it took me hours to convince Nancy that the Slæpan I'd given him had nothing to do with his death and to make her promise not to tell. But when we were really scared was when she came and told me Dr. Harrigan had decided to operate right away! Think how I felt! As soon as she heard about the emergency operation she came to tell me and I told her I'd given him the Slæpan after all. We were both nearly crazy for a few minutes. She was afraid she couldn't manage to stop the operation, and I told her she'd got to and without telling what I'd done, too. I—er—was extremely nervous. And then I had a sort of—attack of hysterics and she finally said she'd tell Dr. Kunce and just then Miss Keate sort of screamed. And Nancy went out into the corridor. And Dr. Harrigan had been killed. Nancy was for telling the police about the Slæpan and what I had done. But I made her promise not to; we are old school friends, you know; were classmates at Miss James's school. But I suppose she finally told you all about it."

"No," said Lance O'Leary.

"Then how did you know? Just figure it out? I don't believe it. Nancy told. She's been half out of her mind to-day; she said she couldn't keep her promise to me any longer and was going to tell Sergeant Lamb as soon as she saw him. I think she's quite taken with this young Ladd. Well, now I've told you, what are you going to do about it? *I* didn't murder Dr. Harrigan. All I did was stop the operation."

Well, she had stopped the operation certainly. Muddled though her plan appeared to have been, she'd certainly accomplished the main purpose of it. And I could readily imagine her wringing a reluctant promise of silence from Nancy—her hysterical tears, her allusions and claims upon an old friendship, her ostentatious grief. Selfish Dione knew how to get her way about things. I have often wondered just how she felt about the whole affair and have come to the conclusion that her feelings were not particularly deep in any case. It was natural for her to wish to stop the operation so long as she felt her father was in danger from it, and it was like her petty obstinacy to resort to rather desperate measures to do so, if she'd once made up her cluttered little mind to that effect.

"I don't know just what we'll do about it," said O'Leary. "Whatever your motives were, you certainly made the murder a possibility. If Dr. Harrigan had not been drugged that night, he might have been able to defend himself." He spoke with unusual severity, and I felt a mean satisfaction in seeing a look of genuine alarm come into Dione's weakly pretty face. Somewhat to my surprise he did not linger to question her further at that time.

I followed him into the corridor. An interne, followed by a nurse carrying a dressing tray, emerged from 305 and entered 304. A student nurse bobbed out of the diet kitchen with something on a diet tray that clinked as she disappeared into a sick room. O'Leary's eyes were shining, and his face wore an intent vivid look, a look of extreme awareness which was at the same time remote and withdrawn.

"That ought to relieve your mind about your Miss Nancy," he said.

"But it doesn't explain why she had hidden the blue snuff-bottle."

"No," said O'Leary. "That room is Mrs. Harrigan's, isn't it? And the room opposite is Miss Ash's room? Or, rather, her patient's room. And the room opposite Mrs. Melady's room was Peter Melady's? All quite close together, aren't they? Now show me, Sarah, the fourth floor, the operating rooms and all. And you must get your own private collection of exhibits and let me see them," he said, smiling faintly. "I'm afraid you are giving me considerable edge on Sergeant Lamb. It really isn't fair, you know."

"I tried to tell him," I said indignantly. "But he wanted facts."

"He didn't know your—er—general reputation," murmured O'Leary enigmatically.

There followed a rather curious half-hour or so, during which he made me repeat certain portions of the story and point out the various spots that were involved. Where was the truck in the operating room when I found it; where had I found the cork; how long had I waited for the elevator before it came to the fourth floor that last time I had signaled for it; did I think it had been at the third floor, or the second floor, or the first floor; was the light on the fourth floor too dim to permit me to see through the open door into the elevator cage; but on the third floor the light was stronger, wasn't it, so, when I returned to look in the elevator I could see its interior quite plainly—plainly enough to recognize Dr. Harrigan at once; was I sure Dr. Kunce had gone downstairs by way of the elevator after his visit to the wing; was I sure it was a Negro on the truck when I looked at the body; how near the stairway had the truck stood while I pulled back the sheet and looked; was I sure Dr. Kunce had still worn his black dinner jacket when he came to the third floor immediately after we found the murder; was I sure no one besides Lillian Ash approached the elevator during the little interval after the finding of the body?—my answers to all these and many more inquiries, particularly those regarding the question of time, he considered at some length, although I did not know exactly what conclusions he was drawing.

He ended by getting into the elevator and experimenting, obliging me to remain on the fourth floor and ring for the cage when I judged he had got to the floor he designated. When I signaled for the elevator that last and only successful time, the night of the murder, I had been sure it came from a shorter distance than from the first floor, but it is difficult to time one's self by memory. And I did not see that the result of all his experimenting and questions was so illuminating as to make O'Leary's eyes a brighter, clearer gray than ever. Positively the man looked jubilant. Especially after he'd experimented for a while with the emergency stop—at least I judged that was what he did there at the last, for I rang a number of times before the cage finally glided upward to the fourth floor. I remember it was very hot and still and smelled sickeningly of ether and was very gloomy and dark as the storm drew nearer and the sky blacker, and I had begun to wonder uneasily if the elevator was quite safe when suddenly the red rectangle of light began to show beyond the glass door and O'Leary opened the door. Jubilant, as I have said.

"That's that," he said in a satisfied way. "Now about these charts that the nurses keep; do you make a permanent record of them?"

"Yes."

"So that you can go back at any time and refer to them and find such things as—time and all that?"

"Oh, yes. They are very definite. Very specific."

"Are the nurses on duty to-night the same nurses who were on duty the night of the murder?"

"Practically the same, I think. Unless one of them happens to be ill, in which case another would take her place. That is, I'm speaking of the nurses on general duty. The specials, the private nurses, you know, come and go."

He looked at his watch.

"I want to see the nurses on the second floor and, of course, those on the third floor. I also want to do considerable prowling. And I want to talk to the office girl who's on night duty. But first, Sarah, let's see your collection."

He accompanied me through the darkening halls to my own room and then refused to let me enter until he had gone in and glanced about the room. He smiled as I emptied the contents of the lavender hot-water bottle into his hands, but the smile vanished as he touched the gold hair and studied the torn slip of paper with Dr.

Harrigan's message on it, and he became very grave as he looked at the cork and sniffed it and then put the whole collection in an inside pocket with, I suppose, the Chinese snuff-bottle.

The little smile came back to his eyes as he looked at me.

"If the police knew that, all along, you've been carrying about such items of interest they would undoubtedly shoot you on sight," he said with a sort of amused air which was still rather thoughtful and a bit respectful. "If Sergeant Lamb ever knows what happened to his gold hair——"

"He'd best not know," I suggested somewhat hurriedly.

"And the snuff-bottle! While the police were scouring the place! Did you know that Court Melady himself finally went to the chief of police and demanded that they make more strenuous efforts to recover it? That was yesterday. And you've had it——"

"Just since last night," I said quickly. "And that was sheer accident."

"It usually is sheer accident—with you," he said meditatively. "That's the strange thing about it. But it's such damn perspicacious accident—if you don't mind my saying so."

Since I couldn't recall at the moment just what "perspicacious" meant, I didn't mind at all, and I said nothing. In the little silence I became aware of a murmurous sound of rising wind outside. We both turned toward the window. The green of the trees was moving now, restless, awakening to troublous life. Birds were darting about anxiously, the tall cannas were beginning to move and sway slightly. The sky was black, and as we watched a long, jagged streak of lightning zigzagged across the horizon there toward the southwest. We both waited, motionless, in the small, darkening room for the low roll of thunder, and when it finally came, far away but deep and threatening, it brought with it the strangest sense of impending fate—of foreboding, of threat. And I remember how clear and white and delicate the marble cross of St. Malachy's looked against the black sky and above the surging green of the treetops.

Even O'Leary was stirred, for he moved restlessly and said in a musing way as if he'd forgotten I was there:

"A storm—the beginning of a storm—does something to me. I don't like to watch it and can't help myself. The way the trees come to life and start to toss themselves about and murmur and then begin to be a part of it all; the waiting; the portent; the wind; the first streaks of lightning——" He broke off abruptly, looked at me as if rather ashamed, and shrugged his shoulders. "And naturally one feels that something is about to happen because it's going to storm. That is what's about to happen. And you'd better put your windows down before you go downstairs. Isn't it about dinnertime? Good Lord, I've got to hurry. I've got to make a trip out to the Melady laboratories."

At the top of the stairway he said:

"See here, Sarah, you hurry up and go downstairs with those nurses. They are just on the landing; you can easily catch up with them. And mind me, see that you stay with them. Don't take any chances. You'll be perfectly safe if you'll remember that."

As if I could forget!

"But just a moment! That hair—was it—do you think it's Nancy's?"

"Not unless Nancy dyes her hair," he said briefly. "Hurry, now."

I obeyed. He stood there watching me until I had caught up with Miss Blane and Miss Bianchi and was descending with them. I didn't hear a word either of them said, though I believe they were talking quite busily. I knew that Nancy had never touched her hair with dye. And I also knew someone who did, and when Lillian Ash came late to dinner I could scarcely keep my eyes from her bright yellow hair; it looked harsh and rather dry, but she'd defiantly and tightly waved it during her hours off. I think she must have made a desperate effort that night to get herself up to look more natural. She must have known that the whole story, rehashed, of her divorce from Dr. Harrigan and her presence in Melady Memorial Hospital at the very hour of his murder would be in the papers that night; and truth to tell, coming on the heels of Dr. Harrigan's violent death, the story was not a pleasant one.

Dinner that night was not a happy meal. In the first place flies had been clinging to the screens as they do before a storm, and a few had managed to find their way into the place and hummed in a maddening fashion here and there. I am neither nervous nor temperamental nor oversqueamish, but there is something about a fly which I cannot endure, and when one lit on my salad and walked nonchalantly over the lettuce before I could bat at it with my napkin, my appetite for food vanished. I sat there drinking black coffee and trying to keep from staring at Nancy's white, stricken face and Lillian Ash's blonde hair and listening with half an ear to the bits of conversation going on. Someone plucked up the heart to turn on the radio, and it sputtered and crackled every now and then. And all at once the orchestra stopped wailing dance tunes and the news man came on the air and started in at once to tell us that "Kenwood Ladd, accused slayer of

Dr. Leo Harrigan, has been arrested and is now in the Euclid Avenue jail waiting indictment by the grand jury. The evidence against this popular young architect is said to be convincing and——"

It was just then that Nancy's chair went back with a screech and she was out of it and across the room and had turned off the radio with a quick little thud of the switch.

CHAPTER XVI

As WE straggled upstairs from the dining room the first great spatters of rain were beginning to fall, and as we reached the east wing of the third floor the storm burst with a great sweep of wind through the corridors, a shattering crash of thunder, and sharp bright flashes of lightning. Nurses were scurrying about, their white skirts blown back by the wind, trying to get windows down and nervous patients quieted, and Nancy and Ellen and I plunged to work.

Having held off for so long, the storm came with a deluge of rain, and it was some time before we got all the windows adjusted, window sills and floors mopped up, and at last turned to the business of removing dinner trays and examining charts and noting the various orders for the night. And through it all I managed to keep within sight and hearing distance of either Nancy or Ellen. O'Leary is not a man who warns needlessly.

Ina Harrigan was sitting in a chair reading some newspapers she had contrived to secure, when I entered her room to remove the vases of flowers and set them in the corridor for the night. I remember that I hesitated at the door and looked across the corridor to where Nancy was stacking trays on the dumb-waiter before I entered. And then I did so warily.

She looked more worried than I had yet seen her look and asked me sharply if it was I who had traced the bit of white chewing gum.

"It was," I said.

"I'm not surprised," she remarked, eyeing me darkly. "Well, you may be interested to know that I haven't the faintest idea of how that bit of chewing gum got stuck to my late husband's sleeve. I suppose he leaned against the table and I had dropped the gum there. But it took me a good hour this morning to convince Sergeant Lamb that that's all I know about it. This business of arresting Kenwood Ladd is absurd. My lawyer says it is all a matter of circumstantial evidence."

"Circumstantial evidence has convicted before now," I said. "Can I help you prepare for the night?"

"No," she said. And as a great roll of thunder shook the very foundations of the old hospital, she leaned sharply forward, clutched at the arm of the chair, bit her lips until some of the heavy crimson paste came off on her teeth, and said: *"What a storm!"*

My other patients I found to be extremely restless, 301 having refused to eat a bite of his dinner and now regretting his contrariness as the pangs of hunger began to gnaw, Dione Melady becoming decidedly cantankerous, and 303, hitherto the most tractable of patients and but recently sundered from his appendix, had become suddenly fractious in the extreme, kicking off his covers and demanding to be taken home, storm or no storm.

Promptly at nine-thirty Court Melady, who'd been sitting in Dione's room, left. I happened to be at the chart desk when he passed, buttoning up his thin, shining raincoat and saying something about a taxi and the storm. He avoided the elevator door and went down the dark stairway. The green light above the chart desk was reflected in a glancing highlight from his glistening coat. It was with a slight feeling of relief that it occurred to me that here was one of that short list out of the hospital

and gone. Court Melady gone, Kenwood Ladd in jail,
Dr. Kunce and Teuber downstairs and far away from
the wing. And I had seen and talked to Ina Harrigan,
who looked more worried than murderous. And I
couldn't believe that Lillian Ash was bent on murder,
though I took care not to be alone with her.

But there is no good saying I was not nervous, for I
was. I found myself wincing at every crash of thunder,
casting quick glances continually over my shoulders and
into corners; my ears were alert to any alien sound,
straining lest they hear a furtive footfall or the whisper
of a stealthy motion. As I say, I adhered firmly to my
resolution to take no chances and kept almost constantly
near Nancy, or, when that was not possible, in the middle of the corridor or at the chart desk where no one
could approach me without being seen.

Along about eleven o'clock things in the wing quieted
down; Ellen was reading aloud to Dione Melady, stop-
ping whenever it thundered, and Nancy had relented and
was giving 301 a hastily concocted cream toast, and our
other patients had drifted off—if not to sleep, owing to
the tumult outside, at least to quiet. And high time, I
thought, as I walked warily along the empty corridor
and paused at the window. The storm had lashed itself
into a fury and was beating and surging against the windows and hurling rain against the shining black glass and
making the night hideous with its turmoil. As I looked
I caught a glimpse of the lights of an automobile splash-
ing its way through the washing pavement. It stopped
apparently at the curb in front of the hospital, and at
that instant there was a bright flash of lightning and I
saw the hurrying figures of several men climbing out of
it, bending to the storm as they fought their way toward
the entrance. One of the figures, the first one, had some

air of familiarity to me, but the flash of lightning was gone and with it my momentary impression. An emergency case, I thought to myself; probably an accident owing to the slippery streets.

303's light was on when I turned to the corridor again. I found him sitting up in bed, holding outright over the floor the rubber hot-water bottle with which I'd tried to lull him to sleep. It was dripping dejectedly onto the rug and had, he explained in a bitter way, burst when he accidentally rolled on it. He was injured and aggrieved, his teeth were beginning to chatter with cold, his sheets and pajamas were soaked. He knew, he informed me agitatedly, that he would get pneumonia.

Well, it was not a good thing for a patient so recently under ether to get a thorough chill. I hid my alarm, however, and said briskly:

"You're going to do no such thing. Let me throw this blanket over you. Wrap up in it while I hurry for dry bed clothing."

"And pajamas," he said plaintively as I closed the door.

I reached the door to the linen closet, pushed it open, reached for the electric-light switch and, even in my haste, peered into the room before entering it. The quick light showed only the room and the neatly stacked shelves. I went hurriedly to the end of the narrow room near the black window panes where the sheets were stacked.

And in the very act of reaching for a sheet my hand stopped. In the black window pane my eyes had caught a reflection of a movement behind me, a flash of white. Before I could turn or speak the light was snapped out.

Someone was in the room. Someone had been behind that door. Someone was between me and the corridor.

There was a cautious, stealthy movement and another.

I could not stir. A flash of lightning came and went. It lit the room dimly and was gone, but not before it had gleamed sharply on something like steel upraised in a white arm.

I tried to scream. I did scream, but I knew that a roll of thunder drowned my voice.

I find that, after all, I cannot tell of those moments.

Lance O'Leary has told me what happened. He says that, with his new and certain knowledge, he hurried at once to the hospital. Policemen were with him and they were coming to make the arrest. He reached the third floor, he said, just as I entered the linen closet. He did not dream I was in so deadly a peril, so he walked no more rapidly than usual along the corridor to the door of the linen closet. Then he heard me scream, faintly, thinly through the storm.

I have no memory at all of his flinging open the door, of the shouts, the quick revolver shots, the running policemen, the shrieks and the turmoil that must have risen in the old hospital and outrivalled the fury of the storm.

I do remember sitting back in a big wicker chair in Peter Melady's empty room. My uniform was wet about the neck and Ellen was dashing cold water on my face as if bent on drowning me, and Nancy was rubbing my wrists and sobbing and crying: "Are you hurt? Are you hurt? Are you hurt?"

I pushed Ellen and the water away, gasped, choked, and straightened up. In the corridor were lights, nurses from other wings running distractedly about, the truck with a sheet over it, and policemen crowding about the door of the linen closet and about the door of an empty room next to Dione Melady's room—the door to this room was closed.

"What's the matter? What happened? No—I remember——"

"Oh, Miss Keate, it's terrible," gasped Ellen, waving the wet towels and sending a shower of cold water on me again. "Somebody's killed and we don't know who it is——"

"What's happened?" It was Dione Melady at the door. She seized Nancy's arm and shook it. "You've got to tell me. I heard the shots. They have got the murderer. Who is it?"

"I don't know, Dione. Let go my arm. I don't know. None of us knows."

The door across the corridor opened suddenly and Lance O'Leary emerged, gave a swift look about him, saw us, and came at once to me.

His raincoat was still wet and dripping; I had an impression of unusual dishevelment, but I actually saw only his face, which was a sort of gray-white under his tan, and his dark eyes.

He leaned over me, taking both my shaking hands in his own hands, and searching my face with his intent gray gaze. He did not speak for a moment or two, and when he did it was only to say, in a voice that did not belong to him:

"You are—all right, Sarah Keate?"

"P—Perfectly."

His fingers tightened.

"What possessed you to take a chance! After I'd told you—never mind, I know why you did it. But I want you to know I'd intended to be here by ten o'clock. I knew you'd be safe till then if you stayed with other people. The storm delayed us; we skidded into another car, couldn't get a taxi or police car. Couldn't even get the hospital on the telephone. You are absolutely sure you are not hurt?"

"Just scared," I said, achieving a smile.

He did not smile, however; there was something like fury back of his luminous gray eyes. Then he relinquished my hands and was gone into the room across the corridor again, and Ellen let out her breath in a long sigh and said:

"Gee! He likes you, Miss Keate."

"Well, I should hope so," I said briskly and felt better.

Miss Blane popped her head into the room; her white cap was over one ear and her eyes bulged.

"303 is raging," she said hurriedly. "Shall I change the sheets for you? I can't get into the linen closet. I'll borrow some from the charity ward. Are you all right, Miss Keate"

"A little unsteady is all."

"Heavens, I should think you'd be out of your mind." At a noise from the elevator shaft Miss Blane popped her head back into the corridor, and after an electric second or two into the room again. "Here comes the district attorney himself," she announced excitedly. "And the coroner and a whole string of policemen and reporters. One of them's setting up a camera."

"Run," I said, "and close the sick-room doors. The place will be full of smoke from the flashlights. I don't think Dr. Kunce ought to let them do it."

"What have they got Lillian Ash in that room for?" asked Miss Blane. "The door was open just then as the district attorney went in and I saw her. And she's crying. And oh, my Lord, here comes old Dr. Peattie! Pull up your socks, girls, and get going!" With which she was gone with a flash of white skirts.

It was only the grim necessity of protecting and caring for our patients' needs and the force of rigid habit that carried me through the next hour. We were very busy. I did see the policemen wheel a truck to the elevator, enter it themselves after the truck, and drop out of sight, but the sheet covered what lay on the truck. Sometime in that hour the conference in Room 310 came to an end, but none of us was the wiser when it was over, and there was so much confusion in the corridor that the only people I remember seeing clearly were Lillian Ash, her face red and blotched from weeping, and Lance O'Leary, looking very grave and grim and, somehow, sad. As if his duty had been exceedingly painful.

Shortly after we got the wing quiet again and the corridor cleared, Lance O'Leary sent for me. I found him in Dr. Kunce's crowded office. The room was blue with cigar smoke, but cool air and a spatter of rain mist were coming in through the window. The district attorney was there, a sprinkling of policemen and reporters, Sergeant Lamb, and Dr. Peattie. And, of course, O'Leary.

"—and so, gentlemen, we are able to reconstruct the crime, although there're one or two bits of it we will never know," Lance O'Leary was saying as I entered the room, closing the door behind me almost on the nose of the office girl. He rose at once, and also Dr. Peattie, and then, reluctantly, the others. "I've asked Miss Keate to be present while we straighten out these details because she was actually a most prominent figure in the investigation. It was entirely owing to her keen observation, her orderly notes, that we were enabled to—er—solve the problem." Lance O'Leary is not as a rule oratorical; a little murmur of comment arose, during which Sergeant Lamb was distinctly understood to remark that something was a hell of a note. Upon which O'Leary, looking very deaf and very bland, added swiftly:

"That and the splendid coöperation of the police, particularly of Sergeant Lamb whose . . ." and so forth and so on. Sergeant Lamb's lengthy face brightened a little, someone offered me a chair, and O'Leary went on:

"To some of you parts of this will be familiar, but in order to get things in their proper sequence I had better begin at the beginning. It is an extraordinarily difficult tale to tell."

His face was very grave now, his eyes no longer clear and shining but clouded and thoughtful.

"You must bear in mind that from the beginning we have actually had to deal with a very simple crime. An unpremeditated crime. One conceived impulsively by an intelligence which had long been dominated by a fixed idea. It was, of course, the logical outgrowth of that idea, but the crime itself was entirely unplanned. It's true that after the crime was done desperate efforts were made to conceal it. But not, mark you, on the part of the murderer. Except in a single instance, and that was in the attempt to—do away with an important witness." The icy, implacable note that got into his voice once in a while was there then. I shivered, told myself sensibly that it was safely over, resisted an impulse to say: "Get on with the story. Who did it?"—which would have been quite outrageous under the circumstances—and settled myself to listen.

"When the facts of the matter were laid before me it seemed there were two points of inquiry. While it was at once evident that only one person could have been the murderer"—it was just here, I believe, that Sergeant Lamb gave a sort of muffled squawk, and the district attorney threw his cigar away and sat up in his chair

—"still I did not know the motive, I did not know why Lillian Ash was so determined to conceal what she knew, I did not know who came so near to murdering Dione Melady, although I strongly suspected and my suspicion proved to be quite correct. I also had to prove beyond a doubt that I was right in my decision. Miss Keate provided me with a very useful clue. She found this cork in the operating room, the morning after the murder. You gentlemen will note that it has a rather curious odor. Mrs. Melady mentioned, in telling of the struggle with her assailant, a peculiar odor; upon showing her this cork this evening, just before I left the hospital, she immediately said it had the same odor. Since I knew where to look I had no difficulty in identifying this definitely with the criminal, thus proving that person's presence on the fourth floor the night of the crime. I say the night of the crime because I found that the operating rooms had been thoroughly cleaned following an operation the late afternoon preceding the murder, and that there had been no occasion for the criminal's presence, or anyone's presence, in fact, during the short intervening time."

The cluster of men were looking at the little cork, sniffing it, passing it from one to another.

"Don't lose it," said the district attorney.

"I'll try to make this as simple as possible," resumed O'Leary. "The whole thing rests upon what was in itself a rather trivial circumstance. Time, too, had an important part to play. You will recall that Miss Keate rang for the elevator at the first floor at very close to twelve-eighteen, the night of the murder. We say twelve-eighteen because it would take at least two minutes for her to walk up the remaining flights of stairs to the third floor, and she reached the third floor at twelve-twenty. Miss Brody says that she saw Dr. Harrigan enter the elevator at twelve-eighteen. We can only surmise that Dr. Harrigan was by that time feeling the effects of the dose of Slæpan which has been explained to you gentlemen, that he entered the elevator, turned out the light probably in a dazed effort to give himself seclusion until he should feel better. Remember that we now know it to be a fact, after Miss Ash's confession, that Dr. Harrigan had returned, after leaving his patient in the operating room, to the third floor and Peter Melady's room, where he found and took this blue Chinese snuff-bottle——"

"Ah-h-h," said the reporters avidly.

"—with the formula for Slæpan concealed in it. He had this little jewel-like bottle in his hands when he—er—passed out, so to speak."

"Was murdered?" asked Sergeant Lamb, adding up the twos.

"Went to sleep; became unconscious from the effects of Slæpan. At twelve-twenty, Miss Keate arrived in the third-floor corridor, found her patient gone, was given the message that he had been taken to the operating room and herself, at no later than twelve twenty-one, approached the elevator door at the third floor and pressed the signal button. She waited but there was no response, because the cage was there already, at the third floor. Dr. Harrigan must have put on the emergency stop immediately upon entering the elevator cage. He probably never knew that his erstwhile friend and enemy, Peter Melady, was dead in the elevator beside him, when he entered it. When you rang, Miss Keate, the elevator held two men—one dead, that was Peter Melady; one alive, that was Dr. Harrigan. Wait, let me tell this my own way.

"Miss Keate immediately hurried up the stairs, found

the operating rooms deserted. She rang again for the elevator and again, because the stop lever was on, the elevator failed to respond. She hurried downstairs and inquired more at length regarding the projected emergency operation, and then, determining to look in the operating rooms again, rang a fourth time for the elevator. The same thing occurred; there was no light and apparently no elevator. Miss Ash came out of her patient's room into the corridor, at this point, and Jacob Teuber, the orderly, approached, pushing a truck on which lay a dead Negro. Miss Keate met him and pulled the sheet aside and looked at the Negro while the orderly went to the elevator door and Miss Ash stood there watching Miss Keate and Teuber. She said, if you'll remember, 'There's no use pulling at the elevator door; it won't open when the cage isn't at this floor,' or words to that effect.

"I must go back now in the story, pick up the other side of the tapestry from the moment when Dr. Harrigan, at a few minutes after twelve, stepped into the elevator with his patient, Peter Melady, on a truck. Someone else was already in that elevator cage. A person whom Dr. Harrigan had no reason to distrust, a person who, upon being told of the situation, accompanied the two to the operating room and was asked to remain with the patient while Dr. Harrigan went, as I suppose he told the two, to arrange for the operation. While Dr. Harrigan was gone, this person, seeing Peter Melady's condition and feeling that he had a distinct claim on Slæpan, demanded the formula. We know little as to that. We do know that the murderer, in an effort to frighten Peter Melady into giving up the formula, must have seized the operating knife from one of the cases. We know that Peter Melady finally said that the formula was in the

Chinese snuff-bottle. At any rate, Peter Melady died from shock and excitement.

"With that we come to another aspect. The murderer was thoroughly frightened; he knew that while Peter Melady's weak heart had simply flickered out, there would be inquiry, talk, gossip, and also that, if he ever would be able to secure the Slæpan formula it must be within the next few moments. So he returned with Peter Melady's dead body to the elevator, leaving the truck standing there beside the operating table, and went down to the third floor. He left the body in the elevator, determined to be connected in no way with Mr. Melady's death. The knife was still in his possession; he was, I hope I've made clear, possessed of a fixed idea and that idea was to regain possession of the formula."

"Regain?" I said aloud.

Lance O'Leary glanced sharply at me.

"Regain, certainly," he said in a surprised way. "He was the original discoverer of the Slæpan. He worked it out in an imperfect way some time ago. He was once in the employ of the Melady Drug Company. Peter Melady took over the formula, as was his legal right according to their agreement. When, after experiment and perfecting, it promised to be such a great thing, Peter Melady stubbornly refused to give the originator any share of it. He, the original discoverer of the stuff, left the Melady laboratories almost immediately after his discovery, but he kept hearing of the progress and increasing importance of the drug in, mind you, Peter Melady's possession. Probably he brooded. Certainly he became desperate when he thought Peter Melady was about to die and the formula would go to his daughter who, morally, had still less claim on it than had Peter Melady. What wonder that when he saw Dr. Harrigan slouched there in the corner of the elevator with the blue snuff-bottle openly in his hands, a perfect frenzy seized him. There was no time for reflection. He must act. He realized nothing but that his formula was there in Dr. Harrigan's possession. That he was to be frustrated again. All his accumulated bitterness of desire must have directed his hand. He opened the elevator door, saw Dr. Harrigan holding the snuff-bottle, saw nothing else and struck."

Someone cried out; I think it was I, for I remember thinking I must keep quiet and that the wild conjecture which had entered my head could not possibly be true.

"And this Ash woman knew the whole thing all along?" asked the district attorney abruptly.

"Naturally," said Lance O'Leary. "In fact, I'd have thought she, herself, was guilty had she not made such desperate efforts to protect the murderer. Never to protect herself, except possibly in the case of the fingerprints on the knife handle. They had left the knife there purposely to connect the affair with Peter Melady who was known to have been in the operating room with Dr. Harrigan. However, it was not her fingerprints she wiped off that knife. A hair fell from her head and caught around the knife as she did it. Who but Lillian Ash, came forward within the hour that the substitution of the bodies was discovered, with a story which eventually sent Kenwood Ladd to jail? It was difficult for her, knowing the truth as she did, to tell that story. She did it only to divert the line of inquiry; she did not think it would convict Ladd. It was however, the truth, so far as it went, and the story of the patient in 301 must have been to her an unexpected stroke of good luck. Who but Miss Ash put the snuff-bottle in Peter Melady's empty room *after* the room was searched by the police? It had to be someone in the east wing who knew the room was already searched and thought it was the safest place to hide the thing until the murderer, for whom she was keeping it lest he be suspected and searched, came to claim it. Miss Ash did not reckon with Dione Melady's determination to get the formula into her own possession and her conviction that it must be hidden somewhere about the empty room. Who but Miss Ash protected Dione Melady's assailant? She let him into the place through the fire-escape window when he came for the snuff-bottle. He waited until you were out of sight, Miss Keate, then came forward and found Dione in the very act of discovering the snuff-bottle, *which still held the formula.* He very nearly strangled Mrs. Melady in order to recover the formula, which by now had become the most precious thing in life to him. And when Dione Melady screamed and the other nurses came, Miss Ash stood there point-ing to Peter Melady's room and crying 'There it is,' so that the nurses had eyes only for Dione Melady and they clustered into that room, trying to bring life back to the senseless victim. Which was quite right, of course, but in the meantime the fleeing man escaped. He was entirely safe by the time the alarm was sounded. One of the most obvious things about this affair was the fact that the murderer must have been very familiar with the hospital and the hospital routine."

"Then was it Miss Ash who put that empty snuff-bottle in Nancy's room?" I interrupted to ask.

"Yes," said Sergeant Lamb, coming suddenly to life. "After the formula had been taken from it. And it was you that found it, Miss Keate. And never said a word to me. I wonder now—I lost something. I lost a pillbox with a gold——" He stopped abruptly with a side glance at the alert-eared reporters. But he continued to regard me with a look in which retrospection, suspicion, and finally certainty were blended darkly.

"So that was why Miss Ash said that about the elevator door not opening," said the district attorney thoughtfully.

"Yes," said O'Leary, nodding. "Protecting again. In the very moment of the shock of her knowledge she said that, hoping to give the impression that the elevator was *not* at the third floor. And who but Lillian Ash helped dispose of Peter Melady's body? There were only two ways to explain Miss Ash: either she had killed Dr. Harrigan, or she had some reason for protecting the real murderer. That reason, as she has confessed, was primarily one of self-preservation. Remember Miss Ash was without financial resource; she really did not know of Dr. Harrigan's will, and owing to the most pressing need she had returned to her former profession of nursing. She was obliged to return to this state on account of her license to nurse having been issued here, which she had kept valid, and her failure to pass the examinations for a registered nurse in another state or two. Her work brought her to B—— and even, since she dared not refuse cases offered her, to Melady Memorial Hospital. As we know, she had been treated with grave injustice by Dr. Harrigan and she hated and feared him—feared him desperately now, because his discovery of her presence would threaten her sole means of livelihood. It would be so very easy for Dr. Harrigan to blast her nursing career; one hint that she was incompetent would be enough. She knew that her presence would be intolerable to him, and she knew he was not a merciful man."

"So she kept out of his way," said the district attorney.

"Exactly. She avoided him with marvelous dexterity. But they finally met. There in the corridor. The night of

July seventh. He was furious. She was terrified. Incredibly bitter against him."

"Don't blame her," murmured someone back of me.

"And," went on O'Leary rather wearily, "not much more than an hour later she—saw his murder. Saw his murder and was so enraged and embittered that in the first moment of seeing it she felt relief. There was some shock and natural horror, but her predominant feeling was one of relief. She had no time to think or reflect; she must act. And her instinctive feeling was that the murderer of Dr. Harrigan was her ally. Had, unwittingly but truly, protected her from him. Her instantaneous resolve to protect the murderer came from a primitive but natural impulse. Later when she had time to reason she realized her terrible mistake. But again self-preservation influenced her. She dared not admit what she'd done. She'd involved herself too deeply."

The district attorney stirred, murmured something about an accessory and waited again while O'Leary continued.

"So—her only safe path lay in protecting the murderer; concealing her knowledge. The murderer told her why he had killed; it was a grain of comfort to her tortured mind to feel that he had some small justice on his side. So she became his ally. She continued to aid and protect him as she had aided and protected him in the first paralyzing moments of the murder, when she helped dispose of Peter Melady's body."

"Just why was that gruesome substitution of bodies made, O'Leary?" asked the district attorney, leaning forward. "Why was that?"

"That was part of that hasty, desperately conceived plan. They had only a moment or two and had to plan with incredible, frantic haste. They made their mistakes thereby, of course. The enmity between Peter Melady and Dr. Harrigan was well known; if Peter Melady's complete disappearance followed the murder of Dr. Harrigan, what more likely than the conclusion that Peter Melady was the murderer? It was Lillian Ash who thought of that. Thus the rapid, grisly plan was set in motion. Let Peter Melady's body be buried. Let the dead Negro be found in the church back of the hospital. And who would be the wiser? The danger was that the undertakers would question it, but they must take that chance."

"Mr. O'Leary," said one of the reporters, "it's all worked out all right, of course. I mean the murderer was caught red-handed—that is,"—he shot an apologetic glance at me—"almost red-handed," he amended (which did not improve matters), "and was shot and confessed before he died. And Lillian Ash has come clean with the whole story. But what we want, for our news story, you know, is how you did it. How you got next to it."

"Why, that was very simple," said O'Leary quietly. "After hearing Miss Keate's curious story of her several attempts to get the elevator at the various floors, it was very clear. The trouble was I had no motive; I suspected that the motive was the possession of the Slæpan formula, but I had to be sure. You must remember that, while the conclusions to which I came seemed to me to be the only logical and conclusive solutions, still I had to prove them. And since I knew where to look, in what direction to seek, I was enabled to do so. With, as I say, the efficient coöperation of Sergeant Lamb. We found that the man who I thought to be the murderer had actually worked some time ago in the Melady research laboratories. Then, of course, I was obliged to check the various depositions of the office girl and night nurses. I was obliged to make sure that no one approached the elevator between twelve-eighteen and twelve thirty-two besides those of whom I knew. It was possible, of course, that Kenwood Ladd was the murderer, for he was one of those who certainly was near the elevator during that important period of time. But I was not satisfied that he was guilty, and if I eliminated him there was only one other possibility. And that possibility proved to be the right one, and Kenwood Ladd was eliminated logically."

"Let's have that bit again," said the district attorney. "It seems so simple. So simple I don't see how——"

"It's so simple that in its very simplicity it is one of those things that one might readily overlook," said O'Leary. "It's just that when Miss Keate rang for the elevator the third time—she was at the fourth floor then, remember—it failed to respond. The emergency lever was still on. When she rang for it the fifth time, again at the fourth floor, it responded. The emergency stop had been taken off during those intervening moments. Well, then, who had been near the elevator during that time?"

"But someone might have released that stop lever, might have seen Dr. Harrigan murdered there and been afraid to tell. It might not have been the murderer at all," said one of the reporters.

"True," said Lance O'Leary, "but it was not at all probable. An innocent person would be far more likely to raise an alarm as Miss Keate did. At any rate the thing to do was to inquire as to the persons who were known to have been near the elevator during that short period of time—to assume that the person who released that stop was guilty and to attempt to prove it. And we —proved it. And remember it was Lillian Ash who said that no one but herself, Miss Keate, and the orderly was near the elevator at the third floor between the time of

Miss Keate's departure to the fourth floor by the stairway and her return about three minutes later by way
of the elevator."

"Very clear," said Sergeant Lamb in a flat voice.

"Altogether too clear," said the district attorney. "It
eliminates Kenwood Ladd at once. Seems to me someone
might have seen it sooner."

"Oh, say, Mr. O'Leary—I mean, Lieutenant—say,
that's swell," said the reporter.

"No," said O'Leary honestly. "I had an advantage
over the police. I came into the thing fresh with an un-
prejudiced mind, and was not, thereby, so likely to be led
aside by the very confusing developments. I also had the
enormous advantage of the work the police had already
done. And of Miss Keate's invaluable observation."

Several looked curiously at me and I said:

"But Mr. O'Leary, I haven't heard just how those
bodies were changed. Teuber was right there in the corridor when I left it to go upstairs that second time. And
Miss Ash——"

"It took only a moment or two, Miss Keate. Miss Ash
stood guard there in the corridor while Peter Melady's
body was placed on the truck *with* the body of the Negro
and the sheet pulled over both of them. Mr. Melady was
small, you know, and once the sheet hid the two bodies
the greatest peril was past. Miss Blane, though she
stopped the orderly to remark as to his use of the freight
elevator, did not lift the sheet. Once in the ambulance
room the Negro's body was swiftly dressed, and the 'man
in the light suit' half dragged, half carried the Negro to
the basement room, left the body there, and hurried back
to the hospital and was quite safe by the time the undertakers' men arrived and, without question, removed the
body of Peter Melady."

"Then Jacob Teuber actually wheeled those two bodies downstairs and into the ambulance room?" I said incredulously. "But Mr. O'Leary, how did Miss Ash get Teuber out of the way while the murderer got Mr. Melady's body onto the truck?"

"I thought you knew, Miss Keate," said O'Leary gently. "I did not realize that you did not know what we all know. You see—do you remember that I said that if the Negro had not died there would have been no murders?"

I nodded. Something was pounding in my throat.

"It was quite true. And the thing that was to me the important clue was the fact that the truck in which Peter Melady was taken to the operating room was found *still in that room*. It had not been used to transport Mr. Melady elsewhere. But something must have been used. A dead body might be dragged through an alley in the dark of night but scarcely through hospital corridors. So another truck had been used. The truck that was beside the murderer as he stood in the elevator when it arrived at the third floor a few minutes after twelve and was met by Dr. Harrigan, who pushed the 3E truck with his patient on it inside and asked the murderer to help him for a few moments. The truck which, after Peter Melady's dead body had been left in the elevator a few moments later, was pushed hurriedly on about its business in the charity ward, where it and the murderer remained for the next twenty minutes. The murder, Miss Keate, was committed in the moments, twenty minutes or so later, during which you leaned over the ambulance truck, making up your mind to look at the Negro and finally drawing aside the sheet. There was no sound behind you. Lillian Ash saw the murder and in the immensity of her relief felt only desperate determination to protect."

"Why—then——"

"You are right," said O'Leary. "The cork came from a bottle of inhaling fluid—camphor, menthol, and the like. The light suit was one of white duck. The man was Jacob Teuber."

THE END